Wicked Prince of Frost

USA TODAY BESTSELLING AUTHOR

ALI WINTERS

Wicked Prince of Frost

Published by Rising Flame Press

First Edition

Paperback ISBN-13: 978-1-945238-24-6
Hardcover ISBN-13: 978-1-945238-29-1

Ebook and hardcover jacket Illustration: Natalie Bernard
Typography and case design: Raven Pages Design

www.aliwinters.com
www.thevampiredebt.com

ALSO BY ALI WINTERS

ADULT ROMANTASY

Shadow World: The Vampire Debt

The Vampire Debt

The Vampire Curse

The Vampire Court

The Vampire Oath

The Vampire Crown

Shadow World: Standalones

The Vampire Trap

Wicked Prince of Frost

Stand Alone Titles

High Stakes

YOUNG ADULT

The Hunted Series

The Reapers

The Exodus

The Moirai

The Fallen

Flirting with Death (a short story)

The Hunted series Omnibus

In The End duology

Sound of Silence

Light in Darkness

In The End Omnibus

Stand Alone Titles

Cast In Moonlight

Favor of the Gods

KINGDOM OF

ARUM

Shadow World

Kassia

SHADOW FIELDS

cabin

WASTE LANDS

THE Capital

Arum PALACE

Brumal

Eolda

Direvale

Rimeholde

Cyrindor

Maldan Ice Wall
Fae Lands
Mortal Lands
Gelid
Lummi
Holiston
Sunfall Mountains
Stone cliff
Winterfell
Firnhallow
Clearkeep
lmcrest
Avalan
N

To all who fight unseen battles.
Keep going. The night will give way to the dawn.

CHAPTER ONE

VIOLET

I HAVE A BROKEN HEART, AND ONE DAY SOON, IT WILL KILL ME.

The steady ticking of the clock on the mantel is an ever-present reminder that I am living on borrowed time.

Blinking my gritty eyes, I rise from my seat and stretch. My muscles are stiff and aching after hours of bending over a book, taking meticulous notes as I dissect each sentence, looking for any possible hidden meanings.

Despite the fire burning in the hearth, the early spring chill clings to the air in the study. I cross over to the window and gaze past the frost-rimmed glass to the street beyond the drive. Night gives way to twilight, and the outside world quiets with the dying howls of wild demons as they go into hiding. Pale, watery light leaks over the edge of the horizon, signaling the approaching dawn, and silhouetting the forest west of the city's border.

Determination and desperation have kept me going long past the time I should have gone to bed, and throughout the night. It would be easy to crawl under the warm blankets and stay there until midday. A few pages left to go over, followed by a full day's work ahead of me. Sleep will have to wait.

I glance back at the book open on the desk. It's not a particularly thick text, but it's from a time when language still held traces of a more archaic style, and medicine was believed to be magic that only the fae could perform. Any human practicing it either learned it from the fae themselves or stole that knowledge. The pages are yellow with age, and the leather binding is dry with flourishes of cracks. The title itself is innocuous: *A History of Winter's Flora.*

Other than needing a rebinding within the next few years, nothing about its appearance hints that it's special in any way. Let alone that it's one of the forbidden fae texts.

Taking it from the archives was a risk. It should have been returned centuries ago when the fourth king divided the fae and mortal lands, and along with it, he created the Old Laws.

No human shall possess one of the ancient fae texts.
No human shall trespass onto fae land uninvited.
No human shall take from the fae what is not given.

A human found in violation of any one of these laws is to die at the hands of the fae.

The fae may come and go as they please without consequence, though few do. Save for the Crown Prince with a heart made of ice, who they say is as handsome as he is wicked and cruel.

I've never met anyone who has personally seen him. It's always a friend of a friend of a friend who has. While the truth of his looks is unknown, there is not one person in all of Arum who is not familiar with his cruelty.

The likelihood that someone will discover it in my possession is minimal. They would have to know it existed and go looking for it first.

And if I don't find a cure, I'll be dead soon anyway.

With renewed purpose, I return to my seat and get back to work.

The remaining pages are a mix of passages written in ink that is too faded to read and entries on common plants or those that haven't been seen in ages.

When I am finally satisfied that I've gleaned every potentially useful word, I gently close the old leather-bound book. I read over my notes that barely fill a small handful of pages in my journal.

It has been over a year since I came across a promising lead. One entry in particular stood out to me while reading, holding a glimmer of hope.

Excitement races along my spine as I study the sketch from the book that I copied along the edge of my notes. It's a simple white flower with six rounded petals and long, slender leaves.

The frost bloom is a rare species, found as a small cluster that produces one to three flowers per plant. The period from the first sprout until full maturity is approximately a decade, followed by three to five years between viable harvests. It is said to have the ability to hold the effects of a curse at bay.

I press a palm to my chest and frown, wondering at the exact meaning of the word *curse* as it's used here.

The book was written in an age when it was widely believed that the majority of maladies were caused and cured by magic and often referred to as curses. There have only been a handful of true curses recorded throughout the Arum kingdom's history, as the victim is not the only one to bear the price. The methods of how curses are cast and broken are a closely guarded secret.

It's equally possible that the entry refers to a malady as it does to an actual curse.

Since the mortal lands were cut off, humans have made significant advances in understanding illnesses and injuries.

After years of studying all known plants with medicinal properties, I have never found a record of anything like this. Not that I, or anyone else in Firnhallow, for that matter, would have reason to possess knowledge of anything of fae origin.

I refocus on what matters now. I tap the tip of my pen at the end of a twice-underlined sentence.

The frost bloom grows nestled between the roots of other plants where magic is thin.

On this side of the border, there is a stretch where magic still seeps from the fae lands. Which means, there's a possibility of one of these plants growing on this side of the border. Getting there is simple enough. It's only a little more than an hour's ride at a leisurely pace.

I don't see what harm it would do to at least scout the area. I have time to cover a small segment before work if I leave within the half hour. If there is no sign of the frost bloom, then I can search the next section another time until I can determine whether this plant exists or is simply beyond my reach.

Closing my notebook with a snap, I decide to go over the rest later, after I determine whether the frost bloom is real or a thing of legend.

I fill my satchel with gloves, flower shears, and a small tin box with a silk handkerchief folded inside. I dress in woolen stockings and a warm riding skirt that will block most of the morning chill without being cumbersome, then don my long coat.

The click of my bedroom door closing behind me accentuates the emptiness of the otherwise silent house. I hesitate for a brief moment, then stride toward the bedroom on the other end of the hall. I knock as I open the door just wide enough to speak.

"I'm leaving to get a few things I need before work." I pause. "I will try to be back in a few hours."

There is no answer.

There never is.

It's still early by the time I near the border. The late spring morning feels refreshing. However, even on perfect days, one must always be prepared in case a nasty winter storm comes out of nowhere. They are unnatural and come regardless of the season, fueled by the wicked prince's tumultuous moods and his cold magic for the past fourteen years.

While I've gone to the forest many times in the past to gather herbs and roots, and though I've come close, I have never ventured quite this far.

Curiosity sparks within. Do the fae know the moment someone sets foot on their lands? Are there guards hidden by glamour right out in the open, waiting for humans foolish enough to break their law? Is being close considered a violation? Or so much as one toe over the line? Or are they lenient and only consider it breaking the second law if both feet are planted firmly on the other side?

There is no use worrying about the consequences of something I haven't done.

While I am curious, I have no desire to risk my neck to find out.

Even without a signpost or barrier to mark the line between the two territories, the border is unmistakable.

The trees on the other side are massive and pale, as if most of the color has been leached out. They look as if they belong to another world entirely. Without crossing, it's hard to tell if they gradually *become* ice or if they are covered in frost that thickens the further in they grow until they are armored in a thick sheet of it.

Slowing my mare Zasu into an easy walk, I guide her as close to the perimeter as I dare, then begin scanning both sides for any sign of the flower.

With a slight shift of my weight, Zasu obeys my commands as if she can read my mind. She was a gift from my parents when I was five. They tried to persuade me to give her a typical horse name like Thunder, Victory, Cinnamon, or Midnight, but I insisted on Zasu Moon. Though I can no longer remember how I came up with it, the name stuck.

After several miles, the trees grow closer together. The frost on both sides has grown thicker. Everything ahead and on either side appears the same for as far as I can see, blurring the line. I have to look closely to spot the boundary.

Halting my mare, I dismount and loosely tie the reins to a low branch, then make my way into the grove. The frosted ground crunches lightly beneath my boots as I wander between the trees, avoiding the patches of snow that pepper the loam.

The snap of a small branch comes from behind, sending my heart hammering painfully in my chest. I whip around, gaze darting in search of the source. But nothing is out of place. All I see is Zasu, exactly where I found her waiting, calm and patient.

I take a moment to slow my racing pulse to avoid having an unnecessary episode.

Stop overreacting, Violet, I scold inwardly.

"It's not as though I'm doing anything wrong. I come into the forest all the time," I lecture myself under my breath.

Ducking under low branches, I weave my way forward.

A low plop comes from the side, slightly behind me. I blink, and as I turn, I catch the shift of a shadow from the corner of my eye.

I release a deep sigh that's part nervous laughter.

It was only snow falling from a branch, partially melted from the gradually warming morning.

Being so close to the fae lands has my nerves on edge.

It's about time I returned home to get ready for work. I can search again tomorrow.

I only manage a few steps when a large mound of snow falls. This time at my feet. The shadowy end of a demon sticks out, their back legs kicking as they try to wriggle free.

Where there is one, there are bound to be a harmony of demons nearby.

I search for somewhere to escape. Zasu is too far, but about twelve yards away is a clearing with a patch of direct sunlight breaking through the canopy. If I wait there, I will be safe until the stragglers are forced to retreat for the day. They won't be able to withstand the bright sun without being severely weakened.

The howl of demons hunting prey is eerily absent in the air, but I'm not about to take any chances. As I run, I throw a quick glance over my shoulder. The demon is nowhere in sight.

I don't stop until I reach the center of the clearing. Bracing one hand on my knee, I press the other over my heart and rub to ease the sharp pain that pierces my chest with each panting breath.

When my pulse has calmed and the ache has faded, I straighten up. There's no sign of demons anywhere—not even that cursed little creature, who quite literally tried to get the drop on me.

How odd. Demons are not known for their patience or subtlety once they've locked onto their prey.

I wait and listen. Several minutes pass, and all remains normal. Bird song and a gentle breeze rustling through the leaves are the only sounds that accompany the sound of my own breath.

When I finally take in my surroundings, nothing looks familiar. It seems I have gone farther than I realized. Until now, everything on either side of the border has only been touched by fae magic. This is something else entirely.

The trees on either side are vastly different than the natural border. It sends a chill crawling up my spine.

Like the surrounding areas, frost blankets the surface of everything. But here, the trees lean away as if blown by a great wind, and a solid sheet of ice, as clear and as smooth as glass, encases the vegetation—perfectly preserved destruction.

New foliage has sprouted and grown through the places where the ice does not touch. Years have passed since the savage force swept through here. In different circumstances, if it were natural, the sight would be beautiful.

But it's not.

It cannot be melted by fire, broken by weapon, or removed by any means available to humans. The same that everyone brave enough to protect the mortal cities will all, eventually, fall victim to. As familiar to me as the back of my own hand—the same ice that took everything from me.

Only the monstrous Winter Dragon that the Crown

Prince summoned from the Otherworld to plague this kingdom could cause such ruin. And it is just as cursed as the beast itself.

All anger instantly vanishes when my gaze snags on a vibrant patch of green.

Tucked into a crevice between two thick roots of a wide, twisted tree is a plant, untouched by ice or frost. The vibrant spring color shines through. Long, slender leaves sprout from slender stalks, and at the top of each one is a delicate, pale, white flower.

Hope leaps in my chest at the sight.

I make my way over to it on shaky legs and kneel, quickly taking the supplies from my bag. I clasp my hands together to stop the trembling before reaching for the flower. If they are as rare as the book claims, then I highly doubt I'll find more if I harvest it incorrectly.

Once I have the tin set out and open on the ground, I pull on my gardening gloves and pick up the shears. I take a deep breath to steel my nerves. Pinching one stock a few inches from the top, I snip just below the first set of leaves, then place it in the tin. Then repeat with the remaining flowers. The more I gather, the more potent the cure.

Carefully, I fold the handkerchief over the blooms, then snap the lid on. I quickly gather my things and get to my feet, smoothing out my skirts.

My hands still.

The lateness of the morning has not escaped me, nor has the possibility of a few demons still lurking about. What has escaped my notice is the exact location of the border. The telltale markings are harder to spot due to the unnatural ice, and I stopped paying attention entirely when I ran.

The border is still nearby—only now, I'm on the wrong side.

Worse than a potential demon waiting in ambush would be getting caught breaking one of the Old Laws.

I hastily shove the rest of my belongings into my bag and head back the way I came, not slowing even when I cross back to the mortal side.

The sight of my mare, alive and unconcerned, fills me with relief.

Snow crunches beneath my boots. A muffled whimper startles me, causing me to stumble. I barely manage to catch my balance. Looking around for the source of the sound, I spot the thing I'd tripped over.

The small, upended demon from earlier is still stuck and mostly covered in snow from their flailing attempts to get free. The creature whimpers again, more pathetically this time.

Anxious to flee as far from my crime and this demon as I can get, I continue toward Zasu.

I've only taken a few steps when it cries again like an injured animal. I close my eyes with a groan.

Deep down, I know the empathy tugging at me for this demon is beyond idiotic. They are like any other wild animal, except far more dangerous. This time, the sound they make is like an injured puppy.

Cursing my soft heart, I turn back. I crouch down, pluck them from the snow, then hold them up to eye level.

They have the same animal-like form as all higher demons. From distorted bones, a knobby spine, ribs that stick out of their middle, to the claw-like hands with deadly talons at the end of long limbs that bend and twist at the joints in painful-looking angles.

Large, shining ruby eyes stare up at me. Their tongue lolling from their open mouth and limbs dangling loosely, seemingly unbothered by being held upside down.

There's no mistaking that this is a demon. Not a formless lesser demon. They wouldn't be able to withstand the light, even protected by the shadows of the forest. But they seem far too small to be a higher demon. Perhaps a baby?

Do demons have babies?

Surely not.

Every demon in existence spawned from the depths of the Otherworld, having escaped into this world when magic was shapeless and feral. This one must be one of the weaker ones.

"I am going to put you down now," I say slowly.

The demon cocks their head to the side.

"I saved you—so don't attack me."

The demon blinks.

Taking that as an answer, I slowly turn them over and set them right-side up on the mound of snow.

"Stay," I order, as I rise and begin to back away. Careful not to make any sudden movements, I inch toward Zasu and climb into the saddle.

The demon is a dark gray blot in the shadows, exactly where I left them.

Thanking the saints for my luck, I urge my mare toward home.

CHAPTER TWO

JOON

A DARK SHADOW LOOMS JUST BEYOND THE EDGES OF MY VISION AS I traverse the darkened corridors. Nothing but silence reaches my ears. Beyond the leaded windows, stars shine impossibly bright against the clear, dark night without the moon to command the attention of all who look toward the heavens.

This is the only home I have ever known, yet everything is unfamiliar.

Terror thrums through my veins, urging me to run… to flee back the way I came. I am helpless to fight the compulsion controlling my body, keeping me moving forward. The halls twist and turn in on themselves with no end in sight—a labyrinth of shadows.

The polished wood is painfully cold beneath my bare feet. I stop before an opening in the floor. Stairs spiral deep into the dark depths where something ominous and vicious waits.

Whispers in my ear layer atop each other like a hundred tiny voices. Words I cannot quite understand, yet I feel their demand in my bones. The pull to descend is undeniable.

Spiraling steps lead down to dizzying depths below the palace. Continuing until it's all I know anymore. An endless eternity, stretching out.

I blink and I'm standing on solid ground before a rough-hewn opening, a path of dirt and sharp rocks that cut into my bare flesh with every step. But still, I'm driven forward.

Darkness swallows the world, until all that is left is the path a few feet ahead. The umbra pushes and shoves me onward until I stop before a rippling mirror coated in frost.

My hand, small like that of a child, reaches out, and I press it to the smooth surface. It crackles under my palm as it clears to reveal my reflection. The face is mine, but the smile spreading across my mouth is not.

"It didn't have to be this way," the boy who is me but not me says in a rasping, harsh voice of a man I do not recognize. "They didn't have to die for you."

Die... for me? Who?

I don't understand what he means. Why would anyone have to die for my sake?

The reflection twists and lengthens, reshaping to a tall figure. A man I do not know, shrouded in shadow. He lifts his head and... it is my face, twisted in rage and disgust and hate. "You killed them!"

No! I try to shout, but my mouth refuses to move.

I jerk back. A crack forms in the glass where my palm was. The fissure spreads, spiderwebbing out to the edges. The mirror shatters in a violent explosion. I raise my arms to cover my face, but I'm not fast enough—a searing pain pierces my eye.

Blood fills my vision as I drop to my knees. Slowly, I lift my head. The mirror is whole again. My body trembles violently at what I see in the pristine surface.

A large fragment of glass protrudes from my eye. I rip it out and fall forward, catching myself with my hands.

"You are nothing. Less than nothing."

Slow footsteps circle me as the words echo around me. I can only stare at the scar cutting through my eye from brow to cheek.

"The world will see you for what you are. Weak and pathetic."

I try to scream but can't find my voice.

"You do not deserve the peace of death for what you have done."

I try to think about what he means and fail.

The voice continues speaking, but the words become too muffled, growing farther and farther away until they fade entirely.

I lift my head. I am alone before the mirror that is somehow whole again. A faint ghostly shimmer of lines dances over the surface.

My reflection behind the ghostly shapes is nothing more than a fourteen-year-old boy.

The slash through my eye has become a pale scar. As a member of the royal family, I was born with the ability to heal, the innate magic erasing all traces. This line is a sign of weakness—that I lack even the ability to heal completely.

A deafening roar fills my ears as something deep within struggles to break free.

Blinding pain rips through me as impenetrable darkness swallows my consciousness.

I bolt upright, drenched in a cold sweat. A deep ache lingers from the dream as all detail fades from my mind, leaving behind nothing but fear, self-loathing, and regret too strong to escape.

Light streams in from the window. It is mid-morning. Although I slept in, I do not feel rested.

A shrill warning bell goes off, signaling that the magical wards placed around the forest have been broken. The sound is silent to all except for me and two others.

Who would dare cross the border just to forfeit their life at my hands?

I throw the blankets off and climb out of bed. Dressing quickly, I ignore the fact that I am the only royal in my family's line to ever perform such a menial task on my own.

After the first year, I grew to prefer it this way. Now, the idea of having anyone dress me would feel awkward, as if I were nothing but a mere plaything for servants.

A frost-white dragon, nearly the length of my forearm, passes into my room through a wall. "The wards have been breached," they say.

"I am aware, Imugi," I snap.

They are entirely unfazed by the terse reply as they float in large circles above my head. "Perhaps it is a faulty warning?" they offer. "It's been years since a human dared."

I snarl at the demon, and in response, they draw up, curling their long body to face me. Their winter-blue eyes flash the red of molten gold.

The moment is broken by a knock at the door.

"What is it?" From the pure irritation in my voice, no one could mistake my mood for anything pleasant.

Instead of a response, the door slides open and my second steps through, closing it before rushing over. The king's messenger bows, then straightens without bothering to wait for the order to do so. Few could get away with such informality, though he is careful to show proper respect when necessary.

"My Prince, King Sameun wishes to see you. Allow me to scout the forest to find the cause of the alert." Mingi is very careful with his words, making the last part nearly soundless in case one of the palace spies happens to be listening in.

I grab my riding jacket and unceremoniously yank my hat onto my head with more force than necessary. "Unfortunately, my uncle must wait to ask, yet again, if I am ready to accept the crown," I bite out. "There are matters I must attend to first that cannot be put off. I am sure he will understand."

With that, I stride past Mingi and throw open the door. A passing woman squeaks in surprise and rushes off, darting around the nearest corner.

Imugi rushes to curl around my neck, secure in the safety of the shade of my hat, while Mingi trails behind, hand resting on the pommel of his sword.

As we leave the Western Court's corridors and step outside, everyone in the vicinity is careful to avert their gaze and bow at the waist.

We stop at the entrance to the stable, and within moments, two horses are saddled and brought out. No words are spoken as Mingi and I mount our waiting horses, then ride through the front gate.

Once the palace is out of sight, I close my eyes and focus on the location where the alarm sounded as I summon the fae road, changing the path ahead.

It is not simply that a human dared to break one of the Old Laws—for that, I might have sent Mingi—it was the specific location breached.

This is a matter I must attend to personally.

The timing seems anything but coincidental. It could be a plot concocted by one of my enemies within the palace walls. Luring an unsuspecting human to do their dirty work.

My gut twists at the possibilities. I am already running short on time. Whether by mistake or design, I will hunt down this trespasser and make them regret crossing me.

Trees slip past at blurring speed. I urge my mount faster.

My tenuous hold on my power slips further with every passing year. The beast within me stirs earlier each time. It is too soon. Yet, it is not entirely unexpected. It will not be long before I lose control entirely.

Fury and fear mix like a bitter storm in my blood.

"Imugi!" I grind out, "Can't this infernal animal go any faster?"

They act without needing to respond. A puff of frost extends from the dragon-like demon's mouth, drifting with intention toward the horse's muzzle as if we stood still. The animal inhales, pulling the misty cloud into its lungs.

Instantly, we pick up speed. I hear Mingi shouting as we leave him behind. He will catch up. But this dark foreboding clings to my back like a monster intent on swallowing me whole.

I must see for myself if what I fear is true or if it's a lingering fragment left behind by the nightmare.

The horse's hooves pound like thunder in time with the beating of my pulse.

After what feels like a torturous eternity, I catch sight of the border in the distance. I pull on the reins and leap from the saddle before my mount has come to a stop. Paying no heed to the cursed ice that engulfs the land, I race to the small clearing.

A harmony of lesser demons has gathered in the shadows

around the area, fighting over some object even as they shriek and recoil from the diffused sunlight.

I lift a hand and send out an icy blast, sending them scattering.

My chest heaves with labored breaths. I come up short and stare in disbelief.

The flower is gone.

Nothing remains but the stubs of cleanly cut stocks. Even without a closer inspection, it's clear that this work was done by the hand of a human.

Demon shit.

It takes great effort to suppress the storm building inside.

"Imugi, search the area," I grind out.

I approach the scene of the crime with measured steps and crouch. Those infernal lesser demons have trampled the traces of footprints. In my attempts to conserve as much power as possible, I have been lax in my duties.

Pressing a palm to the ground, I let my power build, then send it flowing into the land, strengthening the barrier against the Otherworld that allows the frost bloom to grow.

A cold sweat breaks out across my forehead. I grit my teeth against the bone-deep ache of my limited magic leeching from my veins.

When it is done, I exhale and sit on the ground, resting my arms over bent knees, not caring how unroyal it is to let the dirt soil my clothes.

"I caught a lesser demon trying to bury this just beyond the border," Imugi says, floating from between two trees.

They drop their findings onto my outstretched hand—a lone, delicate glove.

What would a demon want with this?

I bring it to my nose and inhale deeply. Beyond the smoky

scent of demons is that of a human woman. Light and floral with a hint of ink. An unusual combination.

There is no doubt that it belongs to the one who stole this flower.

No other frost bloom will be ready for harvest this year—let alone in the next five days. The curse on this land made sure of that. All but a few of these plants were wiped out, leaving only a single plant to come to maturity once a year, counting down to the time when I will lose control completely—and permanently.

Without it, we are all doomed.

Pain pierces my skull as the beast within me struggles to break free. I grunt. Imugi is speaking, but I can't focus on what they're saying.

Too soon. It's too soon. The dragon fights against its binds. *It shouldn't be waking so soon.*

Relief flows over me as Imugi envelops me in a fog of their power, lending me the temporary strength I need.

"Thank you," I murmur, finally getting to my feet.

The hurried thunder of a rider approaches from down the road. It took him less time than expected to catch up.

"My Prince," Mingi calls out. He leaps from his horse and races the rest of the way. "What did you find? What happened?"

I crumple the glove in my fist. I will find that woman before the day is through—and for her sake, she better hope part of that plant is still viable.

"I will need you to cover for me until tonight."

"Your Highness, let me accompany you—"

I face him. "You will be more useful here. I will return before the moon is at its peak."

He frowns, clearly not liking this. "Will you at least tell me what you plan to do?"

Besides Imugi, he and his sister Iseul are the only ones I trust enough with the truth. He knows what I must do and how. Yet, still, I hesitate. "I will explain upon my return."

Mingi presses his mouth into a tight line. It's as far as he will allow his defiance to go.

I return to my horse, waiting patiently and fully restored. Imugi expended their powers more than I noticed. "Go with Mingi," I order gently.

"But—"

"I will not do anything that requires my power. The sun will only drain you further. So go and rest. You have done enough for today."

Mingi and Imugi depart quietly. I wait until they are out of sight, and the road they travel vanishes. Then I turn my mount in the opposite direction and ride, following the faint scent that matches the glove. Such minor magic is negligible, and most common fae are capable of the same in some limited capacity.

The woman's trail takes me to the nearest human city. I pause on the crest of a hill overlooking the people bustling about as they go about their mundane lives.

I use my glamour to transform my clothing and disguise my features that would give me away.

Upon entering the city, a myriad of scents mingles, muddying the trail—food, oil, smoke, perfume on skin, and more I don't care to identify. I move through the streets, for the most part, ignored by the inhabitants. For a moment, I lose the trail before picking it up again. After it happens several more times, my patience runs out.

I use my power to distinguish the traces of the woman I seek, and call up a shimmering blue thread, visible only to those with fae blood in their veins or who were given the gift of fairy sight. It leads me past several humble homes and further into the city center.

The end of the glowing blue thread is wrapped around a woman as she enters a building across the street. She disappears inside and does not emerge again.

The force of my full ire rises to the surface. I wait. She cannot remain in there forever.

I will break my promise to Imugi before I leave this place.

CHAPTER THREE

VIOLET

Tiny bubbles form on the bottom of the pot. The grandfather clock in the other room ticks away. I watch closely, waiting for the first large bubble before I remove it from the heat.

Years of studying have led me to this point—watching water boil so I can make tea from a rare plant that could cure me, do absolutely nothing, or just as likely kill me.

A teacup holding the crushed flower paste sits patiently on the table for the next step.

I run my finger over the directions one more time to make sure I have followed them to the letter... as much as possible, anyway. They are not quite as clear as I would prefer.

Using a stone mortar and pestle that has been purified by fire, then cleansed with melted snow.

It's unclear if that means to do these through ritual or simply by placing it in fire and then washing it with melted snow to clean away any lingering ash. I interpreted it as the latter, but now doubt gnaws at my insides.

The fae are known for their powers of glamour and compulsion and deception, among other things, but not rituals, or anything in that vein. However, that means very little when they keep most of their abilities secret from humans.

Crush the fresh leaves and petals of the frost bloom. Take care never to let the white petals come in contact with skin.

The entry goes on to explain that they would turn as transparent as ice and rot the delicate magic within. As fascinating as it would be to see, it isn't worth giving up my last chance to grow another year older.

Place the mashed poultice in a cup. Boil the water, removing it from the heat when the first large bubble forms, then pour the water. Stir until the contents dissolve, then let the mixture steep for ten minutes before drinking.

I hadn't written the warning down. I didn't need to. Such things as *"under-steeping will cause the plant to retain its poisonous properties, and over-steeping will cause the magic to rot and speed the curse to its ultimate end,"* tend to stick with a person.

Giving the page a curt nod, I bite down on my bottom lip and turn back to the pot. My anticipation grows.

Not much longer.

I barely allow myself to blink until I see what I've been waiting for. Gripping the pot with a folded hand towel, I take it to the table and carefully fill the teacup, then flip over the minute glass to time it.

The paste dissolves with a few stirs. Instantly, the water becomes a deep blue with a beautiful floral aroma rising on white curls of steam.

The sand slips through the narrow glass neck. Gradually, the tea lightens to a bright blue—more vibrant than any summer sky or paint pigment I have ever seen. It's hard to believe that small, white flower holds magical properties capable of affecting curses—and that it would be such a simple thing to prepare.

I don't know if I am cursed, but after so long without a single answer or cure, it feels like one.

As the final grains of sand fall, I bring the teacup to my mouth and whisper a desperate plea, "Please work. Please work. Please work." My breath sweeps the tendrils of steam from the surface of the water.

Then I drink until all that remains are glass-clear crushed petals that haven't dissolved after all.

Warmth spreads through me, but it's no different than with any other tea. A tingle so slight sweeps over my skin, though it's impossible to tell if it is working or if it's nothing more than anticipation and nerves fueling my imagination.

The grandfather clock chimes the hour. It's later than I realized.

Demon shit.

Before heading upstairs to get ready for work, I do a quick clean.

I place the final pin to secure my hair into a simple, albeit slightly messy, twist at the nape of my neck. With that, I don my jacket and hat and grab my satchel. A little over half an hour after my little experiment, I'm on my way out the door.

The streets and sidewalks are busy, as usual, during mid-morning. Each step causes the book to bounce against my hip like a thudding heartbeat while I focus on keeping my pace steady. I return the smiles and nods of the familiar faces, waiting for one of them to stop me, reach into my bag for the satin-wrapped parcel, and reveal my crime to the world.

Perhaps it would have been better to wait until this

evening to try the experiment. At least then my nerves could fray in the privacy of my own home.

An eternity passes before I reach the top of the steps to the archives. Warm air washes over me as I enter. The familiar scent of aged paper, ink, and leather is calming. This place has given me a sense of peace each time I step foot through the door.

Mr. Shaw is already reshelving books from the previous day. His hair is parted to one side and combed neatly. A few black strands persist in the mass of thick grays. He moves slowly, and though his back is slightly bent with age, his hearing is as sharp as ever. He pushes his thin, circular wire glasses up the bridge of his nose as he turns.

"How are you this morning, Mr. Shaw?"

The older man is one of the kindest people I know, though most find him unapproachable because he doesn't talk much. It's not that he's quiet so much as he prefers to wait for others to give him room to speak.

"Ah, Violet, it's always good to see your smiling face," he says, then nods toward the large clock behind the main desk. "You'd better get going. Miss Byron arrived fifteen minutes ago, and she's been looking for you."

My brows rise. "What mood was she in?" I ask in a conspiratorial whisper, leaning in.

He hums thoughtfully while scratching under his chin. "She is either happy or up to no good again.... It's difficult to say."

Talya is likely plotting something to torture Sebastian again.

There are times I envy them for having each other... then again, when they argue, I'm glad to be an only child.

I wave to Mr. Shaw and hurry toward the back room.

The lights are on, but it's silent. Talya isn't waiting for me as expected. She must have gotten bored waiting.

Quickly shrugging off my jacket, I hang it on the coat stand with my hat. I don't waste time taking the wrapped book from my bag and striding down the last row of books. Reshelving the book exactly where I found it brings an immediate sense of relief.

It was mixed in among a handful of antiquated human books that line the three bottom rows of the bookcases in the far back corner. The section reserved for books kept for prosperity that are considered low priority. Texts with information that has long been proven to be outdated.

It's hard to say if they were intentionally hidden or stored there by mistake and forgotten when the fae demanded their return generations ago.

The door of the back room swings open on squeaky hinges. It's followed by a thud of books being unceremoniously plopped onto the worktable, causing my heart to thud painfully against my ribs.

"Oh, good, you're finally here, Violet," Talya calls out from the entry. Her voice fills the room. "Where are—"

Instantly rising onto my toes, I begin wiping the highest shelf I can reach just as she rounds the far end of the aisle.

"There you are!" Talya heaves a sigh, letting her shoulders slump in exaggerated relief. She looks around, arching a brow. "What are you doing back here?"

I wave the cloth in my hand and start swiping at the next shelf down. "Just… dusting?"

"I've been waiting hours for you!"

"You have not." I snort. "You only got here a few minutes before me. Besides, I got here at the same time I always do. "

"Fine, fine… it *feels* like I've been waiting hours." Talya grabs me by the wrist and pulls me to the other side of the aisle as if it will somehow give us additional privacy.

Playing innocent, I ask, "Is something the matter?"

Talya ignores my obvious act and bounces impatiently like a little kid waiting to go to the fair. "Something amazing happened, and I am about to burst if you don't let me tell you in the next five seconds!"

"Don't keep me in suspense," I say.

"Do you remember when Mr. Marston came by with his eldest son two weeks ago?" I nod as she continues without waiting for an answer, "*Well,* when Father took them to the study after dinner, I thought for sure they were discussing trying to marry me off to Henry—but as it turns out, he was secretly courting Pearl Buntham and the two of them will be engaged by the end of the month. I cannot tell you how relieved I was when Father told me, but that didn't explain why he'd been talking to Mr. Marston almost daily since then." Talya offers a broad grin, her round cheeks causing her eyes to close.

"That's great," I offer, not knowing what else to say. I knew she never wanted to marry him, but there's more to this story for this level of excitement.

Her expression falls. "Honestly, Vi, sometimes I can't tell if you are messing with me."

I grimace apologetically. Talya shakes her head, laughing lightly.

"Well, Mr. Marston felt horrible and mentioned how Lilly is now 'of age,'" she says in a mocking tone before grasping my hands in hers and squeezing so hard my joints pop.

"She apparently cares deeply for Sebastian—it seems the two of them shared more than one dance at her coming out ball—so now the two of them are engaged, and the Marstons are going to donate an amount equal to her dowry to the archives—and that's not even the best part! Father said he'll give me the next year to learn how to handle the books under his supervision before he retires and leaves me in charge of running this place!" Talya finishes in a rush that leaves her nearly breathless in her barely contained excitement.

I couldn't be happier for Talya and even Sebastian.

"That's fantastic, you've wanted this for so long." I pull her in for a hug.

"Just think, if Sebastian and Lilly hadn't danced together, Father might have given all this to him, leaving me stuck at home raising Henry's children. Don't get me wrong, he's nice enough, but he's as much fun as a soggy piece of bread." Talya releases a long breath and leans against the bookcase. "I've never been so glad for two people to believe in love at first sight."

My friend doesn't have a romantic bone in her body.

A wicked grin spreads over her lips. "Now we can keep working together, and I will get to be the best aunt ever and play with his children anytime I want, filling them up with loads of sugar before sending them home."

The Byron family has run the archives for generations. While Sebastian never complained about the work, he also never took to it the way Talya had. For him, it was a family business. An obligation that was simply a part of life. She implemented new systems to catalog the books more efficiently, making them easier to find based on subject matter and titles.

The three of us practically grew up together. They were like the siblings I never had. As children, we would play among the stacks and pretend to work, though we mostly created more work for Sebastian.

Talya loves being at the archives more than anywhere else in the world. Once we were old enough, we joined her brother. He tortured us relentlessly the first year, paying us back for all the trouble we used to cause.

It wasn't long before she convinced her father to hire me to restore and rebind worn books. I suspect he initially agreed to it due to the fact that it is one of the few places in Firnhallow willing to employ someone like me.

After proving my usefulness, Mr. Byron had me begin restoration on historical texts before moving on to the highly valued editions. He even allowed me the option to study whatever I wanted in the main area of the library or to restore any book considered obsolete in the time between jobs.

Our conversation winds down with the tolling of the city's central bell tower, signaling the official start of our day. Talya walks me to my worktable. She leaves me to start on this week's rebindings as she returns to the front to assume her duties.

The work is consistent yet not frequent enough to keep me busy all the time. Over the years, I have made my way through every book on the body, illnesses, and medicine available.

I would even take the texts home and spend long nights studying, hoping to find anything that could cure my condition. Or at least give me more time.

Putting all thoughts of forbidden books and fae from my mind, I lose myself in my work. My hands glide over leather and paper in a series of movements I could probably do in my sleep.

I don't look up until a soft knock on the door breaks my concentration.

Talya pokes her head in. "It's nearly five. You can go whenever you are ready." She steps fully into the room and props a hip against the table. "I'm going to stay a little longer. I want to make a list of everything I need to do in the next year.

I'm going to prove to Father that he is right to trust me with this."

I stand and stretch. "All right," I say, gathering my things. "Promise not to stay past six?"

"Seven."

"Six-thirty." I cross my arms.

"Deal!" she says, and we shake on it.

Excited or not, Talya doesn't need to take chances—especially when it's not absolutely necessary.

The streets are well lit at night, and the town is encircled by lamps that are kept lit all hours of every day, but that is no guarantee of safety from the wild demons that roam the shadows after dark.

For the first time since the start of my shift, I allow my mind to drift back to the cure. I wonder if it has worked or if I did nothing more than put in a lot of effort for a single cup of tea.

I button my jacket, then step out into the early evening. The sky is clear, but the air holds an icy chill that's not typical for this time of year. I search my bag for my gloves, but there is only one.

"Pardon me," a deep, rich voice says from behind. "I believe you dropped this."

I turn to find the stranger holding out my other glove. He's tall, with dark hair and full lips. The muscles of his sharp jaw are tense. He is clad in a long, dark jacket and a square top hat with the brim pulled low, hiding his eyes.

He clears his throat, and I realize I'm staring.

"Oh, thank—," I reach for the glove, but the man's fingers wrap around my wrist. My words are cut off by the abruptness of the gesture.

The man lifts his jaw and peers at me with brilliant, electric-blue eyes, burning with anger. A long pale scar runs from his brow to his cheek over one, changing the iris to a slightly different shade. Yet it does nothing to distract from his devastatingly handsome face. If anything, it adds to it.

I can only gape.

He releases me, breaking the spell. Then he's gone, leaving me alone, with glove in hand, wondering what in the Otherworld just happened.

CHAPTER FOUR

VIOLET

I look around at the other pedestrians milling about. No one has noticed the strange encounter.

I've never seen that man before in my life. I would remember if I had. So, what could I have possibly done to earn his ire?

Attempting to shake it off, I turn and head home as fast as I can without drawing unnecessary attention. I can't get the image of the man's eyes and the way they flashed out of my head.

Clouds glide across the sky, moving on a high wind to dim the early evening sun.

Those eyes...

Such an inhuman shade of blue. The ring of molten-red around the iris was so intense, it was almost...

Almost as if...

As if...

They belong to someone bonded to a demon.

No. It wasn't my imagination. The color was too bright from under the shadow of his hat—the only way it could possibly be that vibrant is if the rings glowed with demon-gifted power.

No... I shake my head. *I am overreacting.* If it were something to worry over, surely someone would have reacted.

Paranoia digs its claws into my back, making me imagine things that couldn't possibly be real.

The realization slams into me, and suddenly, the few blocks to the safety of home have turned into miles.

Goosebumps cover my arms. I have never seen anyone with demon-gifted power, but it is something we all learn as children.

Never go out at night unless it is unavoidable and the streets are well-lit. Avoid the shadows. And never—*ever*—venture into the wild after sunset. To do so is to court death by wild demons.

Footsteps clack along the sidewalk behind me. I glance back. A man is walking on the other side of the street, too far to tell if it is the man from earlier or another.

Facing forward again, I gradually pick up speed until I'm running. My heart pounds heavily.

Fear seizes my throat in its icy grip.

The weather turns, a wind kicking up as more dark clouds gather to swallow the sky.

A dark shape, little more than a dog-sized blur, shoots across the street, cutting across my path.

Wind howls as it cuts through the narrow alley. The bitter cold it brings promises a storm. But it is too late in the year for natural storms.

It can only mean one thing: the prince has summoned his dragon.

Panic rises, twisting my insides. I ignore the blooming ache in my chest and force my feet to move.

I pass through the iron gate at the edge of our property

and continue up the short path toward the front door of my home.

Nearly there...

My lungs squeeze. Painfully. Uselessly trying to pull in air. Black spots dance before my eyes. As hard as I try to keep from slowing, my limbs refuse to obey. I grasp at my chest as if I could take hold of whatever has wrapped itself around my heart and untwist it.

There's a sharp movement of a large shape along the edges of my vision. I flinch. In the next breath, I barely manage to keep from colliding with the tall figure standing between me and safety.

I open my mouth—to speak or scream—but before I get the chance, two strong hands grab me, slamming my back against something solid.

A strong arm encircles my shoulders at the same time as a sharp edge digs into the skin just below my jaw.

"Did you think you would get away so easily?" The question is more venomous growl than words.

Even if I could answer without slicing my throat open, I wouldn't be able to draw enough breath to form words.

I am blinded by pain. And if I hadn't felt it a thousand times before, I would think the man at my back had used that blade to pierce my lungs.

Every muscle in my body weakens as rasps scrape their way up my neck. I can't feel my legs. My half-numb fingers grasp uselessly onto the arm holding me up.

"It has been a long time since anyone dared to break the Old Laws. Now you will pay. If you even think of struggling, then everyone in this demon-cursed town will die with you. Do you understand?"

I nod.

He releases me, and I fall, knees and palms crashing to the

frigid stone drive. I can't think as I attempt to breathe through the unrelenting pain.

Maybe this will be the time when this weakness claims my life for good, I think bitterly.

The man moves into my line of vision. Perfectly pressed slacks and shoes made of the finest materials. He gracefully lowers to a crouch.

The pressure in my head begins to swallow my consciousness.

No. No, no, no, no.

Long, slender fingers pinch my chin. His touch is icy against my skin as he tilts my face up. Piercing electric eyes glare with cold detachment as he sneers. There is no mistaking the pure, unfiltered hate in the expression of the man from outside the archives. The gentlemanly hat is gone, and he wears the hood of his cloak over his head.

He scoffs and motions behind him. Then he's hauling me up by the arm and dragging me up the front steps. The door opens for him without resistance or key, then slams shut with a loud bang.

My ears ring. I whirl, panting, and face my captor.

Trapped—I am trapped with a man who hunted me down to murder me in my home. And there is no one close enough to hear if I scream for help.

"What do you want?" I demand. The sound of my voice is clear and strong, as if I hadn't just suffered one of my episodes.

The lingering pain is gone too.

I take a step back. Whatever that was, it couldn't have been an episode, despite what it felt like. Either way, *he* is undeniably responsible. "What did you do to me?"

The man's lip curls. "What did *I* do?" he repeats incredulously, taking three steps closer—a predator seconds preparing to ambush its prey. "You dare accuse me of something so petty? Others would die instantly for a lesser insult than that."

I stand silent, refusing to waver as I wait for an answer.

His back straightens as he moves to close the remaining distance between us and looks down his nose at me. "I did not come to watch a woman crumble at my feet in hysterics."

"I was *not* hysterical," I snap.

It's enough that I have gone most of my life being told how fragile and helpless I am because of my heart. Yet somehow, it hurts having it reduced to nothing more than a display of excessive emotion. Suddenly, it's all made worse because it means the cure didn't work. It was my last hope.

"Then enlighten me. What was that display?"

Why should I answer him when he hasn't answered my questions?

He arches a brow, and whether it's in disbelief or waiting for an explanation, I don't care. I owe him nothing.

"You said you've come to make me pay. Which means you've already decided on my guilt. So, tell me how you plan to do so."

A loud, humorless laugh bursts from his chest. I take several steps back, creating much-needed space.

"I wonder if you would be so bold if you knew who you were speaking to," he says. Slowly reaching up, he pinches the edges of his hood and lowers it.

His shining black hair is pulled into a high ponytail so long that it drapes over his shoulder. The last several inches fade to a shining white. A pale scar slashes through one eye, from above the center of his brow to the top of his cheekbone. It makes him look dangerous—like he could cause great pain or pleasure with little effort. His irises are not ringed with the glow of a demon bond as I imagined earlier. They are a brilliant, electric-blue with one a slightly lighter shade than the other.

My gaze snags on the pointed ears that give away what he is—*fae*.

His clothes are different now. He wears a pale blue shirt beneath a deep blue overcoat with silver frost embroidered along the edges.

The blood drains from my face because I know exactly why he is here.

"It has been a long time since anyone dared to break the Old Laws."

His earlier words come back to me.

A sharp smirk cuts across his mouth, noticing my recognition.

He somehow figured out that I crossed the border into the fae lands. It doesn't matter that it was by accident.

I'm thankful I at least had the wherewithal to clean up this morning. There shouldn't be any traces left of the tea. But exactly how much *does* he know? I have to say something before he does.

Demons and saints, think, Violet, think!

I scour my mind for the facts. He had my glove, so he knows I trespassed. He's here for my life, but hasn't killed me yet, which means he might not know about the book or the flower. If he suspects either, he can't prove it… unless he finds my notes.

I should have burned them before I left for work. Trying to do so now would only lead him to the evidence he needs to learn the full truth of my guilt.

Unless I can somehow secure my safety before.

"Were—"

"I want to bargain," I speak over him.

The fae man goes utterly still, lips parted.

All parents warn their children against bargaining with the fae. Both parties are bound to their promises by the magic—but they will trick you in any way they can.

It's imperative to be as specific as possible for anyone desperate enough to make a deal.

"Bargain with me," I say again. It is enough to bring him out of his shock.

He scoffs, scanning me from head to foot with narrowed eyes. The fae shifts, moving closer, not stopping until my back hits the wall and he's barely a hand's length away.

My eyes are level with his chest. Slowly, I lift my gaze to meet his. I pick my words carefully. "What happened earlier wasn't hysterics."

He blinks, frowning.

Good. I've thrown him.

"Then what was that pathetic display?"

"You frightened—you followed me home and held a blade against my neck," I snap. "I don't want to die."

The anger and annoyance fade from his expression, leaving a neutral expression behind.

"Do you think me foolish?" His voice is soft and low, as if he is promising something dark and forbidden. Yet, it cannot hide that it is a dangerous question.

My heart sinks like lead.

"What could a mere human even possibly have to offer?"

That… *wasn't* an outright refusal.

I swallow the lump in my throat. "I will help you with one thing you need—no matter what it is."

"What makes you think *I* need help? Do you have any idea of who I am?"

"Everyone needs help at some point in their life… no matter who they are." The argument sounds weak, even to my ears.

"And if I did, how is someone like *you* qualified to help *me*?"

Despair claws up my throat. "Accept my offer and see for yourself."

He inhales sharply. His piercing blue gaze searches my face for a long moment.

It was a reckless offer, but… *is it possible that he needs something desperately enough to consider my offer?*

When he seems to come to a conclusion, he braces a forearm against the wall, trapping me in the cage of his body.

He leans in, brings his mouth close to my ear on the opposite side, and says, "Do you have any idea what you have done?" His warm breath caresses my cheek, but it is the question that sends an icy chill down to the marrow of my bones.

My mouth goes dry. "What I've… done?"

"Have you not wondered why I am here—how I found you so easily?" He leans in, bringing a hand up to trail a finger along my jaw to grip my chin between his thumb and forefinger. "You trespassed onto fae lands."

He smells of a warm spring day. Of sun and trees and wind. The graceful features of his handsome face turn hard.

"Trespassed…" I murmur.

His proximity is making it hard to think. His touch is cold, and I can feel it radiate from his body along every inch of mine. *Is he using glamour or compulsion on me?*

"I…"

"You left your glove at the scene of the crime. From there, it was child's play hunting you down."

"My glove?" I frown. I thought my glove fell out of my pocket at the archives, but it seems it was nothing more than a ruse. A way to ensure he had the one he wanted. "I didn't mean to—"

"Didn't mean to?" he mocks. "You did not mean to *what?*"

I squeeze my eyes shut and shake my head, trying to clear my mind. "No, I—"

My eyes snap open at the loud thud of his fist against the wall.

"Do not think of trying to deny it," he grinds out. "You took what was not yours."

"Took?"

He pauses to breathe as if reining in his temper. When he speaks again, each word is slow and measured. "Will you stop repeating me as though you are some half-wit?"

I lower my chin and press my back against the wall, wishing it would swallow me. I do not think anyone has ever spoken to me with such venom or contempt in my life. Yet even I can admit that it's not entirely unearned. He has not accused me of anything I'm not guilty of.

As much as I want to deny everything until he believes me, I cannot bear to lower myself to such dishonesty.

Is there anything I could say to make things right without forfeiting my life?

My eyes remain locked on our feet. "I am sorry."

"There are traces of the frost bloom all over you."

It's not a question, but still, I nod.

"Is there anything left of it?"

I shake my head.

He falls quiet, the tension leaves his body as I wait for his next words. His judgment.

I knew the consequences when I decided to take the book from the archives.

"Let me—" He shakes his head. "Will you allow me to check you?" he asks in an unexpectedly gentle tone.

Slowly, I lift my gaze but cannot quite make myself meet his eye. He is within his rights to end my life.

"Please, don't hurt me." I cannot stop the words from rising up my chest and escaping.

He becomes so utterly still that I'm not sure he is even breathing.

"I will not hurt you," he says after a moment, almost tenderly.

Perhaps it is a mistake to trust him, but I do. I want to believe him. I nod, but when he doesn't do anything, I say, "Yes, you may check."

He cups my jaw with both hands and moves closer and closer, lowering his face until our noses are just shy of touching. His mouth parts ever so slightly. I am too stunned to be embarrassed by the intimacy of his proximity. Everything about him is made to seduce. His touch. His grace. The fullness of his lips. Even the scar that cuts through one eye from brow to cheek adds an air of allure that could put anyone's heart in danger of becoming beholden to him with just the right touch.

I hold my breath, unsure what or how he intends to find whatever he is looking for while doing my best to ignore that ridiculous voice in the back of my head, wondering if he plans on kissing me.

His eyes light up, a molten-gold ring encircling his irises flares, making the blue illuminate to an impossibly bright shade… the color of an intense summer sky. A soft glow radiates from within.

My head swims as his power takes hold. I am clay in his hands. It should frighten me with the way he could do anything to me in this moment, and I couldn't stop him.

"I… feel it inside you," he says so quietly, I would think I imagined it if not for his breath ghosting over my lips.

The spell is broken when he blinks, and his eyes return to their normal inhuman hue.

He releases me and straightens. "Not only did you prepare the drink, but you did it flawlessly. I do not know how, but you have come to possess knowledge only…" His words trail off, but he doesn't need to finish that thought.

Demon shit. He knows everything.

CHAPTER FIVE

VIOLET

"PERHAPS YOU CAN BE USEFUL AFTER ALL," HE MUSES. HIS EYES flick to my mouth, then back. "There is something I must do."

He is considering my offer with something specific in mind, even after acting as if he were above my help. But there's no time to feel smug.

"Obligate yourself into my service and bind yourself to me. If you fail to do what is needed, then you will die. However, if you succeed, I will consider the price of your crimes paid in full—and to show you how generous I can be, not only will I personally ensure you stay alive until you have fulfilled your end, but I will allow you to keep your life beyond that."

"How long will I be bound and obligated to you?" My throat is so dry that my voice is barely a whisper.

He hums. "I thought you wanted to live."

"I do," I say. "But I deserve to know the extent of what I'm agreeing to. What kind of life would it be if it were not mine in the end to live as I chose?"

He nods. "Then, if I succeed, you will be free of any obligation and binding."

I can't possibly imagine what I could do for a fae that he could not ask of a thousand others, far more capable, but I don't intend to waste this opportunity.

"What must I do to fulfill my end?"

He steps back, and warmth fills the space between us. "You will find out once you are bound and obligated. The details are too important to speak before then." When I don't answer right away, he adds, "So, what will your decision be? Will you bargain or die where you stand?"

"Does it count as a bargain if I'm forced into it?"

"You were the one who wanted to bargain in the first place," he says flatly. "I am merely providing you with... *motivation* to decide."

"Still, death threats are a bit much from someone who didn't even need my help five minutes ago," I mutter.

"Would it help if I offered to kill everyone you know and love?" he quips.

My eyes dart toward the second floor before I can stop myself, and he catches it.

"Who else is here?" he snarls.

"No one," I say.

He's already moving toward the stairs. I try to block him, but he pushes past. I race after him. He has already opened the doors to the other rooms and is striding toward my parents' room.

"Wait—"

He opens the door and pauses on the other side of the threshold, giving me time to catch up.

The fae continues further in, though I cannot bring myself to follow. He stops a few feet from my parents, their bodies frozen and trapped within enchanted ice. The tension slips from his posture, shoulders sagging.

They, like countless others over the years, are among the brave who volunteer to protect their town from the dragon who brings winter storms throughout the year, terrorizing the innocent people of this empire by turning them into *this*.

"If I succeed, then I will break this curse on them all."

The way he says it makes it sound like a small, insignificant thing. That promise tells me what I have failed to realize before now—he is no ordinary fae, but the wicked fae prince who commands the Winter Dragon.

No one else has the power to free its victims.

The prince crosses to the mortal lands once a year, and for one reason—the Choosing.

The depth of the obligation he demands crashes down around me. It is far more than servitude—I would be his wife.

At least until he sacrifices me to his monstrous beast, as he had his six wives that came before me.

It's no wonder he didn't want to give me details before I agreed.

My hands ball into fists at my sides. I cannot afford to lose my temper now—especially not with the most powerful fae Arum has ever known. The one who is the reason, I've been alone for the past three years, never knowing if I will get the chance to hear my parents' voices again or hug them one more time before my heart ceases for good.

"Why not now?" The question slips unbidden.

He glances over his shoulder. "You cannot expect payment without having done the work first," he says, though not unkindly.

The cruelty is gone from his face. There is something so sorrowful in his features when he is not delivering threats.

Is this nothing more than a facade to disarm me, or is he a tormented soul using his claws to keep the world at a distance? I squeeze my eyes tight to shove away the absurd thought. *Of course it's a trick.*

He turns and strides past me, moving so fast that I barely manage to catch him as he reaches the front door.

I can't let him leave. Not yet.

I may die at the end of it all, but if there's a chance my sacrifice can help the people who have suffered for too long under him, then I will have done more than I ever dreamed possible.

"I'll do it. I'll bind myself to you—I will be your wife and obligate myself into your service if you promise to break the dragon's curse." Then, for good measure, I add, "And keep me alive until the end of it—no sacrificing me to your dragon." I am as clear as possible so that later, he cannot claim that I didn't ask for what I wanted.

One corner of his mouth ticks up, but there is no triumph or glee in it. Once more, he approaches.

"I will do all you have asked. In exchange, you will freely bind and obligate yourself to me until my task is complete." Taking my hand, he rests it over his forearm. "In three days, I will come for a bride. Do whatever you must to ensure you are in a position to become that bride."

I nod. I don't know precisely what marriage to him will entail. I doubt it will include anything typical.

"Will…" I hesitate, "will we be truly married?"

"Why?" His long, elegant fingers wrap around my wrist. "Is the thought of being my wife repulsive enough to give you second thoughts?"

I shake my head. "No… I just…" I feel my cheeks warm slightly.

"It is a formality to provide a reason to keep you close. The moment we succeed, our bargain will come to an end, and so too will our marriage. You will not have to endure being tied to me eternally." His upper lip curls in a sneer.

A hum of energy races through me as his fingertips glide over my skin. Where he touches, a shimmering thread forms. It lengthens as he guides it around his. Each end snakes out as if it were alive, and knots around the base of our middle fingers. The thread catches the light as it moves, alternating between silver, black, deep blue, and then red.

He releases me, and as the space between us grows, so does the thread, keeping us connected before fading from sight.

The bargain is sealed.

"Keep in mind, you will not be able to speak of this bargain to anyone. I do not suggest testing it. You may find the effects unpleasant." He turns to leave, pausing with his hand hovering over the doorknob. "Remember—three days."

I blink, eyes tired from sleep eluding me all night, just as it had the two before. Smiles are not enough to hide the dark circles under my eyes or the pallor of my skin.

If Talya notices my weariness in my work, she doesn't say anything. She never does.

I've never known if it's because she doesn't want to remind me of my impending death looming ever closer, or if she cannot bear to acknowledge the unpleasant reality of my condition, or if she's determined to be the one person who doesn't look at me with pity.

The weight of the fae text bumping against my hip with every step has my nerves on edge. I feel as though anyone who looks at me will instantly know it's there. Once more, I've smuggled it out of the archives.

There was only a small window of time to grab it before Sebastian and Talya glued themselves to my side for the festivities before the Choosing. I didn't dare risk anyone catching me breaking the Old Laws again by taking it sooner.

I thought I should return it to the prince as a gesture of good faith. And perhaps a little leniency, if I'm being honest.

Like every other business in town, with the exception of the shops at the heart of the square, the archives are closed today. The three of us met bright and early, taking two hours to reshelve yesterday's books and prepare everything for the next day.

A few years after my episodes, I woke in the middle of the night from a bad dream. My parents' voices floated up from downstairs. They didn't shout, but there was tension in their words I wasn't used to hearing. I tiptoed to the top of the stairs to listen. Mother was crying, and they were talking about me as though I were already dead.

That was the moment I realized I'd let fear and misery take over my life, and I'd been blind to the hurt it caused everyone who cares about me.

As I sat at the top of the stairs, I vowed to do everything I could to find a cure and to live my life as if I were promised the same number of years as anyone else.

My nerves have been tangled into a tightly wound ball since the moment I sealed the bargain with the prince. In the past few nights, I have been seeing the inevitable in the same way I used to view my impending death. In the final hour before dawn, I finally stopped tossing and turning.

I stick my hands in my skirt pockets and press the folded letter against the fae text. It took me the last three evenings to draft it. I didn't want to say goodbye—that would feel too final.

The prince promised to spare my life if we were

successful. I didn't want to give that possibility strength, because the reality is that I might not live through it. Instead, I settled on asking her and her family to watch over my parents and home in my absence.

"You look terrible, Vi," Sebastian says. It earns him a sharp elbow to the ribs. "What in the Otherworld, Talya?" he groans, rubbing his side.

She gives him a look that would send demons running. Sebastian straightens and clears his throat, obviously understanding her meaning.

Talya and her family have known of my condition since the beginning, but she has always been my fiercest protector.

I laugh. "I couldn't sleep last night. I was thinking about the food I want to eat today. I want to stop for three—no, *five* —of the candied fruits before we do anything else."

Sebastian rolls his eyes. "With that sweet tooth of yours, I'm surprised you have any left in your head at all."

I may only have a handful of hours left before my life is turned upside down, but I will *live* every ordinary minute I have.

Talya hooks her arm through mine. "If you are going to be a demon's ass, Sebastian, then you can stay here while *we* stuff our faces with all the delicious food we can find."

She pulls a face at him, then drags me off toward the nearest cluster of booths selling food.

Sebastian calls out for us to wait, but Talya picks up our pace, waving her free hand in the air without a glance back.

The aroma of caramelized sugar, roasted meats, and an assortment of other fried sweet and savory delicacies fills the air, reaching us several blocks before the edge of the main square. Clusters of people meander the streets in every direction.

Talya practically drags me into the crowd… and right past the first vendor with an assortment of candied fruit.

"Talya, we just—" I tug on my arm, but she is stronger, and my efforts don't even slow her down.

"Trust me, the one we want is just a little further up," she says over her shoulder.

I glance back longingly at the treats I've been dreaming about for weeks as bodies move in to block my view.

Other vendors sell jewelry, bolts of cloth, notions, various garments, paintings, dishware, or charms. But I'm too busy making a mental list of all the things I want to gorge myself with to give them my attention.

Pastries stuffed with various fillings, both savory and sweet. Skewers of roasted and caramelized meats, and battered and fried vegetables. Colorful bite-sized cakes.

My stomach growls painfully as I mentally tick them off. An older couple walking in the opposite direction looks around in shock at the sound. The man even glances toward the sky as if he expects the cursed dragon to descend on us during the day. I duck my head and quicken my steps to walk beside Talya.

Perhaps skipping dinner and breakfast in preparation for all the things I needed to get done before today wasn't the best idea after all.

At the heart of the square, a temporary stage is set up for a play that will be the final event of the day. For now, a traveling troupe is performing a balancing act, and off to one side, a woman dances with a baton lit with fire on both ends.

In another corner of the square is a smaller stage with a makeshift seating area surrounded by children watching a marionette play. Musicians and dancers fill any space they manage to find.

I bump into Talya when she stops abruptly. "Here we are!" she announces proudly.

My eyes widen at the rows of assorted colorful skewers. Some are mixed with different fruits, while others are all the same. The ones coated in chocolate are popular, but the ones I want are all covered in a clear, hardened candy shell.

The man running the booth turns around to set out another batch to replace the quickly disappearing selection that an older man is selling.

"Four of your finest, please, Mr. West," Talya says in a faux formal tone.

"I'll take five," I correct.

Talya side-eyes me. "Make it seven total then."

"Miss Byron, you made it. Lillian has just left to make a delivery. She'll be disappointed that she missed you," the young man says. He hands her two of the skewers and the rest to me. "On the house," he says with a wink when I reach for the money to pay.

"Thank you, William! Tell Lillian I'll stop by again a bit later."

Their conversation is cut short when the older man calls out for more. William is gone with an apologetic smile and a wave.

I bite down on the first skewer. The sweet coating crunches and melts on my tongue, mixing with the juice from the different fruits. I devour three before I pause long enough to speak. "These are even better than I remember."

Talya is looking at me like I just sprouted a second head. "You skipped breakfast again, didn't you?" she asks with an arched brow.

I shrug. "Something like that."

Also lunch.

"Demons and saints, Violet, what are we going to do with you?" Talya sighs in exasperation.

I polish off the remaining two as Sebastian catches up to us.

"Here you two are." He throws his hands. "You know Mother would turn into a demon if she knew you ran off like that."

Talya takes the empty skewers from me and shoves all of them into his hand and closes his fingers around them as she says, "Oh, for demon's sake, Sebastian, I'm a grown woman and it's the middle of the day."

I press my lips together to stifle a laugh at their bickering. It didn't even take them an hour.

"Besides," she continues, "How would she know unless you tell her?" She steps up to him and glowers. "And if you do, I will make you wish you lived with the wild demons."

He looks down at his hands gripping the sticky ends of our skewers, then back to her face. His eyes narrow, and I can tell it's only going to get worse if I don't stop them first.

I push my way between them and thrust an arm out, pointing to a random food stall. "Let's go to that one next. I'm still famished!" This time, I drag Talya. "Come on, Sebastian, or I can't promise there will be any left for you."

The two siblings quickly get caught up in the excitement of the day. I will say, even though they are quick to fight, they are just as quick to forgive and forget.

We sample as many of the different foods as we can before I even complain about being full.

"If you two gluttons are quite finished, perhaps you could deign to help me pick out a gift for Lilly?" Sebastian takes the opportunity to lead us to a stall selling brooches. His cheeks darken with a slight blush.

Talya and I barrage him with questions about his fiancée's

likes and dislikes until we've narrowed down the choices to a handful of different options.

I shiver from a change in the air. The din of chatter changes to a murmuration of hushed voices. We turn to see the crowd parting as the clomping hooves approach the center stage.

"What's happening?" Talya asks, excitement mingling with worry in her voice.

I close my eyes for a brief moment and swallow down my nerves. "Let's go see," I say, moving forward before I lose what little courage I possess.

Sebastian stops me by my elbow when a carriage surrounded by several soldiers riding identical white horses comes into view.

The entourage halts at the center. The guards and their mounts are dressed in the same shades of blue and silver as the carriage where my fate waits inside.

I shake his grip and force my feet to move forward.

"Vi, wait. We should stay back," Talya says.

I smile for her as if nothing is wrong. "It will be fine. I only want a closer look."

Then I slip into the crush of people before either of them can hold me back.

CHAPTER SIX

JOON

"When you say you found the thief..." Mingi trails off. The air is heavy with his unspoken question as he and Imugi await my answer.

Did you murder them?

He and Imugi exchange a glance. Both remain silent, waiting for me to answer.

There is no reason for him to assume otherwise. My hands have been stained with blood since the day I cursed myself and this kingdom. Yet, this time, it grates against my nerves.

Turning away from them, I lean against the pavilion's balustrade and stare past my rippling reflection into the water. Silver fish glide past. Their shimmering, slender bodies catch the light of the setting sun.

This is one of the few places in the palace where it is unlikely anyone can eavesdrop unnoticed. Nevertheless, we remain careful to speak vaguely.

I release a long breath through my nose attempting to push down my ire.

It doesn't work.

"It means exactly that—I *found* the thief," I grind out the words.

The facts are straightforward and simple. An ordinary woman who stole from the fae prince—a weak woman who could quite literally die of fright.

No. It's bad enough that I am cursed—admitting that someone without powers of any kind or malicious intent is responsible for my downfall by mere happenstance would be too embarrassing.

"Do not worry. I have ensured they will not speak a word of it to anyone."

Water laps against the pavilion's stone base.

Imugi whips around to hover before me. "And did you get it back?" their whisper is a sharp hiss.

"No." I hold up a hand before they can interject. "However, it is not entirely without access."

Mingi's boot taps against the wood floor with a single step forward. "Then, it wasn't destroyed beyond use?"

I can practically hear the gears in both of their heads as they attempt to put everything together. I clench my teeth until my jaw aches.

Demons damn that woman to the Otherworld. There is no way to avoid this humiliation.

Whirling around to face my second, I say, "In three days, I will choose a bride from Firnhallow."

Mingi's eyes narrow with suspicion.

The demon and Mingi remain silent, waiting for me to elaborate.

I remain still and quiet.

Imugi brings their face so close to mine that I must cross my eyes if I want to focus, which is no doubt the demon's intention. "What use is a bride without *it?*" they demand.

"Everything must go on as usual," I deflect, both answering

and not answering their question. "That is all I can say for now."

There are still a few details they do not know yet, but it will become clear in time.

"I am afraid I don't quite understand, My Prince," Mingi says haltingly. "You've already… *chosen* a bride?" He shakes his head.

Imugi hovers beside him, staring at me with an identical expression of confusion and disbelief.

"Yes."

The two exchange a not-so-subtle side glance.

I sigh. Their misgivings are understandable, as my behavior for this Choosing is outside the norm, and I am not in the habit of withholding pertinent information from either of them.

However, I cannot afford for anyone to suspect that anything is amiss this time. The less they know for now, the more natural it will seem.

"My Prince, where exactly is it that you went riding off to the other morning?" Mingi asks slowly. Then, his eyes bulge at the realization. "Was she—? How is that possible? How did —how could she? She would need—" he cuts off.

How a human managed to stumble upon the knowledge to —not only harvest but prepare the tonic properly when such information is only found in the ancient healing texts, all of which have been forbidden to humans for generations—*is* exactly what I intend to find out.

It was surprisingly easy to make her admit to her crimes. I had been intent on carrying out the punishment up until the moment she pleaded for me not to hurt her. Her soft words were not cowardly but held a tangible, desperate longing to live in a way I have not felt outside my own thoughts.

"You will understand before the day is out. Until then, I ask that you trust me."

Mingi's features relax. "Of course, My Prince, that was never in question." Silence fills the space for several moments before he asks, "What is her name, so I will know her when she approaches?"

My lips are parted as I go to answer, only to hesitate before finally saying, "Her name is of no importance."

Imugi gives an annoyed huff and curls up on the cushioned bench beside me. Mingi arches a brow in a clear indication that there is something more he wishes to say, even as he holds back.

The carriage stops, and the sounds of the festival die to a susurration of waves along a shore.

Every human city in Arum celebrates the Choosing each year, glad when they know their community has been chosen in the previous years, and when the day ends without my arrival.

It is difficult enough to keep gossip to a minimum. With the curse of the dragon paying visits to towns at random, the last thing I need is for rumors of kidnapped and missing women to circulate. Doubtless, it wouldn't take much for the humans to let their imaginations get out of control and spur them into an uprising.

I lift the curtain corner over the window a sliver to peek out.

The people of Firnhallow gawk from where they stand, ignorant to the necessity of the spectacle they are about to witness.

Their expressions are a mix of emotions—none of which can be mistaken for anything flattering.

It is as expected. As it always is when they realize they have been selected to provide a willing bride.

Nevertheless, it sours my mood further.

A middle-aged man rushes up to the stage in the middle of the square. He holds his hands aloft, signaling for everyone's attention. When few bother, he clears his throat and calls out. One by one, the people tear their gazes from our procession.

The man stumbles over the first few words as he begins his speech. In his nervousness, he needlessly introduces himself as their mayor, then begins to read directly from a letter detailing what he is to say, sent the day before.

He tells the story of a curse—a truth. And how it is said only a human woman can break it—a lie. The story is a pile of demon shit with enough small grains of truth to make it believable.

The Choosing was Mingi's idea when we realized what needed to be done to stave off the affects of the curse. He understood that they would be more willing if we gave them a noble purpose to fight for.... That and more wealth than human settlement would refuse.

I let the curtain slip from my fingers and face Mingi. "You know what to do. Treat this the same as every other Choosing."

He nods, then steps out. The crowd parts, allowing him passage.

Imugi curls up on the bench beside me. Their body begins to emit a frosty blue glow. "Your pearl."

I take it and hold the dull, listless thing in my palm. It is nothing more than an ordinary, small, white stone. All I need to do is cast a simple glamour at the right time, and no one will be the wiser.

Such a forgery is considered treasonous. Other than Imugi, only Mingi has seen it up close to know the truth. But he has kept my secret all these years.

Mingi climbs the steps up to the stage. The mayor rushes to meet him. He nods emphatically as Mingi explains how to proceed, then scurries back toward the center of the platform with a large smile of pure showmanship that fails to reach his eyes, plastered on his face.

He clears his throat again—which seems to be a nervous habit—before addressing the crowd. "Our Prince, heir to the Arum throne, has graced our humble city with his presence on his search for a future queen. Those willing will be presented to him in turn to see if there is a woman suitable among them."

Mingi steps up beside him. "We wish to bestow a gift for Firnhallow's generosity in hosting the royal procession." He raises a hand to gesture toward ten men approaching the stage, each with a chest laden with gold and jewels.

The mayor's jaw goes slack as the heavy burdens are lined up behind him.

"This gift is for the people of Firnhallow, regardless of our success or failure here," Mingi says, to move things along. "However, if we are successful, the family of the Chosen will be gifted a bride price to ensure they are taken care of for the rest of their lives, and that of their children, and children's children."

At this, the crowd turns to murmur among themselves, faces bright at the possibility of riches they never dreamed possible.

The bride price is nothing more than payment for keeping up the pretense that I am in search of a queen to sit on the throne beside me—as if I have not taken a bride once a year for the past six years. For them to forget their belief that I will sacrifice her to the dragon terrorizing the kingdom and turning the inhabitants into eternal ice sculptures if they dare to cross its path.

Few mind at all, whether they have eligible daughters or not.

Mingi gestures for the mayor to continue.

"We ask any eligible and willing to join us on stage now."

The clot of people shifts and gradually five women make their way forward. But *she* is not among them. I close my eyes and summon the thread that will seek out the woman with the frost flower's power within her.

It wends through the air, weaving around the people until it finds her, then wraps around her. The world shifts to a muted gray as the soft glow of the thread envelops her, making her stand out as a colorful beacon among a colorless world.

A man holds her back by the forearm, preventing her from doing what she must. A frowning woman beside him says something before he can. The two accompanying her seem close to her age, maybe a year or two older. Their small group is too far away to make out what any of them is saying.

My hands clench into fists. She knows exactly what will happen, to her and everyone else, if she fails to do as instructed. Even with the certainty of the bargain binding her, uncertainty scratches against my nerves. I cannot risk the power within her to escape my grasp.

She exchanges a few words with them. They shake their heads, worry etched over their features. The woman appears to be pleading with her. She waves a hand in a dismissive gesture as she steps backward, putting space between them until she is on the verge of the crowd. The man reaches for her again.

What exactly is her relationship with these humans?

She avoids him by stepping into the path of a few others walking toward the stage. An obviously intentional move, but the look of surprise on her face as she's ushered forward with the others appears genuine.

Her acting skills might prove useful.

They are led up on stage for all to see. There is a mix of reactions from the crowd. Words spoken in false whispers for others to overhear mix among the clapping.

"The city of Firnhallow thanks you for your willingness to honor us all," the mayor says. "Let us see if one among you has a heart that calls out to the illustrious pearl."

With that, he and Mingi lead them down the steps and toward my carriage. A guard walks on each side of the line of women. Either to avoid onlookers from trying to grab one or to keep them from the shame of running once the gravity of the situation settles on them. A few of them have already gone ghostly pale as regret hits.

I call my magic up to pull the shadows around me, so the only thing past the length of my forearm that is visible is the glint of the silver spiked circlet on my brow, then pull back the curtain. I reach out a hand to beckon the first to come forward.

Fear shines in the mayor's eyes as he leans in to address Mingi. "Will he not be exiting?" he asks, a nervous lilt to his voice, a little too loud.

A guard urges the nearest woman to move. She stumbles a few steps before managing to walk the rest of the way with a halting gait.

"No one is to see His Highness's face, except the Chosen Bride," Mingi says flatly.

A few of the women take a half step back as if they are suddenly faced with a monster.

Because they are.

The first stops just over an arm's length away.

Jaw clenched, I reach out my hand and unfurl my fingers. The false pearl in my palm remains a dull white. Her brow furrows in confusion.

I withdraw my hand.

"Next!" a guard shouts.

She lets out a relieved breath and scurries away. The guards and crowd part, allowing her to disappear within the sea of bodies.

One by one, the process is repeated. It is tedious, and I would love nothing more than to bypass it entirely if it wouldn't raise suspicion. About half appear relieved. One appears accepting, while another woman is visibly disappointed.

Finally, it is *her* turn. She walks toward me calmly.

I can't help but notice the two who were with her earlier have moved closer, following her from the sidelines. They are the only ones concerned. With the others rejected, the people now have a relaxed demeanor. A few still interested look on in curiosity, while many return to what they had been doing before the interruption.

Suspicion settles upon my shoulders. Either she is a pariah, or her innocent act with me was part of a devious plan that began with her trespassing.

She stops only when she is near enough that I could reach out and stroke her cheek if I wished.

Once more, I present the false pearl, but this time I infuse it with enough power to make it glow bright and undeniable.

Beads of sweat form across my brow. This small use of power is nothing, yet it drains my withering power more than it should. I retract my arm and draw the curtain closed, blinking to dismiss the unnatural shadows.

Imugi has disappeared into a hidden compartment attached to the ceiling of the carriage.

The door opens, and my new bride is guided to enter.

"Violet!" a man's voice calls.

At the same time, a woman shouts, "Vi! Wait!"

She hesitates, one foot on the step, and looks over her shoulder toward her companions.

"My Lady," Mingi says, stepping in to block her view while gesturing for her to get in.

She nods and climbs in, sitting across from me. Then we are alone, enclosed in the small space, facing each other. She glances toward her friends as if she could see them through the side of the carriage.

"Do not worry," I say flatly. "You will have your chance to say your goodbyes to anyone you wish. Give us their names and—"

"No. That won't be necessary," Violet cuts me off sharply as she pulls an envelope from her pocket. "Would it be possible to give them this?"

I glance from the letter to her face, searching for signs of deception, but finding none, I nod.

Strained silence settles in the space between us. I study her, observing every movement and expression as if I will find her true motivations hidden among them.

When Mingi opens the door to join us, I stop him and hold out the letter. "Will you please see that this is delivered?"

He bows his head and departs, returning a moment later to settle on the bench seat beside the prince.

The carriage jerks into movement as we begin the journey.

CHAPTER SEVEN

VIOLET

The prince crosses his arms and leans back. His eyes bore into me. The night forged silver circlet he wears glints in the low light.

He is certainly in a foul mood. Though I can hardly guess the reason, I'm careful to keep my expression neutral. It's all I can think of to avoid making it worse.

The man at his side watches me with a sort of bored curiosity. It's unnerving to have the attention of others on me with such a singular focus.

I do my best to ignore it and lift the curtain to peer outside. We pass familiar buildings and landmarks of the home I thought I would live and die in.

My heart sinks as realization crashes into me. I made a mistake. The prince promised to let me live. He never promised a cure—he doesn't even know about my condition. He won't kill me or sacrifice me, but can he fix my heart?

I doubt it. I have exhausted every possibility, every source. There is no human way to heal me, so what are the chances the fae possess the solution I need?

Will I live long enough to see my parents freed from their enchanted prison? And my friends…

Will I live to see any of the people I know and love again?

Are Talya and Sebastian upset about how I left? Saying goodbye to them in person would have been too hard. They would have demanded answers I couldn't give. We would have clung to each other, my fear getting the better of me, and Talya would have defied the prince outright to keep me from going to my death.

No. I cannot think this way. He swore to keep me alive.

I sigh and relax in my seat, staring down at my clasped hands. When the ground changes from cobblestone to smoothed, packed dirt, I know we have left the walls of the city,

If this strained atmosphere is going to continue, then I hope the journey will be quick.

About an hour in, the man on the prince's right clears his throat. He waits until I look up before addressing me. "My Lady?"

He is beautiful, in the same way all fae are, with their sharp features and long limbs. He wears formal robes that are an echo of the prince's, in the same blues and silver, though not nearly as ornate.

"You can address me by my name," I say. Being given the title of Lady feels like a mockery. I am not truly the chosen bride.

He looks uncertain, flicking his eyes toward the prince, who is currently feigning as if he's not paying attention.

Pinning the prince with a knowing glower, I say. "You don't know my name, do you?"

"Of course I do," he bites out, then turns his face away.

I roll my eyes, knowing I caught him in a lie. I don't know

his either because neither of us bothered to introduce ourselves at any point in our previous meetings.

Before I can address the other man, whom I assume to be his personal guard, the prince speaks first, "Her name is Violet."

I blink at him in surprise.

The prince lifts his chin a little higher, his nose wrinkles in distaste. "It would be nearly impossible not to know when your acquaintances were shouting your name at the top of their lungs."

Determined not to allow his grumpy disposition to make this situation worse, I ignore him and address his guard, glancing uncomfortably between us.

"Violet Hawthorn," I say, letting them both know that I am aware that giving them my full name does not grant them power over me as it would with fae.

It wasn't until after we made our bargain and he departed that I realized we never introduced ourselves. If he didn't ask then, I doubt the prince would deign to ask my full name at this point.

"Hawthorn," the guard says, testing the sound of it. "An interesting surname."

I shrug. "Thank you. I inherited it from my parents."

He laughs.

"I'm sorry, I don't know either of your names. What should I call you?" I ask, as if I am entirely unaware that it's a pointed remark toward the prince.

"I am His Highness's captain of the guard, and second. Captain or Mingi is fine."

"You may address me as 'My Prince' or 'Your Highness.' There is no need for you to address me by anything else," the prince says, without bothering to look in my direction.

I offer him a fake smile.

Anyone who knows a fae's true name will have unfettered power over them. They have all gone by their given names for so long that most true names have been lost to time.

There is no reason for him to avoid giving me his name, as it grants me no power over him without the other, except out of pettiness.

Mingi clears his throat again. "Yes, well, I wanted to inform you that we will stop at an inn shortly after nightfall and you will be given clothes to change into."

"Are we staying the night somewhere? How far are we going? I thought you traveled by the fae roads."

The prince scoffs under his breath as if I should already know the answers.

"We do, but it is not safe for you to use them until you are bound. This will give you the chance to wash and make yourself presentable for your arrival at the palace. In other circumstances, we would ride through the night and arrive before dawn," Mingi explains.

I nod. It wasn't intended as such, but it's hard not to feel insulted when I've taken the time to bathe and pick out my best dress.

Of course, even the most expensive dress in Firnhallow would pale in comparison to one befitting royal standards.

The carriage comes to a halt, and I'm startled awake. I sit up straight and look out the window. The light is fading, but it's still early evening. We can't possibly be near our destination just yet.

"I will see what the holdup is," Mingi says, as he exits.

The prince glowers at me as if my very existence is an offense to him. "I trust you had a pleasant nap?" His tone makes it clear he means the opposite.

I groan. "What have I done to upset you? I did what you asked of me so far. I haven't pushed you to tell me details I need to pull off this—this—" I wave my hands around to indicate everything.

"Farce?" he supplies.

"Yes!" I agree in a harsh whisper.

"You know exactly what you have done—the reason why it is *you* sitting across from me and not someone more suitable." Each word is spat out like poison-laced needles.

I take two calming breaths. It won't help matters if we both lose our tempers.

"Yes—and I am paying for it now," I say slowly. "I am doing all that you ask. Continuing to be nasty toward me will not make things easier for either of us."

The prince leans forward. "Do you think I miss the way you look at me with disgust behind that pleasant facade? You might fool the rest of the world when you bat your lashes, but not me."

The way I look at him?

He sits back, turning his face away. "You are no different than the rest of them. They would gladly take my head for a prize if given half a chance."

All my irritation vaporizes at the underlying hurt in his angry words.

When the entourage arrived, no one booed him or committed any acts that could be interpreted as treasonous or unkind. Everyone obeyed and acted as expected.

Surely, he didn't expect to be loved. He is far too observant for that.

It's understandable that we fear him. Every wife he's chosen has ended up dead to appease the dragon that terrorizes the cities and towns of the kingdom. Though little good their sacrifices have done. The dragon's attacks have only increased in frequency over time.

His words speak to an old wound. He hears hate in the voices of others and sees it in furtive glances, regardless of whether it's there or not.

Had my earlier silence, caused by fear and uncertainty… added to that?

It's an irrational feeling, not entirely unfounded, that I can relate to. However, my experience is with pity rather than hate.

I smooth out wrinkles in my skirt.

"Everyone has always been pleasant to my face most of my life," I say. "When I was old enough to work, the only ones willing to hire me were family friends. It was around that time when I finally understood the looks for what they were." I sigh and flick a quick look at him. He listens, his head cocked. "Most people don't know how to handle what they do not understand, and it can make them seem uncaring even when the opposite is true."

From the corner of my eye, I can see him shift, turning his full attention on me. "Why are you telling me this?"

"Making conversation, I suppose." I shrug.

The carriage door opens, putting an abrupt end to my attempt to ease his mood.

"What is going on?" the prince asks.

Mingi stands with utter calm. "The bridge ahead is out." He looks over his shoulder, then back at the prince, shaking his head in answer to an unspoken question. "The men are looking into the cause. It will be a little while before the repairs are done."

The prince nods. After the door is closed again, he sits back in his seat and resumes glaring. Whatever progress I could have made is gone. His walls are firmly back in place. Instead of trying again, I choose to ignore it in favor of trying to gather what information I can while we are stuck in close quarters.

"Did your previous wives die helping you this way?"

"Hardly," he scoffs.

"Then, how did they die?"

He shrugs, then shifts forward. "Perhaps it was the dragon," he says, moving closer until he is bending over me, caging me in with his hands braced on the back of the seat.

He is playing with me. The fae are infamous for toying with humans. I stand my ground, refusing to be intimidated.

A chill radiates off him as if he were made of ice instead of flesh and blood. He lowers his face until his mouth hovers over mine. His breath caresses my lips when he speaks. "Or perhaps I stole their lives with my cursed kiss."

His eyes spark. The same feeling that washed over me when he tracked me down swallows me up again now. A brush of something, an invisible touch wrapping around me, squeezing me as if demanding my compliance.

I bring my hands up and shove his chest. He backs up and drops down into his seat, blinking at me.

A tightness grows in my chest, and I try to hide the quickening of my breath.

"I don't believe in deadly kisses," I barely manage to get the words out, though they sound weak and lack conviction in my attempt to hide the effect he has on me.

His lip curls, baring his teeth. "What would you do if I had killed them with my bare hands?"

I cannot think of an answer, nor tell if he even expects one.

I close my eyes and take slow, shallow breaths, fighting against my weak heart.

"You can relax. I cannot curse with a mere touch, nor am I in the habit of forcing myself on unwilling ladies. You are a means to an end. Nothing more."

Once I've regained control of my pulse, I remind myself of our shared objective and ignore the cruelty of his comment.

"If we are to work together, perhaps you ought to consider treating me as an ally instead of your enemy," I say evenly, sitting back and mimicking his posture.

He notices. A muscle in his jaw ticks, but he doesn't speak anymore.

I am prodding at a dangerous monster of a man. But I am safe from him, if nothing else. He won't—can't hurt me.

Has anyone ever returned his attitude in kind?

I quickly dismiss that thought. Of course not. He is a prince. One that is powerful and heartless enough to summon the Winter Dragon from the Otherworld and send it to attack the people he will one day rule.

Despite his known cruelty, I trust him to keep his word even if without a bargain to bind us. There was a sincerity in his voice when he made his promises.

It quickly becomes clear that I must be the first to narrow the chasm between us. I reach into the pocket at my hip for the wrapped book and hold it out to him. "I thought you might like to have this," I say.

The prince flicks a glance at it before looking away again. "I have plenty of books in the royal library."

I barely resist rolling my eyes as I fight the barest smile trying to form. "Then consider it a wedding present."

"What is it?" He glowers.

"The text where I found the information about the flower

and the tea prep," I say, ignoring his open hostility. "I thought I would return it as a show of goodwill."

The prince slowly reaches for it, taking it with two fingers as if it were covered in filth, then shoves it in a nearly invisible compartment overhead that I hadn't noticed before. He doesn't offer a word of gratitude or any indication that he wants to work on building trust. I don't take offence. He might need a little time. All I can do is continue to show my intentions through actions.

We sit in silence long enough that, even with the extravagant seating, I grow restless.

"If it is going to be much longer, I would like to get out and stretch my legs for a bit."

He looks at me as if I hadn't spoken. Just when I think he won't respond at all, the prince shifts forward. "Very well, I will accompany you," he says as if doing so is a great burden.

"There's no ne—"

"How would it look if I allowed my future bride to wander around alone while I remained hidden?"

When he realizes I don't intend to argue, he steps out and stands facing away as I follow, unassisted. There's barely enough room for me to exit without pressing against him.

I shake my head and try to smother a smile. I do not need anyone to hand me down, but it seems he is using the excuse of joining me for appearances to do the same.

Several smaller carriages trail ours, with guardsmen leading and taking up the rear, and several more scattered in between. Their horses wait in position for their drivers to return. Standing torches are in place, surrounding the procession and workspace ahead.

I walk past the prince to the edge of the makeshift perimeter. Beyond the border of light, the woods stretch out. Shadows thicken in the spaces between as darkness falls.

There's a soft rustling behind a tree. A startled rabbit or some other small animal, perhaps?

A shiver crawls along my spine. Something in the air has changed. It takes me a moment to realize what feels off—the evening birds have gone silent. If it weren't for the sounds of voices and thuds of wood from repairs to the bridge, it would be perfectly silent.

"They anticipate another hour before repairs are," Mingi starts as he jogs up to the prince.

As I turn toward the prince, a large, shadowy shape soars over my head, rustling my hair. The power of its movement extinguishes the torch.

Something bumps against the backs of my legs, causing me to stumble and trip over a tree root as another dark shape passes overhead.

The torchlights are snuffed out in quick procession, bathing us in near darkness.

Howls rise up from every direction. The sound is a chorus of dark victory scraping along my bones.

My heart pounds, squeezing painfully. I grasp at my chest, clawing for breath. What feels like branches tug at my clothes and snag in my hair, ripping out a few strands. I squeeze my eyes shut and crouch, covering my head.

Then everything stops.

"Get up," the prince growls over me.

Peeling my eyes open, I tilt my head back to look at him as I straighten. Barely able to make out his face from the spots dancing in my vision. Either the world rocks beneath me, or I'm swaying and on the verge of passing out.

Then, I'm falling.

A strong arm wraps around my waist, catching me. I never hit the ground. I find myself surrounded by the prince as he holds me upright.

Sliding a hand up my neck to cup my cheek, he brings his face within inches of mine. The molten-gold ring encircling his irises flares, giving the brilliant blue a hypnotic glow.

"Breathe." The power in that command flows into me like an icy balm. It eases the pain, slowing my heartbeat until I can fill my lungs with air.

He turns me, keeping me pressed against his side as he guides me back to the carriage.

"Get in and do nothing until I return."

I nod as he yanks open the door and practically lifts me inside.

He is gone before I am seated. As instructed, I wait, absentmindedly rubbing my palm over the lingering ache in my chest.

The howling gradually dies down, and light flickers to life outside the windows. Exhaustion seeps into my body as I continue to wait.

What chance do I have of surviving? Let alone doing so for long enough for the prince to remove the dragon's curse on my parents?

The carriage door opens, and I nearly jump out of my skin as the prince reenters.

"I believe it is time we had a little chat," he says. "If you want to work as allies, as you say, then I think it is time you told me what is wrong with you. I cannot keep my end of the bargain if I am unaware of what I am working against."

He's right. It is hypocritical to expect him to tell me all I want to know when I have been unwilling to do the same. Everyone knows the fae deal in bargains and trades. To get something, you must give something in return.

"I wasn't born weak," I say.

Images of the storm that came out of nowhere and ravaged the land flash through my mind. I can still feel the stab of ice pelting my younger self. "I don't remember exactly how it came about... but when I was young, I was caught in a storm...."

Whenever I think about it, the fear I felt that day is as fresh now as it was then.

I glance at the prince. He waits for me to continue.

"I got lost trying to make it home and passed out. I woke up three days later. My parents were so relieved. At least until I suffered my first episode."

Years of consulting the best physicians in the kingdom yielded nothing more than a handful of guesses and names for my condition, from an incurable malady of the heart to nothing more than being born weak, among many other terms that mean nothing. Some physicians prescribed medicines that had no effect, while others shrugged regretfully and told us to pray to the saints.

"There is no case like mine on record. The physician declared that I had a broken heart, damaged by miraculously surviving lethal conditions. He said I probably wouldn't live past twenty... I'm twenty-three now." The reason for my desperation, for breaking the Old Laws, is unavoidable. "That's why I've spent the past several years studying."

The prince is silent as I speak, processing my story, even after I finish.

Mingi sticks his head inside and warily glances between us, then announces he will ride alongside us until we reach the inn. We are alone again. Moments later, the carriage jerks into motion.

"It was the dragon," the prince says reluctantly.

I blink, confused. Does he think I'm accusing him?

"The dragon is responsible for the fate of my previous wives." The prince looks away as he explains.

Ah, payment.

A truth for a truth.

"Will the dragon kill me, too?" I ask just above a whisper.

He turns his face away to stare out the window as if fascinated by the passing landscape. "We have a bargain. I will do everything in my power to keep you alive and safe until you succeed or our time has run out."

Safe.

CHAPTER EIGHT

VIOLET

There is a charge to the atmosphere the moment we are well and truly beyond the border. A gentle hum gradually settles over my skin. It's familiar. Something so light at first, growing undeniable as we travel farther from the mortal lands.

Magic. I felt it the day I trespassed, but I was too distracted to notice at the time.

I peer out the window, curious to see the fae lands.

We've left the forest behind for a vast stretch of land. The nearly full moon is high above, lighting the way and bathing the world in hues of silver and blue. Lights of distant cities appear as clusters of fireflies. There are forests and farms and everything else I'd expect to find in the human lands.

I find it a bit disappointing. It's pointless to keep us all separated when there is little difference between our lives, and the same crown rules us all.

After a little over an hour more of traveling, we finally arrive at the inn at the edge of a small town the captain of the guard had mentioned earlier.

Other than the buildings retaining more of the natural shapes and textures of the source materials, they are not so different from those in human cities.

The prince offers the option to stay the night and resume in the morning. I decline, saying I would prefer to get the traveling out of the way. Even as exhausted as I am, I don't think I could sleep a wink.

Everything feels like a waking dream as I'm given a small snack of fruit and sliced meat. Nerves have turned my stomach into knots the further we go, and I only manage to force a few bites down.

The tub is more of a small pool than a tub, carved from a flawless pale stone with a plugged drain in the center, rather than an actual tub. Hot, fragrant water is pumped in through a pipe.

A fae woman washes my hair, then afterward helps me into the dress the prince or one of his people picked out. It's a beautiful blue with a design of winter foliage stitched onto the corset and the ends of the long sleeves, with a capelet to serve as a collar and shoulder covering, all trimmed with white fur.

I expected royal clothing to be confining and limiting, especially those intended for women, but it's surprisingly comfortable.

Once I've been adequately prepared for my arrival, we resume the journey. Neither the prince nor I attempts to fill the silence.

I blink and sit straighter, wondering when I had drifted off.

Across from me, the prince is asleep with his arms crossed over his chest. His features are relaxed, making him look a few years younger than when he's awake and scowling. It occurs to me that I don't know how old he is.

The carriage has come to a stop. Voices come from outside, too muffled to make out what is being said.

When I reach for the curtain to look, the prince's fingers wrap around my wrist. Our gazes meet and hold as I allow him to lower my arm.

I don't see what harm there could be in looking, but I am not curious enough to argue.

A light knock sounds on the door a moment before it opens. The prince releases me, drawing back as if burned.

"Your Highness, dinner is prepared and waiting under the pavilion in the Western Court," Mingi says.

"Thank you, Captain."

The prince steps out, and this time, he offers me a hand down. I accept the help as I take in the sweeping palace before me.

It is not the towering fortress I imagined but a sprawling estate surrounded by a solid wall.

The moment my feet are planted firmly on the ground, the carriage turns around and vanishes back through the gate.

We stand in the center of an expansive courtyard with several buildings situated throughout. Each is connected by enclosed walkways with massive windows. I see through them to more of the same. Areas of gardens and bridges that cross streams and ponds, and trees that shade the grassy patches during the day.

The prince walks forward, leaving me behind as I take it all in. I rush to catch up, trailing by a few steps. His stride is long, and it takes effort to keep pace as we pass several buildings and through one gate, then another. I smell the fragrant aroma of the food before I see it. Finally, he leads us down a path to a pavilion.

In the center is a low table laden with various dishes of caramelized meats, fermented vegetables, seasoned with a blend of mouthwatering spices, fruits, soups, and steamed dumplings.

The dining area is lit by two fires, one behind each place setting. Two cushions on either side of the table. The prince takes a seat on one. I follow his example and take the other across from him.

He has been quiet for so long, it's impossible to tell if he is upset or tired.

He watches me, not eating. I do the same, using his actions as a guide.

"You shouldn't let it bother you," I say quietly.

His brow furrows.

"What others think of you. It's easier to get caught up in rumors than it is to take the time to know someone."

The prince narrows his gaze with obvious suspicion. "And you think *you* know me?"

I shake my head. "No, but I would like to."

He blinks, and his expression softens.

My stomach growls loudly, ruining the moment we were about to have.

One corner of his mouth ticks up before he can rein it in. "Eat," he says finally. "We will not get another chance until early evening tomorrow." With that, he plucks a few things from various dishes, and sets them on his plate.

I hesitate for a moment, unsure how to take his long silences, only speaking a few words when necessary. But the answers won't come by not eating. I gather a little bit of the dishes closest to me onto my plate, then take a bite.

"You will be woken at dawn and readied for the ceremony. Assistants have been assigned to you. As long as you allow them to do their job, there will be nothing to worry about."

With my mouth full, I nod in response.

"You must behave in a manner that suggests you were born and raised for this role," he continues.

I swallow, barely tasting the food.

"How am I to do that if I have no idea what is expected of me, let alone without training?"

He lifts his cup and takes a slow sip. Piercing blue eyes hold me captive over the rim until he breaks the spell.

"You have done well so far, Violet. Continue to follow my lead and cues. I will do my best to inform you of anything you need to know beforehand. However, if things go as intended, after tomorrow's ceremony, it will not be an issue for long."

I lick a smear of sauce from my bottom lip and narrow my eyes. There is an unspoken meaning within his intentionally vague words.

To figure it out, I work through what I know.

So far, he's refused to give me any details of how I am to assist him or what he needs my help with, so it stands to reason that no one knows of our bargain, and considering I am bound from speaking of it. And he intends for it to remain that way.

The only reason to speak vaguely now is if there's a chance we might be overheard.

Whatever his secret, it must be a matter of life and death.

I believe he is trying to communicate that we will only be around to fake our marriage for mandatory appearances and only for unavoidable events, while spending every available second on our mission.

"I understand, My Prince," I say quietly. His title falls off my tongue, stilted and awkward. Then, I add a message of my own. "I will be what you need."

He raises a brow as if he hadn't expected an equally veiled response. An emotion shadows his features, but it's gone before I can identify it.

As we eat in companionable silence, I contemplate my new role.

There is so much I wish to say and know. Surely, I am not expected to keep from speaking unless addressed directly. Of course, I'll treat him with respect, but demons help me, I will not cower before him or be treated as lesser.

If others are to believe this is real, wouldn't they expect to see us talking to each other naturally?

"My… Prince?" I start, unable to keep from grimacing.

If I'm not mistaken, even he flinched.

Pushing aside my uncertainty, I straighten my shoulders and, in a casual tone, say, "Considering we will be bound this time tomorrow, is there perhaps another way I may address you when we are alone?"

I flick a glance to each side.

The prince lowers his hands to his lap as he mulls over the request. The warm fire at my back highlights the sharp yet graceful edges of his perfect features.

"You may call me Joon," he says, then leans forward to add, "Do not be careless with it—we wouldn't want anyone to misunderstand."

"Joon," I say quietly.

Despite his warning, the ghost of a smile, tinted with sorrow, touches his lips as if it has been a long time since he heard anyone else speak his name.

Exhaustion is a heavy weight pressing down on my body, as my consciousness struggles to break through to the waking world.

"My Lady, you must wake up now," a gentle voice calls to me from a great distance.

Rustling fabric reaches my ears. Whispered words strip away the layers of sleep that cling to me.

"The seventh bride," a woman's soft voice says.

"It's an auspicious number... perhaps the gods will keep her from the same fate as the others," another adds.

"Silence. It is too soon to know. We must not say anything that might upset the saints," yet another says. Her voice is deeper and scratchier with age.

"My Lady," the first woman says again. Clearer and louder than before.

A heavy flutter of fabric brings warm light shining across my face that pierces my closed lids. When I finally open my eyes, I find a woman who only looks a few years older, leaning over me with a placid expression.

My head swims. Everything in sight is unfamiliar and strange. A jolt of panic rushes through my veins. I sit up and glance around, trying to make sense of everything through my disorientation.

A line of five women stands near the door. They all wear the same uniform, a simple light blue dress with wide sleeves that reach their elbows in the front, trailing down to their wrists at the back.

An older woman waits near the foot of my bed, her hands clasped before her. I get a vague impression of disapproval coming from her, though she tries to disguise it. Her uniform is a much darker blue, with a fuller skirt and longer sleeves. Her black hair with bright silver streaks running through it is pulled back into a knot at the nape of her neck.

A hand settles on my shoulder, pulling my attention. The one who woke me. Her black hair is pulled back in a braid that drapes over her shoulder.

She smiles warmly. “My Lady, you must get up now if we are to stay on schedule.” Her outfit is a variation of the others. The color and sleeve length are both somewhere in the middle. Their clothing seems to indicate different ranks.

Her calm demeanor helps me think clearly and remember where I am and why. I nod and push away the covers.

The older woman signals to the lined-up women. They bow before splitting into two groups. Three of them hurry through a side door while the other two exit through the main door.

“He said you might want to eat,” the one at my side says, guiding me over to a low table near the window.

He? Did the prince arrange this after last night?

Before I settle, two women reenter. Each carries a tray. One with food, the other with a teapot, a glass pitcher of water, and a cup for each. They place it all before me, then leave without acknowledgement. Considering the turnover rate for the prince’s wives, I might as well be nothing more than another decoration in the room. Temporary. A flower that will wilt and be replaced soon enough.

“Once you are finished eating, we will begin the preparations, starting with the bath. After that, we will dress you and do your hair and makeup,” the senior woman announces.

As she continues to go over the schedule for the day, the first woman pours an amber tea into my cup.

The food smells amazing. One plate holds a colorful array of steaming, bite sized dough, stuffed with aromatic vegetables and meat. I lift the lid from the bowl before me to find a broth soup with vegetables. I start with a long drink, then pick up the spoon and start with the closest dish.

It’s uncomfortable being waited on when I don’t know

how to address anyone. I should ask their names. Only, I don't get a chance as every minute of the day is outlined in detail.

As the final vestiges of sleep fade away, my nerves tangle into knots.

Growing up with my condition, I never even considered marriage. Yet, I've somehow found myself here... about to marry the fae prince I agreed to help with some mysterious task in exchange for restoring my parents. The same prince, who is known for his cruelty, and whose six previous wives have all ended up dead.

A small part of me is afraid he will bring me the same fate through some subtle wording of our bargain I've yet to realize. However, I am not worried about finding an early death at his hands because, irrationally, a much larger part trusts him.

Prince Joon might need me because of the flower, but he didn't need to promise my freedom. He didn't just say he would keep me alive—he swore to keep me *safe*.

I've already lived three years past the age I or anyone else expected. And he is giving me more time.

After breakfast, I'm ushered into the side room and bathed in perfumed water. The five attendants scrub me, wash my hair, then massage oil into my skin. Any attempt on my part to do anything myself results in my hands being pushed aside.

My mind swirls with thoughts of Joon's contradicting nature. He is harsh and cold, but he will say and do things to belie all I thought I knew of him.

It takes all five women a painfully long time, tugging, twisting, and tying twenty layers of sheer material fabric into knots to create a dress that gives the illusion of being crafted from ice. Without a moment's break to breathe, they move onto my hair, drying, brushing, and styling it into an intricate knot of twists and braids.

My back aches even before they start the makeup portion. I don't think I have ever been forced to remain so still for so long before in my life.

The older woman chides me whenever I squirm.

At last, the five attendants finish their work and step back. I hardly recognize myself in the mirror. My hair is styled into complicated knots, and my features look flawless. They are beyond talented. This is what I would look like if I had been born to a life like this.

The older woman dismisses them, then turns to the one who woke me. "Make sure to stay on schedule, Iseul." Her eyes flick in the direction the others had gone as worry tugs at the corners of her mouth.

"Yes, Mistress," Iseul says with a low bow as the woman retreats.

Alarm turns the blood in my veins into rivers of ice.

"Are you ready?" Iseul asks.

When I don't respond, she places a hand on my shoulder. I startle and whirl to face her. "What?" The question comes out breathless.

She holds up a large veil in her hands, and I allow her to place the material over my head. It's thin, making everything appear covered in fog.

"We must go now, My Lady."

My throat goes painfully dry. I nod, then follow her out.

CHAPTER NINE

JOON

Imugi floats through the wall as if they were made of nothing more than mist and shadow.

Upon birth, all fae of royal blood are bonded to a demon who has proven their heart is free from greed and hate. Our magics are irrevocably linked and multiplied for life. It is a test to ensure those who rule are strong enough to do so without being corrupted by the immeasurable power. At any sign of a mismatch, the ritual is stopped, and that child remains unbonded for life, never eligible to sit on the throne. There have only been a few instances since the kingdom was established.

Imugi comes to hover near my shoulder.

"And where have you been? It's not like you to hide for so long," I ask, without taking my eyes from the view outside the window.

The sky is a ceiling of thick, gray clouds, occasionally allowing the sun to shine through temporary openings before swallowing it up again.

It is the last few minutes before the preparations begin. I

would gladly skip this part if I could. It is not as though anyone of note will be there. Nobility and officials have not bothered attending since my fourth bride came to the palace.

"I have been investigating," they say. "An unusual presence has been lingering since the incident at the bridge."

That snags my attention. "How so?"

The demon dragon shakes their head. "Something about it is familiar, but it is too faint to pinpoint."

Could the curse be reaching out its long fingers, ready to consume me once and for all? Or is it the beginning whispers of a treasonous movement?

"The frost bloom already flows within her," Imugi states. Their glacial eyes flash with flecks of a glowing golden-red, then back to normal.

One must look for it to find it. I glance sidelong at them. "You checked."

"It is fortunate the thief knew how to use it effectively, wouldn't you agree?" The demon is less than subtle.

"It does not matter *how* she stumbled across the knowledge, but that it is in my possession, and nothing of this kind will happen again."

Imugi's head swivels toward the door at the sound of approaching footsteps. "It is time to ready yourself for your bride."

"Go, see what more you can learn about this *presence.*"

Wordlessly, the demon departs through the walls like mist.

Mingi enters without knocking and hurries to my side.

"I have done as you asked, My Prince. Iseul was all too happy for this assignment." He shakes his head and chuckles under his breath. "She seems to think the two of them will become the best of friends. It will be a nice reprieve from her constant nagging to help."

"I appreciate your willingness to put your sister in this

situation. It is not entirely without risk," I say, then, quietly, I add, "I know she is all the family you have left."

Mingi's expression softens. "You will always have our loyalty. We know who you are, even if you've forgotten."

By the time the arduous preparations were finished, the sky had cleared. From where I stand, I have the perfect view of her. The late afternoon sun shines down, turning her dress a pale…

Violet.

It is no secret that a death sentence is the burden of being my bride. Yet rather than walking toward her untimely end with downcast eyes, Violet's head peeks between the gaps of her entourage as she tries to see around them. More curious than afraid.

Violet's steps falter as she leaves the covered pathways, and the full scale of the Temple Tower comes into view. In contrast to the ground-level structures of the rest of the palace, the temple's several stories make for an imposing silhouette.

The bridal procession stops at the base of the steps, leaving Iseul to lead her the rest of the way.

Within the shadows of the antechamber, Violet blinks to adjust her vision. Warm honey eyes pierce the veil covering her face. Their color contrasts against the icy colors of her clothing. Her gaze briefly passes over Mingi before coming to land on me.

Her mouth forms an uncertain pout as I approach, but she takes my offered arm without hesitation. Used to my brides approaching me with fear, I am momentarily taken aback by her lack of it.

Violet's fingers curl, gripping my sleeve, and without thought, my other hand moves to rest atop hers. She glances curiously at the touch, then faces ahead.

The doors to the vast inner chamber slide open. Standing crystal candelabras bordering the long, frost-white carpet are the only decor in the otherwise empty space.

We walk forward, with Mingi and Iseul trailing. Violet's brow furrows as she takes in the only one awaiting our arrival. There is not a single noble, court member, or government official present to witness the binding. Save for the Minister of Ceremonies waiting at the end of the aisle.

Because this is the seventh time.

"Hold out your hands," Minister Molan says when we stop before her. Her robes are an iridescent white that resembles snow when she shifts, appearing to be transparent without actually being so.

I gently take Violet's wrist when she doesn't respond and guide it into position. Her lashes flutter as she only now notices how she gripped my arm as if it was the only thing keeping her tethered.

Minister Molan's face is a placid mask that fails to hide her true feelings. Disapproval radiates from her stiff movements as she wraps a thin ribbon of frost around our wrists, and again in her voice as she recites the binding incantation in the Old Language.

The spell reverberates within the vast chamber, creating a song that grows upon itself.

As the final note dies away, the ribbon shines. Violet flinches away from the blinding light. As the glow fades, the ribbon vanishes, forming a connection between us.

"It is done," the officiant says flatly. She turns to me, adding, "Now, seal the binding."

I guide Violet toward me by the shoulders, then lift the veil, letting it slip and flutter to the floor. Cupping her jaw, her heartbeat speeds up under my finger that rests atop the pulse point in her slender neck.

I lean in, she squeezes her eyes shut, holding her breath. I stop just shy of brushing my lips against hers, close enough to feel the heat of her skin. The slightest shifting of weight would close the distance.

She peers through her lashes and releases the air trapped in her lungs. Before she can accidentally move, I draw back.

Violet glances around as if waking from a dream. She frowns at the empty spot where Minister Molan had been moments ago.

I could have easily prepared her for how it would be, but I cannot afford to trust her. She could very well be responsible for that strange hovering presence.

Unlike the fae, humans are not held so tightly to their word. Where my kind will shrivel and eventually die, mortals feel a constant nagging ache—a bearable consequence to live with.

Her gaze trails up to an upper atrium overlooking the main room, and squints. I follow her line of sight, but there is no one there and nothing out of place.

"What now?" she asks in a whisper as her attention returns to me.

"To the marital chambers. It is our wedding night, after all," I say, trying to keep my tone light. I am unsuccessful, and my voice comes out rough and low.

The thoughtless comment holds an unintended implication.

Embarrassment stains her cheeks. It is easy to tell where her thoughts have gone.

This is not the first time she has jumped to the conclusion that I expect unfettered access to her body.

It reminds me of the way she blushed when we sealed the bargain. At the time, I thought the idea of being my wife repulsed her… but this reaction makes it seem as though she forgot this was all a ruse.

“I—are we—to…” Her voice trembles as she stumbles for words.

Despite assurances, she remains wary of my intentions.

“I meant what I said,” I murmur, wanting to put her worries to rest before she faints at my feet. “I do not need a bargain to keep my word about that.”

“Oh…” The small sound is little more than a breath, quickly followed by a grimace.

She does not strike me as vain enough to consider herself irresistible. And since she believes I send the Winter Dragon to attack human cities to subdue the people, attraction would be the last thing causing these momentary lapses.

Regardless, perhaps I can use this little detail to keep her on her toes.

If offered the chance to be privy to everything going through her head in a day, I would be tempted to take it.

It would certainly be interesting, to say the least.

CHAPTER TEN

VIOLET

As it turns out, the marital chambers are his personal apartments. His belongings are arranged comfortably, as if he's long lived here, rather than newly settled.

A few lit candles situated around the room add just enough light to see. I take in the space, only to freeze when I see through the open doorway his bed with the covers pulled back, ready for us.

I turn and cross to a bookshelf that spans from floor to ceiling in the study opposite the bedroom and try to think of anything else.

Recalling the shadows on the third-floor balcony, I could have sworn I saw the tall figure of a man bow. It's entirely possible it was an illusion caused by the flicker of light passing through crystals.

The prince stalks up behind me. "Does my word mean so little that you still believe I would force myself on you?" The ice coating his words belies hurt.

I face him. "That's not it at all."

"Then why are you suddenly afraid?"

Demons take me. The last thing I want to do is explain my thoughts, but I can't risk offending him.

"It's not fear," I start.

"Then what?"

"I know you won't do anything *untoward*—you didn't even kiss me earlier. It's just…" I trail off, looking down to hide my face. "I couldn't help thinking how everyone must be certain of what intimate acts will pass between us—and that is a lot of people thinking of something so personal," I finish in a barely audible whisper.

Joon is silent and motionless for a long moment. Then, a low chuckle rumbles from his chest.

My head snaps up, and I gape. *This is funny to him?*

"Never mind what they may or may not think. I am sure you have questions. You may ask freely," he says.

"Was a kiss part of the ceremony?"

"It was," he says slowly.

"Won't that make it impossible to use the fae paths when I am with you?"

He shakes his head. "In this case, it was unnecessary. We were bound the night we made our bargain."

The prince holds up his hand, indicating the invisible thread around our fingers that binds our fates.

I use this as my chance to change the topic instead of delving deeper into the subjects of kisses and intimacy with the prince. "So, what exactly is it I must do to fulfill my obligation?"

Joon breathes out a long breath. "Before I answer that, tell me something. How did the book come to be in your possession?"

Demon shit.

"I… found it."

Joon blinks in disbelief. "You expect me to believe that you just so happened to stumble across one of the forbidden fae texts in your little human city that managed to escape the notice of every other human for centuries?"

"I suppose not." Telling him would endanger the lives of people I love—and I refuse to do that when I very much doubt he will extend the same mercy to them that he has shown me.

"I can't say. *Please* don't make me," I plead. "Can it be enough that I returned it to you?"

He must sense my desperation because the hard lines of his face relax. Then a sinister glint flashes in his eyes. The scar cutting down through one appears paler than usual, enhancing the ominous feeling that I am about to pay for this concession.

He moves in close enough for his proximity to distract me. "Have you figured out why I agreed to bargain with you yet?"

"Because I asked you to?"

He smirks.

At least I amuse him.

"If I were to ingest the tea, it would grant a temporary, minor increase to my power. Which would be a terrible waste of such a rare specimen."

The steady rhythm of my heart picks up as if it senses something my mind has yet to fully grasp.

"That unassuming little flower needs a mortal life force to thrive. Its power multiplies until it eventually becomes more than your human body can withstand."

Dark spots dance before my eyes. By trying to prolong my life, I guaranteed the opposite.

"To make proper use of it, the human possessing the frost bloom's power must remain close to me. What better way to do that than taking that human my wife? So, you see, by correctly preparing the tea and consuming it, you sealed your fate."

The blood drains from my face, leaving me dizzy. I open my mouth. Close it. Open it again, then press my lips into a tight line.

"Fret not, Wife. The effects of the frost bloom last only until the next is ready for harvest," he says, answering a question I hadn't thought to ask. "That is where our bargain comes into play. Since the power I need is inside you." His brilliant blue gaze flicks to my lips. "You are to act as a vessel for it."

This means I am the *only* one who can help him. He'd had every intention of accepting my bargain from the beginning or perhaps even offering one to me.

"H-how do I do that?"

"You are already doing it. Our relationship is a symbiotic one."

I frown, waiting for him to give me the final piece of the puzzle.

"To prevent a fatal buildup of power, I must siphon it for my own." Joon shifts closer. "Which is done with a kiss."

I hold my breath.

"For this to work, you must be willing."

The air trapped in my lungs escapes in a long exhale.

"Why a kiss?"

"Magic is intimate. To share it with another requires a personal price—physical intimacy, blood, or pain, it does not matter which. I assumed this would be the least objectionable choice. However, we can do any of the other options if you prefer."

If this is what it takes to stay alive and honor my obligation, then it is far from the worst thing imaginable. Joon is handsome, so it would hardly be a burden. Disconcertingly, kissing him is not the unpleasant notion it should be. When he's this close, he has a way of pulling me into his gravity.

I place my hands on his shoulders to steady myself as I rise onto my toes and lean in.

His fingers press against my lips, stopping me.

I flatten my feet and frown up at him, a protest ready on my tongue.

"*Willingly*."

If it brings us closer to getting what we both want, then I am willing.

"It is not willing if you feel there is no other choice," he says before I can speak. "You must want to."

Wanting to kiss him? Is he implying that there needs to be a deeper emotional connection, more than simple attraction?

He... he couldn't possibly be asking me to care for him... could he?

"But I..."

"While your enthusiasm is appreciated, I will not impose on you more than necessary." Joon steps back. "It is best to wait for the power to accumulate, or until necessary."

There's a knock on the door as our conversation comes to an end.

"Enter," he calls over his shoulder without taking his eyes off me.

The door slides open, and an older man steps inside and bows deeply. He wears simple robes made of undyed material and a thick purple sash knotted around his waist with the ends tied off to the side of one hip, dangling almost to his ankle.

"Your evening meal, Your Highness."

Joon waves him in, and the man gestures to others waiting in the hall.

Servants with trays enter, careful to keep their heads lowered as if they are afraid to look in the prince's general direction. Their robes are the same as the first, but their sashes stop midway between the hip and knee.

In moments, plates upon plates of food fill the entire surface of the table with far more food than either of us could eat. They move efficiently, laying out the food. They are gone as quickly as they arrived.

The prince and I wordlessly take our places across from each other. During our first meal together, I waited for him to begin. I do the same this time. Better to enforce the habit early, even if it's awkward.

I watch the prince pluck bite-sized portions from several dishes and set them on his plate. Each movement is smooth and practiced like a choreographed dance that lacks emotion. Almost as if he is going through the necessary motions to stay alive out of habit.

What must his life be like that even the slightest gesture is done to perfection without thought, where there is no room for even the slightest mistake with something as simple as eating a meal?

He takes a bite of thinly sliced meat and chews. His face is an expressionless mask, as if the food is bland and tasteless.

Colorful vegetables, steaming balls of stuffed dough, and grilled meats. The food is mouthwatering in its array of colors and savory aromas. I can't imagine being anything less delicious than the way it smells.

Deciding where to start is difficult. I choose randomly from the options nearest to me, generously filling my plate.

I pop a piece of meat into my mouth and barely suppress an unladylike groan. It's cooked to perfection. Juicy with a slight crisp on the outside. I quickly move on to the next item, then the next, and the next. Each is as delicious as the last.

I must have been too nervous to really taste last night's dinner because everything tastes better than I remember.

Determined to at least sample everything, I quickly clear my plate. As I reach for more, I catch the prince watching me with the barest hint of a smirk playing on his lips.

My hand stills midair over the food. Feeling uncertain, I slowly retract my arm and clasp my hands in my lap.

"Please,"—he gestures to my plate—"continue. It's been a long time since I've seen anyone enjoy eating quite this much."

Hesitantly, I help myself to more. I chew each bite slowly, feeling the full weight of the prince's attention on me from across the table.

He seems more curious than intimidating. Still, I find him distracting. I shift in my seat. The prince must notice because he looks away and busies himself with his own plate and sipping his tea.

Eventually, I sit back, unable to eat another bite without becoming uncomfortably full. There is still enough food left to easily feed another five or six people.

"I must leave to take care of a few pressing matters. I will send for Iseul and have her escort you to your quarters in the Southern Court."

I frown. Despite the ordinary nature of his words, I can't shake the feeling that I'm expected to remain confined. To leave one cage for another only when I can be of use.

I don't want to feel like a prisoner. Being treated well is not enough. A prison is a prison, no matter how prettily adorned.

"Will this be the sum of my role—to stay in my rooms, waiting to be summoned?" Even to my ears, I sound disappointed.

His head tilts slightly. "Would that be so bad? You would want for nothing and be safe, as promised."

Yes, I want to say.

Pressing my lips into a tight line, I consider his point. I

assumed I would be an active part of his mission—whatever that turned out to be. I even said I wanted to live... so why *do* I feel disappointed?

Because you never believed you would live, and this adventure could give your life purpose, my inner voice chides.

It might be a childish notion. Even so, wanting to free my parents and the Winter Dragon's other victims is far from the worst motivation.

Sitting in a room waiting for a fae prince to demand a kiss is a far cry from keeping the promise I made to myself long ago. If my broken heart hasn't stopped me, then I refuse to let anyone or anything else prevent me from making the most of the time I have left.

I won't allow this new situation to change that.

Leaning forward, I grin. "Why should I stay locked up while you have all the fun?"

"Rest assured, Violet," he says with pointed emphasis on my name. "I will not enjoy myself one bit."

"I could change that," I say with false innocence.

The prince's eyes widen slightly as he goes so still, he could almost be mistaken for a statue if not for the way the muscles in his throat contract.

"With conversation, I mean," I add, batting my lashes.

I think I will delight in perplexing him every chance I get.

His shoulders relax slightly.

I suppose he is not in the mood for teasing. As tempting as it is to ask him what he's doing and why he must do something unpleasant, I keep my curiosity to myself.

"While I am gone, you may explore the grounds as you like. There are wards set up to keep wild demons from infiltrating the palace. Some still manage to slip past on occasion. For your safety, I ask that you be mindful to stay within the covered areas after sunset, where there are additional wards."

With that, he is on his feet in a single, fluid motion. He dips his chin then strides toward the door, pausing at the threshold to look back.

"If you wish, we can discuss the..." the prince hesitates before continuing, "extent of your *involvement* when I return."

It's not long before I grow bored waiting for Iseul. She probably has more important things to do than babysit a human.

I pace the large room. There is a lack of personal and sentimental items in the open that could tell me more about the man I married. No tokens or souvenirs serve as reminders of cherished memories. Nothing that appears to be a gift of any kind from a loved one.

Snooping through his things would be wrong... although he did barge his way through my house without consideration of my privacy. Perhaps a closer look wouldn't hurt—as long as I avoid anything too personal.

The room is separated into sections laid out identically to mine, though obviously larger. The side door to the right is a room with a long, low-leg desk for studying and shelves along two walls filled with handbound books.

Sitting down at the desk, I take a pen and write a short message on the corner of a piece of paper in small script. I make sure to put everything back where I found it before moving on to the other room opposite this one.

The prince's sleeping chamber is as impersonal and cold as the other two rooms. His wardrobe is perfectly organized and predictably boring. An oil lamp on the nightstand is the only thing close to a decorative item in the room.

The bed takes up a good portion of the space and is larger than any individual could possibly need. I flop onto the mattress. Even stretching my arms and legs as far as I can, I still can't reach the edges.

And it's comfortable too. Easily ten times more so than my own. It would be easy to close my eyes and sleep until morning.

If he complains, I'll just say something about us being married, I think as I reach for a pillow to curl up.

The back of my hand bumps against a hard object. Lethargy leaves my body at the contact. Sitting up, I move the pillow aside and find a small, lacquered box made from black oak that fits in the palm of my hand. A dragon with a long body curling around every side is carved onto the surface.

I lift the lid. The inside is covered in padded silk, cradling a white pearl.

No, not a pearl. A stone.

How odd. Why in the Otherworld would he have this, and hidden under his pillow no less?

A prickle of unease dances along my spine. For some reason, I feel like I stumbled across something far more personal than I intended to find.

I carefully tuck it back under the pillow, then return to his desk. Helping myself to another piece of paper, I quickly scribble a note to Iseul, telling her that I'll be wandering around the nearby covered areas, then leave it on the table in the sitting area so she can easily find it.

CHAPTER ELEVEN

VIOLET

The palace is sectioned off into five areas. It's far from the closed-off, dreary castle with high, looming towers of my imagination. The Northern, Southern, Eastern, Western, and Central Courts are separated by walls the height of an average fae man. From what I've seen, they have similar features.

Wide, windowed corridors connect buildings throughout each court. Outdoor paths meander between buildings, through gardens, and along a wending stream that passes through each court.

After a while, I end up in the Central Court. Those who pass either bow or nod in acknowledgment as they hurry along their way.

The massive Temple Tower, situated in the palace's very center, is the only structure that rises several stories above ground level.

Plants, manicured to perfection, grow along the outdoor paths. A stream flows through the grounds and under walkways. It connects the courts by passing below the walls that would otherwise keep them entirely separate.

Since arriving, I have caught glimpses of the extensive outdoor gardens, but only now, as I wander the wide, windowed corridors, do I notice the entrances to them in the spaces between buildings. They are covered in glass domes that become invisible as night falls. Lanterns have been strung up, bordering the footpaths and low stone bridges that hover inches over the water's surface.

I catch glimpses of others strolling in groups of two to five, chatting and laughing. The clothing varies from a mix of servant uniforms to expensive materials. It seems all who live within the palace are welcome in these areas, though the hierarchy is respected, and lower-ranking individuals move aside to let those of higher rank pass.

Lantern light glittering off the water and the countless stars winking overhead, lend the palace a sense of magic. It would be easy to spend hours walking through a single court to take everything in, but I decide to leave that for another time and stick with learning the basics of navigating the palace grounds.

I stop at a veranda and look out onto the sloping ground that plunges down several yards to a wide section of the stream at the bottom. My eyes close, and I focus on the musical trickle of water.

"You must be His Highness's new bride," a low voice interrupts.

I whirl, pressing my back against the railing. My hand flies to my chest to calm my racing heart.

"Demons and saints, y-you startled me," I say breathlessly.

Long, pointed ears and an ethereal presence mark him as distinctly not human. He appears to be only a few years older than Joon. His eyes are a smoky color, more gray than blue. And unlike most of the other nobles within the palace, his hair is short. The simple crown atop his head renders me speechless for several seconds.

"Good evening, Your Majesty," I say, finally remembering myself long enough to stop gaping at the man who sneaked up on me.

As I start to bow, his hands grip my shoulders, stilling me.

"There is no need for that. It is only the two of us. I wanted to meet the prince's new wife and apologize for being unable to make it to your bonding ceremony." The king smiles warmly and gestures down the corridor. "Would you do me the honor of walking with me for a bit?"

The Crown Prince's uncle has sat upon the throne as interim king since the death of the previous king and queen. If that weren't common knowledge, I might never have guessed they were related because the two men look nothing alike.

I glance around, realizing there isn't another soul in the vicinity. Not even a single guard for the king's protection. Though I suppose having magic is a defense all its own.

While unprepared to meet someone so important like this, I don't see a reason to refuse. "It would be my honor."

He leads the way, and I follow a few steps behind until he gestures for me to walk at his side.

We slow as we approach an inner garden with two guards stationed outside. I peer through the open doors to the glass dome surrounding it. The countless squares are etched with vines and held together by silver framework polished to a mirrored finish.

"This is the Garden of Stars, the royal family's private garden," the king explains as we enter. Then he takes one of my hands between both of his, giving it a fatherly pat. "I will make sure the guards know you are welcome here whenever you wish."

"Thank you, Your Majesty," I say with a slight bow of my head.

The garden path wends between dense vegetation and tall bushes with alcoves branching off to the sides at random intervals. One is a grassy area that would be perfect for an intimate picnic. Another has a flawless, white marble statue resembling the Winter Dragon. Two more have benches.

We pause in the center of a curved bridge over a narrow stretch of stream, no wider than the height of an average man. The king rests his hands on the railing and peers into the water. For a long moment, we stand side by side in companionable silence.

He is doing what he can to put me at ease with his casual manner—and with almost anyone else, it would work.

However, he is still a king. I cannot imagine anyone feeling completely at ease in his presence unless they are his equal.

"Do you like it here at the palace?"

I know my answer should be positive, but to what extent?

When I hesitate, he chuckles, making the corners of his eyes crinkle. "I suppose you haven't had time to figure that out yet."

His smile is broad and welcoming in a way that's nearly tangible.

All my muscles relax as tension drains. Despite my earlier thought, I find myself beginning to feel at ease.

"Nothing is how I expected it to be," I admit.

"And… the prince is treating you well?" The king's tone almost sounds worried.

"Yes. He has been a perfect gentleman." It's a bit of a stretch, but for the most part, it's true enough. Besides, only someone with a death wish would dare speak ill of the royal family.

The king sends me a sidelong glance. "I am glad to hear it," he says slowly.

Silence falls between us as we watch a shoal of shimmering fish with silver scales swim in lazy patterns beneath the gentle ripples of the water.

He turns to me. The warm expression he wore moments ago is gone now, replaced with a slight frown. "You need not lie or cover for his behavior. It is well known that he is cruel to his wives."

I take a step back, waving my hands. "He has not acted in an objectionable way. I swear it," I say quickly. Then, not wanting to find out what would happen if I openly disagreed with someone so powerful, I add, "Perhaps it is because I've been here less than a day and spent so little time with him?"

The king hums and nods, seeming to accept that.

Long before the mortal and fae worlds collided, fairytales spoke of the inability of the fae to lie and their magic that binds them and others to their promises and bargains. In truth, they can lie as readily as any human, but thankfully, we managed to get the second part right.

"I hope you will not hold it against him when that side emerges." He shakes his head and heaves a weary sigh. "It is not his fault. His heart holds a lot of pain ever since the… brutal murder of the last king and queen."

My hand flies to my mouth, smothering a gasp. I'm stunned by his candor. "I had no idea."

Everyone in the kingdom knows of their passing. But all the rumors spoke of a rare illness contracted during their travels.

He nods, his shining pale blue eyes watching me expectantly.

I am curious about learning the details, but I dare not pry.

If they wanted the world to know what really happened, we already would.

When I don't inquire, the king tilts his chin up and peers down at me. "There is something different about you from his other brides."

"I'm not sure what you mean," I say slowly.

The king couldn't possibly know the truth—that Joon and I made a bargain… and that I know more than I'm letting on.

My throat feels tight. A warning from the magic of our agreement, ensuring my silence. Surely, Joon would have warned me if anyone could sense it.

The king waves a hand dismissively. "Perhaps things will be different this time. I've long hoped for a bride strong enough to guide him toward his true path."

I shift, unsure of what he's alluding to or what he expects from me.

"I was only supposed to be on the throne until his nineteenth year when he was of age, but he has shown no interest in fulfilling his role even after all he did to gain it."

If convincing him to take his place as the rightful king is part of my duties as his wife, this is the first I'm hearing of it.

"Please, do not feel compelled to take on such a daunting task." Emotion pulls at his features, something akin to… *regret*? "You are aware of the dangers of your position. It is more important to keep yourself safe from harm. The prince is not all he appears to be."

I suppose that is as kind a way as any to say someone is dangerous. If not for the bargain, I would be afraid.

"Thank you," I say. "I appreciate your concern."

The king's smile is sad but kind as he rests a hand on my shoulder. "I will leave you to return to what you were doing before my interruption. Perhaps we will have another chance to walk together soon."

"I would like that."

"When you leave, take a left and continue straight, and you will find your way back to where we met."

As he walks away, I'm struck with a sense of strangeness. My head feels fuzzy, as if I'd been drinking or about to come down with a head cold. It must be from exhaustion and the stress of the situation. I've barely slept since it all began.

I contemplate my first encounter with the king, going over our conversation as I lazily make my way back the way we came.

There was a warning in the king's words, and I doubt they were given lightly or without reason.

I've already seen different sides of Prince Joon. Yet, it is hard to imagine the prince as the king implied.

Which version of you is real, Joon? The one you show me, or the one everyone else knows and fears?

"There you are!" Iseul calls out, waving as she hurries over to me. Her cheeks are flushed bright pink against her pale face as she struggles to catch her breath. "I've been looking everywhere for you, My Lady. I was worried."

"I'm sorry, I wanted to explore a bit… is that not allowed?"

She frowns. "You have been gone for two hours."

The palace must be larger than I realized. How could so much time have passed?

"Anyway, now that I have found you, I will show you to your rooms." Iseul gestures toward the south gate with both hands.

We don't see another living being on the way to the Southern Court.

"Please don't tell the prince or Mingi that I lost you tonight," she pleads.

"Is Mingi your senior?"

She pulls a face, sticking out her tongue. "Demons, no!"

Iseul makes a show of shuddering. "He's my brother, and he would never let me live it down after I've begged him to pull some strings to help me get this position."

My brows rise. "You did?"

She slaps a hand over her mouth before leaning in. "Maybe I shouldn't have said that… I know it's terrible to abuse his position that way, I hate working in those stuffy kitchens. I want to do something I know I'm good at," she rambles, everything coming out in a single breath. "Being the personal handmaid to the future queen is the most important job in the entire palace, and after what my brother said about you, I just know we will be best friends!" Iseul's dark eyes shine with excitement as she talks.

I can't help but smile at her cheerful nature. She appears to be close in age to me, but with the fae ability to glamour, it's impossible to know for sure. Most of all, I am glad to know our positions here won't have any bearing on our friendship, even if my marriage to Prince Joon was real.

"What did your brother say about me?"

"Well," she says, pausing to look around before ushering me into the main room of my personal quarters and closing the door behind us. "He was irritatingly vague about it all, but did mention that the prince has been acting differently for several days before the Choosing and thinks it has something to do with how you don't let him bully you."

She might not think me brave if she knew the reason I feel safe enough to stand against a prince.

Iseul brings a hand up to the side of her face, even though we are alone, and whispers, "Mingi was *not* pleased to give me this assignment, so I think the prince personally requested me this time—that has to mean something, right?" By the end, she's practically bouncing on her toes, giddy over whatever she thinks that *something* happens to be.

In some ways, Iseul reminds me of Talya. It will be nice to have an ally here. She will undoubtedly bring a lot of cheer to everything.

"I should let you rest now, but if you need anything, I am staying in the rooms down the hall. Oh, and if you ever get hungry, the kitchen staff will gladly sneak you one of their delicious pastries," she says on her way out the door.

Her absence leaves the room too quiet for my liking.

I startle and bolt upright in bed, wondering what woke me. Outside, the mournful howl of wind accompanies the patter of ice tapping against the window.

Another unseasonable winter storm?

I lower my legs off the edge of the mattress, feeling the familiar ache in every inch of my body that tells me that this is no natural squall.

I go to the window and pull back the curtains. Tiny shards of frozen rain whip through the air, while above, the stars twinkle free of the obstruction of clouds.

The large, pale body of a dragon rises into the sky, curling and weaving. The beast circles the capital city outside the palace walls, then turns inward and releases a roar so powerful I feel it down to my marrow.

Two glowing blue eyes land on me, and the Winter Dragon stills. I'm rooted in place. Gradually, the storm dies down, and I realize it's coming closer. My chest tightens, squeezing painfully, the first warning sign of an episode.

I drop down and crouch below the window, pressing my back to the wall as I cover my ears and squeeze my eyes tight.

Breathe, Violet. Joon promised to keep me safe. Breathe. Just breathe.

I repeat the command over and over in my head, even after my pulse returns to normal.

CHAPTER TWELVE

VIOLET

A hand on my knee shakes me awake, though I don't remember falling asleep. I open my eyes in time to see Iseul shove Mingi to the side, sending him sprawling onto his side.

"What do you think you are doing?" she hisses at him as she takes his place, crouching before me.

"Demon shit, Iseul—" Mingi starts.

"I will bring her. Now, get out before anyone finds you in here."

"Make it quick." It's a command rather than a retort.

She turns her attention back to me. "Are you all right, My Lady? What are you doing on the floor?"

It's still night. The only light in the room comes from a lantern set down in the middle of the floor.

"I... the dragon... it looked at me." Saying it out loud like that makes me feel like a child again. "I've never seen it so close before."

Iseul pats my knee. "That would frighten anyone, My Lady."

"Violet," I say. "Call me Violet."

"Violet, then." She smiles and helps me stand, making sure I'm steady before letting my arm go to grab a long robe and wrap it around my shoulders. "Prince Joon has summoned you, but there's no time to dress."

I nod and let her lead me through the halls, wondering what possible reason he could have for summoning me in the middle of the night, especially after he made it clear that he wouldn't force himself on me.

Mingi waits outside Prince Joon's door for us. He holds up a hand, blocking Iseul.

"Just her." He gestures at me with his chin.

She scowls. "I am her handmaid, and I'm not letting her out of my sight."

She looks ready to tackle him to the ground.

"Prince's orders," Mingi says flatly.

Iseul purses her lips, then turns to me with large doe eyes. "I'm sorry, I can't go against him."

Her protectiveness surprises me. I'm touched. I take her hand and squeeze, wanting to reassure her as she did for me. "It will be all right."

Mingi slides the door open just enough for me to pass, then snaps it shut, barely missing the hem of my robe.

The room is dim, with only a single candle on the table. I move further inside and peer into the open doorway to the bedroom.

A bare-chested Joon sits on the edge of his bed with his elbows braced on his knees and cradling his head in his hands. His crown rests on the bedside table. Even without it, his very essence makes it impossible to see him as less than extraordinary.

I walk over and stop in front of him.

Out of the corner of my eye, something white catches my attention. I turn to see a dragon, identical to the one from the storm, pass through the wall. Even though it's much smaller now, it must be the same.

Before I can scream, Joon is on his feet, pinning my back to his chest and covering my mouth with his palm. "My head is already splitting, so I would appreciate it if you refrained from making my ears bleed."

I jut an accusing finger at the tiny dragon, who winds their body in a tight spiral in mid-air and snarls at me in response.

"This is Imugi. They may look like the Winter Dragon, but I assure you, this is as big as they get."

I stiffen. *A demon?* Then I remember the flash I thought I saw in the prince's eyes, but dismissed at the time.

So, he is demon bonded, after all.

The prince sighs. "They will not harm you."

Imugi flicks their tail at me before landing on the bed. The demon releases several puffs of frost from their nostrils.

The prince releases me, and I shuffle to the side, wanting distance from the demon. I've heard stories of some bonding successfully with higher demons, who take the shape of an animal familiar. Their physical size decreases, but they gain power through the bond and become greater demons. I never realized all those stories could be true.

"I couldn't contain it… I used too much power." Joon turns to me. His face is too pale, and he looks like he will fall over at any moment. "I thought I had more time, but it seems you must fulfill your duty earlier than anticipated."

Even in a weakened state, he's still graceful and just as painfully beautiful to look at. It's almost impossible to look away. In a single step, he devours the space, only leaving a hand's breadth between us.

My mind empties of all thoughts with his proximity. He wears nothing to dull the warmth coming from the bare skin of his broad chest. The front of my robe falls open, leaving the thin layer of my nightclothes as the only thing separating us.

He lowers his head until his mouth hovers over mine, but he doesn't close the distance.

This is dangerous. *He* is dangerous. I lose my head when he is close enough to touch. It makes me want things I shouldn't.

"Violet." My name on his tongue is like melted sugar.

"Yes?"

"Have you already forgotten?"

Though the question is barely more than a sigh, it's enough to get my mind working again. I must initiate the kiss. The thought of acting so boldly sends heat rising up my neck.

The prince releases a slow breath and straightens. "It is all right if you are not yet ready." He lowers back down on the edge of his mattress.

The dim light casts shadows over his features, making him appear gaunt—something in my chest twists. I had thought he looked weakened, but I was wrong—this is so much more than that, and he hid most of it from me.

"I'm sorry," I say. Because I am. The prince told me he needed that power—power that I stole. I haven't considered what he must be going through. I thought only of myself and how I felt.

"I said it is all—"

I lean forward and press my lips to his.

The prince's body goes rigid with tension for several seconds before he relaxes. Joon's hands find their way to my hips as he lifts his chin and presses into the kiss, but doesn't deepen it, letting me keep complete control.

A hum of energy rises slowly from the bottom of my feet, up my legs, my middle, to the tips of my fingers and the top of my head. The intensity increases until every inch of my body tingles with it.

A slight tug from within is the only warning I receive before it begins.

The flow of energy—of magic—races forward. It takes me by surprise. My lips part with a gasp, causing his to do the same. Our mouths move against each other's, fueled by the heady sensation. It's addicting. Intoxicating.

As the world shifts beneath me, I brace my hands on his shoulders. Joon cups my jaw with both of his, holding me in place as he stands, bringing the length of our bodies flush together.

My pulse quickens. Each beat of my heart comes with a sharp pain. I tighten my grip on him, fingertips digging into the muscles of his shoulders. The magic continues to surge until a whimper escapes against my will.

The prince immediately pulls away, breaking the connection. A shimmer passes over the side of his face. Soft and iridescent, like frost made of moonlight. It's gone before I can be sure of what I see.

Without the flow of power, I stumble back, clawing at my chest.

I can't breathe.

Fear and panic overwhelm me. Shadows encroach along the edge of my vision, swallowing up the dim light.

How can I do this? I will die if I let him siphon—but I will also die if I don't.

He's speaking, but I don't understand what he's saying over the roar of blood in my ears. Joon takes a step closer.

I hold out a hand to keep him at bay.

What have I done? What did I let him do?

Because I was desperate, because I was not satisfied with the time I had, I welcomed death with open arms.

Prince Joon's words back in the carriage return to me with striking clarity.

Perhaps I stole their lives with my cursed kiss.

I thought he was teasing, trying to intimidate me. He made it sound as such. It hadn't occurred to me that he could have been serious.

My legs give out. Two strong arms envelop me before I crash to the floor. The prince cradles me against his chest and forces me to meet his gaze.

"Breathe, Violet." He scowls down at me and forcefully moves my hand out of the way, replacing it with the press of his palm against my chest.

The cold caress of his magic is a balm on the burning agony of my episode, quelling it within seconds. The pain fades. My pulse returns to normal. I can breathe as if nothing even happened.

"Why is it that you are incapable of remembering anything I tell you?" he chides gently, almost affectionately.

He helps me sit up. I rub my chest, in awe that the ache I'm used to for hours after an episode is not there.

"Would you rather die than—" The rest of his words catch in his throat when I grip his wrist.

"Thank you," I say.

He blinks, clearly not expecting gratitude.

I rush on before he can speak, "To be honest, I've never had an episode that bad before. It frightened me. I thought the worst, and that wasn't fair to you when you haven't given me reason to doubt your word. I'm sorry."

Joon clears his throat. "It is late. You need your rest. Mingi and Iseul will escort you back to your apartments."

DRAGON

Pain lances through the beast's body. It struggles.

Fights against its magical bonds.

Lashing. Claws and teeth.

With a roar, it breaks free and claims the sky.

A beacon of soft light calls to it. Beckoning.

The agony fades... soothed by the glow.

Mine...

Too soon, it vanishes, and the beast releases its rage upon the world.

CHAPTER THIRTEEN

JOON

Shapeless nightmares fill my dreams. My ears ring, filled with distorted shouts and blood-curdling screams from equally distorted faces, and fires that consume with insatiable hunger. Destruction and death mix into a cruel visage that fades as soon as I reach for it. All of it is both familiar and unknown to me at the same time.

Early morning light spills through the window. Far too cheery in contrast to the shadows within my dreams. I need more rest, but convalescing in bed all day is not an option.

My muscles protest, aching and inflexible as I rise and make my way into the bathing chamber.

Violet fared worse than expected last night. Her heartbeat, an unsteady rhythm, weak and irregular.

She will not live long enough to find the last of them. Not without my intervention.

If she dies, I die with her.

Neither of us intended for that to happen, but I cannot chase the look of betrayal on Violet's face from my mind. If it happens again, she will not be persuaded that I do not intend to harm her.

If I wait to siphon only as a last resort and stop it before it takes a toll on her, then there is a slight possibility I can prolong this until another frost bloom is ready. If not, then no amount of magic will help me keep up my end of the bargain.

Determined to check the progress of the next viable plant before settling on a plan that may not even be an option, I quickly dress in a simple riding outfit. Mingi reaches the door just as I exit.

"You are up early, My Prince," he says in a way that makes it clear he would like to know where I think I am going without him. There are times when he acts more like a mother than Captain of the Guard.

"I would like to check on Miss Hawthorn's condition," I say, turning in the direction of her quarters and away from the stables.

Undeterred, Mingi keeps pace with me. "How uncharacteristically considerate of you," he says flatly.

Iseul stands outside Violet's door. The only outward sign of her true feelings is the way she presses her mouth into a thin line.

"The future queen is still resting," she says after a quick half-bow. "She tossed and turned all night."

I cannot blame Iseul for being upset. She doesn't know of Violet's condition, and it is not my place to tell her. It is better if she believes I completely disregarded Violet's life.

"I would like to see for myself… and to apologize."

Iseul's gaze snaps to Mingi, who shrugs, as if to say he doesn't understand either.

"Then I suppose that would be all right," Iseul says reluctantly. "Don't upset her further."

Iseul's tendency to become overly fond of anyone or

anything in her care is why I never assigned her to this post before. As it is, I wouldn't put it past her to fight a harmony of demons with her bare hands if it kept her charge safe.

"I promise to leave the second she asks."

Iseul gapes for a long moment before she gathers herself and allows me to enter.

I cut through the main area, pausing at the threshold of the bedroom. Violet sits cross-legged on top of the covers. She has one elbow propped on her knee, resting her chin in her palm while she traces the stitching on the blanket with a finger.

She must sense my presence because she looks up.

"Tell me if you want me to leave, and I will."

She says nothing, only offering a small grunt of acknowledgement.

"Did… you sleep well?" I try again.

Violet glances up, her warm, honey eyes narrow at the sight of me. "You're going somewhere," she says, ignoring my question.

"Only to check on something." I edge closer. "I wanted to see how you—"

"There is always some mysterious thing you must 'see to'." She sits straighter, folding her arms under her chest.

"I have upset you."

"I vaguely remember being promised a discussion of my involvement the last time you *saw to something.*" She turns her face away. "It would probably cause me a great deal of distress if you put me off again without keeping your word."

Demon shit. How could I let a human corner me?

"All right. What sort of involvement would you like?"

Violet's demeanor changes in the blink of an eye. She scrambles to the edge of the bed, eyes shining and wearing a broad grin. "I want to go with you."

"No."

She frowns. "What do you mean, 'no?'"

"I mean, *no*. It's too dangerous. What if something happened to you?" I shake my head.

Violet narrows her eyes. "That's it then? What you say goes?"

"Yes. I *am* the Crown Prince."

"You promised a discussion, except your mind was already made up."

"No. There—discussion had, as promised."

Violet continues, speaking over me. "You get to come and go as you please, keeping secrets, and I'm supposed to stay here, locked up like some damsel in distress waiting for you to return so you can use me?"

By the time she finishes, her breaths come quick and shallow as she tries, and fails, to keep her bottom lip from trembling.

Demons take me, this woman will be the death of me, even if I break the curse.

I pinch the bridge of my nose. "Fine. You can come with me."

"Not just once—every time."

I drop my hand. "Whenever possible."

"How will I know the difference? You could just say it's not possible when it is."

"Violet." Her name is a warning.

"Joon," she half growls right back.

I hold back a groan. "You're not going to let this go, are you?"

"No."

"Very well. Every time, but only if you promise to take my warnings into consideration."

"Deal." A slow smile spreads across her lips as she bats her long, dark lashes in faux innocence. "That wasn't so hard, was it?"

Demons... this woman is determined to test my limits in every way.

"I really can't have my own horse? I know how to ride," she complains.

I climb into the saddle behind her. "You are more than welcome to stay here if you are unwilling to make concessions of your own."

She sighs.

"If you insist on leaving the safety of the palace, then I plan on keeping you as close to me as physically possible."

We haven't made it more than a few yards away from the stable before Violet twists to face me. "Won't people find it suspicious—" she lowers her voice to a whisper, even though no one is close enough to overhear, "—if you don't have your entourage?"

Perhaps it would have been easier to risk Iseul's wrath.

"Time is short, and it is vital that I come and go unnoticed. The fewer who know about my absences, the better. My people may not be fond of me, but a prince who disappears for long periods of time will raise more suspicion and discord than there already is." I say through gritted teeth. "Rest assured, no one will notice a thing."

"Because?" she draws the word out.

"I will use a glamour to disguise us."

Violet scrunches her nose. "Do you think that's the best use of—"

"Why must you question me about everything?" I snap

impatiently. I feel a headache forming. "It might be easier to glamour you into thinking you loved me to avoid such insolence."

She gapes, then snaps her mouth shut with an audible clack of teeth. "Don't you *dare* even think about it," she hisses.

"Does that frighten you?" I say, intentionally provoking her. Perhaps she will change her mind and ask to return.

"Of course it does."

"It is not too late to take you back to the palace."

"Why would I go back? You'll protect me," she says matter-of-factly, then sharply faces forward, her spine rigid. She saw through my ploy instantly.

I place a glamour over us, changing our clothes to common materials and designs, turning our eye colors to a dull gray, and our hair to pale shades of brown and blonde. Finishing off the disguise, I alter our facial features by erasing all unique marks and scars, thinning our lips, and adding wrinkles around our eyes and mouths. It settles over us like the ghost of an image only we can see past.

Neither of us speaks as we ride from the stables and through the palace's main gate. Violet still hasn't spoken or relaxed. Her silence continues as we make our way through the capital city.

It's quiet in the early morning before most citizens have woken. The sun's rays splash a myriad of colors across the sky, chasing the wild demons back into the shadows where they hide from the harsh light that weakens them.

There are few out and about to see us, and fewer still who even bother to glance our way. The glamour is a precaution I'm not willing to forgo.

Violet pulls her cloak a little tighter around herself, warding off the damp chill in the air. "Anyone would feel the same to find out emotions are so easy to manipulate. But that's not the reason I'm upset."

"Then what is it?"

She peers over her shoulder. "What you said was as good as threatening to do it."

"Not a threat. I simply *stated* that it would be easier," I say, knowing the point is uselessly pedantic.

She frowns and lowers her gaze.

Demon shit. Frustration got the better of me, and I went too far. I cannot very well expect Violet to be willing to fulfill her end of the bargain if I frighten her.

"However, I suppose I can see why a human might take it that way..." I concede.

We reach the edge of the forest, and I close my eyes, focusing on our destination as I summon the fae paths. When I look again, the plants give way to a narrow, dirt-packed road. To her human eyes, it would appear no more magical than rounding a bend.

The horse's hooves clomp over the packed earth in a steady rhythm, accompanied only by the chirp of birds waking, signaling the impending dawn.

"It is not as easy to do as it sounds," I say after a few minutes. "The easiest way to explain it is that fae magic is made powerful with truths and weaker from lies. Forcing someone's emotions to change is to force a lie upon them. Emotions can be manipulated, but only for an hour at most, and the victim will remember everything they said or did during that time."

"I see." Her tone, like her face, is expressionless.

I wait, wondering if she will say more, but she doesn't.

"It wasn't my intention to imply I would force my will upon you. It was thoughtless, and I went too far. I am truly sorry."

Violet tilts her head, looking perplexed. "A Crown Prince apologizing to an ordinary human? I can't tell if you are being genuine or if you said that because it's what you think I need to hear."

I narrow my eyes.

"Can you blame me?"

Instead of answering, I look to the road ahead and urge the horse into a run. Because the truth is, I don't know. It could be either or something in between. We are both aware of my reputation.

We ride for an hour, Violet chatting, trying to strike up conversation… even naming my horse.

Star Runner. What a ridiculous name for a horse.

I slow the mare to a walk. Even with the fae paths, there is not always a direct route crossing great distances in no time.

"I would appreciate it if you would refrain from attempting to scare me in the future," she says.

I scoff.

"What?" The word is sharp on her tongue.

"You insist on accompanying me, knowing nothing of what I must do. I will oblige your request. However, be aware that there will be things outside my control that will frighten you."

Violet's hand alights on my forearm, drawing my gaze to hers. "I do not expect to avoid every terrible thing in the world." She is thoughtful for a moment. "I am far more afraid of letting them control me, keeping me locked away until I barely exist anymore—I want to live my life. All I ask is that you don't add to them."

I swallow.

Any response I might have had dissipates. The frost bloom's power pulses from the earth in a sudden rush through my veins as we approach the copse where it grows.

The clearing is barely more than a gap between trees. I dismount. The cold ground crunches beneath my boots. Violet leaps down after me, then stumbles on stiff legs. I reach out to steady her.

"Oops," Violet says with a laugh. Color stains her cheeks as she straightens. "I guess my legs fell asleep. That's a bit embarrassing."

This human is perplexing. To look at her now, smiling as if she doesn't have a care in the world, it would be impossible to guess she suffers from the strange affliction plaguing her.

She tilts her head. "Are we resting?"

"No, we're here," I say, striding toward the plant.

Hurried footsteps race to catch up to me. "The thing you wanted to check was in the middle of a forest?"

The flower is nestled in the crook of a tree's roots. I crouch to examine the frost bloom. Violet stands off to the side, brow furrowed as she glances around.

Fuck.

I don't realize she is beside me until she rests a hand on my forearm. I am not accustomed to others touching me, let alone so casually.

"This is…" Violet's voice trails off.

"Another frost bloom." Then, before she can ask the thousand questions that are no doubt waiting to jump off the tip of her tongue, I add, "I hoped it would be closer to maturity."

Her fingers gently curl into my sleeve. "How much longer?"

I shake my head. "Too long to be of use."

"I'm sorry," she says, barely more than a whisper. "I ruined things for you… I wouldn't have—" All the cheer from moments ago has drained away, leaving her looking despondent. It doesn't suit her.

I rise and pull her with me. "How could you have known?"

"Now you're stuck with me." Violet blinks up at me with glassy eyes.

She is incapable of hiding her emotions. That will be dangerous if anyone realizes how easy it is to read her.

Perhaps bringing her with me is better after all.

We make our way back to the horse. I offer to help her up, but she ignores it, watching me for a long moment.

"We should go." I motion for her to take my hand.

"You wanted to see if it was ready because of what happened last night, didn't you?" she asks slowly.

A scratching sound, faint and unusual for this area of forest, catches my attention. I twitch an ear, listening closer.

"What is—" she starts, but I am faster.

I flick my wrist, sending a spark of power toward her. The magic forcefully snaps her mouth shut with a clack of teeth, sealing her lips. Without control over her lower face, she can only blink rapidly. I release the magic hold the moment I realize what I did.

Her eyes narrow as a slow, vicious smile curls the corners of her mouth. "Never do that again," she says in a low voice.

A twig snaps, breaking the tension between us, demanding our attention. I spot the source—a runt of a demon diving into the nearest bush to hide. *What in the Otherworld are they doing out when the sun is up?*

Violet inches toward them, bending to peer through the leaves.

I send a jolt of power toward the wild thing. It scurries away with a yelp, exposing itself in the process. "That is no harmless little forest creature—that was a demon."

She frowns, looking as if she watched me kick a bunny. "It wasn't doing anything bad."

"It's a demon. All demons are dangerous, Violet."

"Imugi is a demon."

"All *wild* and *improperly bonded* demons," I clarify through gritted teeth.

A sharp pain pierces my skull, taking me to my knees. My ears ring, drowning out the world.

Violet's voice distorts, quieting as if she is far away.

When the pain fades, it leaves behind a tug in my chest.

"Joon? Joon, what's wrong?" Violet's warm hands hold my face.

It calls to me.

Finally....

CHAPTER FOURTEEN

VIOLET

Joon lurches into motion, leaping into the saddle, then reaches down and unceremoniously drags me onto the horse behind him.

I gasp as the road we took here dissipates in a glittering, whisp of smoke. Another unfurls in its place, turning in a different direction. Like the first, it blends in, as if it has always been a part of the natural landscape.

"Hold on to me," he says.

That's all the warning I get. The horse bounds forward at a speed that nearly sends me tumbling off. I fling my arms around his waist and hold tight.

The wind whips through my hair and sends my cloak billowing out behind us. The only thing keeping me from freezing is the warmth coming from Joon as his body shields me from the worst of it. But even that's not enough to keep the numbness out of my fingers as we continue to race through the forest.

"What did you mean by 'time is short'?" I ask.

"Like you, my time in this world is limited." He pauses. His chest expands with a deep breath. "Unless I break the curse."

His honesty takes me by surprise. I tighten my arms around his waist, pressing the side of my cheek to his back. "Joon...."

We break out of the trees onto a sprawling expanse of land with mountains bordering the east and south. To the north lies the giant ice wall, which stretches from horizon to horizon.

Joon pulls the horse to a stop. Towns and cities are spread out across the valley. I can even see Firnhallow from here.

He searches the sprawling landscape, reorienting, homing in on a single, massive tree, standing alone at the top of a hill about a mile ahead. Curling roots become a wide trunk that twists upward into long branches that reach skyward. Newly grown leaves bask in the sun to soak up every bit of warmth they can get. Even from here, I can tell it's no ordinary tree.

"What is that?"

"That is the Guardian Tree. The fae used to come here to send wishes and prayers to the Guardians of past kings and queens," he says. Then quietly, he adds, "Not all were like the dragon you know and hate."

The fae road we are on shifts, changing direction toward the tree. Then we are off again, this time at an easy canter.

I contemplate that information for a long moment. The only dragon I know—besides Imugi, who is actually a demon in the form of one—is the Winter Dragon.

People say the prince summoned it to curse all of Arum. But if the Winter Dragon is a guardian, and all the past rulers had them, then perhaps something went wrong, and Joon never intended to attack the people.

The path ends about a hundred yards from the base of the tree. The prince dismounts gracefully and makes his way forward with a singular focus. I slide off the horse and hurry after him.

He stops halfway there, his dark eyes searching for something. When I catch up, he continues to face straight ahead. "The curse limits my powers. The frost bloom is the only thing that allows me to harness the Winter Dragon, giving me a little more time to find the items I need before it kills me."

My gaze snaps to his profile. The words of the frost bloom's entry rush back. *It is said to have the ability to hold the effects of a curse at bay.*

Demon shit.

I really made a mess of things. How much more time would he have if there were someone stronger in my place?

He doesn't clarify whether he means the dragon or the curse will kill him. But that hardly matters. He just told me something very important about the monstrous dragon that has terrorized Arum for the last fourteen years. Either he needs control of the dragon to send it out to attack, or to keep it from escaping and causing harm.

But which one is it? More importantly, what brought about the curse?

I want to ask, but now isn't the right time. Not that I think he would tell me if I did.

Prince Joon continues forward. His long strides force me to jog to keep pace. I nearly collide with his back when he comes to a sudden stop.

He glances from side to side, a frown furrowing his brow, completely lost in thought.

To give him space, I meander toward the tree, stepping over roots as I go.

The trunk is massive up close, more than I first realized. I lift my face to the canopy above. Pale blue sky peeks out from between young leaves shivering in the gentle breeze.

I circle the tree, letting my fingers run over the rough bark. My entire bedroom back home could fit inside, with space to spare.

On the opposite side, my finger slides over something blunt protruding from the bark. The oddity of it is enough to stop me in my tracks. I lean in to examine the anomaly. A small hole the size of my little finger is pierced through the wood, which is not abnormal in itself. It's the bark surrounding it, splintered and bent outward.

Bracing against the trunk, I peer into the opening and see through to the other side. A thin coating of ice on the inside. Almost as if whatever made it came from within.

Something punctured it with enough force to enter one side and out the other. I can't think of anything so small that would have the power to pass through an object this size, as easily as a nail through leather.

Joon steps into my line of sight, still searching as he walks closer. Each step he takes is hurried, as if he can't quite hold back the anxiety that drives him.

Continuing the rest of the way around, I find the prince peering through the cavity.

"Demon shit." He pounds his fist against the trunk and straightens. Devastation and frustration cross his face. "It's gone."

"If you tell me what you're looking for, I might be able to help," I offer.

The prince's gaze darts to me. "Do you possess a magic ability that I am unaware of that lets you find anything you want?"

"Well, no. Obviously not," I say, unable to help the pout that forms at his harsh words. "But—"

"Then I doubt telling you would do any good."

"It's in my best interest to help you."

"And it is in my best interest to tell you *what* you need to know, *when* I feel you need to know." Prince Joon's mood is a storm in his eyes.

Every time I think we make the slightest bit of progress, he throws up a wall and shuts me out.

He inhales deeply and closes his eyes. When he opens them again, magic flares as a golden-red ring around his irises, making the vibrant blue glow. The color is almost spellbinding in its beauty.

The prince scans the tree. Then the rest of the landscape, turning in a slow circle. A sheen of sweat forms on his forehead with the effort of using his power in unseen ways.

With a muttered curse, he releases his magic. "The trail has gone cold," he says, leveling me with a scowl. "I almost had it. If you were not slowing—"

My jaw drops, but I recover quickly. I don't wait for him to finish. "Do not blame this on me."

"If I were on my own, I—" he starts.

"*Still* might have failed," I finish for him. I step closer, tilting my head back at an uncomfortable angle to keep my gaze locked on his. The only thing giving away the strain of using his magic is the paleness of his face. "I am here to help you find… whatever it is you're searching for. Whether that is to physically help or simply as a vessel, but why not let me do what I can?"

The prince is the first to look away.

"Then it is not your fault," he says in not-an-apology… which seems to be the best I can expect. He pivots on his heel and heads back to the waiting horse. "Come. We must return to the palace before our absence is noticed."

With a sigh, I shake my head and follow. I suppose there

are limits to the number of apologies a prince can be expected to give in a single day.

"Wake up."

I force my eyes open to find a broad figure bathed in shadow looming over me. Fear spikes through my veins. I struggle to sit up. Hands on either side of my hips pin down the blanket, trapping me. The figure leans forward, bringing his face within inches of mine.

A scrap of moonlight that leaks in through a gap between the curtain and the wall, lining the edges of his face. The scream building in my chest dies out as I finally make out the intruder's features.

"Joon," I hiss, swatting at him. Not that he seems to notice.

He is close, and it's still dark out, with only the moon's light casting the world in silver.

"What are you doing in my bedroom?" Prickling heat rises up my neck.

The prince arches a dark brow as if he can sense the direction my thoughts have wandered.

"I thought you wanted this."

My breath catches in my throat.

"Get dressed." The prince reclines on the bed at my side. "We leave in half an hour."

"What time is it?" I slide out from under the covers.

"Three hours before dawn." Joon stretches his legs out, crossing them at the ankle, and folding his arms behind his head. "There are clothes for you in the bathing room. Let me know when you're ready," he says with closed eyes.

Still sleep-addled, I glance back at him over my shoulder before shuffling into the adjacent room.

The top is a pale blue, paired with riding pants of the same shade, accompanied by a deep, glacial blue jacket and a knee-length, flared skirt in the same dark color for the outer layers.

I dress quickly and return to the main room. The lantern hanging in the center of the ceiling is lit. The prince stands at the window with his hands clasped behind his back, gazing out to the private garden behind my personal quarters. Lanterns hang from lines above the paths, with more along the water's edge. I take in his clothing and realize the riding outfit he brought for me matches his.

A folded pile of material, the color of the pale sky with snow-white fur peeking out along one edge, is set out atop the long dresser under the window in front of him.

After a moment, he turns to face me. "I sense another."

I nod. Another *what* exactly? I don't know, and I don't ask. He's made it abundantly clear that he will either tell me or he won't.

The prince grabs the bundle and shoves what turns out to be a warm cloak.

Imugi is waiting out in the hall, hovering at eye level. It is still too early for either Mingi or Iseul to be awake for their duties.

I hesitate, looking nervously out the window. "Will we not wait for dawn?"

"And risk letting the trail go cold again?" The prince scoffs.

"The demons..." I trail off, gesturing weakly toward the night.

"This is why humans cannot rule—they are afraid of lesser demons," Imugi says under their breath.

I glare at the demon dragon.

"No wild demon will approach us," Joon says. His tone is unexpectedly reassuring.

Imugi snorts, expelling two small wisps of smoke from their nostrils. Then, with a silent signal from the prince, the demon leads the way, breathing a fog of magic over each guard we pass. As the mist touches them, they stop in place, blink, and then shake it off to continue their patrol. None of them reacts to our presence. It's almost as if they cannot see us at all.

Imugi stays behind as we leave the main gate, with orders to take any necessary measures to prevent people from asking questions about our whereabouts.

Less than half an hour later, we are on the main road beyond the city that surrounds the palace. Once again, we share the same frost-white horse. With the distant howls of wild demons in the distance, I am too nervous to speak, let alone ask for a horse of my own.

I tighten my hold, curling my fingers in the material of his jacket, and press myself up against his back.

Whether he's using his power or his mere presence to keep the wild demons at bay, I'm just glad to have him as a shield.

At the edge of the forest, Joon calls up a fae road. I don't think I will ever get used to seeing something so fantastical.

The horse's hooves thunder over the ground as we cut west through the trees. It takes minutes, rather than hours, to reach the tundra on the other side.

Out in the open, the stars glitter against the blanket of night, unobstructed by clouds. Straight ahead, the ice wall has the same soft glow as the moon.

With no place for demons to hide here, their howls grow distant. I relax slightly, straightening to take in a version of this world I never dreamed of seeing. I remain silent, ignoring the occasional questioning glance the prince sends me.

The chilly air seeps through my gloves, numbing my fingertips. Gradually, the sky fades from black to purple and pink, then red and gold, before finally blooming into a cheery blue that couldn't be more opposite of the prince's mood.

We stop alongside a partially frozen river to stretch and quickly eat the packed breakfast, then we are off again.

By the time the sun is at its zenith, the ice wall is only a few miles up ahead. I tilt my head back. My breath catches from the dizzying height.

Joon urges the horse faster. His heart hammers in my ear as I lean against his back. Anticipation speeds up his breathing as we bear down on the wall.

"Joon?" His name is a question, though I'm not sure what I'm asking. But he's so focused on his mission anyway that he doesn't seem to hear.

The horse skids to a stop with a protesting whinny. The prince jumps down and races the rest of the way on foot. I scramble down from the saddle and run after him on legs stiff from the cold.

When I catch up, the prince has his hands pressed against the ice wall, speaking quietly in a language I don't know.

I reach out, only to recoil and shield my eyes from a sudden burst of blinding light that sends an explosion of ice shards raining down around us.

Joon digs through the new hole in the ice like a man possessed. He pulls back, grasping something in his hand, and collapses to his knees. Desperation shadows his eyes as he stares at his clenched fist. His breaths come fast and shallow. Joon tightens his grip until his knuckles turn white. A thin line of red forms on the side of his hand and drips to the ground.

I tear off a strip of fabric along the hem of my skirt and kneel beside him.

A stray lock has fallen forward over his brow. Without thinking, I reach up and brush the strands away from his face. The prince blinks a few times before his gaze clears.

"Let me," I say in a soothing voice, placing my hand over his.

"Do not bother. I will be healed in moments."

Releasing a slow breath, I uncurl his fingers, glad when he doesn't resist.

When he first realized I had used the frost bloom, he seemed so furious... Yet, seeing him like this now, I understand it was fear, not anger.

In his hand is a single shard of mirrored glass coated in his blood. Joon holds his breath, body tight with tension as he watches my every movement.

I take it from him, clean it off on my cloak, and carefully wrap it before placing it back in his open palm. Healed. Just as he said it would be.

"Thank you," The reluctant words fall awkwardly from his tongue.

I open my mouth to respond, but he quickly averts his gaze, and I decide to let it go for the time being.

The prince pockets the wrapped shard as he rises to his feet and smooths out his clothes. "We should return to the palace. It would be best if our absence remains unnoticed." His tone is gruff, but I don't take it personally.

It's never easy to have someone you barely know witness a vulnerable moment.

We take a different route on our return trip, stopping in a small town a little over halfway to the palace.

Joon casts a glamour over us as we ride in.

There are only a handful of places to get a meal. The first is a tavern filled with patrons already deep into their drinks.

The second is a packed inn with no free tables. He settles on the only other option: a small restaurant. It's what I would have chosen—not that he bothered asking. There are too many eyes glancing our way. Strangers in a small town stand out to the locals.

As soon as we are seated, Joon orders the house specialty for each of us. I'm just grateful that it doesn't take long for the food to arrive, because I am famished.

I wriggle in my seat, anticipating the meal as my mouth waters from the aroma of the cooked meat and roasted vegetables. The promise of a full belly and the day's victory instantly bolsters my mood.

"One success does not guarantee another," the prince grinds out under his breath as soon as the server is out of earshot.

My hand stops with the fork halfway to my mouth, and I lift my gaze to meet his scowling face. "I know."

"Pretending it will be easy will not make it so."

I place my fork beside my plate. "I know that, too," I say slowly. "I never said—"

"I cannot tell if you were born naive or if you are intentionally acting as if you were," he continues.

Narrowing my eyes, I lean forward. "My being positive and trying to make the best of this situation is not naivety," I hiss, trying to contain my irritation and not draw attention.

The prince leans back in his seat and folds his arms over his chest. "Then what would you call it?"

My throat feels uncomfortably thick and dry. I take a sip of the warm, spiced cider before responding. "What harm is there in seeing good wherever I can when my life is destined to be short? I don't want to waste what little time I have left being miserable or giving in to the fear of my… *inevitable end.*"

Joon relaxes, lowering his arms, his expression slipping into one of neutrality. He doesn't say another word about the topic, and we finish our meal in silence.

CHAPTER FIFTEEN

VIOLET

I WANDER THROUGH A CRYSTAL GARDEN ALONG THE WALL THAT separates the Northern and Central courts. Flowers, bushes, and trees are carved from the clear stone, each piece cut and polished to perfection until every surface glints with the appearance of ice. The early afternoon sun shines through the curves and facets, throwing rainbows over the ground.

The stunning display does little to lift my spirits. It's been days since I've seen the prince. After we returned, he walked me to my quarters, leaving me with a gruff word of thanks, and has been avoiding me ever since.

It's hard not to be frustrated or hurt over being ignored when he doesn't have a use for me.

"Is this not helping?" Iseul asks, leaning forward to peer at my face. She frowns. "I thought for sure it would."

"It is beautiful. It's just..." I hesitate, searching for wording she will understand that won't trigger the silencing effect of the bargain. "How can I fulfill my role when he hides? I don't seem to understand anything about him."

Iseul taps her bottom lip, humming in thought. "I'm not

sure." She hums thoughtfully. "Why don't we talk through it... But not on an empty stomach. If we go to the kitchens, the chef will give you one of Joon's favorite treats if you ask." Iseul has taken to calling him informally by his name when we are alone. "Perhaps knowing what he likes will be a good place to start."

I highly doubt the prince's favorite snack will offer the kind of help I need, but I suspect it's really an excuse for Iseul to sneak some for herself. "Then, what are we waiting for?"

Iseul takes me by the wrist and practically drags me out of the garden. She releases her grip and composes herself the moment we reach the common areas where we might be seen.

I much prefer when she's free to be herself around me, rather than adhering to hierarchy protocol.

The kitchens are quiet, with only the head chef and three other cooks prepping for the next meal. Two women are at a stone counter along the wall, rolling dough. A young man stands between the stove's two firepits, adding various ingredients to different pots. Another counter is laden with jars of pastes, seasonings, quick-growing herbs in pots with several bowls filled with others freshly picked from the garden, and piles of vegetables.

Several waist-high, dark brown clay pots line one of the walls. They are the kind meant for aging the mouth-watering sauces and marinades I've tasted in every dish I've had here.

Iseul skips inside. "Chef Jeong!"

The head chef looks up from his work of slicing a large slab of meat. The only thing giving away his age is the gray that streaks the black hair at his temples. A warm smile sweeps across his face, etching small lines at the corners of his eyes.

He's quick to set his knife down and round the table as

Iseul all but barrels into him. He catches her, enveloping her in a hug. "It's good to see you, too, Iseul."

She pulls back, batting her long lashes. "We were feeling a little hungry. Do you think we could get a snack?"

"Strawberry or blueberry lemon?" Chef Jeong asks with laughter in his voice.

I was right about this being an excuse. And this is obviously not the first time Iseul's done this. Not that I mind. The aroma of a dozen different dishes being prepared has made me realize how hungry I am.

Iseul brings a hand to the side of her mouth and whispers, "We were hoping for... *the special one.*"

He chuckles and goes into the back, returning with two small, wrapped bundles. He holds them out only to pull them out of reach when she goes for them. "Keep this between us. I don't need half the palace expecting similar favors."

"We promise," Iseul says with a playful wink.

Chef Jeung turns his attention on me. "I don't believe I've seen you before," he says politely, though I'm sure he knows who I am by the simple fact that I am the only one in the palace with round, human ears.

"This is Violet—Lady Hawthorn. She's the prince's new bride."

"It is a pleasure to meet you, My Lady."

His bow is interrupted by a cry coming from the other side of the kitchen.

The young man at the stove cradles his hand against his chest, wrapped in a tea towel. The others all gather around him, trying to examine the damage.

My feet carry me past the man and over to the gathered cooks before I realize what I'm doing.

"I grabbed the wrong pot," Myung sniffles. Up close, he's even younger than I first thought. "It burns."

"Will it heal quickly?" I ask.

The gathered cooks lift their heads, seeing me for the first time, gaping in bewilderment.

"No," a young woman says. "I'm afraid no one here possesses that kind of magic. Myung will need a healer for something this bad." She holds him against her

"Myung," Chef Jeung says with a mixture of worry and weariness. He looks to the woman on the young man's other side. "Hana, please go fetch her. Bitna has everything under control. The rest of you can get back to work."

"Have him put his hand in cool water until the healer gets here," I say. Then, on a whim, I ask, "Is there a clean bowl I can use?"

Chef Jeung jerks his chin toward the counter behind me. "Help yourself to anything you need, My Lady."

I pick up the nearest one and help myself to several herbs. I add several things to the bowl, crushing them before breaking off a thick leaf from a plant I recognize. A jell-like substance oozes from the broken end. I squeeze it into my mixture and stir until it forms a smooth paste.

Iseul, Bitna, and Myung gather closer, watching in fascination.

"Can I see your hand?" I ask Myung.

He holds his hand tighter to himself.

"You can trust her," Iseul urges.

He glances at Bitna, who shrugs, then nods.

Taking his hand, I smear the salve over the angry-looking skin. Myung sighs in relief.

"You'll want to keep it wrapped for the next few days while it heals. Make sure you change your bandages out once a day —more if they get dirty. And reapply more of the paste. I'll leave it unbandaged for now so your physician can examine it."

A movement in the doorway catches my attention. I look up to find the scowling prince just outside with his demon perched on his shoulder. No one else seems to be aware of his presence. I excuse myself and go to him as he slips from view.

The prince waits for me further down the hall. In this light, he's paler than the last time I saw him. A scowl twists his lips.

He is upset. Again.

Wordlessly, he turns and strides around the corner. The silent order to follow is clear enough. He pulls me into a side room with at least forty long, low tables lined up in neat rows. We are alone in the servant's dining hall.

He slides the door shut and whirls on me. "What are you doing?"

The anger in his voice takes me by surprise. I take half a step back, but he advances by two. "What do you mean? I'm not doing anything."

"That is not what it looked like to me." The prince continues to close the distance between us. "What if they say something? What if someone else saw you?"

I shake my head and stand my ground, refusing to let him back me into a corner. "I did nothing wrong."

"Nothing wrong?" He barks a humorless laugh. "You are supposed to be playing the role of future queen. How would it look if word got out that you spend time in the kitchens *working* as if you were one of the staff? Is it not enough for them all to hate me? Do they need to think my magic is so weak that it would choose a servant for their queen?"

"He was injured, and I wanted to help. I didn't think—"

"That's the problem. You didn't *think*."

My cheeks burn with embarrassment. "I'm sorry."

He's right. It's not as if he hadn't warned me to be mindful of my words and actions.

"The last thing I need is for my people to rise up and rebel against me. Need I remind you that if you fail to perform your duties, then so will I?" With that, he turns on his heel and strides away. Imugi hisses at me before following.

Even if the threat was unnecessary, he is justified in being upset.

There's not much I must do to hold up my end, yet I've already made a mistake.

I sigh. I can't change what happened, but I can resolve to do better.

About to turn back, I stop, realizing the prince never said why he was looking for me.

I suppose I should find him and see what he needs—considering how I might as well not exist outside my usefulness. Besides, there's something I want to discuss with him as well.

Taking a right when I leave the dining hall, I walk until the end, stopping at the cross section. I'm not sure where to go from here. There are countless places he could have gone.

With no other choice but to find someone who knows, I start walking, turning down corridors at random until I end up so lost that there's not a single other person around. I groan and lean against the windowed wall. Warm sunlight filters in through the leaded glass, warming my back.

"What an unexpected pleasure," a man says, his voice is one I could never forget.

My head snaps up at the familiar sound of the interim king's voice. I push off the wall and bow.

"Now, now. What did I tell you the last time we met? There's no need for ceremony when it is just the two of us."

"Good afternoon, Your Majesty."

The king holds an arm across his abdomen, using his other

hand to gesture down the hall. A silent invitation to walk together. "I am glad I ran into you."

"You are?" I can't imagine what he would want with me.

He laughs as if the reason should be obvious. "I noticed you haven't made many appearances since your arrival. I was worried something might have happened to you." He places a peculiar emphasis on the last part.

"I… had a slight fever." The lie slips out of its own accord.

I'm unsure why I feel the need to hide the truth from him. Joon mentioned that he wanted our trip to go unnoticed, so I must assume that means everyone. Even the king. At least until he says otherwise.

After the prince's earlier threat, I cannot risk our deal further. My parents' lives, and those of countless other innocents, depend on my success. Nothing is worth failing them.

"It's nothing to worry about. It was just from the overexcitement of everything catching up to me. I am well now."

The king raises a brow and hums thoughtfully. "Then something must be weighing heavily on your mind."

I need to choose my words carefully. Too many lies will make him doubt every word from my mouth, and I do not want to find out what consequences come from offending the king.

"Oh, I was looking for the prince, but I am afraid I've gotten all turned around."

"Ah, I am glad to hear it is something easily remedied. I saw him not more than a few moments ago. I believe he was heading toward his private study behind the library." He reaches out and takes my hand, clasping it between both of his. "But before you leave, I would like to say that I am pleased you are hale and whole. I worried you might be in a much worse state."

Unease settles over me like a damp blanket. A lump forms in my throat, and I swallow to breathe past it. "Please don't worry yourself on my account. As you can see, I am fine."

A wave of nausea rolls over me, as my heart squeezes painfully. I fight to keep the episode at bay. Then, as quickly as it came on, it disappears, leaving behind a sharp pinch in my chest.

The king straightens, his gaze unfocused as he stares off into the distance. "Perhaps if they lived, he might not have turned out this way…" he murmurs to himself so quietly that I almost miss it. "Their screams were the worst sound I have ever heard."

"Your Majesty?"

He clears his throat, shaking off the thought. "Oh, nothing, my dear. Only that our Crown Prince has a reputation for being… a bit cruel," he says almost apologetically, as if cruelty is some small thing.

The king isn't wrong. Even the human cities whisper about Prince Joon's frozen heart and callous acts. But since the day he tracked me down, I have seen pieces of him that do not match what everyone believes. He is temperamental to be sure… though I am still figuring out if I am seeing the real him or if he is hiding his cruel side because I have something he wants.

"I thank you for your concern. I will be as careful as I can."

"That is all I ask. Now," he says, finally releasing my hand. "If you still wish to find him, continue this way to the Northern Court. The library is in the building on the far left."

We part ways, and I wait for the king to disappear before resuming my search for the prince.

I pass the open arched gate, and to my dismay, I find a

series of connected buildings lined up against the western wall.

At least I have a general idea of where to begin.

Servants hurry through the halls too fast for me to stop them for directions. Just when I think I am lost again, I spot Mingi at the end of the hall, standing guard outside a door. I hurry over.

Mingi dips his chin in an obligatory polite greeting as he remains vigilant at his post.

"I request an audience with the prince."

Wordlessly, Mingi moves to the side, pulling the door open, then closing it behind me.

Joon is at his desk with a stack of rolled documents on either side of him. He moves the paper he just finished reading to one pile and reaches for one from the other. He freezes, hand hovering in the air, when he sees me.

CHAPTER SIXTEEN

JOON

The door slides open, then closed. I wait for Mingi to speak, but when he does not, I lift my head.

Violet—not Mingi—stands in the entrance.

"I'm sorry," she hurls the words as one would an insult.

I bite the tip of my tongue to keep from laughing at the strangeness of it. "You already said that," I remind her. "Is there some other reason for this interruption?"

Violet rolls her eyes and groans dramatically as she approaches the desk. Without invitation, or anything that could possibly be mistaken for one, she sits across from me with her legs tucked.

Imugi has curled up behind the documents I have finished with, unseen from where Violet sits.

I rest my arms on the desk. "You have my attention."

The demon lifts their head at that, but I send a subtle command not to interfere.

"You never said why you were looking for me earlier."

"That is no longer relevant. Now, if that is all—"

"That is certainly *not* all," she bites out in a tone no one has ever dared to direct toward me. "You're avoiding me—and don't bother saying you're busy because you're more than capable of finding the time when you want something." She shakes her head and exhales, refocusing. "I wanted to find you because I want to know more about everything. I want to do more than to stay behind or have you drag me along. But more than anything, I want to be your ally—someone you can trust. I want you to be someone *I* can trust."

I scoff. "A pretty speech, and though I am sure you think you mean it, you would change your mind once you are in the thick of it. But by then, it will be too late." I lean forward, searching for her real motivation in her bright, honey eyes. "Considering the circumstances when we made our bargain, I am not inclined to take your words at face value. Nor am I in the habit of falling for such childish trickery."

Violet's hand shoots out to grab my wrist. "I am not trying to deceive you, Joon. I know you only threatened me because you are as desperate as I was when I stole the frost bloom."

My name on her lips sounds warm and natural, filled with a familiarity I've not heard in years.

When did she stop using my title?

"Being here was my choice—I begged you to bargain with me and offered to help with anything you wanted, remember?" she says softly. A furrow forms on her brow as Violet searches my face.

She is human. Nothing more than a vessel to siphon the power needed to stave off the curse. No different from the six who came before her.

Yet, she *is* different.

They were content to stay within the palace, safe from the dangers of traversing the wild, never requesting to join my search—never asking why. And siphoning certainly did not bring any of them within an inch of their lives.

Violet releases a heavy sigh. "You do not need to carry this burden alone."

I clench my jaw. "It is not a simple matter of trust. It would endanger both my life and yours."

"How?" she prompts. Almost demanding.

"Telling you means a higher chance of the wrong people learning the details. Few would hesitate to use it against me. If my enemies thought for a second that you knew anything, they would threaten and torture you for the information—you would become their weapon against me."

Violet's grip on my wrist goes slack, her hand sliding away. She lowers her gaze, looking down at her clasped hands. "I understand."

She gave up so easily. Unexpectedly, I find myself wavering at the disappointment on her face.

"I am sorry for pushing the issue. Endangering your life was never my goal. I wrongly assumed the same magic that keeps our bargain secret would keep that information safe in the same way." Violet stands, bowing at the waist, then turns to leave.

Demons and saints...

I had not thought of that. Of all my wives, she is bound to silence, because she alone knows what the others did not.

I am used to keeping the details close to my chest, never needing or wanting to let someone in. Violet's constant needling to know has burrowed under my skin and rooted in the marrow of my bones.

The memory of her taking the shard from my hand and wrapping it flickers in my mind.

By now, Violet has seen enough to know basic details of the curse. It was a kind gesture, but she could never guess the significance of the shards in a thousand years. Yet, in that moment, she seemed to understand its importance on a deeper level.

Against my better judgment, I find that I *want* to tell her—not just part of it—I want to tell her *everything*.

Violet reaches for the door.

"Wait." The word escapes with a will of its own.

Imugi's head snaps up, and the demon sends me a sharp warning glance.

She glances back at me, waiting patiently.

I am at a loss for words, with no idea where or how to begin.

As if she senses my internal struggle, Violet walks back over, this time skirting the desk and coming to sit beside me. "Joon, it's all right. You don't have to tell me if it will endanger you. But if you're worried about me, then don't. I knew any bargain I made would be dangerous. The risk is the same whether I know or not."

I study the set of her jaw and the fiery determination in her eyes, looking for a sliver of deception, and find none.

"If you are sure…"

Violet's face brightens as if I promised her unlimited wishes with those four words rather than unnecessary danger. "I am."

"Your Highness," Imugi hisses at the same time.

Even if *she* does not come to regret this, I have the distinct impression that *I* will.

"Then, for you to truly understand, there is something you must see." I pin her with a glare. "There is no going back. You have been warned."

Iseul is out in the hall with Mingi, looking uncharacteristically flustered. Her voice cuts off as Violet and I emerge.

"The two of you should remain here," I say. "We will return soon. There is a private matter we must discuss."

The two siblings exchange a sideways glance.

Violet follows me enthusiastically down the hall and out into the Northern Court.

"The least she could do is stop grinning like an idiot," Imugi mutters sourly as they settle on my shoulder under the protective cover of the brim of my hat.

Violet's smile falters, though she pointedly ignores the barb.

"Be nice." The admonishment slips out before I can stop it.

After the dim light in the Royal Office, the afternoon sun is blinding. The demon hisses and curls tighter to escape the harsh light that weakens them.

I take her to a door in the wall, hidden by a curtain of ivy. We step over the narrow flowerbed along the length of the wall and into the Western Court.

"Are there many hidden doors like this?" she asks in a whisper, even though we are alone.

"A few. Most are ignorant of their existence, and I would prefer to keep it that way."

Violet walks at my side rather than trailing by a few steps, as is customary. Yet, I find that I do not mind.

Within my personal study, I call forth my power and press my hand to the floor—light flares in the shape of a large square. A section of the wooden slats disappears, revealing a staircase that leads down into the darkness.

Violet witnesses it all in silence. It impresses me how well she holds back the questions I know she is dying to ask.

We descend the narrow stone steps to a cave-like room roughly carved out of the earth far below the palace. Dragon Flame lights flicker, keeping the room alight. The fire burns eternally, without fail, on a single gold coin until quenched. It is superior to the meager light given off by the patches of moss along the walls.

Imugi remains at the entrance, not passing the last step. They have never liked the feel of this place. Perhaps it is the nearness to the Otherworld that unsettles them. Though all demons originated there, none would wish to return.

A path of flattened and smoothed dirt at the bottom of the stairs leads us toward a shimmering, silver pond.

Violet steps forward, gazing around in wonder. I move to the side to let her pass. She stops at the edge of the perfectly still water. The packed dirt path continues around the edge of the pond, while the way forward is a glass walkway that hovers just over the surface, leading to the mirror in the center.

Violet looks back at me. "What is this place?"

"You don't have to whisper here," I say. "No one but Imugi and I—and now you—know that any of this exists." I leave out the part that everyone else who knew is dead.

Because of me.

She doesn't ask again, but there are questions written in her eyes.

I offer her my hand.

"Is it safe?"

I smirk. "I thought you didn't care about the danger to you?"

Her eyes narrow into a cutting glare as she roughly takes my hand and steps onto the glass. Only the minor tightening of her grasp gives away her nerves as we near the center.

Though it proves awkward to walk with someone holding onto me from behind, I don't shake her off.

We stop before the broken mirror. Violet's other hand joins the one already clutching mine as she presses against my side.

The spider-webbed cracks in the glass distort her reflection. A few shards are still missing. I can see her trying to piece together this new information with what she already knows, and failing. She is still missing the part that ties everything together.

"I suppose I should start from the beginning—the beginning of what I remember, anyway. In truth, everything before then, and even that day, feels like a series of half-remembered nightmares where nothing makes sense."

Violet frowns at that.

"There are details leading up to the curse that are beyond my reach. I cannot even remember how my parents died, only what I've been told." I close my eyes for a moment, and everything is as fresh in my mind as it was living in that moment. "I awoke to the smell of smoke, the loss of my powers, and being cursed."

A slight noise escapes her throat, but she remains silent, allowing me to continue.

"Each member of the royal family is born with a pearl. It is the source of our power, and our connection to our guardian."

I glance down at her and gesture to the scar that crosses over my eye. "I am sure you've noticed this."

She nods. Violet wears an emotionless mask. Even though she is usually incapable of keeping her emotions from showing on her face, I cannot read her now.

"I was down here when it happened." I turn back to the mirror. "I was only fourteen years old. Waking up to the pain is the first clear memory I have. The curse stole my pearl and trapped it, along with my power, within this mirror, shattering it and sending the shards far and wide throughout the land. The first piece I recovered was the one that had embedded itself in my flesh.

"At the time, I could not comprehend the magnitude of

what that meant. So, for years, I did nothing." I stop to swallow down the bile that threatens to come up. At the remembered pain. The regret.

There is no one to blame for my situation except myself.

"My powers grew weaker by the day, until I could no longer control the dragon. By the time I understood that it would kill me if I did not recover all the pieces, I had already wasted too much time."

Violet's head whips around toward Imugi.

"They are simply my bonded demon in the form of a dragon. I am speaking of the Winter Dragon. Without my powers, the dragon loses the ability to think and becomes nothing more than a wild creature."

I pause as a shudder rolls over her.

"Why do you let everyone believe you send it out to attack cities and towns if it's not true?" she asks, even though we both know she is already aware of the answer.

"The truth doesn't matter when the world chooses to believe the lie."

"But—"

"In this case, it is close enough to the truth. The dragon has been unleashed upon this kingdom, the king and queen are dead… and I am responsible for all of it."

Violet's brows pinch into a frown. I turn my face away, unable to stand seeing the pity in her eyes.

"I should have been crowned king on my nineteenth birthday. But instead of taking the throne, I took a wife. After all, what good is a king who cannot wield his power and is doomed to die without it?"

Violet lets her hold on me slip as she inches toward the mirror. Her fingers trace the cracks of the shards in the air, pausing over the gaps where the final two missing pieces should go.

"There aren't many left to find."

"It has become increasingly difficult to trace them as time passes. The power of the frost bloom can only do so much for my ever-diminishing magic." I hold her gaze in the mirror. "If I do not succeed, I will die before the next frost bloom is ready."

Violet whirls on me. Her face is twisted in anger, though her eyes shine with sorrow. It makes me think that, should she manage to outlive me, she might be the only one who will remember me as something other than a monster.

"And you haven't told anyone?" Her bottom lip trembles. "If I had known any of this, I would have helped you without bargains or threats."

"I did not tell you this so you would pity me," I say harsher than intended.

"It's not pity, you demon's ass—it's *empathy*," she snaps, shoving me in the chest.

Unprepared for such a reaction, I stumble backward. The heel of my foot slips off the edge of the dais. She reaches for me, grabbing my arm to pull me back, but I am too heavy for her. Together, we careen over the edge and crash into the water.

She struggles, weighed down by the layers of her dress. I wrap an arm around her waist and kick toward the surface.

Violet coughs and sputters, gasping for breath as I drag her to shore. She claws her way onto solid land until most of her is out of the water. Her hair is plastered all over her face.

I roll onto my back beside her. Laughter bursts from my chest. Sudden and uncontrollable at the absurdity of what just happened.

She goes still before turning a cutting glare on me. "I n-nearly drowned, and you find that f-f-funny?"

I sit up and push away the soaked strands of hair stuck to her cheeks. "No one told you to throw me in the water."

"I d-d-didn't—" she sputters, beginning to shiver violently. "I d-didn't m-mean to."

Even looking like a half-downed demon, there is an almost endearing quality about her.

"J-Joon?" she says.

Realizing my fingers remain against her neck just below her ear, I quickly pull away. I stand, regaining my composure, then help her to her feet. "You should change into something dry before you get sick."

She nods and stumbles on the damp hem of her dress and collides face-first against my chest.

I catch her by the shoulders. "It might be a good idea to pick up your skirt when you walk... unless you're trying to get me to carry you out of here?"

Violet bristles, snatching up the water-laden material in her fists. Her eyes burn with defiance as she shakes me off. "D-don't mistake y-your d-desires for mine," she says as darkly as one can with chattering teeth. She turns her back on me and storms back down the path toward the stairs.

"You really should do something about that violent streak of yours," I call after her.

"It w-was an accid-dent," she says with a dismissive wave of her hand.

"People have died for lesser offenses against the crown."

Violet stops and slowly faces me. Her head lists to the side. "T-then I suppose it's a g-good thing your end of the b-bargain is to k-keep m-me alive." She wrinkles her nose, then resumes her assent with a triumphant bounce to her step as if she weren't soaked to the bone and leaving a stream of water in her wake.

Imugi sweeps in front of me, blocking the way. "Perhaps

you should worry less about her falling ill and see a healer yourself. You two seem a little too close." They twist in the air. "You already know what will happen to her."

"I find her amusing. There is nothing more to it than that."

Imugi snorts wisps of smoke from their nostrils. "My mistake."

I send Imugi to let Mingi know that Violet and I will not be returning to the Royal Office, and for Iseul to bring Violet a change of clothes to my apartments.

I am standing before the fireplace, still dripping, when the siblings arrive. Mingi frowns at the sight of me.

"Where is Violet?" Iseul's voice is loud as she barrels through the door, breathless from running. "What happened?"

Mingi motions for her to be quiet and closes the door.

"She is in the bathing room."

The same look comes over both of their faces.

"Your Highness—" Mingi starts.

"You tried to drown her in the tub?" Iseul squeaks out, then races to find Violet.

"You didn't...." Mingi grimaces.

"Of course not," I bite out.

Violet cries out as Iseul bursts in. It's followed by a flurry of loud questions regarding my behavior and Violet begging her to let her get dressed.

I pinch the bridge of my nose, barely holding back a groan at the commotion while Mingi tries and fails to smother his laughter.

When the two women finally emerge, I send Iseul and Mingi out, asking Violet to stay behind.

"You must be uncomfortable. Why don't you change first?" she offers. "We can talk later."

"This won't take long."

Violent cringes. "That… doesn't sound good."

"I owe you an apology for threatening." She opens her mouth, but before she can speak, I clarify, "All of them, from the beginning. I assumed the worst of you."

Her mouth twists into an amused smirk, and she snorts.

I'm taken aback. That is not exactly the reaction I was expecting.

"You don't need to apologize for that." Violet moves closer, tilting her head back to look me in the eye. "You had every reason to think the worst of me. After all, I did steal from you."

"Nevertheless, if there is a way I can make it up to you, I would like to do so."

The fire in the hearth crackles as the puddle at my feet continues to grow while Violet takes her time considering.

"Would you grant me access to the royal library?" she asks at last. "I would like to see if there is anything useful about curses in the historical texts."

The request takes me aback. "This should be for your benefit, not mine."

"I've spent years researching, and even though I haven't found the solution to my *particular problem*, I've learned many useful things. I enjoy it. I want to know more about fae history, dragons, and how fae magic works."

"Those are all things I could easily tell you."

She smiles softly. "While I do want to talk to you outside of us working toward our mutual goals, I do not wish to monopolize all of your time."

"Then I will inform the staff that you are granted unrestricted access."

Beaming up at me, she leans in and slides her palm over my shoulder. I barely dare to breathe, waiting to see what she will do. Her hand curves around the back of my neck.

"Now that that's settled, you should change," she says, eyes gleaming as her mouth curves up at the corners. "We wouldn't want you getting ill."

She pulls back and flicks her wrist. My hair smacks me in the face with a heavy, water-soaked slap, plastering the long strands across my face.

Reaching up, I slowly peel it away only to find her walking hurriedly from the room.

A moment later, Violet sticks her head back through the door. "Before I forget, I told Iseul that I sneaked up behind you in the garden, and you fell into the stream, and I had to jump in to save you."

Demons take me. This woman is turning out to be more than I bargained for.

CHAPTER SEVENTEEN

VIOLET

Two stacks of texts sit to my right. I have gone through the entire section on magic and gathered every book with the slightest potential of holding any information that could help me understand what the curse did to Joon's power.

And none of them has a single mention of stolen or fractured magic, let alone anything to do with curses involving mirrors. At the very least, I expected basic explanations of the effects and general workings of curses. But to find nothing at all, as if they are things of fairy tales?

Pushing away from the short table, I stand. I stretch my back and legs, stiff from hours of study. I frown at the books, then gather them and go about the tedious task of returning them to their rightful places.

The closest I found was a brief mention of mirrors being able to hold and store a limited amount of magic temporarily. However, it lacked any specifics, such as how long it can retain power, whether it can only be done with the power by the one using the mirror, or if someone can take and store another's magic.

The day Joon showed me the mirror, I could tell he had left some details out. Curses are born out of pain and suffering. And with the sharp pain behind his eyes, it seems cruel to ask him to relive it for the sake of my curiosity.

The more I think over everything, the stranger it seems that Joon can't remember anything about the day he was cursed, especially if he is responsible for everything.

Did his injury or the sheer trauma of it all cause him to forget? Or is there something more sinister than even his malediction?

There is no point in stewing over questions that don't have answers. I shove those thoughts away for another time and weave my way through the maze of shelves, making mental notes of the books I would like to go through another time.

Along the entire length of the back wall are family records. The royal and noble families are a given, but I am surprised to see records of the common fae that work in the palace as well.

The bindings, as well as shelf placement, reflect the status of the families. Leather and polished metal corners are reserved for royalty, placed higher, away from the ground. Painted for the nobles, they are positioned in the middle, while unadorned shelves, reserved for all other families, are placed at the lowest level, with the thinnest volumes.

I pull a book at random and flip through it. Name, date of birth, marriages, children, extended family members and their relationship to them, the day and cause of death. They even go into detail with any other notable information, such as crimes or significant achievements.

I find it impressive that everything is written down as fact, without emotion or bias.

The records are far more detailed, but not wholly different from the ones we keep in Firnhallow, with the biggest contrast being that the fae records include their magic abilities and strength. It explains why we keep such detailed accounts. Though we must keep our personal family records updated ourselves, and in the event that we are unable, the next of kin is charged with the task.

It makes me wonder if the similarities are a leftover echo of the time humans and fae used to live among each other.

I place the book back on the shelf and search the royal family's most recent volumes. Perhaps there is someone whose magic abilities could help find a solution to this curse or even shed some light on the unknowns.

My hand hovers over the rich, dark leather of a spine as another snags my attention, and I grab that one instead, opening to a random page.

Sameun, born of Arum

Born to the Arum Lands in the year of the Thirteenth Wind.

First son of King Jiho, born of Eolda and Queen Nabi, born of Arum.

Bonded demon: UNBONDED.

Made interim king in the year of the First Moon.

He became the acting king the year everything had changed for this kingdom. Which makes sense, Joon would have been too young, and with the deaths of the last king and queen, Arum needed a ruler.

I flip through the next few pages until I find Joon's name.

Joon, born of Arum

First son of King Silla, born of Arum and Queen Raya, born of Lummi.

Born in the year of the Seventh Frost.

Bonded demon: Imugi

Named Crown Prince at age seven, in the year of the Fourteenth Frost.

I was born in the year of the Twelfth Frost, which means we are only five years apart.

The page doesn't lie as flat as it ought to. When I turn to the next, I find out why. Jagged remnants of a torn-out page poke out along the crease.

"Oh, there you are." Iseul lets out a dramatic sigh as she rounds a shelf. "I came to get you for dinner, but when you weren't at the desk, I was worried I might have lost you again."

I blink in surprise. It's later than I realized. Just the mention of food makes my stomach growl.

Iseul laughs, and I join in.

"Time got away from me," I say. "I didn't mean to worry you."

Iseul waves off the apology. "Did you find what you were looking for?"

"No. But there are other things I would like to look into further."

She glances around the section we're standing in, then at the book in my hand. "What is that?"

Closing it, I shove it back on the shelf. "The royal family registries." Then, at the confusion on her face, I add, "I wanted to know more about the prince and his family."

It's the closest thing to the truth I can say without having the bargain silence me.

Iseul brightens at that. "What is it you'd like to know? Mingi and I have known him for most of our lives. We could tell you more than any book can." She hesitates and lowers her voice. "He is not as bad as you might think. He's been lonely for a long time—which is normal for most royals."

I nod, wondering where this knowledge was the other day. I've come to somewhat understand his cold exterior and why he appears fine with being hated by nearly everyone. Most would put up a wall to protect themselves if they were in his place.

"Mingi and I owe him our lives. He found us when we were mere children." Iseul says barely above a whisper as she leans back against the wall and stares vacantly out the window. "We were orphans. He saved us by bringing us into the palace. I suppose that is the reason we feel protective of him even after everything."

I think of Joon falling to his knees before the ice wall, grasping onto the shard so tightly that it sliced into his palm. The pain on his face when he told me about the mirror and the curse. And the brightness of his laugh after he pulled me from the water.

It's all too easy to forget who Joon is and to think of him as someone I could have interacted with in daily life back home whenever we argue and tease each other.

"He doesn't act the way I would assume a prince to act," I murmur, more to myself than to Iseul.

"Don't judge him too harshly..." she says, misinterpreting my meaning. "He was always formal and reserved, but after the deaths of the king and queen, he became even more closed off. If you give him a chance and get to know him a little better..."

I take her hand and offer a reassuring smile. It isn't my place to share the things I'm learning about him, so the best I can say is, "I think I am beginning to see what you see in him."

We end our conversation abruptly in mutual

understanding at the sound of the library's main door sliding open, then closed again. Footsteps approach without hesitation.

Iseul and I wait, watching the space where the visitor will appear. She inhales sharply when it's the prince who finds us. He looks between us, his expression hardening into a guarded mask.

It isn't what she said about Joon but how she pleaded with me that helps me see his abrupt changes in mood for what they really are—a shield of ice to protect himself.

"Hello, My Prince," I say, trying to break any awkwardness before it forms. "Iseul was just telling me it was time for dinner. Would you like to join me?"

She bows. "My Prince."

His eyes narrow in suspicion, not at all fooled. "Actually, I came to ask you the same thing."

Iseul squeezes my hand. She is practically vibrating with the need to say something.

"I would like that."

"Dinner will be served in half an hour in the Western Court." His winter blue gaze slowly travels over me from head to toe, then back, leaving a trail of warmth rising in my chest.

Perhaps it was my conversation with Iseul, but it is impossible to ignore how devastatingly handsome he is. Even the scar over his eye adds to his unearthly beauty rather than detracting from it.

He could forgo his crown and wear worn and dirty clothes, but he would still look every inch a prince.

How is it that there are times I can forget something so obvious?

Underneath that, I feel a pull toward him that has nothing to do with his looks. I cannot tell if it is the bond that ties me to him or our shared determination to defy the fates we've been dealt.

Joon nods and takes his leave.

Once he is gone, Iseul exhales a large breath as if she was holding it the entire time. She grabs my arms and shakes me lightly. "I have never seen him dine with any of his wives after the first night." She bounces on her toes. "I think he likes you."

I smirk. We have a mutual understanding between us that allows us to relax when we are alone, but that is all it is. And all it can be.

"No wonder he has been taking you with him on his outings instead of Mingi. He has been insufferable, by the way, pouting about being left behind and unable to do his duty," Iseul does a playful, mocking impression of her brother.

Joon studies me from the other side of the table, legs crossed and hands resting on his knees. He pointedly ignores the embarrassingly loud growl coming from my empty stomach.

I glance longingly at the food, wishing to eat, but I wait for him to begin first.

"Oh, for demons' sake," I snap, throwing my hands up. "What have I done this time?"

"You two were acting suspicious."

"If you want to know what we were saying, all you had to do was ask."

Joon arches a brow.

"We were talking about you," I say, earning a startled look from him. He hadn't expected the blunt truth.

I get up and go around to his side and sit with my legs tucked. I reach out and cup his cheek, turning his face so he looks me directly in the eye. This close, he is paler than he should be.

"It was nothing bad, Joon," I say gently. "Do you know how much Mingi and Iseul worry about you?"

He frowns.

"I told her I was curious about your life—don't make that face. She respected your privacy, but she did ask me to give you a chance before judging you." Lowering my hand, I sit back on my heels.

The muscles in his body relax.

"Then she said you obviously couldn't resist falling for my charm," I tease.

Joon snorts. "Hardly." He fails to hide the smile tugging at the corners of his mouth before I catch it. He motions to my plate. "Eat before the food gets cold."

The rise and fall of his shallow breaths keep me in place. "Joon, what's wrong?"

His gaze snaps to mine, desperation and something else shadowing the different shades of blue. "I will be fine—"

"Let me do what I promised."

"Very well," he says after a moment. He rises to his feet, pulling me up with him.

I reach up and wrap my arms around the back of his neck, bringing his face to mine, and will whatever power I hold within me to help him.

His lips are warmer than I remember.

At first, Joon doesn't react. Then his hands find my waist. I cannot tell if it's working, but when I deepen the kiss, he responds, his mouth moving against mine. He is like winter and warm honey at the same time.

When his tongue finds mine, I melt against him, forgetting everything beyond our bodies pressed as close as we can get. My appetite is replaced by something else entirely.

Then I feel it. The tug from inside my bones as the magic wakes, gathering, then races out of me and into him, and I no longer know which way is up. I hold on tight as he crushes me to him.

My chest squeezes, bringing a sharp pinch with every beat of my heart. Joon starts to pull back, but I can sense that the transfer is not complete. The power still hums under my skin.

I tighten my arms around his neck and push up on my toes. He groans in response.

The pain in my chest intensifies until I forget how to breathe. He breaks the kiss, and I gasp for air. This time, he holds me, ready for how the siphoning affects my condition.

"Breathe, Violet," he says, pressing his palm against my chest at the base of my throat.

Cool power seeps into me, soothing the pain like a balm. Each inhale brings more air to my lungs until there is no sign that the episode ever started.

The light glow of iridescent scale-like frost pattern passes over the back of his hand, vanishing as quickly as it appeared.

I let my forehead fall against his chest. He lets me stay there.

"You should not have pushed it."

"It wasn't so bad this time." I smile weakly. "Don't worry, I know I'm no use to you dead."

"Do not take this so lightly, Violet," he snaps.

"I understand the risks, and I am fine now." I step back, and his arms fall away. The air is noticeably colder than before. Or maybe it only seems that way after the warmth of his embrace. "Are you worried about me?" I ask with a teasing smile.

"Of course I am." The harshness of his voice is a sharp contrast to his words.

I don't have the faintest idea how to respond.

Joon jerks his head toward the window, eyes wide. "I did not expect to sense another so soon."

It should be good news, but he looks distraught.

"We should leave now," I say, remembering how our first search took us all over the fae lands of Arum before the trail went cold.

Joon turns to me and shakes his head. "It is one thing to leave before dawn, but another entirely to leave near nightfall."

"Then there's no time to waste." I grab his wrist and tug him toward the door.

He resists. "Violet."

I round on him. "There is nothing that can be done for my condition, but *we can* do this for you." He still doesn't look convinced. "It could be closer than you think. And if there's not enough time to safely make it back, we can stop somewhere or find shelter or figure something else out."

Joon is silent for a long moment. "Now you sound worried about me."

I wave a hand. "Purely selfish reasons. I don't get what I want until you succeed," I say airily. Though not entirely untrue, it doesn't quite ring as honest as it once would.

It takes more prodding than expected, but less than half an hour later, we are on the road, galloping toward the unknown destination of the next shard. The urgency to outrun the night and to end his curse before he is out of time is tangible between us.

I press against his back with my arms around his waist. We are married in name only for the sake of our bargain; holding on to him shouldn't come as naturally as it does.

Around us, the landscape jumps from one to the next as he opens path after path, letting one fade and the new one form. If he uses too much of his power, I think I should be able to handle another siphoning.

We stop on the outskirts of a town with an hour of sunlight to spare.

"It is close," he whispers, though there is no one around to overhear.

He pants from the exertion of using so much magic in a short time. It would be best for him to preserve what remains to avoid having to siphon again so soon.

"It would be faster to go through than around," I say.

The tingling sensation of his magic envelops me as Joon disguises us with a glamour and urges the horse onward.

His entire body is rigid with tension as we pass through the main road, being as inconspicuous as possible.

I recognize this place. It's where we stopped on our journey to the palace after the Choosing. At the time, I didn't take the opportunity to really take it in. The city has a comforting feel, with citizens milling about unhurried as lanterns, already lit in anticipation of night, line the streets and paths like a thousand stars fallen to earth.

A young man climbs a ladder as an older couple, who I assume are his parents, survey him. The woman frets, wringing her hands as her husband passes a freshly painted sign for their son to hang. The sign reads "The Dragon's Tome," and I wonder what books they have that I can only dream about getting my hands on.

The dimming light casts a strange shimmer over the young man as a beam passes through a thin break between buildings. Even the sunsets have an air of magic to them on this side of the border.

It stings to see a happy family like the one I once had, and I wonder if Joon feels the same or even notices them.

Hours seem to pass before we make it through the quaint town. We slip into the woods and weave between the trees until we reach the edge of a sprawling field of flowers.

Joon dismounts, striding ahead as if in a trance. I leap down and follow, feeling a little guilty about the way we're trampling down the beautiful plants.

My heart plummets when he stops dead in his tracks. I hold my breath, waiting for him to say he lost the trail.

He falls to his knees in the dirt. My feet carry me over, and I kneel beside him. Joon's hand trembles as he reaches for a folded flower, such a dark shade of purple it nearly looks black.

The lightest touch of his finger against the glossy petals is all it takes for it to unfurl as if he were the sun itself.

My breath catches in my throat when I see a shard of a mirror, nestled in the center of the flower.

He plucks it up and wraps it in the strip of cloth I ripped off my skirt on our last journey, then tucks it safely away. I didn't realize he kept the stained rag instead of throwing it away.

I grip his shoulder. "You did it. You found another one," I say.

He turns to me. His fingers tangle in my hair, and he's pulling me to him. Then his mouth is on mine in a crushing kiss that steals the air from my lungs. His lips move against mine, demanding my surrender so he may consume me.

Joon releases me, ending it as abruptly as it began. "It is all thanks to you." He clears his throat and looks anywhere but at me.

A lone demon howls in the distance, and my stomach answers as my forgotten hunger returns with a vengeance.

"We can return to the palace or stop here for the night," Joon says. "Whichever you prefer."

The feel of his mouth lingers on my lips. It has me wondering what it would be like to kiss him as long as I wanted, to surround myself in his scent and feel his touch everywhere.

I shake my head. With thoughts like these running through my mind, I don't think I can trust myself to be alone with him tonight. "We should return."

His eyes search my face, and the knot in his throat bobs as he nods.

"Yes. That is probably for the best." His voice is hoarse, and I wonder if he sensed the direction of my thoughts.

CHAPTER EIGHTEEN

VIOLET

My breakfast sits on the table before me, having long since gone cold, as my mind replays images of a painted sunset sky, Joon's fingers tangling in my hair as he pulls me to him. . . .

Even days later, the phantom crush of his mouth on mine continues to linger. Heat spreads in my lower belly.

Stop being so ridiculous, I chide inwardly.

Something so simple should not have such a strong effect. After all, it's not as though it was the first time we kissed.

But it is different, a small, traitorous voice at the back of my mind whispers. All the others were for the sole purpose of siphoning.

I shake my head. While I can admit that part is true, it is equally true that it was nothing more than a whim—a reflex on his part. Joon found one of the final missing shards. It most certainly wasn't out of desire or affection. It could have easily been any of his previous wives in my place.

I rise from the table and cross to the wardrobe to get ready for the day. A long research session in the library should clear my mind. I am here for one purpose and one purpose only: to help him break the curse so he can live and free the people trapped in the Winter Dragon's enchanted ice.

I nearly jump out of my skin when a knock at the door jerks me from my thoughts.

It's too loud to be Iseul or Mingi. It certainly isn't the prince; Joon lets himself in without announcing himself in any way. Whoever it is, doesn't speak.

After a pause, they knock again. I finish dressing before answering the door to a stern-faced woman. She's dressed in the standard deep blues and silver of the Arum palace guard uniform.

"Lady Hawthorn, your presence is requested by the king," she says flatly.

"What is this about?" I ask, rapidly sifting through all my words and actions since arriving that could possibly warrant a summons, only to come up empty.

The guard stands silently, her gaze fixed straight ahead.

"All right, I'm ready," I say when it's clear she can't or won't answer me.

She spins on her heel and marches down the hall with the unspoken expectation that I will follow.

Unable to come up with a reason, good or bad, for the king wanting to see me, I allow her to lead the way.

We cut through the open courtyard and through the main gate leading to the central palace. The Temple Tower looms behind another building, small in comparison, though nearly double the size of Joon's apartments and mine combined.

This must be the Formal Hall and the king's quarters.

The palace guard stops before five other guards at the double doors. "The king has requested the Lady's presence," she announces.

They step aside and allow us through. More guards are posted every thirty feet within the hall.

I feel their eyes on me as we pass.

We continue deeper into the main hall of the Central Court until we finally reach a room at the very center—a heart within a heart. It even feels symbolic.

"Stay here," She orders, then slips inside, closing the door before I can glimpse what lies beyond.

My escort guard is back within moments, gesturing for me to enter. The door slides shut with a snap.

The room is wide open, with massive, frosted windows on the east and west walls. Most of the space is empty, able to accommodate several hundred court members, formal dinners for anyone of status, including minor nobility, or host a ball.

Sconces made of white metal fashioned into designs resembling delicate lace, spiraling dragons carved into the pillars, and engraved beams overhead serve as the main decorations.

Contrasting against the snowy-white wood of the floor, a cobalt runner starts at the center of the room and ends at the foot of seven steps leading up a dais. Atop the dais, the king sits upon a wide throne with an identical empty throne to the right.

At the bottom of the steps, two fae officials stand on either side of the runner. They wear the traditional robes denoting their position. A layer of white that begins with a high, straight collar and ends an inch above the floor, with wide sleeves that end halfway down the hand. The top layer is a sleeveless, sheer material in a smoky blue with a midnight trim. The robes wrap around the front of their chests, held in place by a wide belt, knotted at their left hip. Each belt has a symbol embroidered on one of the dangling ends.

I walk forward. The female official flicks her wrist in a sharp motion, halting me several feet away.

With no instructions or guidance on how to conduct myself in formal situations like this, I am at a loss for what to do beyond the obvious.

I bow deeply and say, "Good morning, Your Majesty."

The male official snorts derisively. I bristle inwardly but am careful not to react.

"I am sure you are curious as to why I summoned you."

"I am… Your Majesty," I say.

Demons and saints, I hope no one caught the tremor in my voice.

The king stands and clasps his hands at his low back as he casually strolls down the stairs. I force my feet to root me in place, fighting against the nerves that push my heart to beat faster.

Remain calm, Violet.

"There is no cause for concern, Lady Hawthorn." The king pauses at the bottom of the dais and smiles warmly. "I called you here because there is a small matter of official business to address."

Confusion furrows my brow. I can't help the feeling of betrayal. Neither Joon, Mingi, nor Iseul bothered to warn me that I would be expected to perform *"official business"* in any capacity.

I don't notice the king moving closer until he's less than an arm's length away. He reaches for my hand and holds it between both of his in a move that takes me by surprise. I barely stop myself in time from yanking my arm back from the unexpected touch.

Why am I acting like this? We have spoken before and walked together.

"Be at ease, Violet. Have we not talked and walked together before?" he says in an eerie echo of my thoughts.

"I apologize if I failed to adequately perform the duties of my position," I hurry to say, even though I have no idea what they are. "I will do better—"

The king chuckles. "It is nothing to worry yourself over. I wanted to know how you are faring since we last spoke," he says with fatherly concern.

"I am well, Your Majesty." I cringe at the way I repeat myself. It makes me sound as though I only know a handful of words.

"Good. Good. Now, for the reason I sent for you, I wanted to make sure you understood why you have not been given the typical luxuries due to someone in your position."

What else can there be? I have my own palace in the southern court, fine clothes, and the best food.

"I haven't given it a moment's thought," I say honestly. "I have more than I need."

"Rest assured, it will be remedied once you are presented to the court," he continues as though I hadn't spoken. "It should have happened within a few days of your arrival and is long past due. Usually, it falls to the Crown Prince to arrange it, but he has been selfishly keeping you all to himself." The king smirks, finding humor in his own words that I don't understand.

"I had no idea," I say.

Surely, this is not what he wanted to discuss?

"Worry not, I will personally see it taken care of before the month is out. The head seamstress is already hard at work on your gown."

"Thank you, Your Majesty. I am honored."

He shifts closer, almost intimately close. His eyes darken. "Our Crown Prince is quite fond of you."

I frown at the casual turn in conversation. An odd

sensation prickles along the back of my neck. "I'm not sure what you mean."

A wave of dizziness slips over me, and my pulse picks up. I feel like I am going to be sick. I am one wrong move away from offending the king in an unforgivable way by being sick all over his shoes.

"Our prince has rarely spent time with any of his previous wives, yet I have it on good authority that you are often seen in his presence."

He reaffirms what Joon said during dinner the night we arrived at the palace—that we are constantly being monitored.

It doesn't seem too unusual for random servants to report the happenings of the palace to the king, especially anything that could be deemed out of the ordinary.

If I lie and he notices, there's no telling what the consequences will be. Against my better judgment, the urge to explain is overwhelming.

Tingling prickles lodge in my throat in warning. I try to swallow it down, but it's no use. The power of the bargain settles, ready to silence any words that might give it away.

I'm at a loss.

"So, by your silence, may I assume you have come to the same conclusion?"

Though I'm not entirely sure how that could be a bad thing, I am left with the nagging sensation that it will only complicate matters. My heart squeezes, sending a sharp ache radiating through my chest.

Demons, no... please, not now.

"I am afraid I don't know him well enough to understand his feelings one way or another, Your Majesty." I focus on smothering the telltale signs of an impending episode.

He nods. "That is understandable."

"I only wish to do what is required of me," I offer as a platitude.

"You may be my favorite one yet," he murmurs so only I can hear. The rapid thudding of my heart against my ribs makes the soothing tones of his voice into something ominous.

My nerves are completely frayed. Earlier, I could dismiss it as anxiety over the possibility of unintentionally insulting the crown. But now there's little chance of quelling the impending episode.

Demons and saints, I need to get out of here.

My episodes have never come on so fast, over such a small amount of stress. My heart won't last much longer if this is all it takes.

I cannot die yet. We have to break the curse.

"I would hate to see anything happen to you," the king adds.

The blood drains from my face, and my entire body goes cold in the span of a single breath. "Your Majesty?" My voice comes out in a pathetic whimper.

Another sharp pain pinches inside my chest. I don't have long before I can no longer hide what's happening.

Now I do pull my hand from his.

The king keeps his voice low and even, as one would when trying to capture a wild animal. "Forgive me. I only meant that I do not wish to see you end up like the others." His head lists ever so slightly to the side. "Have you seen them yet?"

Too focused on smothering my impending episode long enough to make it somewhere else, I can barely make sense of what he is saying.

I shake my head while trying not to wince at the increasing pain. "Seen who, Your Majesty?"

"They reside at the back of the royal crypt." He lowers his gaze to the floor and sighs. "I have suggested he send them back to their families, but he insists on keeping them as his trophies."

I suck in a sharp breath as another pain stabs at my heart. Thankfully, he takes it for a shocked reaction.

"You may visit them if it is what you need to realize the full scope of the risk your position entails."

The door is flung wide, interrupting our conversation. I whip my head around to see Joon cutting the distance with long strides.

"Ah, there you are, *Wife*. I have been looking everywhere for you."

I nearly choke from the way he says *Wife*. It's sharp. Possessive. It will only further add to the king's belief that he has genuine feelings for me.

"J—" I start, but his name dies in my throat as he wraps his fingers around my wrist and tugs me to his side with so much force that I bump into him.

Joon's eyes find mine, and I realize my near error.

"Did you forget?" he asks just as another surge of pain lances through me. "There is somewhere you are supposed to be."

I gape at him. His features are arranged in a placid expression, but a dark fire burns behind his eyes.

My breaths grow shallower by the minute. I'm lightheaded.

Joon knows what my episodes look like, having seen plenty of them, so I'm unsure if I've actually forgotten something important or if this is an excuse to get me out of here.

"I-I believe I did." He twitches one brow, and I hastily add, "My Prince."

Stars form across my vision. I want to reach out and grab hold of Joon to steady myself, but I don't.

Joon turns to the king and bows his head in respect. "If you are finished here, would you please excuse us, My King?"

King Sameun presses his mouth into a thin line, considering Joon for a moment. "Your timing is excellent. We just finished our talk," he says, then turns his piercing eyes on me. "See to it that you do not overtax her… she does not look well. And we wouldn't want to have *another* incident, especially so soon."

Joon bows at the waist. I do the same, glad when I don't topple over onto my head. My hands are shaking from the pain, and I clasp them tightly together as we walk out of the throne room.

Once we are beyond the doors, the prince grabs my upper arm and practically drags me down the hall until we reach a secluded alcove. Joon stops and presses my back to the wall.

The prince cups my jaw with both hands. Cooling strands of power seep into me, slowing my heartbeat and dousing the fiery pain.

It will never cease to amaze me how he can stop my episodes and leave me feeling as if it never even happened.

Taking my first deep breath, I lift my gaze to his scowling face.

Did he hear what the king said? Is he upset with me?

There's nothing I could have done to get out of that situation on my own. Surely, he understands that.

I study the prince. There are still fathomless depths to him that remain a mystery. He is flawed just like everyone else, temperamental, and walled off, but even so, I have a hard time believing he would keep his dead wives as trophies.

I suppress a shudder at the grim image.

At one time, I might have believed Prince Joon capable of something so morbid and cold. But not now.

It makes me wonder if the king has never made an effort to know the prince or, like most others, if he simply took everything he's ever said or done at face value.

"Are you angry with me?" I ask. "I didn't know how—"

Joon's eyes soften. "You did nothing wrong. I was worried when Iseul said you were not in your rooms when she came for you." His eyes cut to glare back the way we came.

"I'm sorry..." I trail off, still not able to recall. "I am not usually so forgetful."

A smirk spreads over his mouth. "I am taking you into town." Prince Joon takes my hand and pulls me along.

My brow furrows. That's definitely something I would remember.

Before we leave the cover of the central palace awning, Joon pauses and lets his fingers slide away, releasing me. "It's not Lummi, but I thought you might like to see what the capital has to offer. When this is over, and we have time, I can take you back to that bookstore, if you would like."

I blink. "How...?"

"It was hard to miss the way you nearly toppled both of us off the horse as we passed." He begins walking again.

I smile at his back and follow.

CHAPTER NINETEEN

JOON

I SLIP INTO THE SIMPLE RIDING JACKET I BORROWED FROM Mingi.

In the beginning, I had the strength to collect most of the shards on my own. But with each one found, the next took more of my power to track down.

When I became too weak, there was no other choice but to use the frost bloom and enlist the aid of human brides as vessels.

With their help, I managed to find several more, though each success was few and far between. Hopelessness weighed on me, trapping me in a pit of despair until I had all but given up. My sixth wife resulted in nothing but failure after failure.

As long as I am careful with the use of my magic, the power I siphon from Violet lasts longer than any other vessel.

There is only a single shard remaining before the mirror is complete.

I feel lighter than I ever have before. The burden of this curse does not seem so heavy now. Mingi and Iseul have always been by my side, always ready to support me, but were never able to help.

For the first time, I allow myself to hope.

And it is because of Violet.

Perhaps it is because she is more willing.

"If I had known any of this, I would have helped you without bargains or threats."

She alone has expressed a desire to help and outright demanded to know more about this situation… and me.

Imugi passes through the wall like fog. "The presence has returned," the demon says, gliding through the air in agitated patterns.

"You say it is the same one as before?"

As if on cue, there's a tap against the window drawing my attention—the blur of a dark shape darts out of view.

Imugi hisses. "There!" They whip their pale face toward me. "The very same. They must have followed us after the attack at the bridge." Imugi releases two small puffs of mist from their nose. "Maybe even longer than that.

Another tap. This time, the small demon remains perched on the outer ledge. They press their long, finger-like talons against the glass, clicking the sharp tips.

"It is unusual behavior. There is something wrong with them," Imugi mutters.

Why would a demon venture into the sun when direct light weakens even the strongest among them?

I flick my wrist and send a flash of power toward them. Frost spreads, crackling over the pane. They fall, trying to get out of the way.

"Wait!" Mingi snaps from out in the hall. His command is ignored by whoever is frantically knocking.

The second I open the door, Iseul pushes her way inside,

heedless of the impropriety. She looks around the room frantically. "Is she here?"

Mingi follows, stopping right inside the threshold. He knows I wouldn't do anything untoward, but it would cause nothing but trouble if word got out that she was in my apartments, alone with me.

"What is going on?" I demand.

Iseul rounds on me, her dark eyes wide with worry. "Violet—I was supposed to accompany her to the library today, but she wasn't in her room when I went to get her." She flings her arm toward the window, pointing. "And I caught a demon climbing out the window. What if it did something to her?"

Imugi and I exchange a glance.

"Was it about this size?" I spread my hands to match the one that was just here.

Iseul nods.

Violet is entirely human, so they cannot be bonded to her. There would be signs of a demon's magic, impossible to hide. One cannot bond with a demon and remain unchanged.

"Do you have any idea where she could have gone?"

Iseul bites her lip, shaking her head. "I don't… I am sorry."

Unease slithers down my spine. Everything about this is off.

Without a word, I stride from the room. Turning a corner, I stop mid-step when I catch sight of the same demon peering through yet another window near the end of the hallway.

I quicken my stride. By the time I reach the window, the demon has already moved to the shade of a tree along the walking path beyond the main doors. They sit, watching me, as if waiting.

This wild demon's presence cannot be a coincidence.

The Western courtyard is empty, but there is one place that is always teeming with activity. And where there is activity, there will be servants spreading palace gossip like currency.

The demon scrambles to keep out of reach, pausing every few yards to look back.

My steps falter. *Do they want me to follow?*

They are leading me toward the central court. That suspicion is confirmed as I continue.

The demon hides beneath the shelter of plants, stopping at the edge of the Central Court's Garden, out of the servants' view. They gesture toward the main palace.

I reach out and stop the first guard that crosses my path. His posture lacks strength, and he moves with a lack of confidence. The young man cannot be more than a year into his service.

"Where is my wife?" My voice holds the cold threat of a winter storm.

His face pales. "She is in the throne room, with the king, Your Highness."

I am already walking away before he's finished. My uncle has never formally met with any of my previous wives. I lengthen my stride.

Ministers Ilseong and Molan have long wished to see me stripped of my birthright and banished. I do not know what they hope to accomplish, but this situation reeks of their influence.

I do not slow as I enter the Formal Hall, and stride through the corridors with menacing purpose. Servants line both sides of the corridor outside the throne room door, standing in neat rows with their backs to the wall.

"Your Highness, y-you can't go in—" one of the king's attendants stammers out.

I reach past him and push the door open. It comes as no surprise to see Ministers Ilseong and Molan there. Their faces contort in a mix of shock and anger—no doubt they are the ones responsible for this.

Violet snaps her gaze toward me. She is unnaturally pale, lips bloodless, and eyes glassy with pain.

"Ah, there you are, *Wife*," I say with a casual air. "I have been looking everywhere for you."

Violet's eyes widen. "J—" she begins.

I take her wrist and pull her to me, keeping her from addressing me informally.

She is so unsteady on her feet that she collides against my side. Violet's skin is cool to the touch. My fingertips shift to find her pulse. It is erratic, confirming what I already knew. She is in the early stages of one of her 'episodes.'

"Did you forget? There is somewhere you are supposed to be."

A barely perceptible wince pinches her expression. The rise and fall of her chest quickens with sharp, shallow breaths.

Her visible confusion is a bad sign. She doesn't even have enough wits about her to know that she hasn't forgotten a demon damned thing.

"I-I believe I did?" Her voice is breathy and weak. I send her a subtle prompt, before she hastily adds, "My Prince."

I tear my gaze away from the desperation and pleading shining in her eyes and turn my attention to my uncle.

"I hope you do not mind if I steal my bride for a previous commitment, My King?"

He contemplates my request for a moment before speaking—it wouldn't do to allow anyone to order him around through a thinly veiled demand. Not even the crown prince.

"Your timing is excellent. We had just finished our talk," he says, then flicks his gaze to Violet, taking in her deteriorating condition that becomes increasingly difficult for her to hide by the second. He lowers his voice. "See to it that you do not overtax her… she does not look well. And we wouldn't want to have another *incident*."

The comment is a sharp barb that hits its mark. He believes I am doing this to her, as I have done with my previous wives.

Uncle disapproves of my cruelty to my wives and the people of Arum, whether human or fae.

He may be the only one who has stood by me for the last fourteen years, but that does not mean he has forgiven me for the late king's death. I took his brother, and last living relative, from him.

I bow low in deference, more than expected of the Crown Prince. We are both aware that he could have easily denied me out of spite if he so wished.

Violet clasps her trembling hands to still them, then bows as well.

We take our leave. I watch her carefully, ready to catch her if necessary. Her uneven breaths are now coming in short, shallow bursts.

By the time we make it to the hall, she can barely hold herself upright. I scowl and grab her arm, dragging her with me as we pass dozens of eyes, scrutinizing my every move. The servants frown and send her sympathetic glances.

At the first alcove offering a semblance of privacy, I press her against the wall for support. I call to my power and send it into her.

My eyes close as I guide the magic through her veins. Once it finds the way to her heart, I watch as the pain melts from Violet's face. When all signs of her episode are gone, I release her.

Emotions flicker in her honey eyes as Violet lifts her gaze

to mine, peering through thick lashes. "Are you angry with me?" she asks softly. "I didn't know—"

"You did nothing wrong. I was worried when Iseul told me you were not in your rooms when she came for you."

I glare through walls as if I could see Ministers Ilseong and Molan. *What had they said to my uncle that he would publicly summon her?*

"I'm sorry…" she says haltingly. "I am not usually so forgetful."

I return my attention to Violet. Her look of innocent confusion is too pure to resist.

There is still the matter of that strange, wild demon to discuss. But that can wait until later. There is something else I would like to do first.

"I am taking you into town." I take her hand, relieved to find her skin is warm again. We stop just before leaving the cover of the central palace, and only then do I release my grip. "It's not Lummi, but I thought you might like to see what the capital has to offer."

Violet's face alights with amazement as I pull back a curtain of ivy to reveal a narrow door in the outer wall of the western corner along the back wall of the Northern Court.

The hidden passage is known only to the royal family and intended as an emergency escape. As a child, I would slip in and out of the palace through here. I remember the excitement of getting away with something, shared laughter, and whispered secrets.

Those days, as with all my memories before that night

fourteen years ago, are muddied by the horror of what happened.

Imugi drapes their long body over my shoulders, silently pouting. They are against the idea of sharing this secret with Violet. The demon's protests were half-hearted and didn't last long.

I think they are finally warming up to her in spite of themselves.

Stepping inside, I hold the vines aside. Violet follows without hesitation. The passage is dark, but I wait until the cover is back in place before conjuring a fae light that hovers several inches above my palm.

The stone path is damp from the humid air trapped within. Without room to walk side by side, Violet holds onto my free arm with both hands until we reach a short door.

She sucks in a sharp breath when I extinguish the light. I crack open the door just enough to listen. Imugi rises from their perch and impatiently slips through.

"That is not necess—" I begin, but they are already gone.

Violet presses closer. Close enough that her breasts press against me with every breath.

Imugi returns a moment later. "The way is clear," they say with a bite to their tone. Then, under their breath, they say, "Though you are a fool to do this."

CHAPTER TWENTY

JOON

A WHITE MARE WAITS FOR US JUST BEYOND THE PALACE WALLS. I help Violet into the saddle, then climb up behind her.

A fae path makes quick work of the wild woods behind the palace as we make our way toward the king's road.

Upon my request this morning, Mingi had procured clothing typical of the capital's citizens. It is nowhere near as comfortable as my own, which is to be expected of something not tailored to my body.

Violet twists around and puts a hand to the side of her mouth. "Can we talk yet?" she whispers.

"Yes."

"Good. Because I have questions." She takes a deep breath. "Do you use that way often? Do Mingi and Iseul know about it? Shouldn't we have brought them with us? Where—"

I silence her with the press of my fingertips. "One at a time," I say. "To answer your first question, no, I do not use it often. At least, not anymore. As for the other questions, aside from myself, only Mingi, Iseul, and now you know. It is not necessary for them to come along, as their presence would give us away."

I wanted time alone with you, away from duties and curses. The thought comes unbidden. I had not realized it before, but I know it is true. When I am with her, I can pretend I am someone else, someone without the burden of a crown or countless subjects waiting for me to assume my role. I can be someone she might have wanted if I had not stolen her away from her life.

The familiar sensation of a shadow brushing the edges of consciousness returns, pulling me from my daydream.

A wild demon is near. Where Imugi's power is strong, this one is faint—not unlike the one from earlier.

Did the small one summon the others that were with them during the attack on the bridge? I quickly dismiss that thought. Imugi would have been able to sense if there were others. Based on the earlier incident, I believe the demon is somehow connected to Violet.

"What will we do in the capital?"

"It's a surprise," I say, which earns me a half-hearted pout. "Now, it is my turn to ask you questions."

Violet tilts her head.

"What dealings with demons have you had?" Out here with no one else to overhear seems like the perfect opportunity to ask.

She frowns, chewing on her bottom lip. "None… unless you mean the time we were attacked on the way here?"

"Have you ever attempted to deal with one?"

"Of course not. I am desperate to live, but I have no desire to end up demon cursed," Violet says adamantly. "Why do you ask?"

"I believe you may have inadvertently attracted the

attention of a demon." I lower my voice. "They have been following you for a while... as they are now."

Violet inhales sharply. Her gaze darts in search of the creature. Unable to find them, her eyes return to mine, worry etched in their depths.

"Do not worry. It does not appear as if they wish you harm."

Her fingers curl into the material of her cloak with a death grip.

"I am looking into it, but in the meantime, I will keep them away from you," I add. That comforts Violet enough that she relaxes back into me.

We reach the main road, and the fae road vanishes behind us. From here, it is only a short journey into the capital.

I cast a minor glamour over myself to hide my scar, change the shape of my face, make my one pale blue iris match the other, and turn the white ends of my hair as dark as the rest.

For Violet, I want her to look like herself today, only altering her appearance to instill doubt that she is anything other than fae. I give her pointed ears, darken her hair, and change her eyes to a deep brown, letting flecks of the honey color peek through.

Citizens converge at the crossroads where the six major roads meet. They travel on foot, horseback, by wagon, and by carriage in and out of the main gate. We merge with the market day traffic, unnoticed in our disguises.

At the gate, we dismount and enter, turning down a side street to leave our horse at a stable before we venture into the heart of the city.

Violet's face alights with excitement as she tries to take everything in all at once. I tuck her hand into the crook of my arm to guide her safely through the crowd as we pass the gathering of small vendors from other cities who have traveled to trade and sell their goods.

She tugs on my arm as we come to the edge of the square. Her breath catches.

The entire business district of her city could fit in this space. The cacophony of voices rises as citizens bustle from place to place. The open square is sectioned off into a dozen temporary lanes, each separated by a variety of goods ranging from food, clothing, jewelry, hairpins, charms, specialty items for homes, and countless others.

"Joon…" My name is little more than a sigh.

I lean down, bringing my lips to her ear. "Careful with my name, Wife. It might be best if you call me Husband while we are here."

Violet's lashes flutter as she turns her face toward me. Her entire focus narrows, and pink stains her cheeks as the movement causes her nose to brush against mine.

Satisfied, I straighten. "Shall we?"

"There's so much I want to see…" Violet trails off. "Will we have time?"

The sparkle in her eyes makes it difficult to keep myself from dedicating the entire day to fulfilling her every whim.

"Today, we are here for a specific purpose." I watch her face fall. "Perhaps after we have accomplished what we set out to do, and before you leave, I will bring you here again. "

Though she nods, some of her brightness has dimmed behind the smirk she throws my way. "I will hold you to that, Husband."

"I count on it, Wife."

We weave through the throng. I catch the longing look Violet gives a booth selling pastries, and despite what I said, I stop to buy her several of the jam-stuffed pastries in the shape of fat little dragons, tipping the vendor an extra gold coin.

Violet devours the delicacies as if she hasn't eaten in weeks. I can't help staring at a smear of winterberry jam in the corner of her mouth. Her tongue darts out but misses it completely.

The urge to lean down and taste it on her skin strikes. I am partway there when I catch myself, using my thumb to wipe it away before my baser instincts take over.

"Thank you." She echoes the movement and laughs at herself. "Talya always said it was impossible for anyone to take me anywhere."

"I hope that never changes."

Violet blushes again. It makes me want to find every possible way to pull that reaction from her.

When I reach for her hand, she weaves her fingers through mine, letting me guide the way.

She is too distracted by the activity in the square to notice where we are headed until we stand before a bookstore three stories high. Her mouth parts in realization.

"It is not the same as the one you wanted to go to—"

"No. It's even better."

Hands still linked, she half-drags me inside. Reluctantly, I release her. She stops in the center of the first floor, pressing her fingers to her mouth to stifle her gasp, and slowly turns in a full circle.

"You can have whatever books you can carry," I say, then motion for her to explore. She does without hesitation, knowing I will follow close behind.

Violet runs her fingers over the covers of books with gold corners and the most intricate embossing ever created—one-of-a-kind books intended to be works of art as much as something to read.

But she doesn't take a single one of them.

She asked for access to the palace library to research, and I assumed she wanted to visit the bookstore in Lummi for similar reasons. But until now, I had not realized the joy she found in books themselves.

After an hour, she has amassed a small stack of books, most of which are no thicker than a notebook.

Violet has barely spoken since we entered the store, her attention stolen by the books. I could be a ghost standing at her side, for how little she notices. Yet her joy has completely ensnared me. Such happiness is foreign to me.

Is this what life away from curses and the weight of the crown is like?

Never in my life have I seen anyone so happy over anything, let alone being the reason for it.

I bring out my pouch of coins, barely taking my eyes off her long enough to pay. There is enough to buy half the books in the store if she wanted them.

"You must be newly bonded," the man behind the counter says.

I turn to the merchant, an older gentleman graying at the temples. He looks between us with a warm smile as he wraps each of the books except the one Violet is lost in. His voice takes on a dreamy quality.

"I remember those days with my Corine. Things will change with the passing years, and your love will grow and temper, but such moments are worth enjoying each other while the passion still burns."

A heavy possessiveness settles in my chest. Violet doesn't hear him, and I am glad. If she is made to blush, then it should be mine alone to claim.

I mutter a harsh goodbye and usher Violet out into the bustling square. She adds the book she was reading during the exchange to the bag with the others. I insist on carrying it for her as we make our way back toward the city's main gate.

We only make it a few blocks before Violet stops at a corner. I turn to her, expecting something to be wrong.

"I was thinking..." she says with a look of such innocence that it makes her seem guilty.

I narrow my eyes, instantly suspicious. "Yes, Wife?"

"Should we get something to take back for Mingi and Iseul? We haven't exactly made things easy on them."

"All right," I sigh. With the streets this packed, it will be much faster if I only need to worry about getting myself through the crowd. "Wait here. I will only be a few minutes."

Violet leans into me and takes the bag. Her broad smile is warm and filled with victory. She sees me in a way no one else does. She instinctively senses my weaknesses and doesn't hesitate to use them against me.

The streets are even more crowded than before. Patrons push and shove their way through the throng, not even noticing when they bump into others.

Luckily, a nearby vendor is selling the colorful, chewy, steamed cakes the siblings have always been fond of.

I have been gone less than five minutes, but as I return to where I left Violet, I cannot see her through the mass of bodies. A sinking feeling settles in my gut.

Heedless of those around me, I shove through the throng with more force, using my powers to help move those not paying attention. Shouts and cries of alarm ring out, but I ignore them.

When I reach the corner, she is nowhere in sight. The only sign she was ever here at all is the knocked-over bag, with her books half spilling out.

I turn in every direction, scanning every face for her.

A slap rings out through the din.

"What are you doing?" a man demands.

"She bit me!" another snaps back.

Their voices are coming from the alley. I race toward them, knowing I will find Violet with them.

Four men and one woman position themselves strategically within the narrow space. They are dressed identically in all black, with silver masks obscuring the upper half of their faces.

Violet hunches, grasping at her chest as she gasps through her second episode today. If she dies, we are all doomed.

"If you come any closer, she dies," the woman says, taking several steps forward.

"We were wondering how long it would take you to come for her," the man closest to me says.

"There are two ways we can do this: give us your coin, and you are free to take her. Resist…" With a flick of her wrists, she draws two short swords from behind her back and swings one in a circle, stopping with the blade against Violet's throat. "And both of you will die."

"Take it." I fling the bag of coins at her feet. "Now, release her."

They all exchange glances. The smallest of the men bends to scoop it up. He is scrawny compared to the others in a way that betrays his youth.

No one moves to release her.

The man standing directly in front of Violet hums, then turns to address the woman. "He gave that up a little too easily."

The woman nods in agreement. "Makes me think there is a lot more where that came from."

"I gave you what you wanted. Unhand my wife or learn the true meaning of regret," I say in a low warning.

The man strolls forward a few paces. "The problem is we think you're holding out on us. No one goes around flashing money like that unless they have ten times as much hidden on their person. You were practically begging us to help relieve you of it."

The men slowly advance on me while the woman keeps the blade pressed against Violet's neck.

"Let's kill them both so we can get out of here," the youngest says.

"You will regret this."

The woman's sharp, humorless laugh cuts through the dark alley. "And what will you do if we don't? Tell the big, bad prince?" she asks in a voice dripping with mocking sarcasm. "No one has given two demon shits about the people of this land since he brutally murdered the king and queen."

Ringing fills my ears, drowning out whatever the woman says next. She shifts her arm, drawing her blade across the delicate skin of Violet's neck.

The cut is shallow, bringing forth a thin line of crimson that forms a series of beads. Violet sways, on the verge of collapse.

If she dies here, all of Arum is doomed.

I run toward them.

The first man to reach me moves to strike with an ax, but I release a burst of power. It hits him in the chest, a starburst of ice piercing his flesh. The crystals spread, coating his entire body in a thick layer of ice. He crashes to the hard-packed ground with a deep crack.

The others shout, scrambling to get away. Unfortunately for them, the only way out is past me. Beads of sweat form across my brow from using such an immense amount of power.

They intended to take the life of the one I swore to protect. I refuse to stop until I ensure that it will never happen. One by one, each of them falls.

The woman gapes in horror at her frozen companions.

She tries to run, but it is too late for her to avoid the same fate.

I drop to my knees before Violet and drag her into my arms, pressing my palm against her chest. Tendrils of magic pour into her, weaving through her veins and wrapping around her heart.

She inhales deeply, then leans on me for support.

Scooping her up in my arms, I rise and carry her away.

"I think I can walk," she says, weakly pushing against my shoulders.

She is not the slightest bit convincing, but I oblige her anyway. I set her on her feet at the edge of the alley, holding onto her until she's steady.

Violet shifts to look back, but I stop her, cupping her cheek.

I tell myself that letting her see will not help the trauma of her ordeal, but I cannot deny that my true motivation is how much I loathe knowing she will know me for the monster I am if she sees the death I wrought.

I gather up the bag of books as she leans against the side of the building. There is no sign of the box of steamed cakes I discarded the moment I realized something was wrong.

Violet clings to my arm until she is forced to let go in order to get in the saddle.

Weak and exhausted, we ride together in silence.

One more shard.

One.

I will find it, or we will both die trying.

CHAPTER TWENTY-ONE

VIOLET

After the trip into the capital, the warmth of spring fades by the day, replaced by a chill and the scent of ice on the wind. Frost spreads, reaching its long fingers over the world beyond my window.

This morning, I woke for the first time since, to find that relentless exhaustion has finally released its relentless hold on me.

That day in the city sparked the worst episode yet. It worries me that they are escalating after years of consistency. I know I will not last much longer.

Everything that happened is nothing more than a collection of fractured words and sounds and images. I can still feel the numbing sensation of death clawing at my heart. My throat tightens at the memory.

The last clear thing I can recall before Joon healed me was a shock of pain striking the back of my head. It held the charge of lightning moments before a strike, seizing control of every muscle.

Dark figures... so many of them. Moving in and out of focus, dividing and multiplying. Voices speaking in harsh whispers. But one stood out, different from the rest—haughty, formal.

"Take care... not... second chance... rewarded."

"You have... pleasure..."

Low laughter surrounds me from all directions.

Retreating footsteps pause. "Mess this... or you will... it."

"...up!" A harsh shout.

Rough hands grab at my arms. A sharp sting across my face. Then prickling power sinks through my skin like a thousand hot needles—nothing like the feel of Joon's magic.

It's wrong—all of this is wrong.

My heart squeezes so hard it feels as though it will shatter.

I fall to my hands and knees and dry heave. My lungs struggle to work. Gasping. I claw uselessly at my chest with one hand.

"... doing?" a woman growls. "Not..., you're... her. Idiot!"

"Not... fault. She's doing..."

A vicious tug yanks my head back, holding it at a painful angle, then up to my feet toward a blurry face shining like the moon in the shadows. A shouted command. A large hand wraps around my throat, sending another wave of magic into me that feels like a thousand bees stinging all over.

Joon's voice rings out. I'm released, barely catching myself before I collapse to the foul-smelling ground.

They are arguing... but I can't understand them through this endless, unbearable pain that threatens to consume my mind for good. An inferno burns through my veins, setting my heart on fire.

In the shadows of my waning consciousness, I feel it. Claws, scraping up my body. Inch by inch, numbing my skin. My muscles. Working its way through me to remove all feeling. It is worse than the agony because I know it's death coming to claim me.

Cold metal presses against my neck, leaving a stinging trail in its wake. The hand keeping me upright releases me without warning. I drop to my knees, catching myself with my hands.

Darkness crowds in on the edges of my vision. I try to see what's happening, but it only causes my stomach to lurch. It forces me to focus on the pinprick of light reflecting off the small, rancid puddle beside my hand.

My head buzzes, muffling the shouts. Making the thuds and cracking sounds of the fight sound far away.

Joon wraps his arms around me, then the soothing sensation of his power washes over me, cooling the fire that threatens to consume me from the inside out and washing away the foreign power from the other fae man. Feeling returns to my body. I can finally breathe again.

I shudder and push the memory away. Resting over the last several days has helped rid me of the fatigue and remaining aches that even Joon's power couldn't heal.

The books from that day are stacked neatly atop the dresser under the window. Three on healing with common plants found in the wild, another two on gardening plants for healing, and two volumes on all known illnesses, their symptoms, and causes, with another on rare maladies.

I brush my fingers over the top book's buttery soft leather cover. They should be a horrible reminder of what happened, but they aren't. When I look at them, I see the beauty of the expansive bookstore—how so many books were pieces of art themselves—the reason we went into the city....

And Joon.

He said to call each other husband and wife. A role we play for the public, the same one we play for everyone within the palace. I hadn't expected him to watch me as a doting husband might.

Then again, it made sense when he paid. I was about to offer to reimburse him when the owner made casual conversation regarding our new marriage bond. It was so painfully awkward that all I could do was pretend not to hear.

Outside, a snowflake drifts past the leaded glass. Then, more and more. Within moments, the sky looks as if it's sprinkling powdered sugar over everything.

Winter is returning. But seasons do not reverse, which can only mean one thing—the Winter Dragon stirs, slowly waking. I can't help worrying about Joon. He must be struggling to contain it.

Guilt settles on my shoulders, weighing me down.

He must need to siphon, or this wouldn't be happening. Why hasn't he sent for me yet?

Perhaps he doesn't realize I've recovered yet. I should let him know. But it's late. Iseul left for the night an hour ago. It would be rude to intrude on the little time she has for herself just to ask her to deliver a message for me.

His apartments are not far. It will only take a few minutes, and I'd prefer to do it myself anyway.

Besides, I want to see how he is doing. And should he need to siphon, I will already be there.

Setting my jaw, I cross over to the wardrobe to grab a nicer dress and quickly change.

When I emerge, there is a folded piece of parchment on the floor. The messenger must have slipped it inside when I didn't respond.

The message is only a single sentence.

Meet me at the Garden of Stars.

I take pride in my handwriting, but Joon's neat, elegant script puts mine to shame.

At least now I know where to find him. Setting the note on a narrow stand beside the door, I reach for my cloak and wrap it around my shoulders.

My hand hovers inches from the door when a series of light taps against the window behind me demands my attention. I turn in time to see a dark figure, made indistinguishable by the layer of frost coating the glass, hastily duck out of sight.

A moment later, the shape reappears. Again, tapping. The figure presses closer to the frost-coated edge of the glass. Red eyes peer in, large and blinking.

Demon.

How? There are wards all around the palace, as well as over each court.

I run to the window, intending to get a better look to be absolutely sure before alerting anyone.

The demon makes a yelp of surprise and… falls backward in a strangely familiar way.

Pressing my face to the icy pane, I peer down and confirm I wasn't imagining a demon. They are sprawled on their back. Their dark body is a stark contrast against the snow-powdered ground.

Could this be the demon presence the prince warned me about?

Hesitantly, I slide the window open. The demon scrambles to their feet, whimpering like an injured animal.

Are all small demons so uncoordinated?

If this is the presence Joon mentioned, then they most likely got past the wards by hitching a ride on a carriage.

It's not worth making a fuss over one demon who can barely get around without hurting themselves to the guards. They appear harmless enough, but I'm not in the habit of taking unnecessary chances, so I will mention it to Joon when I see him.

"Go away," I hiss, waving a hand in a shooing motion, then snap the window shut and lock it.

Not wanting to make the prince wait longer, I hurry out into the hall and make my way through the enclosed areas toward the Central Court.

In addition to the guards stationed strategically that I pass along the way, there are a handful of servants who still move about during the late hours. They all either ignore me entirely or bow in greeting.

Three female servants whisper as I pass, loud enough for me to overhear. I recognize one as being part of the group sent to ready me for the bonding ceremony.

"Yes, but the storms have been less frequent," one says.

"I knew the seventh was lucky!" the other replies with a high-pitched lilt.

Even if I couldn't hear, the way their eyes locked on me makes it obvious that I'm the subject of their conversation.

Rounding another corner, I come to the Garden of Stars. Two guards stationed at the entrance bow their heads as they let me through.

The door slides shut behind me, and I feel as if I've been transported to a different world.

The warm, humid air leaves a film of foggy condensation on the dome's glass squares. There is a break in the clouds overhead, and the blurry stars look like thousands of fireflies.

Hundreds of crystal lanterns hang on strings in zig-zagging patterns all along the main path, lit for my arrival.

I open my mouth to call out, nearly using Joon's name without his title, before I stop myself. I can't be sure we are alone.

"Your Highness?" The title feels clunky on my tongue. My voice is hampered by the labyrinth of plants.

When there's no reply, I meander further in, peering into the various alcoves until I get to the bridge that curves over the narrow stream.

I suppose it is possible I got here before him.

A whirl of cold air slips over me in a stark contrast to the warmth I've grown used to.

"My Prince?" I call out.

A man's voice, muffled by the thick vegetation, comes from near the outer edge of the garden. There's a haunting quality to it that makes me think Joon is in a worse state than I thought.

This better not be some misguided attempt to downplay the severity of it by distracting me with a nighttime stroll through the garden.

I hurry in that direction. The chill in the air continues to increase with every step, and I soon realize why.

Joon has left the door leading to the outer garden propped open with a sturdy marble figure about knee-high and thick enough to withstand the weight of the door pressing against it. The light snowfall has already stopped.

Making sure the prop is firmly in place before inching out a little way, I open my mouth to call to the prince when I hear his voice again from further out.

The path continues from the inner garden, lit solely by moonlight. After a few steps, I hesitate, looking back. The door is as I left it, and despite the demon at my window, the howl of any others is entirely absent.

Warm light flickers through a crystal topiary just ahead, and I smile. The prince, more than anyone, will probably appreciate the solitude and privacy of such a place. Especially given the nature of his situation.

I step on a patch of half-melted snow that has refrozen. The crunch feels obtrusive in the quiet. Joon stirs from where he waits.

The snow crunches again. Except, I haven't moved. Slowly, I turn to look over my shoulder. There are no shadows or movements of anyone nearby. There's nothing out of the ordinary.

My imagination is getting the better of me.

No amount of wards is enough to undo a lifetime of avoiding the night when the closest thing humans have are the gas streetlamps we light every evening.

Right as I take the first step around the topiary, a hulking figure lunges out from behind it. I flinch away and fall hard on my ass.

I drag my gaze up, finding myself face to face with a demon half my height and the bulk of a horse prowling closer. Burning, molten eyes that pierce the dark, and rows of razor-sharp teeth jutting out at all angles are all I can focus on. Long, taloned fingers clack over the stone path, emphasizing their deadly points.

Survival instinct, honed over the years, kicks in. I scramble to my feet and race back the way I came. Adrenaline dulls the ache rooted in my chest.

Before I'm halfway back to the door, it slams shut. The prop is on the ground inside, rocking back and forth, too far away to have naturally fallen on its own.

Still, I keep running in the hopes that one of the guards heard and will come check.

I lurch to the side as another demon leaps from the shadows at my right, then another to my left. The tapping of their sharp talons joins that of the first demon to create an unsettling death march.

I try to scream and call for help, but I can't take a breath deep enough.

I don't stop until I slam into the door. I tug with every bitch of strength I can muster. It doesn't budge. Locked.

Demon shit.

My heart contracts painfully as I pound my fists against the door, desperately hoping that someone… anyone, will hear.

A low, rumbling growl has every muscle along my spine tensing from its nearness. I whirl, pressing my back against the door.

Knowing they have their prey cornered, the demons converge slowly, drawing out their hunt. They pause several yards away, shifting their powerful muscles.

I glance around, searching desperately for anything I can use to defend myself or create light, but the grounds are kept immaculate.

The pain of yet another episode comes on faster this time. Tears of anger and frustration burn my eyes. Loathing washes over me stronger than anything I have ever experienced. An emotion I've never felt but understand at once.

Demon shit. After all this time—after *everything* I've been through, everything I've endured, this is what will kill me—demons.

Useless.

If it weren't for my weak body and broken heart, I would like to believe I stood a chance at getting away. Or, at the very least, I could die fighting instead of helpless and gasping, unable to draw a full breath.

I've spent so many years pretending as if my broken heart only shortened my life. That I wasn't trapped in a weak body, and if I tried hard enough, I could do anything.

No matter what I did, I could not make myself strong.

I curse this body of mine for betraying me.

Clenching my fists at my side until my nails dig into my palms, I straighten and face the demons.

When I don't attack, they grow braver. The center one prowls closer, reaching out to claw at my skirt.

I kick at them. They recoil, only to realize just how helpless I am a second later.

Cruel smiles spread over the three skull-like faces.

I try to call Joon's name, but all that comes out is a harsh rasp.

The first demon coils their body, muscles bunching over elongated limbs, ready to pounce. The two others follow the cue. A horrible rumbling builds in their throats.

With a howl, they shift their weight, then leap.

CHAPTER TWENTY-TWO

VIOLET

The world shifts all around me as the door at my back opens and I fall. Blinding light flares, consuming the dark. The victorious howls quickly transform into piercing screeches of agony. Then there is only silence.

In one seamless move, two strong hands catch me before I hit the ground and drag me inside, letting the door snap shut.

Joon's endless blue eyes hover above, searching my face. Imugi hovers behind his shoulder, dipping in and out of view.

Familiar tendrils of magic weave through me, easing the vice-like grip around my heart.

Pressure builds behind my eyes with prickling heat. "I hate this. I—I thought I was going to die—I couldn't do anything to stop it." Years of pent-up emotions I buried surge forward all at once, spilling over in rivulets of hot tears. "I'm so tired of being afraid and weak."

After days of rest, I thought I was fine, but that day in the alley, a crack formed in the dam I created to hide it all, until the pressure became too much.

Joon holds me to him as fear and anger pour out. Most of

what I manage to say is barely intelligible, but it hardly matters. He listens silently and waits until I take shuddering breaths, completely spent.

"Your *body* may have a weakness, but that doesn't make *you* weak." Joon strokes my hair. "This… condition is only a small part of you. There is so much more to you than this. It does not define you. Look at me, Violet." He pulls back and pins me with his gaze. "It takes more strength and courage to keep going and fight for your life every single day than most could ever hope to possess, and when you thought it was over, you faced it with bravery."

I sniffle pathetically and offer him a thin, half-hearted smile.

These feelings have been building for years. They are not about to change after a few kind words from a prince. It will take time to be rid of them—time I don't have.

It's not that I don't believe him. For so long, I have lived trying to get the world to see *me* and not my broken heart. Pretending I could live a life as normal, as long as anyone else's.

Though perhaps he, more than anyone, is capable of understanding how I feel.

"Come," he says. "Let us get you back to your apartments." Supporting my forearm with his, Joon wraps an arm around my waist and helps me stand.

Happy to lean on him for support, I shuffle along, but before we can even take five steps, the rustling bush leaves sends fear spiking through my veins—there is no breeze within the enclosed garden. Nothing to logically cause that to happen.

I plant my feet and refuse to take another step.

Several leaves near the ground flutter, and from within the

cluster of branches, two red eyes blink through small gaps in the foliage.

"Demon," I squeak, stumbling back, pointing a shaking finger at the beast that somehow managed to get past the wards and inside the palace.

"How did they get *inside*?" Hysteria builds at the base of my throat.

Joon grips me, holding me steady. "I invited them in," he says in a calm voice, as if giving a demon permanent access to the palace was a reasonable thing to do.

"Three demons tried to kill me a minute ago, and you invited one in?"

"They… helped me find you."

My head snaps up and I look him in the eye, so he knows I'm aware that he's lost his demons damned mind.

"They were scratching at my window as if trying to escape the Otherworld. Each time Imugi chased them away, they kept coming back more insistent. Then I realized I had seen this one before."

I frown. "What are you talking about?"

Imugi gives a derisive snort, then floats toward the door to the outside garden, muttering something about the perimeter.

Joon shakes his head, disbelieving, and… *smiles*? "When I asked you about possible encounters with demons, it was because this same one led me to you when you were with my uncle."

My jaw goes slack. Was I wrong to put so much trust in his ability to keep me alive?

Joon studies the demon thoughtfully, then motions for them to come closer.

I half jump when they obey like a trained dog. The demon stops halfway and plops down in a sit.

"They won't hurt you, Violet. In fact, I think they've been

protecting you. I do not understand how or why, but I think they are attuned to you," he murmurs.

Aghast, I step sideways out of his hold. "Are you insane?"

The prince continues to ignore my incredulity. "Look closely." Joon jerks his chin, gesturing toward the demon. "Are you sure you haven't seen this one before?"

He is so confident in his fascination that his calm rubs off on me until I doubt myself.

I close my mouth and tear my gaze from his to play along and do as he asks.

The demon shifts up on their haunches, lifting both hands and wriggling their taloned fingers as if attempting to communicate.

Maybe I'm the crazy one?

The demon falls onto their back, plucking a leaf from the bush and sticking it to the side of their head.

Then it hits me—this is the demon outside my room from earlier. I take a tentative step forward, squinting at them.

They pop up, point at my legs, gesturing again. The demon points to me, then to the ground at my feet as they back up. They repeat it twice more, pausing after each time to see if I understand what they are trying to communicate.

Joon shrugs. "I am not sure what they mean here."

The demon huffs in annoyance.

A demon expressing emotions?

Though I suppose that's not too far-fetched. Imugi is a demon, and I've never questioned their ability to feel emotions.

The demon clambers up the bush and then tumbles to the ground with their rear in the air, holding the pose a moment before righting themselves.

There's something familiar...

Details of an incident I'd brushed aside push to the

forefront of my memories. I crouch to the demon's eye level. "Have we met before?"

They nod their head enthusiastically.

"The morning in the forest…" I flick a glance toward Joon, then back to the creature in front of me. "That was you?"

Another vigorous nod.

"You came all this way… because of me?"

The demon lifts their chin a little higher.

"The day I was in the forest," I explain. "They… fell out of a tree and ended up in a pile of snow. They were stuck, so I pulled them out." As I speak, the demon approaches tentatively, then slowly reaches out to rest a hand on my knee.

"You helped a demon?" Joon asks slowly.

I shrug. "I don't make a habit of it, but I couldn't just leave them there like that."

They are so small… I suppose a baby demon is still a baby.

"Demons deal in bargains and trades. But it seems you have made a friend by doing them a kindness and asking for nothing in return."

The demon stretches their neck out as if asking me to pet them, so I do. Their charred-like skin stretches over elongated limbs with joints that bend at painful angles, but they are smooth to the touch.

This demon is identical to the three who attacked me. Yet, their small size, puppy-like demeanor, and intelligence make it easy to see them as a wholly different creature. One that I need not fear.

"Come, it's late and you should get your rest."

"What about them?" I ask.

"They can go back outside, where they belong."

The demon sits back on their haunches and looks at Joon with a sad expression reminiscent of a puppy, then chatters their teeth.

I bite down on my bottom lip to keep from laughing. "You would toss a poor, defenseless baby demon out on such a cold night?"

"Demons do not have babies," Imugi snaps.

I blink up at them. "Oh."

Well, there goes that theory.

"It's a wonder humans manage to survive as long as they do when they know nothing about demons," the demon grumbles to themselves.

"You might as well keep them near you," Joon relents with a sigh. "Otherworld knows they will continue to follow you. Just make sure no one else sees them."

"Other than Mingi and Iseul?"

"Of course."

As we walk through the halls, I can't keep myself from glancing back over my shoulder at the demon prancing happily along as they trail us.

They really are like a puppy.

When a patrolling guard turns the corner, the demon zips forward, hiding under the folds of my skirt. I choke on a sound somewhere between a gasp and a whimper.

Joon presses his lips in a tight line, trying—and failing—to contain a snort of laughter.

I shoot him a glare. I doubt he'd enjoy a demon hiding inside his clothes.

Even after we are alone again, the demon refuses to leave their hiding place until we reach my apartments.

As soon as the door opens, they dart out and race over to the bed, leaping up, then curling into a shadowy ball in the center.

Joon follows me further in. I'm relieved. Perhaps more than I should be.

All the energy that kept me going until now drains away in the span of a breath. I drop down onto the foot of my bed.

"What were you doing outside alone?"

I frown. "Your note said to meet at the Garden of Stars."

He shakes his head. "I never left you a note."

I realize my error the moment he speaks. Whenever he sought me out in the past, he either sent Mingi or came himself. I'd just assumed he was responsible for the note.

"Then…" I trail off.

Joon doesn't answer for a long time. A muscle in his jaw ticks as he considers. "Show me."

It takes far more effort to rise than it should. Imugi joins us as we cross to the stand beside the door. The smooth wood surface where I left the note is now bare.

"It's gone," I say, backing up to see if it fell on the floor, even knowing it won't be there. "I don't understand."

Imugi blows out two frosty puffs from their nostrils. "There is no trace of anything unusual." Then muttering, they add, "That wild *thing* is muddying everything up with their smell."

A small decorative pillow flies from the other room toward Imugi, who barely dodges it in time.

Joon releases a long sigh through his nose. My gaze snaps to him. There's no judgment or disbelief in his expression, yet I feel defensive.

"I'm not making this up—there *was* a note," I insist.

Joon's sharp eyes scan the room before returning to me. "I believe you."

There seems to be more that he wants to say. I wonder if he knows who left the note and why.

"From now on, either Mingi, Iseul, Imugi, or I will personally come for you. Trust no one else. First thing in the morning, you will move to the Western Court so you are closer to me." He moves toward the door. "We will search again soon… but for now, get some rest."

Something in his voice sounds as if he is talking about more than finding the final shard and breaking the curse. More than that, I can see the hope he is trying desperately to hide. The kind of hope that is terrifying if you are not careful —a feeling I am more than familiar with.

Without thinking, I grab his sleeve. At the light tug, he stops and turns back to me.

"Will you stay with me?" I ask. Then, realizing how that could be taken the wrong way, I add, "Just until I fall asleep. You don't have to stay all night. I… don't want to be alone."

Joon reaches up and strokes the side of my head. His full lips curl gently at the corners. "Yes, I will stay with you."

"Violet." Firm hands grip my shoulder, shaking lightly. "Wake up, Violet."

I struggle to peel open my lids. Joon's face hovers over me, going in and out of focus. The world tilts uncomfortably when I shift.

"You have a fever."

The icy touch of his hand on my forehead sends a violent shiver through my body, instantly chasing away the last vestiges of sleep. I struggle to sit up, but he's there, helping me, doing most of the work.

Wind howls outside, pelting the windows with frozen rain.

A strange bone-deep ache has woven itself through every inch of my body. Everything is so cold despite the beads of sweat that dampen my brow. It's accompanied by an uncomfortable fullness inside as if my body no longer fits me.

"Let me see," Joon says. He takes my face in both hands, not waiting for my answer, and searches my face. His expression crumples. "It's my fault—I should have been better about monitoring you. I allowed too much of the frost bloom's power to build up."

I blink slowly. "Am I dying?"

"No." He shakes his head. "It is not nearly that severe. I should have siphoned sooner, but I didn't want to be the cause of a third episode so soon after the others."

I reach for his hand. The thin layer of frost coating his skin melts at my touch. "It's all right, you did what you thought best. There's not always an easy answer to everything."

He swallows thickly as if he doesn't want to be absolved of the blame he placed on himself.

I tuck my legs and lean toward him, holding on to his shoulders for balance. He cups the side of my jaw, fingers curling around the nape of my neck as he shifts to meet me.

Our lips touch. Joon's mouth moves against mine for a moment before I feel the caress of his power opening a channel inside me. Magic flows toward him, slowly at first.

The slight release is a relief that leaves me wanting to rid myself of more. I lean into him, but he continues to siphon at a leisurely pace. He takes his time, consuming the power, as if savoring the taste and feel of our languid kiss.

All too soon, he pulls back. A small noise of protest catches in my throat. The iridescent frost passes over one side, just below his jaw, before disappearing.

Strength returns to my body. Not much, but enough to make a difference. The pressure of the built-up power is still there.

Joon presses his palm to my chest over my heart, sending

tendrils of his power to heal me. He's barely siphoned any power. Nowhere near enough to trigger an episode. He realizes it too when he feels my forehead again.

"You are still burning up."

"I know." I lean forward and kiss him again.

The first swirls of magic slip from me to him, pulling a gentle sigh from me on its current. His breath hitches. I sense him stanching the transfer due to his worry.

I trace his bottom lip with my tongue. He groans but still doesn't allow the flow to increase. I do it again, but this time, I scrape my teeth over his lip.

The hand above my heart slides over my breast as it finds its way around my waist. With only the thin material of my nightdress and his shirt between us, it is impossible for either of us to ignore the way my nipples tighten at his touch. His other hand tangles in my hair, pulling me closer.

I slide my arms over his shoulders, leaning into him. His reluctance gives way with a nearly audible crack. The frost bloom's power flows in a steady stream, finally easing the pressure from within.

At the first painful squeeze in my heart, Joon blocks the flow through the channel. He begins to break away. Not ready for this to end yet, I lean into him. He gives in, and the siphoning becomes a real kiss.

Desire alights from within, pooling in liquid fire at my core. He's not unaffected either. The evidence presses against the side of my hip.

Joon holds me with one arm, letting his free hand wander lower, coming to rest where my thigh meets my hip. His fingers press into my flesh, gently massaging, thumb teasing dangerously close to my core.

Our tongues search for each other's in ways that feel far more intimate than our normal kisses, as if we are imitating the physical desire we wish to act on but dare not go that far.

If he moved his hand slightly toward my inner thigh, he would find his way to that ache between my legs that craves to feel his fingers slip inside and explore until that desperate longing eases.

As if in silent agreement, our hands and bodies remain as they are, leaving our mouths to express this aching need as it mixes with fear, uncertainty, and a deep longing for so many things that, against all odds, are identical for us both.

We stay like this for some time, whether it's minutes or hours, I can't say, until finally, the kiss ends. I am left satisfied and aching with need all at once.

Lying down, I rest my head on Joon's shoulder and snuggle into his side, soaking up his familiar warmth. His arm tightens around me.

Sleep settles like a heavyweight. I can't help but wonder at the way things have changed between us since he caged me with his body against the wall in my home. How, even now, things continue to change.

But none of this is permanent. It can't last. Whatever this is, whatever it could have been, will end when the curse ends.

Once this is over, I will return to my home in Firnhallow, and he will take his place as king. Then the world will get the chance to see him for who I know he is, not for the misunderstanding they see

My throat grows thick with disappointment at the fluttering in my chest. I know it instantly, despite never experiencing it before.

I can't pinpoint when or how it started, but I care for him. Deeply. If I am not careful, I will lose my heart.

A surge of selfishness sweeps through me. I want him to be mine, for however long I can have him.

Giving in to this is a terrible idea. There's no way this can end happily for either of us, even if Joon wanted the same. There is no future we can share that would not end in heartbreak.

My chest tightens with the thought.

Can you break a heart that's already broken?

Except, the way I feel when his fingertips shift against their resting spot at my hip makes me wonder if I have already lost my heart to him.

Stopping it might already be a lost cause. And I'm not sure I could, even if I wanted to.

CHAPTER TWENTY-THREE

JOON

Violet is still sound asleep when I wake at dawn. Her hair is loose and wild around her.

I slip my arm out from under her head, then. The demon, who has attached themselves to her, opens one eye, peering at me as I tread with silent footsteps toward the door.

"It would be best if no one else knew about you," I whisper as I pass.

Violet might be my wife through our bargain, but as far as anyone else is concerned, she is merely another I will eventually turn to ice, as all those who came before her. A pawn to use against the people of this kingdom—to remind them of my power.

Should my enemies assume she is anything more, they won't hesitate to use her as a weapon.

Iseul stands in the middle of the hall, watching me slip from Violet's room like a thief.

Were she anyone else, I wouldn't hesitate to threaten them into silence. She and Mingi have been like siblings as well as close friends since we were all children. One of the few things I have a clear recollection of.

Iseul stalks forward, her dark eyes silently demanding answers I have no obligation to give.

"You can forget whatever lurid thoughts are in your head."

"That makes you sound guilty when I haven't even said anything yet, Your Highness," Iseul says with an arched brow as she reaches me.

"She came down with a fever last night," I say anyway, offering a partial truth. "I was already with her when it started, so I did not see the need to send for you."

I leave out the part regarding the demon attack. It would only make Iseul feel guilty when there was nothing she could have done.

"Is she…?" Iseul trails off, looking past me as if she could see Violet through the door.

"Violet is well. Let her sleep a bit longer."

Iseul scrunches up one side of her face.

"Why are you giving me that look?"

She snorts. "No reason. It's unexpected, that's all."

"What is?" I ask flatly.

Iseul lowers her voice to a mock whisper. "Does my brother know our Crown Prince has been playing nursemaid to her all night—in her bedroom? *Alone*?" she draws the last word out, making her implication clear.

I briefly debate telling her about Violet's new pet, sleeping in her room like a loyal dog, but I think I will let her be surprised.

"Who would have thought that our little Joon would grow up to be so sof—"

"Finish that sentence, and you might not like the consequences," I warn, though we both know the threat is empty.

I move past her, then stop when a thought pushes itself to the forefront of my mind.

Looking back, I ask, "Did you deliver a note to Violet yesterday evening?"

Iseul frowns. "No, Your Highness."

It is as expected. I've never wanted to be wrong before in my life. I needed to confirm on the off chance I am being paranoid.

Head bowed and one hand resting on the pommel of his sword, Mingi raises a fist to knock on the door to my apartments.

"Your Highness?" he calls, a note of uncertainty in his voice.

"You may go in."

He spins on his heel, then strides over to walk with me the remainder of the way. "Your Highness," he says again.

This time, there is a litany of questions hidden within those two words, which I ignore until we are inside.

I glance through the open door of my bedchamber. Imugi is stretched out across the bed, tail swishing lethargically over the edge of the mattress. They lazily lift their pale, shimmery head, then let it flop back down.

I take a seat behind the low-legged table at the back of the main area. Mingi follows, shooting Imugi a sharp glare as he passes before sitting across from me.

"You should have let me know when you left this morning, Your Highness." The way he uses my title shows his irritation over how difficult he finds me as of late.

Few would dare to show such feelings to any royal or

noble above them without expecting swift repercussions. It has been this way with both him and Iseul since I brought them into the palace.

An unspoken agreement between the three of us.

In private, they are friends. Confidants. They allow me the freedom to move about without reporting my movements, and I allow them to speak freely in my presence without fear of punishment, regardless of what they have to say.

"I left last night and am only now returning. I was with Violet all night. She was not well." I send a side glance in the demon's direction. "Imugi should have informed you."

As a compromise for my constant secrecy, Imugi will inform Mingi of my general whereabouts.

"I will send for the head physician."

I wave him off. "There is no need." A sense of guilt, burdened with shame, fills me. "She had a fever from a build-up of the frost bloom in her blood."

"It's not like you to hold off for so long." Mingi frowns.

There is no logical reason I can give him to make him understand. Delaying puts the entire kingdom in jeopardy. No single life should be put before the needs of Arum.

Siphoning wears on Violet in a way it never wore on the others. Not that I spent significant time with them, the way I do with her, so perhaps I am wrong.

"Did you happen to notice anything out of the ordinary yesterday?" I must first rule out those closest to me,

He blinks.

"By chance, did someone ask you to deliver anything to Violet yesterday?"

Mingi's unimpressed expression quickly changes to mild confusion. "No. If I had, I would come to you first."

"Are you aware of anyone who might want to meet with Violet in private?"

"Not off the top of my head. Did something happen?" He shifts and leans forward.

I nod. "Last night, Violet received a message asking to meet with them in the Garden of Stars. She said it wasn't signed, but she went, thinking it was from me."

"I may be able to identify the handwriting if I saw it."

"Unfortunately, it was gone by the time she returned. There was also a complete lack of evidence of anyone having entered her room without notice."

"She is certain it was real? Not a hallucination from the effects of the frost bloom?" he asks hesitantly.

"When I found her, she was outside and the door was locked behind her," I say. "This was intentional. Someone lured her out by making her think I was waiting."

"Odd. Nothing like this has happened with the others."

I appreciate Mingi's ability to focus on the important details.

"We both know I have many enemies within the palace walls. But beyond rumors, none have dared to act against me before now. I have a few suspicions, though nothing more than a gut feeling. I'd like for you to keep an ear out for any whisperings or anything out of the ordinary. For now, we should keep last night's incident quiet.

"As for the why of it, I believe it was to endanger her life, if not outright kill her. The wards were down around the garden, and three wild, higher demons made it within the palace walls. Have Minister Yeona reinforce all the wards in the palace immediately."

"Consider it done." He dips his chin in acknowledgment of his orders, awaiting dismissal.

"One more thing."

Mingi lifts his gaze to meet mine.

"I want Violet moved to the adjoining apartments by the

end of the day. If someone comes after her again, then I want her as close to me as possible at all times. I won't risk everything by taking any chances. Fill Iseul in on the details when you can, but for now, say nothing to Violet about my suspicions. She doesn't need to constantly look over her shoulder. The added stress could take an unnecessary toll on her that could negatively affect the power of the frost bloom."

Imugi takes cover between the tall collar of my outer coat and my neck as I aimlessly wander the palace grounds. I find myself halfway to the Southern Court before I bother to notice my surroundings. I turn and head in the direction of the Winter Garden.

"Nephew," Uncle's voice calls from behind, breaking through my thoughts.

I turn and bow. "Good afternoon, Uncle." With no one else around, we address each other by our familial titles.

"I was hoping to see you today." He smiles pleasantly, though he remains as guarded as ever. It is more kindness than I deserve. "What brings you out here?"

As if sensing I've yet to collect my scattered thoughts, Imugi prods the back of my neck and hisses, "The weather."

"The—" I stop myself in time from speaking the obvious lie and quickly correct myself, "I wanted to get some air."

I feel Imugi's amused chuckle more than hear it.

The king's gaze narrows, either from a flash of sunlight peeking out from behind a cloud or because he heard Imugi. It's gone before I can be entirely sure.

Or perhaps it is because you took everything from him, and he still chose to try to care for you anyway, a voice at the back of my mind whispers.

Even after all these years, I still feel like a child when I stand before him. The guilt is as heavy as it was the day I stood in the middle of the aftermath of my destruction.

I do not deserve to be free of it. My actions were unforgivable.

"I was about to walk through the garden. Would you like to join me?"

"I think I will. There is something I wanted to speak with you about."

I defer to him, letting him choose the way through the open Central Court's public outdoor garden. The wending paths are seemingly random while intersecting at the right spots to offer ideal views of the garden's beauty.

We walk in silence along the stone path that follows the largest stream cutting through the grounds.

"Miss Hawthorn has been at the palace for some time now."

"She has," I agree.

"Why has she not been introduced to the court yet?"

Why indeed...

I will not make it another full year. I felt the truth of that in my bones even before I found Violet.

He has never shown interest in my previous wives until they had been around for nearly a full year. And by then, the power of the frost bloom had grown so weak I could no longer siphon enough to control the dragon. It would break free of its prison and freeze them shortly before or after they were presented.

It would be pointless, especially knowing someone within these walls wishes her harm.

My uncle may be one of the few I can trust, yet the thought of introducing her to my enemies who lie hidden behind pleasant smiles and operate under the cover of shadows has a thread of annoyance coiling through me.

"It is customary to wait a year. None of my wives were ever introduced early before," I say dryly. "There is hardly a reason to start now."

"Look around you, Nephew." Uncle spreads his arms out wide. "The frost is gone more often than not, and sightings of the Winter Dragon have nearly halted altogether. Everything is different now."

"*She* is... different." The thought slips past my tongue without meaning to.

"Different? Different how? That is precisely what I mean," he cuts me off. "We can all see as much, but you leave us in the dark. They deserve to know—*I* deserve to know. We must begin searching ahead of time for another with the qualities she possesses that inspire such a drastic change."

Ire sparks in me at the petty interference of those who have been whispering in his ear.

"She hides away, claiming to be unwell. It sets a bad example. My brother's wife—*your mother*—would never let a headache or minor illness keep her from her duties to the people. I will not allow this woman to ruin everything I have worked to accomplish—for this kingdom and for you," he snaps. Then, with a breath, he releases his frustration. "I tell you this because the nobles have begun to talk, and the Ministers are suspicious."

My boots scrape against loose gravel between the stepping stones as I halt in my tracks. "What are they saying?"

The king stops and faces me, clasping his hands behind his back in a casual manner. "That she has done something to you. There are whispers she is a witch, or if not that, then she enlisted the help of one to cast an enchantment to bewitch you."

"That is absurd," I scoff.

"Perhaps," he agrees. "But what do you expect when you have changed so drastically since the Choosing?"

I want to deny it, but he is right. Even I can see the changes in me, though not for such a preposterous reason.

"To prevent a scandal, we must act sooner rather than later —before talk reaches the people." He shakes his head, and a loose strand of hair falls over the rim of the wide circlet crown. The metal band bears an embossed image of the official—a symbol of his temporary status.

"I will think on it."

"Your absences have not gone unnoticed either, Nephew. You do not seem to be present at the palace for long these days. If you are not careful, there will be consequences, and I can only do so much to mitigate them. The entire court worries that you are not taking your position seriously," he continues. "I cannot help but think that this is her doing."

If only they knew how seriously I am taking my duties.

"There is nothing so sinister about her." I lower my head in respect. "She is merely a sheltered woman who grew up with naive ideals. The changes to her life as she settles into her role have been overwhelming." Even as I say the words I once believed, I know it would hurt her if she heard me.

Uncle places a hand on my shoulder. "Then consider the presentation an act of goodwill. It would go a long way to cut these rumors off at the ankles."

I lift my head to meet his gaze and remind myself that he has been on my side since the beginning.

"The others had almost eight months to prepare and learn the expected etiquette after they settled in. I ask that you grant her adequate time."

"How much time?"

"Five months."

His hand falls away. "You ask for too much." The rejection is soft, though it does nothing to ease the blow.

"Two months then."

He purses his lips as he considers. He is no longer my uncle in this moment, but the king. Whatever his next words are, they will be as good as law.

"Very well. You have two months. Not a day longer. I do not need to tell you that the court's expectations of her are high. She should be the image of perfection."

The tension in my back eases. I am careful to keep all emotion from my face and voice. "Yes, Your Majesty. Thank you for your generosity." I bow, then straighten. "I will attend the next council meeting to personally inform them."

Violet will be gone before the time comes. Either we will have broken the curse, and she will be free to return home, or we will both be dead.

None of this will matter in the end, and in the meantime, I will play their game.

CHAPTER TWENTY-FOUR

VIOLET

I stretch my arms and legs over as much of the mattress as I can. The space beside me is empty but not yet fully cold. I frown.

"My Lady," Iseul's gentle voice is accompanied by her soft knock.

A flash of shadow streaks across the floor and dives under the thick comforter. With a startled cry, I bolt upright at the feel of their cold, bone-like skin brushing against my leg.

Iseul bursts into the room. "What happened?"

"What are you doing?" I snap at the demon at the same time.

"I—" she begins, hurt flashing across her face.

But I am focused on the unwelcome creature in my bed. Grabbing a fistful of blanket, I yank, flinging it to the floor. The demon starts and scrambles from the foot of the bed and dives for the pillows.

My irritation gets the better of me. "What are you—"

"Demons and saints... that's... that's," Iseul's voice rises to a screech, cutting me off.

I whip around, finally remembering that she doesn't know about the demon yet.

Iseul gapes, her wide eyes are stark against the backdrop of her concerningly pale face. She points a shaking finger at the pile of blankets, taking a deep breath.

Now, it's my turn to scramble. I am less than graceful as I launch myself toward her. Stumbling over the blanket, I barrel into her. My hand clamps down over her mouth to stifle her scream before it alerts every guard in the area.

"It's all right. Don't scream," I say.

A knock on the door has me flinching. "Is everything all right in there? Do you need help?" The guard's harsh voice carries through the door.

"I am fine, thank you. You may go!" I try to insert a lightness to my tone, but even I can tell it sounds fake.

Iseul struggles against my grip, speaking muffled words against my palm. I wrap my arm around her shoulders and pull her against me. It's a bit awkward with her being several inches taller than me.

"Are you sure?" the guard asks after several beats.

"I thought I saw a bug, that's all," I call out. I loosen my hold on Iseul just enough so I can look her in the eye. "Everything is fine," I add, more to her than the woman outside my door.

Listening, I wait for the sound of heavy footsteps to fade.

"I'm going to let you go, so please don't scream," I beg.

Iseul grunts.

Slowly, I release her. Iseul backs away, looking at me in betrayal.

"W-what in the Otherworld are you doing with a wild demon in your bed?" she hisses.

"I think you startled them."

"*I* startled *them*?"

"It's all right. Joon knows—"

"How long has that *thing* been here?"

The demon leaps onto the middle of the bed and growls at her for the insult. I wave my hand, motioning for them to behave, without looking at them.

"Only since last night—"

"Joon knows about this?"

I sigh. "Yes. Please let me explain."

She looks between me and the demon several times before giving a curt nod.

"Joon and Imugi noticed them following me for a while," I begin. "I was almost attacked by demons, but this one alerted him and led him to me."

Iseul looks skeptical. "Demons prey on humans—*they don't send for help.*"

"We were confused at first, too…" I send a quick glance over my shoulder at the demon. "Until I recognized them."

Iseul throws her hands in the air. "Oh, well, why didn't you say so? Knowing a wild demon is entirely different than letting one you just met sleep in your bed," she says mockingly.

Though I would love to tell her everything, I must censor myself from saying anything that could lead to questions I can't answer. She needs to believe I was chosen before drinking the frost bloom tea, rather than because of it.

I miss Talya and the way I could share everything with her. I miss having that closeness and honesty with someone. And Iseul has been more like a friend looking out for me instead of a handmaid. I want to confide in her.

"Back home, I did a lot of research on healing injuries and conditions. I would frequently make trips into the forest to gather herbs and roots for poultices, teas, salves, ointments, incense…" I tick each thing off on my fingers as I list them, stopping when I notice Iseul's incredulous stare. "During my last trip, this one fell out of a tree and landed head-first in a pile of snow and got stuck. I felt bad leaving them there like that."

"You felt bad for a demon?" Iseul asks, rubbing her temples. She is clearly questioning my sanity… or perhaps trying to gauge my level of insanity.

"I thought they were a baby," I offer weakly.

"Demons don't have babies, Violet."

Crossing my arms over my chest, I look away. "Well, I know that *now*," I mutter, then motion to the demon. "Look at them—it was an easy mistake. Anyway, Joon said to keep them near me."

Iseul blinks, dumbfounded. "He must care a lot for you to let you keep a demon."

I choke on air at the bluntness of her unexpected comment.

Joon might feel friendship toward me, perhaps a slight attraction, but that is all it is. The lingering moments after he siphoned, me on his lap, my body begging him for more until his cock hardened, straining against my hip, was nothing more than a purely natural physical reaction to the intimate moment we shared.

Whatever affection there is beyond friendship is solely on my end.

"It's not like that between us."

There's a knock. We freeze and turn toward the door. A second passes before it slides open. I exhale a relieved sigh when Joon enters, rather than someone else who would be less understanding about a demon.

Did he hear us talking?

Iseul jabs a finger in the demon's direction and glares at Joon. "You allowed this?"

He chuckles.

"You could have warned me," she snaps.

Joon shrugs. "I suppose I could have." He turns to me, a smirk playing across his lips. His eyes darken as he takes me in. "I wanted to let you both know that starting today, Iseul will give you lessons on palace customs, protocol, and decorum. I will personally oversee these sessions when I can, if necessary, give notes."

Iseul and I exchange a glance.

"Any particular reason, Your Highness?" she asks.

From the uncertainty in her voice, I think it's safe to assume that this is out of the ordinary.

"It is merely a precaution and mostly for the sake of appearances." There's a pause, then to Iseul, he adds, "It seems a few officials have a lot of spare time on their hands. I hope this will prevent unnecessary complications from arising."

She seems to understand what he means by that. However, I remain in the dark.

Hearing that I lack in ways his previous wives did not stings more than I want to admit.

I start to lower my eyes, then stop when I realize how ridiculous it is to let it get to me. I am not here to win the approval of anyone. I am here to help Joon break this curse so he can free the Winter Dragon's victims from their frozen prisons.

The prince looks as if he wants to say something more about it, but instead, he says, "Others will be here in a few hours to move you to the Western Court."

Joon dips his chin and takes his leave.

Iseul pierces me with her narrowed gaze.

Unable to bear the scrutiny, I gather up the blanket from the floor and pile it onto the bed. I sit on the edge and pretend to be focused on the demon jumping onto the pillow, then tumbling off, only to do it over again.

Iseul joins me, sitting where she can see my face. "I never thought I'd see the day when our Joon would fall in love." She sighs wistfully, then snorts. "I never thought he would be one to be so obvious about it."

"It's not what you think," I say, hoping she doesn't see the way my cheeks warm.

"*Moving* you to live with him. Overseeing these lessons is not something for a prince to concern himself with. What other reason could there be?" Iseul leans in.

"He is trying to keep me out of trouble," I point out.

"Then why did he look at you like that just now?"

"Because I'm wearing my nightdress," I counter.

Iseul tilts her head to the side. "Which he has already seen after spending the night with you." She smirks. "He told me as much."

"I had a fever."

She makes it sound as if I'm not alone in these ill-fated emotions I've miserably failed to prevent. Allowing myself to believe that will only hurt more in the end. Besides, there is a reason for it. She would understand if she knew about the bargain and my condition.

"I'm serious, Vi," she says softly, using the same shortened version of my name that Talya and Sebastian do. "He's changed since you came to the palace."

My throat tightens at the way my heart leaps. "How so?"

"You know of his reputation throughout the kingdom?"

To hide the warmth burning my ears, I busy myself with gathering the blankets from the floor and piling them on top of the bed. The demon wastes no time pushing them around for maximum comfort before settling in. "Everyone does, but that's a facade. You and Mingi know as well as I that he's not what they say he is."

"True. We know many sides to him, not just the one he shows the world." She doesn't outright disagree with me, yet her face and voice reflect her skepticism.

"I told him it was important to me that we trust each other. I think we were able to become friends because of that. Perhaps the others"—I avoid saying *wives*—"never tried to get to know him beyond all the rumors?"

"Perhaps," she concedes. "So, why did you?"

I shrug, buying myself a few seconds to come up with something close enough to the truth. "I'm here for a purpose, and I want to do everything to the best of my ability, which is a lot easier to do if you trust the person you're working with." I swallow and confess another truth. "The thought of being nothing more than a vessel, of each of us doing our part separately, seemed so horribly lonely."

The demon yawns, stretching their arms and legs out before wriggling deeper into the blankets.

"I think there's more to it than that—he's gentle with you. Softer. More himself. Like the person Mingi and I knew as children."

It might seem that way, but Joon and I are just looking for the same things. Someone to be there for us. Comfort. To know gentleness in a harsh world. Things we have both lacked for too long.

We are both lucky to have good friends, but they can't take the place of family or a lover. The way Joon touches me is different than anything I've known, the intention behind those touches is the same.

The only words I have to offer her are the ones I don't want to share. That I like having someone who doesn't see me as a walking tragedy, waiting for the moment when I collapse, dead. To see me as another person with a normal life ahead of them.

So, I shrug and say nothing.

"It's nice to see him like that again." She sighs. "You're good for him."

If she knew about my condition, she would understand why it would be pointless for anyone to fall for me. Let alone a prince who will go on to make a queen of someone with noble blood.

"Even the guards and other servants have noticed a change," Iseul continues. "It's likely that the king and other nobles will have as well. Which would explain why he wants me to give you lessons."

"Or he doesn't want me to embarrass him," I suggest.

"I can see you won't be convinced otherwise. Fine then, the two of you are *friends*." Iseul shakes her head, smiling softly as she turns to the demon. "I will say, you certainly have a way of capturing the heart of the most fearsome of creatures."

I realize I referred to myself as a vessel, hinting at his curse, details I shouldn't be able to divulge.

Iseul didn't react to what I said, nor did the bargain silence me. Which means she must know about the curse and why I'm here, at least to some degree.

"What will you do with them?" she asks, gesturing toward the demon.

"I don't know… I guess, keep them?" the demon rolls onto their back. "I always wanted a dog when I was little."

Iseul pinches the bridge of her nose and takes a long, deep breath. "Violet, I mean this with nothing but respect, but you *do* realize that is a demon, *not* a dog, don't you?" She drops her hand and pins me with a look. "If not, then I might have to drag you to the physician to get that head of yours examined.

And believe me, you do not want that. She will make you drink the most foul-tasting tonics." Iseul pulls a face.

"Of course, I know that. Though you can't deny they do act a little like a puppy." I pat their head. "Maybe I should think of a name for you."

"How about, Bear?"

The demon rolls onto their stomach and bounces onto their feet.

"I think they like it," I say. "Bear, it is."

"I was… never mind." She hadn't intended for me to take it seriously, but somehow, it fits them.

"Now, little Bear, there will be times when I will need to leave you with Iseul. I want you to be nice and watch over her for me, all right?"

Bear nods and prances up to Iseul. She rolls her eyes but doesn't fight the smile that spreads over her face. She reaches out and pats their head, laughing when they lean into it.

"Yes, yes. Very cute. Now that this has been settled, I should go get your breakfast before everyone arrives to collect your things."

CHAPTER TWENTY-FIVE

JOON

A WEEK GOES BY WITHOUT FURTHER INCIDENT. I AM UNCERTAIN if I ought to be relieved or suspicious by that.

It is possible that whoever sent Violet that note is afraid I will discover their identity if they act so boldly again so soon.

Violet stands beneath the pavilion on the opposite side of the stream, listening to Iseul's instructions. From the second story of another pavilion, I observe them, taking mental notes of any weak points as well as strong ones.

The two of them have been at this for almost three hours. Every once in a while, Violet's eyes will dart over to the flat stone bridge, halfway to the west side of the Northern Court, which earns a stern, yet kind, correction from Iseul.

Violet has not uttered a single complaint to me about the tediously mind-numbing lessons I forced on her.

They are exactly as I remember from my childhood. I can't quite recall, but there is the vague sense that I did not always suffer through them alone. Of getting into mischief—most likely a noble's child. Trying to remember anything from before the curse only makes my memories more unclear.

Iseul bows to Violet, ending their lesson and dismissing her. They exchange a few words before Violet hurries over the bridge and turns onto the path leading to the library.

Iseul motions for a servant waiting in the distance to gather the lesson books.

Violet does better than anyone could ask—at least while she is concentrating. But she will continue with them past the point of mastery, because I have no intention of parading her before the nobles like cheap entertainment. Or until we break the curse.

"This curse is never-ending."

"It *must* end," Imugi says from my shoulder, responding to the thought I muttered aloud. "They can go on for a long time, but they are not meant to last forever."

Without another word, I turn and descend the stairs. Imugi follows silently. My stride is long as I traverse the path leading back to my apartment.

Inside, I lock the door while Imugi draws the curtains. The room darkens to pitch. I don't need to see to know where to stand. Calling to my power, I coax it forward until a soft, icy blue light fills my palm.

I press my hand to the floorboards. A rectangle border forms, glowing, as the section of wood vanishes, exposing a set of stairs that lead down a narrow passage.

Imugi is accustomed to my retreating to the underground cavern of the mirror when I am uncertain of my next move.

Our lives are irrevocably tied, yet Imugi has never once mentioned wanting to break the curse so they can live. Only wanting to aid me in my efforts as needed, because it is *my* goal.

If I live, they live. If I die, they die.

I stop before the mirror, nearly complete. Save for the single, empty space above and left of the center. A piece that is barely the length of my thumbnail and half as wide. It is all that stands in the way. Every day that passes without sensing the final piece is another day wasted.

The cracks that spiderweb over the glass distort my reflection. I stare at the long, pale line that cuts through the center of one brow, through my eye, to the middle of my cheek.

I am so close, yet I might as well be back at the beginning with nothing more than the first shard, covered in my own blood. If I close my eyes, I can still feel the echo of pain as I pulled it from my flesh. I shake off the sensation, but it continues to intensify.

Agony pierces my scarred eye. Sharp and hot, a needle heated to the point of glowing. Ringing fills my ears, muffling the natural sounds of the air moving as if they are stuffed with cotton. My vision vibrates until the world is distant and indiscernible.

When it fades, it leaves behind a phantom ache and a tug in my chest. Stronger than any shard has ever called to me before.

"Is it the last?" Imugi asks.

"Yes." The word claws up my throat, raw and rasping.

Time to end this, once and for all.

The Western Court is a hive of activity. Servants walk in line to and from the Southern Court, carrying loads to Violet's new quarters.

Iseul turns from the woman holding a stack of books beside her to look ahead, jolting when she sees me. She scrambles to wait on the side of the path, pulling the other woman with her, murmuring orders. The woman bows to me before hurrying away.

"Tell my wife to be ready within the quarter hour," I tell Iseul, but I don't slow or shorten my long stride.

"Wh-what does that mean, Your Highness?" Iseul takes a few steps toward me. The question dies in the air, unanswered.

Mingi emerges from my foyer, running at full speed. The feather on his hat, showing his rank, flutters behind him like the wing of a bird trying to take flight.

He skids to a halt before me. Dust clouds kick up at his feet as he bows. "Your Highness," he grits out, speaking low even though no one is close enough to overhear. "I must speak with you at once."

"Later." I wave him off without pause. "Ready my horse and have her waiting at the same place as last time."

Once the shard is in my possession, none of this will matter anymore.

Mingi whirls, trailing by a single step. "That is what I need to speak with you about."

He follows me into the privacy of my rooms. I can practically feel the frustration rolling off him as I gather a change of clothes and other items that Violet and I may need.

There is nothing in this world that he can say that is more important than ending this curse.

"You've sensed another," Mingi states, at once understanding. He knows the look in my eye, the fear behind the outward impatience, better than anyone.

I pause for a heartbeat, then focus again on the tug. The pull is stronger now. Which means it must be in the vicinity of the palace—perhaps an hour's ride at most. Still, there is no time to waste. The shards can only call out for so long before they go dormant, slowly building up their power before they signal to me once more. But each time, the draw is weaker than the last.

"I will ready the horses."

"You will stay here," I say before he takes more than a few steps.

He jerks to a halt, then his boots fall heavy on the wood floor as he draws closer. "Not again." He groans in frustration. "I cannot do my duty to protect you if you continue to leave me behind."

I step behind the folding screen to change.

"You must be careful, Your Highness. There are whispers that the Crown Prince attacked people in the capital unprovoked. I thought the rumors would die down within a few days as usual, but they've only spread." Worry and concern lace his voice. "Let me go with you."

I slip into my riding boots and step out into the open. Mingi stands firm and resolute, with more than a hint of defiance in the set of his jaw.

"I am lucky to have the loyalty of you and your sister," I say.

Mingi frowns at the compliment. Not at all appeased.

"Next time. I promise. In the meantime, take Imugi and do what you can to quell the unrest."

Imugi glides from the shadows and hovers at Mingi's shoulder.

There's a knock on the door half a second before it slides open. Violet enters, flinching when she sees Mingi.

Mingi bows to each of us in turn, then hurries out to do as asked.

For the first time, I notice she has lost weight since she came to the palace. Not quite enough to be worrisome yet.

The toll my siphoning is taking on her is already showing. Until I regain my full powers, there is only so much I can do to heal her. But that only reminds me of what Uncle had said —what the people are saying about her.

Part of me wants to present her when we return for no reason other than to prove their cruel words wrong.

There will be time for that once the curse is broken.

Except then, our bargain will be fulfilled, and she will return home, healthy and alive. *Where she belongs.*

Which is all the more reason to end this curse as soon as possible.

"You're early," I say.

She shrugs one shoulder and smiles warmly. We meet in the middle of the room as if drawn by a magnetic pull.

Since the morning after her fever, dark circles have gradually appeared under her eyes. Shadows that have nothing to do with the long hours of practice or the hours of searching she spends in the library afterward. Not enough for most to notice unless one is looking for such signs.

"Does this mean…?" Violet's honey eyes shine as bright as ever.

I nod.

In moments, we are outside, moving unnoticed along the back wall of the Northern Court. I lift the hanging vines out of the way and allow Violet to enter first. She moves through the glamour covering the door without hesitation as if seeing past it.

Violet holds my hand as we traverse the passage to the forest beyond the northern wall. I sneak glances at her, trying to discern if she is doing so because she wants to or because my conjured light isn't enough for her human eyes. We are out before I can decide, and her hand slips from mine.

Mingi arrives at the meeting spot right as we do. He hands over the reins without a word, though his thoughts are clear as day on his face.

I climb into the saddle behind Violet and turn the horse toward the pull in my chest.

When we are a few miles from the castle, I summon a road, crossing large swaths of land in a fraction of the time.

We emerge on the other side, and my stomach sinks when the pull changes. Reorienting, I summon another road. I push the white mare onward as fast as it can run.

Violet is silent during the whole ride. I am so wrapped up in locating the shard that if it weren't for the warmth of her body, I might not notice her at all.

Again, the direction changes. I curse and call yet another road. Again, and again.

We ride for most of the afternoon, crossing from one corner of the kingdom to the other. The landscape changes from the open tundra plains to forests to rolling hills and valleys to the wide roads that stretch from one town to another.

Each time, it is the same: the moment we are nearly upon it, the pull changes, moving to a completely different direction, farther away.

How is this possible?

This time, when I summon a road, I don't dare to hope. Yet, disappointment finds me as we come out on the crest of a hill overlooking the small town of Kassia, nestled just northeast of the Shadow Fields.

Before the road vanishes, I know luck has run out.

Rather than changing direction again or gradually fading, it is simply… *gone.*

Frustration burns sharp and white hot. Violet will end up getting burned if I do not put some space between us. I pull the horse to a stop and dismount, striding away from her, up the hill ahead.

Demon shit.

The pull had been strong. It should have been impossible to lose the trail. It was there, waiting for me to take it, yet it slipped away like dew under the sun's warmth.

From this vantage point high above the valley, I can see most of Arum. Distant towns and cities with countless fae and humans. What will happen to them all if the Winter Dragon is loosed on them?

The fire raging within my chest is smothered by the oppressive dark of hopelessness.

I drop to my knees. Weary and defeated.

My arrogance will be the downfall. Over half of my power —wasted and used up in less than a day. Because I believed this would be the day I put an end to the curse.

Light footsteps crunch over the frosted ground.

Violet crouches at my side and reaches for my hand. I refuse to budge, so she clasps it where it rests on my knee.

"Impossible—it should not be able to move like this." I'm forced to swallow down the bitter devastation or choke on it. I hang my head. "I lost it."

A bitter wind kicks up, sweeping over the plains.

I expect Violet to offer hollow words, intended to encourage, that will do nothing to help. I am about to cut her off before she can open her mouth, but guilt silences me.

I cannot even accuse her of not understanding. Of all the people in this world, she more than anyone else, can understand.

"You need to rest," Violet says. "Let's ride again, without the paths this time."

She stands and tugs on my arm. I let her pull me to my feet. Her cheeks are rosy from the cold, and even with her cloak wrapped tightly around her, she cannot suppress her shivering.

"You're cold," I say. Violet shakes her head, but I pull her into me anyway, wrapping my arms around her. She practically melts against me as if trying to siphon my body heat the way I siphon power from her. "There is a town near here where we can stop to rest and warm ourselves."

Separating, we turn toward the horse.

Just as I am about to help Violet into the saddle, Imugi's unexpected shout stops me.

"Joon, you must return to the palace immediately!"

I whirl to see the demon glide through the air at incredible speed. What are they doing here—and alone?

"The Ministers will gather tomorrow with the king in your absence."

"What is this about? What happened?"

"The only talk among palace staff is that no one knows." Imugi twists in agitated knots as they speak, releasing puffs of frost from their nostrils. "It is suspicious."

I look to Violet. She is not born of the frost as the fae of Arum are and will die if she gets too cold.

"I'll be fine," she says through lips that are too pale, as if she can hear my thoughts. Her hand alights on my forearm. "If Imugi came all this way during the day, then it must be urgent." Violet's fingers curl, squeezing gently.

I am loath to give up after coming so close to finding the last piece.

Yet, this cannot be ignored. Instinct tells me that the note and the silence following the demon attack are somehow connected to this unscheduled council meeting. The timing is too perfect to be coincidental.

"Very well."

"We will keep searching," Violet says as if sensing my inner turmoil. "Just as we did after the first time. And we found them twice after that."

"If only it were that easy," I scoff. "Time is a luxury we cannot afford when I've failed more than I've succeeded."

Violet's spine stiffens at the venom in my voice. Her jaw sets. "Your life is not the only one on the line." She doesn't move away, but I feel her withdrawing inward.

This is not her fault.

"I cannot promise my magic will cure your condition even if we break the curse," I say quietly.

She remains silent for so long, I think she has no intention of responding.

At last, she says, "I know." The muscles in her neck tighten. "But even if you fail, you will try until you succeed. All of Arum is counting on you—I'm counting on you. You're not in this alone, so don't you dare give up now."

In this moment, I notice something in her that I never had before. Not naivety as I once thought, but inner strength. Unfailing hope and determination in the face of defeat.

I have had my obligation, fear, and the promise that all will be made right if I can only break the curse. They are the fuel to my motivation. I have always wanted to live, but my will has never been as strong as hers. She has nothing—nothing to seek, nothing to work toward with the knowledge that, once she finds it, she will have the one thing that will let her live. Only the belief that the *something* exists.

Nothing to give her reason to hope.

And yet she does.

She is determined to fight tooth and nail for the smallest sliver of hope.

Violet has continually disarmed me since the first time I came face-to-face with her. I cannot fight her influence over me.

"There is no guarantee we will find it. However, I will

admit this situation is not entirely hopeless," I concede. Not because I believe it, but because she makes me want to believe.

CHAPTER TWENTY-SIX

VIOLET

"It's not like you to be so agreeable," Imugi mutters.

The demon's words are almost inaudible as the wind finds its strength. Either Joon doesn't hear, or he chooses to ignore the demon as he climbs into the saddle in a single, elegant motion.

Again, I'm struck by how much he appears every inch a prince, from his innate grace and physical strength to his posture and overall demeanor.

A smug grin pulls at his mouth.

I duck my head to hide the blush trying to creep up my neck from being caught staring as I take his offered hand and let him pull me up in front of him.

Imugi glides to Joon and settles over his shoulders, nestling into the space between his neck and collar, with only the end of their long nose peeking out.

Even within fur-lined gloves, my fingers sting from the chill that has only worsened as the day stretched on. I was looking forward to warming up in town. More important than my disappointment, Joon needs to rest.

I've come to recognize the signs when his power is depleting. When we started out, his face radiated warmth from within. Now, he looks as though frost will form on his skin if he gets any colder.

Joon closes his eyes as he does when summoning one of the fae roads.

"Wait," I say. Both his and the demon's attention snap to me. "Siphon first. You've used a lot of power today."

"She has a point," Imugi says, surprising me when their voice lacks the usual bite.

Joon leans forward, taking my chin between his thumb and forefinger as he lowers his face. It's a bit awkward with someone else within inches of us—even if they are a demon. Just as I think his lips will brush mine, a soft cerulean glow lights his irises.

He checks the frost bloom's power within me, then pulls back, leaving me feeling oddly disappointed. I shouldn't want the risk that comes with siphoning.

"Not yet."

"Then take the main roads," I say.

Joon shakes his head. "That would add half a day to our journey. We would have to ride through the Shadow Fields."

"I will lend the horse my power," Imugi says. "Conserve what you can. There's no telling how much you'll need for what lies ahead."

Joon's nostrils flare. "Since when do the two of you get along so well?"

"We can't always disagree on everything," I say with a shrug, not bothering to hide a triumphant smirk.

"Fine."

Imugi slips out of their perch and slowly circles above the horse's head. Twin streams of fog pour from their nostrils, condensing into a thick cloud. It moves curls as though alive toward the horse's muzzle, then into the beast on an inhale.

Joon urges the mare into a run, and we race in the direction of the palace. The sun begins its descent toward the horizon. There's a good chance it will be dark before we reach the palace.

My nerves strain at the thought of being out in the open when that happens. Despite the fact that both Joon and Imugi are with me and able to drive demons away, the recent attack is still too fresh in my memory.

That feeling worsens as we enter the edge of the forest. The canopy overhead blocks most of the light. Leaves cast shadows in all directions that shift in the air currents.

Joon gathers the reins with one hand to slip an arm around my waist, holding me tight against him. His fingers splay over my abdomen, and his thumb brushes over my ribs absentmindedly. The feel of his muscled chest against my back chases away the chill better than a hot meal.

Has he always been so warm?

He must not realize how his hands make me feel when he touches me so casually. It makes me think there could be more to this than our bargain and the friendship that developed between us.

The rhythm of the horse's gate causes our bodies to shift against each other. Warmth gathers in my belly, bringing to mind images of how it would feel to have his hands on me. To feel his skin sliding over mine, as he moves over and within me…

Or maybe Joon realizes exactly what he's doing. Because it's impossible to worry about demons when I am having such lurid thoughts about the prince at my back—thoughts I have no right to have.

I close my eyes, trying unsuccessfully to push the images from my mind.

We break free of the trees, their shadows giving way to the weak light filtering through the overcast sky. A storm looms atop the Maldan Ice Wall far behind us.

The Shadow Fields turns out to be a sprawling tundra. I've never seen anything like it. Thousands of dips hold layers of dark, frozen water that reflect the shifting, angry clouds above. Our progress slows as we weave through the tightly packed pools. They range in size from standard puddles to the size of Firnhallow's main square.

There is something eerie about it that sends a chill crawling up the back of my neck.

The prince's hold on me tightens as we make what feels like painfully slow progress after using the fae roads to travel. We ride for several hours, with the descending sun serving as a constant reminder of our impending deadline. The muscles in Joon's arm only loosen when the end of the Shadow Fields comes into view.

A worn cabin sits on the shore of a wide lake about a mile beyond. Without lights shining through the windows or smoke rising from the crooked chimney, it has the look of being abandoned for a long time.

In the far distance, straight ahead and to the west, I can just make out the crossroads that lead to the palace. It will take at least another four or five hours of riding at this pace to reach it.

Movement from the corner of my eye catches my attention. When I look, I find nothing out of the ordinary.

The sun disappears behind a wall of gray as the wind whips viciously. Small flurries pelt against our faces like needles of ice. The howling wind grows louder and louder until it sounds like a mix of screams and growls.

There is something unnatural about this storm. I twist toward Joon. The words on my lips turn into a cry of alarm as a massive demon, half the size of the horse, bursts from a frozen pool, spraying us with ice and water. I shield my face with my arms. Joon lets out a harsh curse, jerking on the reins.

The horse whinnies and leaps to the side, then runs wild, trying to fling us off as more and more demons burst from icy cores between mounds of earth.

Imugi is out, using their power on the horse once more. We move faster. Joon tries to steer toward the cabin and away from the field of ice wells.

A demon materializes a few yards ahead. The horse screams and rears up. Another demon seizes the opportunity to plow into our side.

We land hard. The horse flails as it gets back up and bolts, faster without our burden, and leaves us stranded.

My ears ring. Everything hurts from the impact. I push myself to sitting, pressing a hand against my head. I touch something warm and sticky. My palm comes away with a smear of blood.

"Imugi!" Joon yells over the cries of demons. "The horse!" He is already on his feet, taking up a wide stance beside me. "We need it! Now go!"

The demon responds, but I can't hear what they say. Imugi heeds Joon's command.

Now, it's the two of us against a harmony of wild demons. And without a weapon or magic, I can do nothing to help drive them away.

The demons' formless bodies twist and reshape, moving like shadows, slowly solidifying.

I struggle to my feet and clench my fists at my side, fighting against the first agonizing squeeze in my chest.

Their restraint breaks, and they lunge at will, snarling in delight. Joon lifts his hands. A ball of pale blue light hovers over each palm as the demons bear down.

Anger rises in my chest. *What in the Otherworld made me think I could be useful to him*? I'm only another thing for him to worry about. A distraction that could get him killed.

Joon moves with speed and agility. The first ball of light hits its mark, throwing the demon back with a furious roar. More follow, while others manage to dodge the light. He fights the demons off, keeping them at bay, sending bursts of light in rapid succession. There's only so much he can do when he's forced to stay with me.

"Violet," Joon calls over his shoulder. "The dagger in my right boot—get it."

I don't know why he thinks a dagger, of all things, can help. It would require getting too close to be of any use. Regardless, I do as he orders, dropping into a crouch and yanking it free.

It's the same dagger he once held to my throat. The blade gleams from within like liquid moonlight. I shove the hilt of it into his palm. The weapon draws the light above his hand into it, and now, it really does shine as his power crackles over the surface in streaks of blue lightning.

"Stay close," he says. And then he leaps toward the closest demon, flinging a lance of light at them. They dodge, but not fast enough to avoid the dagger that sinks into their massive shoulder. The demon releases an ear-piercing scream as it drops with a heavy thud.

I struggle to keep close, but my heart continues to squeeze as if it's fighting to beat against some physical force trying to contain it. My panting quickly turns into rasping breaths.

Joon glances at me over his shoulder. It's only a second,

but it's enough time for a demon to reach out and rake their talons over his forearm.

The dagger clatters to the ground.

With a furious cry, he sends a blinding burst of light into the demon's face. Two more demons race to attack in tandem now that he's unarmed. But his back is to one, and he doesn't see.

I will not be the reason he dies here. I will not sit back helplessly waiting to die.

Ignoring the sharp pain piercing my chest, I dive for the blade, wrapping half-numb fingers around the hilt as I roll. My body protests against the jolt against the frozen earth, but I push on and swing my arm.

The blade cuts across the demon's belly as it leaps over me. It slices through like a hot knife through butter. An echo of screams fills the world loud enough to make my ears bleed as the beast careens, trying to escape too late and crashes off to the side. The impact rattles the ground, quickly followed by another behind me.

A hand wraps around my upper arm and yanks me to my feet. Joon's eyes search my face.

My head swims with a wave of dizziness. Motion from the side rises up from behind him. I gasp for breath, unable to form words. I throw my shoulder into him with all my weight, shoving him out of the way and thrusting the dagger at the demon. A single nick of the blade is all it takes to fell them.

I will not let them have him.

I will not die helpless.

I take a step, determined to keep fighting alongside Joon. The world tilts as darkness encroaches on the edges of my vision.

We move together. His light. My dagger. Every time I see Joon, he bears another deep slash, while I remain untouched.

Demon shit.

He takes hit after hit, allowing me to strike.

My vision wavers. I gasp for breath. I keep fighting, refusing to let his sacrifices be in vain. But it's useless, and my legs finally give out.

No... please no...

Several demons litter the area, but several more are still coming for us. Joon picks up the dagger and reluctantly turns from me to face them.

When had I dropped it?

The flurries quickly turn into a mix of ice and snow, obscuring everything, but not before we both see a dozen more demons bursting through ice in the distance.

"Cabin!" I shout above the wind.

Joon cuts another down before glancing in the direction I indicate. He reaches down and pulls me into his side, half-carrying me as he begins to run.

I point at a demon, nearly upon us, and slip out of his grasp. Joon whirls and sends a burst of light at them, enough to blind, then drives the dagger into the space between the demon's two burning red eyes.

He hooks an arm around my waist and drags me along with him once more.

A cool, soothing sensation weaves through my veins like soothing balm on a burn. The pain wracking my body eases. It's only when I can take a full breath again that I realize he's wasting the magic he needs to fight these demons on healing me. But it's too late to say anything now, so I run on my own beside him.

The harmony of demons is gaining rapidly, but we are almost to the cabin.

My knees go out. A force shoves us from behind and sends me sprawling.

"Violet!"

Rolling onto my back, I'm blinded by light exploding out in a massive wave toward the demons. The world dims again in time to watch as Joon drags the dagger across a demon's side as they slash at him.

Joon twists to avoid the gleaming talons. His body jerks, and he stumbles toward me, falling to his hands and knees.

Rips in his clothing expose four long gashes carved into his back. Blood soaks the ruined material, plastering it to his skin. I grab his wrist and tug, ignoring his pain and forcing him to his feet.

The blast of light didn't stop the demons, but it bought us a little time.

Draping his arm over my shoulder, I grab onto the front of his jacket with my other hand to avoid his injuries. I drag him the last few yards to the cabin and inside.

Releasing him, I throw my full weight against the warped door, then slide the long bolt into place. Heavy thuds bash into it seconds later. The wood splinters in places but holds.

He braces against the rough-hewn table, barely managing to stay upright.

The cabin is small, with a kitchen opposite a stone fireplace on the interior wall, with open doors, one on either side of it. Behind the first door is a cramped bathing room with a tub in the center. Beside that is an iron stove with a tank sitting on top of it, and a dial to control the spout protruding from the tank, overhanging the tub. The other leads to a relatively clean bedroom.

There is little in the way of personal touches. Moth-eaten curtains partially cover windows coated with a layer of dust.

Supporting Joon's weight, I help him to the bedroom and

have him lie face down on the bed. He half flops onto it with a groan. The mattress springs creak loudly in the quiet space. Then I carefully peel the torn material away from his wounds.

The gashes across his flesh are deep. His skin is not stitching itself up as it should. In fact, he looks close to death.

I kneel beside the bed and bring my face close to his. "You need to siphon, Joon. You're not healing."

He blinks slowly, gazing at me through unfocused eyes.

"Please," my plea is whisper soft.

Whatever he hears in it is enough to get him to comply. He inches to the edge, and I close the distance. Our lips meet, and the channel within me opens to him, allowing the power to flow. Drawn to him the way a river is drawn down a mountain.

The kiss is empty. Void of everything other than the transfer of magic. He breaks away before he can take enough to fully restore his magic.

While I trust he knows what he needs, I watch his injuries to be sure. Gradually, the bleeding stops. At the first sign of his skin knitting back together, I get to my feet and return to the bathing room to look for anything that might be useful.

Like the bedroom, there's not much beyond some basic soaps, a salve, and a few other hygiene necessities. I grab a few towels from the cupboard, then head to the kitchen.

I raid the cabinet, sorting through the glass jars of dried herbs and spices. The writing on them has faded beyond legibility. One by one, I sniff to identify what they are, rejecting most, until I have a small collection of jars. Fresh herbs are best, but dry ones will do in a pinch.

I place them on the table, then search the rest of the drawers and cupboards where a few mismatched dishes were left behind. Grabbing a bowl from one of the cupboards, I portion out the dried leaves. I frown at my mixture. It won't do much good as is. I need to reconstitute the ingredients.

Remembering the salve, I quickly return to the bathing room for the unlabeled jar, and scoop several spoonfuls into the bowl, and mix while adding more a little at a time, until it becomes a smooth green paste.

Gathering my concoction and the towels, I return to Joon and get to work. I slice the towels into strips, then smear the poultice over Joon's injuries, starting with the ones on his back and moving to his arm. I'd prefer a cleaner environment and the supplies I have at home, but this is the best I can do for now.

He is unconscious by the time I finish, torso rising and falling in slow, even breaths.

The ice and snow from the storm have melted, soaking through my clothes. My teeth chatter as I cross the room to the fireplace. I thank the saints that the last tenant left the flint sitting on the mantle and the dry wood piled beside it.

I make quick work of it and soon, a fire lights the room, crackling and snapping, as the dancing flames chase away the chill in the air.

After removing my outer layers, I pause as I reach for the ties to my dress and look over my shoulder.

Joon's eyes are closed. All the tension has leached from his muscles as he slumbers.

I strip out of my clothes until I'm only wearing a thin slip, then drape them over the rocking chair beside the fireplace to dry.

While Joon sleeps, I quietly move about the room, searching for anything left behind. There's precious little and nothing that we can use in the dresser, but I do find a white shirt hanging in the closet, which I fold and leave beside Joon.

I lift the lid of an intricately carved hope chest at the foot of the bed. The hinges squeak, and I cringe, but Joon doesn't stir.

Inside, there are three thick fur blankets. I pull them out and pile two in front of the fire, then sit on top of them with my knees pulled to my chest, wrapping the third blanket around my shoulders.

Once I'm warm again, I let the blanket slide off my shoulders and pool around me. I lean back, propping myself up on my hands, and stretch my legs out.

I watch the flames dance and crackle, letting them hypnotize me, until the wild storm and horrible demon howls fade from the outside world.

"Violet?" I'm not sure how long I've been sitting here before Joon's voice drags me from my reverie.

"You should be resting," I admonish gently. "I left a clean shirt for you beside the bed."

Joon settles beside me, his upper torso still completely bare.

Instead of responding, he brings his hand to the back of my head. I wince at the light touch. Pain shoots through my skull, condensing where it hit the ground after being thrown from the horse. It fades in seconds as he heals it.

"Thank you."

He huffs a humorless laugh. "You don't need to thank me. It's part of our bargain to keep you safe."

"Would you have agreed to bargain with me if there had been another flower?"

"Yes," his answer is immediate.

"Why?"

"Because you said please. Because of every time you have said please." There's a depth to his answer that holds far more than he gives voice.

"You need to siphon."

"I have taken enough. We cannot risk you having another episode. Are you hurt anywhere else?"

I shake my head.

The intensity of his gaze, traveling from my face down my torso and legs, leaves behind a phantom caress. His eyes darken, and I see a desire in those blue depths that matches my own.

I twist and lean forward, pressing my hand to his chest, sliding up over his shoulder and around his neck. "Then you can stop if it gets to that point."

His skin is smooth and warm, filling me with the sudden urge to run my palm over his defined muscles. Instead, I pull him down as I lean in the rest of the way and kiss him. When Joon doesn't respond, I pull back, releasing him.

Between one heartbeat and the next, his fingers wrap around my wrist and tug me closer. His mouth crashes down on mine. Firm and demanding.

I melt against him with a sigh. He takes full advantage, slipping his tongue inside and claiming my mouth.

It takes me entirely too long to realize that he's not siphoning.

CHAPTER TWENTY-SEVEN

VIOLET

I PULL BACK AGAIN, BUT BEFORE I CAN BREAK AWAY, JOON OPENS the channel. Power gathers and flows into him, as he siphons faster than ever before.

Joon's hand splays over my chest as he abruptly closes the channel. His power floods into me, healing me. Then he's siphoning again. Over and over, he repeats the pattern, not giving my heart a chance to fall into an episode. I can feel the strength in him returning through every shift of muscle.

The kiss lingers. After the fifth time—*or is it sixth?* —I wait for the channel to open again. Only it doesn't.

The hazy thought that I should pull away enters my mind, but I'm not quite ready to stop.

I want to continue tasting him. To revel in the feel of our chests pressed together as his arms encircle me, holding me in place, the heat of him along my inner thighs as I straddle him.

When had I climbed on top of him?

My eyes snap open, and I jerk back. Joon's strong embrace keeps the rest of my body in place.

Demons and saints... I am wantonly straddling the Crown Prince.

Ever since he kissed me in the field, I have become greedier by the day—trying to take more than I should. But this time, I have gone too far.

Embarrassment rushes through me, even though he doesn't seem to notice. I am supposed to help him break the curse, and he is supposed to keep me alive until then. *This* was never part of our bargain.

"Y-you're injured," I protest, but it sounds weak even to my ears.

Joon's hands splay along my spine as he holds me against him. I don't have it in me to even feign a weak attempt at trying to get away as his lips slowly trail along my jaw.

We should not be doing this.

"I am healed." The low rumble of his voice mixes with the heat of his breath along the shell of my ear.

This is dangerous territory.

Dangerous for whom?

Me... a voice in the back of my mind whispers.

"Let me see," I demand.

I feel him smile against my cheek. His arms loosen enough for me to crawl off him. I move around to his back.

Dancing flames cast a warm, flickering glow in the small room, but I can see the color has returned to his face. He is no longer concerningly pale.

Flakes of the dried salve still stick to him. I brush my palm over the area. A slight shudder rolls over him as I swipe the remainder away. Other than four faint, pink lines, he is whole again.

I sit back on my heels and take a deep breath, then let it out slowly. "I'm glad."

Joon turns so that we are sitting side by side, facing

opposite directions. He leans over my legs, planting his hand beside my hip. The position brings his face within inches of mine.

He was clear about how the siphoning process worked from the beginning—a necessary evil. Power requires a sense of intimacy to transfer. He is not doing this because he feels anything beyond his obligation to me. Yet, I've managed to lose myself in the process.

"Satisfied?" he asks.

Every inch of my body says no, but I manage to say, "Yes." I lower my eyes to his shoulder, finding it hard to meet his gaze. "I was worried."

The fire crackles in the hearth. Joon gently guides my chin toward him, so I have no choice but to meet his piercing gaze.

"Thank you," he says. Two words that once sounded awkward the first time he uttered them are now full of sincerity.

"For what?"

Joon huffs a soft laugh and shakes his head as if it should be obvious. "For saving my life."

"If it weren't for me, your life would never have been in danger out there. Besides, you're the one who saved my life."

He lifts his hand beside my hip and curls his arm around my waist, pulling me into a hug so tight it's as if he's afraid I'll evaporate if he lets go. Joon turns his face to rest his cheek on my shoulder, resting his brow against the side of my neck.

"We saved each other," he murmurs. "You are not responsible for us getting caught by a harmony of wild demons."

That is a difficult point to argue, so I don't. Instead, I say, "We should get some rest."

Joon hums in agreement, then he shifts, and the next thing

I know, I'm on my back with him next to me. He flings the blanket over both of us.

I still can't decide if he is oblivious to the effect he has on me, or if he's well aware and enjoys teasing me for it. Either way, with him shirtless and me in my chemise, the temptation is too great.

"I should get dressed," I whisper because I don't trust my voice not to tremble. "And you should sleep on the bed."

When I try to sit up, he holds me down by my shoulder. "It is better to share body heat, and our clothes are still damp." Joon closes one eye, peering at me with just the other. "We have slept beside each other before."

Heat prickles over my chest and works its way up my neck. "That was different… I had a fever."

Joon props himself up on an elbow and leans over me. A wicked smirk spreads over his mouth. "I will grant you that, but I think there is another reason you are trying to run." His eyes scan my face, then move down my neck to my chest before meeting my gaze again.

Any hope that the orange firelight disguised my blush is immediately dashed. He is *definitely* teasing me.

Joon's expression turns serious again, and he lowers himself back down. He reaches up and brushes his fingertips over my forehead, then down the side of my cheek to guide my chin, turning my face to meet his gaze. The desire from a moment ago is back.

He is relentless, and I cannot hide from him.

"Violet…" His breath skims over my lips with the sound of my name.

My lashes flutter as a tremor passes over me. How could I ever stand a chance of resisting him when he does nothing but endlessly find ways to make sure I can't?

"You were breathtaking out there."

I shake my head. "You shouldn't exaggerate."

"It is no exaggeration. You fought beside me. You carried me when I could not stand on my own." His lips graze the corner of my mouth. "There are a thousand ways to be strong, and you are all of them. I saw it in your face, the way you moved—you are the strongest person I know."

He kisses me, soft and light. Then again, lingering a little longer. Without meaning to, my mouth searches for his, pulled by some unseen force, and I lean to the side, and he is there, meeting me halfway.

The kiss starts gentle and tentative, gradually deepening as uncertainty falls away.

A groan escapes me at the taste of him. Of ice and candied ginger and honey. Joon's fingers tangle in my hair, cradling my head, urging me closer still, until our bodies are flush.

I let my hands roam over the plains of his chest, along his side, and over his stomach, feeling each muscle until my little finger bumps into the waist of his trousers.

A rumble, like a growl, vibrates in his chest. He rolls us, and I am on my back again as he holds his upper half over me, creating a cage I have no desire to escape.

Joon pins me with his stare as he slides his palm over my side, splaying over my stomach before gliding up to my ribs. His thumb brushes the underside of my breast, where he pauses for half a heartbeat.

My breath catches and releases on a shudder filled with need. Then Joon is kissing me again. I moan into his mouth, which only encourages him. His hand cups my breast, massaging gently before taking my nipple between two fingers and pinching. I arch my back as the unexpected desire pools between my legs.

Joon trails kisses down my neck, nipping at my collarbone as he moves lower and lower. I gasp again as he takes the stiff peak into his mouth, using his tongue and teeth until I'm writhing beneath him.

He lifts his head, and our eyes meet. The material of my chemise is wet from his mouth, transparent, and plastered to my skin. I drag my teeth over my bottom lip. He watches me watching him, leisurely trailing his fingers to the thin strap, then sliding it off my shoulder, then the other. He hooks a finger along the collar, inching it down. Lower and lower, until the material bunches around my waist.

Joon takes his time, letting his hand wander over every inch of exposed skin. I practically vibrate under his caress.

His mouth descends on my breast again as if he means to consume me. Then he moves to the other, sending fresh waves of insatiable need down to my core.

I have never felt such overwhelming sensations. It's impossible to hold onto any coherent thought. All I can think about is that I never want him to stop.

So caught up in the way he slowly drives me mad that I don't notice where his hand has gone until I feel his palm over the bare skin of my ass, sliding down the back of my leg to bend my knee up.

"Joon," I manage to gasp by the time his hand rests just below my belly button.

Our eyes meet and lock as his touch shifts lower, grazing over the apex of my thighs, as he finds the evidence of my desire. It only takes the barest amount of pressure for two fingers to slip inside me.

The last scraps of propriety vanish as he sinks deeper and deeper. The sensation is unmatched.

"Joon?" I breathe his name. I mean to ask him what he's doing, but then he begins to move his fingers, slowly stroking. I shudder around him.

"Tell me to stop and I will."

"Don't. Please don't," I am begging shamelessly, and can't find it in me to care.

A rumble emanates from deep within his chest. "There you go again, making it impossible for me to deny you."

I reach for him, stroking him through his trousers. He grinds his erection against my hand. I want to touch him the way he is touching me. Joon moves, shifting his hips before I can, and I let out a frustrated groan that's cut off as he spreads my legs.

He gazes down the length of my body, snagging at my core before returning to my face. "You are beautiful, Violet."

Joon settles between my thighs. Before I can reach for him, his mouth descends on mine. His fingers find my center again. This time, he adds a third as he begins to stroke me. He swallows my moans, then claims my breasts, moving from one to the other. Teeth scraping over sensitive flesh. He has me at his mercy as he takes my body with hand and mouth.

My stomach clenches as tension builds, coiling tighter and tighter at my core until I think I'll combust. I try to say his name, to say it's too much, but can't think past his caresses. I've forgotten how to form words, so I nod.

"You are fucking stunning," he whispers, then drags his teeth over my earlobe. "Let me see your surrender."

His hand moves faster. I pull him against me, so his hard length grinds against my clit.

A whimper escapes my throat and turns into a cry as I come undone. Wave after wave of pleasure washes over me, nearly drowning me. Joon doesn't stop until he has pulled every last shudder from me.

Completely spent, I let my hands fall limply at my sides. Joon returns to lie beside me. I look at him, my mind hazy from pleasure, as he pulls my chemise back into place.

Slowly, awareness returns as the full impact of what just happened hits.

Demon shit. What did I do?

I shouldn't have been caught up in him so easily. He jokingly says he cannot deny me, but I am the one who can't deny him—and the truth is that I don't want to. I want to be selfish, to claim him and everything he has to offer. Even now, I ache to touch him. To taste him. To draw pleasure out of him as he has done to me.

Joon gathers me into his arms before I get the chance. His arousal strains against my lower belly, trapped between us.

"Joon," I start.

He hums. "Sleep. You were right, we need to rest."

"But…" I trail off, not sure what I'm trying to say. *I want to touch you,* or *are we allowed to do this?*

"Be still, or I might do something to you that you'll regret." Joon's words are rich and sensual, promising things my body already desperately craves.

Yet, uncertainty wraps around me.

There is nothing special or unique about me or my role. I am only here now because I stole the frost bloom, and he had no other choice.

I don't regret what happened, but I also don't want to be a way for him to pass the time. Someone easy to walk away from… and forget.

Light streaming through the window drags me unwillingly back to consciousness. The warmth of the fire has faded slightly. I am warm, but the air is still chilled.

A heavy weight is draped over my waist, pinning me against something warm at my back.

No... not something.

Someone.

Joon.

His breaths are slow and even, as he remains in the clutches of sleep. Lying like this feels almost sinfully decadent. But I know I can't stay here. If I do, I'll never want to move. I risk losing myself entirely.

As carefully as I can without waking him, I inch away.

I barely make it halfway out from under the blanket we share when his arm tightens and pulls me back, the other joining to trap me in place.

"Where are you going?" he murmurs into my hair.

I am his seventh *wife,* I remind myself.

"I need... some air."

Joon cups my jaw in his hands and looks at me. "Something is wrong. What is it?"

"I..." I don't know what to say. The technical words are easy enough, but they clot in my throat, refusing to come out.

They are too bold. Too greedy.

What right do I have to demand that I should mean something to him? You can't have it both ways, Violet.

I can't selfishly take what I want regardless of his own wants.

"It's nothing." I shake my head. "I should check to see if Imugi is back."

I sit up. Joon catches my wrist, stopping me.

"Why won't you tell me?" He waits for me to respond. The moment stretches out, the silence growing heavier by the second. Eventually, he lets his grip fall away.

I rise and walk over to the chair to check my clothes. They are warm and dry.

"You are upset with me." Joon clears his throat. The next time he speaks, he is right behind me. "I crossed the line, and for that, I am sorry."

I squeeze my eyes shut and swallow thickly. Hearing Joon apologize for something I liked—something I wanted—makes it worse.

"Don't do that. Don't apologize." I whirl on him. He catches me by the shoulders to keep me from crashing into him. I still haven't opened my eyes. "I am not ashamed, I just…"

His posture stiffens. "I would have stopped—"

I can't stand the hurt in his voice. "It's nothing you did. I don't regret it—"

Joon's arms wrap around me, crushing me to him. "Violet, I cannot fix this if I do not understand. If not that, then what?"

I inhale a deep breath, then slowly release it. "When this is over… it will be hard enough to say goodbye, and impossible to forget you."

For several seconds, Joon barely even breathes. "Do you want to forget me?"

I shake my head.

"But you think I will forget you?"

I nod slowly. "I don't want to be another…" I can't finish. It took the last of my courage to say that much.

His breath leaves him in a long exhale. "I see."

Demon shit, now I made him feel guilty. We made no promises about this. We both acted on our own urges willingly.

He chuckles—*actually chuckles*—as if this weren't embarrassing enough. "And should I be jealous of your past lovers?"

"What?" I try to pull back, but he holds tighter. "I don't—"

"Then do you think I use all my wives to satisfy my

desires? Or do you think I seduce any lady who happens to cross my path?" He might be laughing at my expense, but there's an expectation to answer the questions. Worry that the answer might be yes. All while pointing out that I am acting jealous.

Otherworld, take me. I made such a mess of this.

"No—I don't know," I say truthfully.

"Intimacy is not something I take lightly." Joon kisses my forehead. "If you think anyone could forget you, then you are sorely mistaken."

I am relieved, perhaps more than I should be, even though nothing has changed. Not really. "But… this…" I flounder. "It can't happen again."

Imugi passes through the wall, effectively ending the conversation with so much left unsaid.

"I won't ask what the two of you have been up to," they quip, continuing before either of us can respond. "The horse is in the shed behind the house. The way is clear of all demons."

As if on cue, there's a rapid tapping on the window. We turn to see my demon, pressed up against the glass, trying, unsuccessfully, to pass through.

Imugi groans. "Except for that one."

CHAPTER TWENTY-EIGHT

JOON

Violet doesn't argue when I summon the fae road as we ride toward the palace in the early morning. Imugi drapes themselves over my shoulders, while the other demon has insisted on Violet holding them in her arms.

It is well into midmorning by the time we make it back. Mingi and Iseul wait on horseback just beyond the gated entrance to the capital, riding out to meet us the moment they spot us.

Mingi hands me a pouch holding my crown. I put it on, but the weight of it feels strange. I have worn it less and less over the recent weeks, and now it no longer feels like mine.

"You will have to go straight to the Central Court. The king and the council are waiting."

Iseul opens her arms to the demon. They leap across to her. She catches them, hiding them in the folds of her cloak as we near the gate.

"What happened?"

"I am not sure. No one has spoken a word about it. I don't even think most of the council knows," Mingi admits.

"There were whispers of you presenting her to the court earlier," Iseul interjects. "I thought it was strange because neither of you mentioned it, and you'd already left."

"We think it's a ruse… However, we haven't figured out who is behind it or what they are trying to accomplish," Mingi finishes.

When we reach the entrance to the Central Court, I dismount, then turn and take Violet by the waist, lifting her down without thought.

"Wait here," I order Mingi and Iseul.

"Be careful," Iseul says.

I take Violet's hand and lead her forward. She glances at me, entwining our fingers. Her honey-brown eyes fill with apprehension, but she squeezes my hand as if to offer me comfort. I return the gesture.

A sinking feeling settles in my stomach. I have always had enemies, yet this is more than stirring up rumors and creating unrest among the people. We are walking in blind to the accumulation of a devious plot coming to fruition.

The entrance to the building is dark, with few lanterns lit at the far end. The moment we are both inside, the door slams shut behind us, and more lights flare to life.

Violet is ripped from my grasp as several guards seize her by the arms, restraining her as if she were a dangerous criminal.

Her eyes go wide with fear.

I summon my power, knowing it shines in my eyes like a threat as I round on the King's Guard. "What do you think you are doing?"

If they are fazed, none show any sign of it.

A woman steps forward. The silver dragon feather dangling from her hat marks her as the chief guard. "His

Majesty and the council are waiting for you, Your Highness. We are to ready Lady Hawthorn before bringing her in."

Not even I can go directly against the king's orders.

I scowl. "Very well."

I must don the mantle of the heartless prince they expect. The one they have always known. Cold. Wicked. Murderous.

It is a role that no longer comes naturally as it once did—one I no longer wish to play.

She has changed me more than I realized.

I leave her in their custody as if doing so is the easiest thing in the world to do.

Servants scatter out of my way as I stride through the halls. I don't even slow as I approach the throne room. With a look, a man scrambles to open the door in time.

Officials and nobles line both sides of the center aisle. All heads turn as I enter, but I pay them no heed. My full attention is on my uncle, the interim king.

He sits back on the throne with his legs crossed and his hands resting atop his knees.

"What is the meaning of this?" I demand.

The king straightens at my tone, planting both feet on the floor. "I am relieved to see you have returned at last, Nephew."

"Why has *my wife* been arrested?"

He moves with exaggerated slowness. Entirely too relaxed. "I intended to surprise you both by presenting her to the court last night when you returned from your little *joy ride*." Disdain fills the last two words. "However, something has been brought to my attention that cannot go unaddressed." The king gestures to the throne beside him. "It seems we are to have a trial instead."

For the moment, he is no longer my uncle but King Sameun.

The game is in full motion—there is no stopping it now. All I can do is play along.

I climb the steps and take my place, settling into the uncomfortable throne.

The king motions to the guard standing right inside the door, who signals to the others waiting outside.

There's a commotion of rough voices and the clink of metal. A guard drags Violet in by chains, leading her to the foot of the dais where I stood a moment ago.

"Kneel," he snarls, kicking the back of her legs.

Her knees hit the floor with a hard crack. Though I do not allow myself to react, I take careful note of his face, burning his visage into my memory.

"Minister Ilseong, you may begin," my uncle says.

The official steps forward, practically preening with arrogance. "This woman is guilty of treason against the crown."

He turns to Minister Molan. She holds a small wooden box I am all too familiar with. He takes it and presents it for everyone to see.

I already know what is inside before he opens it.

A flawless pearl, identical to my own before the curse shattered it. Without my power to infuse it, the thing sits dull and lifeless on a bed of pale blue silk—an obvious fake to any who lays eyes on it.

And it is mine.

"This was found among her things," Minister Ilseong says, twisting to allow the room to see before returning to address the king again. "She is accused of deceiving His Highness."

He looks at me with a challenge in his eye, daring me to call him on the lie. We are both aware that he found it in my room.

If he came to the court, accusing me, without proof—

something that would only implicate him in violating my privacy—I would deny it, and none would side with him against the Crown Prince.

So, he is attacking me in the only way he can—through Violet.

If she is found guilty, then she will die right here.

Murmurs erupt throughout the room. Their words and suspicions build on each other. Voices rise, matching their growing outrage.

My uncle lets it go on for longer than necessary before finally motioning for silence.

Only Imugi and Violet knew of its existence. I have not even shared this secret with Mingi or Iseul.

All it would take from me is a few simple words, admitting it is mine, to prove her innocence.

Yet, to do so would spell disaster. To hide something like that is unthinkable. The pearls are the source of the royal family's power. Sacred. This is not a simple copy, but a forgery meant to deceive the people of Arum and even the guardians of the past. They are part of us, not a thing to be kept in a box.

The implications of the Crown Prince in possession of such an object would reveal my secret—that I am cursed and without my pearl.

Violet's crimes are breaking the old laws, which she has paid for with her bargain to me. Everything she has said and done since then has been to make up for it.

Violet glares at Minister Ilseong as he spews his lies.

She could easily deny it.

The only thing she cannot do is speak of the curse—our bargain would prevent it, but she does not move or attempt to speak in her defense. Yet she does not.

"There is more, Your Majesty," Minister Ilseong says. He

waits for the signal to continue. "She has been seen acting in an unqueenly manner, consorting with servants."

Demons damn him to the Otherworld. Of course he would learn of the incident in the kitchens.

"Do you honestly expect me to believe that she is plotting against me because she—" I pause, flicking a glance at her. "—is *kind* to the servants?"

Some of the nobility and other officials chuckle among themselves.

"My pearl and the power within it chose *her*. Yet you stand here and spout these vile accusations against her, knowing full well that any human, so long as they are willing, may be selected—regardless of their status." I scoff.

"That woman would turn the people against you—she is not to be trusted! Her every action is an insult to undermine the crown." Minister Ilseong half-shouts, unable to restrain himself.

"She may not have been born to nobility as the rest of us, but she has proven herself more than worthy of being my wife. The only insult is the presumption that you have taken it upon yourself to decide what I should find insulting."

"Enough!" King Sameun bellows. "While it is certainly undignified to consort with servants as equals, it is not a crime. Present your evidence of her crime, Minister Ilseong, so we may make a judgment."

The minister's face distorts as if he naturally expected my uncle to side with him, no matter what he said, simply because his position grants him the king's ear.

"I believe she planned to steal His Highness's real pearl and replace it with the forgery she created."

Again, murmurs break out all around the room. Growing as they turn to discuss the seriousness of the accusation among themselves.

I adopt an overly relaxed posture, practically lounging back on my throne. But inside, I seethe.

No one points out the numerous weak points in his argument that do not align with how the magic of the pearl works, how nothing he says is evidence, but baseless speculation.

No one speaks in her defense. Because Violet is human.

Could this be the reason Uncle suggested I present her early? To weaken any argument my enemies might cling to.

I am a fool for not heeding his earlier advice.

"She has no access or ability to create such things," I point out in a mocking tone. "Especially when she has spent so much of her time under careful watch.

"A witch is capable of doing so unnoticed. Even within the palace walls." Minister Ilseong is relentless.

"She is human." It's growing ever more challenging to keep my temper in check.

Ilseong looks to King Sameun again as if expecting a specific response. "If that is so, then she clearly conspired with a witch and brought it with her."

"What evidence do you have that led you to that conclusion?" the king asks.

It is not the response the official was hoping for. I straighten in my seat. Minister Ilseong will continue to talk in circles, falsely accusing her, until he gets what he wants. But I have no intention of allowing it to go that far.

He moves to stand beside her. "Well, that is merely conjecture. However, there is no other explanation for why she possesses a forbidden forgery. That treasonous act alone is enough to warrant her death." His hand shoots out and yanks her head back by the hair. A dagger appears in his hand. The metal glints with malice as he brandishes the blade against her throat. "I call for her immediate execution!"

King Sameun is silent for a long moment. I know his answer before he moves to speak. There are laws that even kings and queens are subject to.

"No," I say calmly, rising to my feet and descending the stairs.

I take my time. Our audience holds its breath, waiting to see what I will say, what I will do. I stalk toward the Minister of Justice.

"I think it was you," I say. The man sputters, but I don't give him the opportunity to speak. "Do you believe I haven't heard the whispered rumors you spread? Or the ways you choose to speak out against me for years?"

"That-that's—" The look on his face makes it clear he believed I had not been aware of his movements all this time. That I was oblivious to his machinations. Too weak and too stupid to figure it out.

I lean in to whisper so only he can hear, "Did you think I wouldn't find out how you sent people to murder her in the streets or the demons you lured into the gardens?"

His eyes bulge, and he looks to the king in panic. But my uncle does nothing. It's more than enough to cement my suspicions.

The recent threats to Violet's life, and now this farce, were too manufactured and too close together to be coincidental. All of it was his doing. I straighten.

"And now, you plant this abomination among her things, where it happens to be discovered so you can stage this trial as yet another way to undermine me."

I turn his lie back on him. We can see the truth of it in each other's eyes.

The silence in the room is heavy.

Now, he knows what it is like to have no one come to his defense.

Minister Ilseong knows he has lost. If he changes his story now, it will only make his guilt that much worse.

I lift a hand to shoulder height, keeping my eyes locked on his. A jagged crystal of ice forms under my palm. It flies through the air and finds its mark in the chest of the guard who kicked Violet. Shouts of alarm fill the room. Ilseong gasps and turns to look. But my hand is already around his throat, squeezing until he releases Violet. His weapon drops with a clang against the marble as he grapples uselessly against my grip, trying to pry himself free.

My fingers elongate, turning into razor-sharp talons. The tips press into his skin, slowly piercing. Hot blood seeps from the wounds. I pull his power from it, then send it back into him.

The power of the bargain commanding me to protect her is a weak pull, smothered by my own will.

The quiet crackle begins in his throat, first cutting off any ability to make a sound. It moves into the muscles of his limbs, then his organs. I let the ice form slowly. Painfully. Only when he passes out do I let it consume his lungs and heart, then over his skin until he is encased in ice.

It is not the enchanted ice of the Winter Dragon but of the undeniable death of a traitor.

I release him. His frozen body crashes against the floor with a hard crack.

Violet whimpers and shies away from her would-be murderer. She is pale, and her eyes are wide. I offer her my hand. Slowly, she pries her gaze away from the minister's body.

For once, I cannot read her expression. Is it for what Ilseong would have done to her or for what I did to him?

I crouch and grip the irons chained around her wrist. With

a burst of power, I freeze them and twist, shattering them into a thousand pieces between us.

This time, she takes my hand and rises to her feet, holding her head high.

I turn and stalk halfway up the dais steps before facing the room, pulling Violet along, refusing to let her go.

"I am still your Crown Prince. I am not so easily tricked by words or schemes," I announce to the room. "I alone will decide her guilt as well as any punishment."

Violet's grip on my hand tightens. Her skin is cold to the touch. I can feel the small tremors that vibrate through her.

Her fear infuriates me.

"She is first and foremost my wife, and she is to be treated with the respect of her position. If anyone dares to speak out against her or attempt to harm her in any way, then expect to meet the same fate as Minister Ilseong."

With that, we make our way down the center aisle. Each official and noble bows deeply as we pass.

CHAPTER TWENTY-NINE

VIOLET

Anger rolls off Joon in palpable waves as he half-drags me all the way to his apartments, only releasing me when we are inside.

I remain where I stop and stare blankly toward the curtained window. My heart hammers against my ribs. I'm shaking from the bone-deep chill of fear of the past half hour. Somehow, it was worse than the demon attacks.

The door slides shut with a gentle click. I hear Joon's footsteps approach. He sighs but doesn't speak for a long moment.

The walls and ceiling darken the edges of my vision. It feels as though they are closing in on me.

"Violet, I…" he begins, his voice is a hoarse whisper.

Heat gathers behind my eyes with a pressure that blurs my vision. Somewhere in the back of my mind, I know I am in shock. I've lived most of my life expecting it to be short. Yet, it is one thing to wait for my heart to stop and another thing entirely for someone to actively plot my murder.

And for what? A crime I am not guilty of.

"I would not blame you if you hated me for this." I blink. Hot tears spill down my face, only to have more well up, replacing them. It's a flood I can't stop now that it has started.

Strong arms wrap around my shoulders from behind—the warmth of Joon's body at my back seeps into me, and with it, my pulse slows. He rests his cheek against the top of my head.

"I am sorry," he whispers into my hair.

I twist in his hold. He must think I want to push him away because he shifts backward, letting his embrace slacken. I reach out and grab his hand to keep him from retreating.

I'm not ready to lose his warmth.

The tension in Joon's stance melts away. He hooks a finger under my chin and tilts my face up.

Joon wipes the tears from my face. A wild storm swirls in his eyes as pain and guilt war within those deep blue depths. "I failed you. I was silent, and for that, you could have died. It would have been over in minutes if I had just told—"

When I found the pearl, I sensed there was more to it than it being a simple trinket. But I never could have guessed its existence could be such a serious crime.

"You said what you could. Telling them any of it only would have made things worse." I understand that now

A muscle in his jaw ticks.

Joon murdered one of the highest-ranking officials because of our bargain. Anyone could see the long-standing conflict between them by the way they looked at each other. Minister Ilseong went after Joon in any way he could, using whatever and whoever was necessary to achieve his ends.

"You—" my words crack on a hiccup. "You stopped him."

Joon cups the back of my neck. Anger distorts his expression as he speaks, "I murdered a man."

"You had to save me because of our bargain."

"No, Violet. I killed him because I *wanted* to. I wanted to make him suffer for touching you. To writhe in pain for looking at you. Just as I killed those criminals in that alley for daring to threaten your life—because I am every bit the monster the world says I am. Death follows me, claiming everything I touch."

He killed them without a sliver of hesitation or care for the consequences. His willingness to murder should frighten me, but I find that I don't mind. He didn't do it out of enjoyment or boredom, but because he was protecting me. The prince with the frozen heart does not exist.

I've seen many sides to him, but underneath them all is someone who cares deeply—whether he admits it to himself or not.

"I understand."

A lump forms in my throat, and I swallow it back down.

"Do you?" he half snarls as he tilts my head back further. Even in this mood, he's careful to remain gentle. "Do you understand what it means to tangle your life with mine?"

I've never wished harm to anyone before—never like this.

Yet… I see it in him. How he's as trapped in his situation as I am in mine. How he's been alone for so long. Afraid. Tears well up and spill down my cheeks.

If he is wicked, then let me be wicked too. I will become whatever I must if that's what it takes for him to never feel alone again. To forgive him when he can't forgive himself.

"Yes, Joon, I do. I understand the consequences of failing." I press a palm to his chest, right above his heart. "More than that… I am *glad* you did it." Venom coats my tongue as I calmly admit the dark truth.

His breath hitches, then, as he exhales, the tension melts from his muscles, and his chest rises and falls, matching mine. "Say it again." He leans down and kisses one of my eyes. "I want to hear you say my name." Then the other eye. "It is the only time I can remember who I am."

"Joon…" I whisper his name again and again as he kisses away my tears until the sharp emotions roiling through us have cut away.

Then his mouth finds mine, lingering with gentle caresses as if he's afraid that he might break me. I open to him, and our kiss deepens as we seek solace and comfort in each other. It's chaste and sweet, but within it, there is something pleading, questioning, and desperate.

It isn't enough. It can't be so long as we are in this place—this palace. It surrounds us, feeling alive and sinister. I want to escape. The need to run from here claws desperately inside my chest. It's so strong, I think I will suffocate if I stay here much longer.

We break apart.

"Will you take me somewhere?" My chest feels tight, as if I am turning to stone from the inside. "Anywhere else… *please*. I don't want to be here right now."

Joon nods.

"Imugi," he calls to his demon through his connection with them. The bright, glowing blue lights his irises. The demon appears seconds later. "Make sure no one knows we are gone until we return."

The demon obeys without a word of protest. My demon remains behind as well.

He takes my hand as he gathers our cloaks. Within minutes, we are in the secret passage leading to the forest behind the palace, hurrying through. As we step out into the wild, I can finally take my first deep breath. But we don't stop.

Joon summons a fae path, leading us deeper into the woods. We stop on a hill overlooking the palace at the high end of the valley of the Arum kingdom.

A light breeze rustles loose whisps of my hair against my neck. The path disappears, leaving us beneath an opening in the canopy that lets the sun's warmth envelope us.

He is silent, waiting for me to tell him if I approve.

I gaze out over the landscape, grateful to have this space away from the palace. "Thank you."

He releases my hand and moves to stand behind me, gripping my shoulders, offering safety and security.

The day is beautiful and warm, and the air is thick with the fragrance of early spring. I almost didn't live to see it.

And at my back is the man who saved me and comforts me now. Not because of the bargain but because he wanted to. Whose touch still lingers on my body, who sought my pleasure while taking none for himself.

"Take as long as—"

My heart swells with so much emotion, and I whirl. The front of my body brushes against his. Warmth spreads through me. I am acutely aware of every inch of muscle under his shirt.

Last night, I said nothing could happen between us again because I was afraid of how much it will hurt when I have to let him go. But now I realize it will be worse to die without telling him how I feel, without giving myself over to these feelings, without taking what I want.

From now on, I will be selfish. I will take what I want without regret.

I reach up and grab him by the collar, pulling his face down to mine as I rise up on my toes. And I kiss him. Fiercely. I nip at his bottom lip.

"Joon," I say. His name is the only word I can form, but even I can hear the raw need in my voice—not for the prince, but for the man who has ensnared my heart against all probability.

Joon wraps his arms around me, pulling me tighter against him. With a groan, his tongue slips inside my mouth, caressing mine as if he will consume me. And I want him to—I want him to devour me as I devour him.

My hands slide over his chest, curving over his shoulders to lock together behind his neck.

His desire matches mine in the way his mouth moves, the way his hands roam over me, and the length of him hardens, trapped between us, pressing against my belly.

Joon breaks away, breathless as he rests his forehead against mine. He feels too far away. "You said—" he protests, struggling for words, trying to stop wanting what his body demands.

"Just this once," I say quietly. "Let me pretend I am yours, just for a little while. Let me pretend I can have you—that I'm allowed these feelings."

He goes perfectly still. "And what feelings are those?"

We belong to two different worlds. Joon is a fae prince. And I am a human, not even born into a noble family. We were never meant to come together. This—our bargain, our bond—was all because of a choice I made that put us both at risk.

I bury my face against his chest, aching to tell him everything, yet knowing I shouldn't. "Isn't it obvious?" I want someone to know these emotions lived inside me at least once in my life.

"Tell me anyway," he says.

"I love you."

"And what is so wrong with that?"

"I'm neither fae nor noble."

"I should think my wife, more than anyone, is allowed to love me in return." Joon's voice is nonchalant.

It stings to hear him take it so lightly. "I am only your wife because of our bargain." I pause as I fully comprehend what he said.

...in return.

"You are my wife in every way that counts. Our bargain is that I will free you when the curse is broken. I will not force you to remain my wife forever when your only choice was between that and death."

I search his face for any hint of a cruel smile and cold eyes, but there is only the familiar expression he only wears for me, and I finally understand the full meaning behind it.

"You… love me?"

One corner of his mouth lifts. "How could I not love someone as stubborn and kind and strong and brave as you? You see me in ways no one else does. You treat me as a man. I am free to be myself around you without pretense. I never needed the bargain to save you. I would have done it anyway."

"How long?"

"I am not sure exactly." He shrugs. "Perhaps it was when you wrapped that first shard without knowing the importance of it. Or when I pulled you out of the water, looking like a half-drowned rat…." Joon looks at me with such tenderness, then softly adds, "But it could have been the way you said please the first time."

Joon cups my jaw with both hands. "You have made me feel as if I was never cursed." He presses a kiss to my forehead. "As if I could be worthy of love."

We come together again. Mouths crushing, tasting, searching. Bodies pressing and sliding. Trying to get closer still.

His hands slide from my hips and over my ass. In one swift motion, he lifts me. I wrap my legs around his waist. In this position, I can feel his hardness against my core, straining against his trousers. He slides a hand up my ribs to my breast, massaging my flesh through my clothes. It sends heat pooling in my belly. I grind my hips against him as I moan into his mouth.

He breaks away, moving his lips along my jaw and down the column of my throat.

Slowly, he lowers me to my feet.

We will take what we want, where we can, and that is what will make it perfect.

"You own my heart." He kisses my mouth, then trails his lips down my neck. He kneels at my feet, holding me by the hips. "And if you let me, I would bow to you every day for the rest of my life to show you how deeply I love you."

Joon gazes at me as if he is lost, and my heart flutters.

I reach for his crown and let it fall to the ground beside us. "Do not bow. All I ask is that you stay with me for as long as you can. Show me with your words and your deeds." I unclasp his cloak, letting it fall away. "And with your hands." My hands slide over the hard muscles of his chest and lean into him, bringing my mouth to his ear. "Show me."

CHAPTER THIRTY

VIOLET

A shudder runs over him. Joon unhooks my cloak, hands lingering on my shoulders, sliding down to my waist. His fingers roughly dig into my hips as he yanks me to him. One arm goes around the backs of my thighs, the other snakes around my waist, hand splayed up my spine.

Joon kisses my stomach, then between my breasts, before taking one in his mouth. He teases me with his tongue, nipping and sucking the peak until it tightens, then moves to the other. The wet material is chilly against my skin.

I moan, sure that I will come undone from this alone. Then I remember the way his fingers felt inside me, and I want to know how it will feel to have his cock inside me.

"More," I say breathlessly. "I want your skin on mine."

Pulling me down to him by the back of my neck, Joon claims my mouth with his, lowering me to the ground, holding himself over me.

His tongue slides over mine, and unlike every other kiss we've shared, there is something so carnal about it. My legs part, allowing him to settle between them.

He pushes my skirts up. Every part of my body awakens at his touch. I lift my hips to help, and the movement causes me to press against him.

The palm pressing down on my bare hip brings his thumb tantalizingly close to my core that demands more, *more, more.* He makes a noise low in his throat, grinding his arousal against the junction of my thighs.

I squirm, searching for the angle that will bring me the relief I need.

No one has ever stirred such desire in me before, and my heart has never longed for someone as it longs for him now as he holds me in his embrace.

Joon kisses his way down my neck, nipping at my collarbones as he unbuttons my blouse. "Tell me you are not pretending, Violet. When I claim you, I want it to be real."

With a rough tug, he undoes the tie that holds my skirt in place. The material falls away. I am left completely exposed, yet I have never felt safer. "This is real… I am yours. My heart. My body. Every part of me is yours."

I want to feel his skin against mine—to explore him with my hands and body. I *need* to—*need him.*

He holds himself over me, ensnaring me with his gaze as he trails a hand down to my breast, kneading once, catching my nipple between two fingers before moving down my ribs, to my stomach, and lower still, finally slipping between my thighs.

He slides two fingers along my core. He does it again and again, sliding through the arousal gathered there. Even if I wanted to, I could not deny how much I need him in every sense of the word.

Joon continues to stroke me until I feel like weeping from the overwhelming fire he stirs in me. He presses against my slick entrance, sinking into me until his knuckles meet my center. I arch into him as he begins to pump his hand.

"I do not know when I started wanting you, only that I do." Joon's mouth descends on my breast, and I see stars as his lips and tongue explore. Tension coils in my belly.

His teeth scrape as his mouth inches lower, leaving my dampened skin exposed to the cool air.

I don't realize that my hands are free until he spreads my legs.

"To think I could have had you on my tongue weeks ago." His fingers slip from me, and then he descends on my core, exploring me. Learning me. It's as if he is a starving man intent on consuming me. He uses his tongue relentlessly until I am writhing against his mouth. His teeth scrape against my flesh, sending sparks of electric pleasure through my body. Joon gives a low growl of approval.

He finds a spot that sends a wave of ecstasy over me. I arch my back as he continues to discover, searching for all the places that give him the reactions he wants from me.

It is too much and not enough. I want to touch him the way he touched me in the cabin. The way he is touching me now.

He moves back up my body. I watch as he drags the tip of his tongue over his bottom lip, licking me off him.

"Tell me what you want, Violet," he whispers against the shell of my ear.

My eyes threaten to water from the unspoken words I want to say to him.

"I want you. All of you. I want to know what you feel like. What you taste like." This time, when I unbutton his top, he doesn't stop me. "I want to feel you all over." I push the material off his shoulders, and together we make quick work of his clothes, leaving him as exposed as I am.

I shift back and admire him. He is larger than I realized when I felt him through his clothes. Joon's dark eyes watch intently as I reach for him. I slide my hands over his shoulders and chest.

His fingers press into the soft flesh of my hips as I take my time learning him as he did me.

I lean forward and bite his shoulder as I take him in my hand. He is both hard as steel and soft to the touch. The feel and shape of him, the hard plains of his body, the way his skin tastes, the sounds each touch elicits from his throat.

He lets out a low hiss. I move my grip up and down, using the same rhythm he had on me. Bringing the side of my cheek to his, I drag my tongue along the shell of his ear to the pointed tip. A tremor rolls through him as my mouth and hands continue to explore.

"Violet," Joon rasps my name, tangling his fingers in my hair.

In a move so quick, he pulls me to him before I can blink. I wrap my legs around his hips, trapping his hard length between us, so close to my aching core.

Heart hammering against my ribs, I brace my hands on his shoulders.

I rock my hips, dragging my center over his cock, pulling a ragged moan from his throat. Loving the sound, I do it again.

Joon's hands shift, moving to grip my ass. He lifts me to position himself at my center, parting me with his tip. He holds me there, aching on the edge of the only thing that can quench this overwhelming need. "I want you to be absolutely sure this is what you want. Because I have no intention of stopping until I have memorized every inch of your body."

"*Please,*" I say breathlessly.

Joon bites the side of my neck, then licks and sucks to soothe the skin. "Then take what you want."

His grip loosens as he leans back, relinquishing control over to me. I sink down partway, unable to take all of him at once. I take a breath, then lift myself up, then lower again. His cock fills and stretches my body around his thick girth until I wonder if my body can accommodate all of him. But this need refuses to abate, and I keep going. I pause when there's a slight discomfort as I stretch to accommodate all of him. It only increases the ache between my legs that only having him inside me can ease.

Joon finds the apex of my thighs, using his thumb to massage circles over the most sensitive part of my body. His touch sends a jolt through me. The shock of pleasure is so intense and unexpected that my thighs give out. I drop, sinking the rest of the way, gasping at the dull pain from the force of it. My thighs tremble with every sinfully delicious inch of him buried inside me.

The sensations he creates with his fingers override that momentary soreness, and I'm moving again.

I watch him, his eyes locked where we are joined, mesmerized by the sight of me, taking all of him again and again and again.

"Demons and saints, Violet." He lets his head fall back.

He sits up and clutches me against him. His mouth seeks mine, consuming me as I rock against him. My fingers dance over his back, feeling the lines of his muscles.

"More," I plead.

With a grunt, he twists us. I am on my back as he holds himself over me. I reach for him, but he captures my wrists and pins them above my head with one hand as the other slides over my breast, kneading my flesh. He pinches my nipple, pulling a moan from me, and I'm rewarded with a pleased rumble vibrating in his chest.

"You are breathtaking," Joon purrs. "You have no idea

how long I've wanted to be inside you—to feel you come undone around my cock." He moves slowly, savoring every languid stroke. Every caress is laced with love and tenderness.

"Joon," I moan his name, lifting my hips to meet his. The angle allows him to hit deeper, with a pleasure so intense I cry out.

He groans and releases my wrists, bracing himself with both arms. "You make it difficult to control myself when you say my name like that."

There is something about his wants and needs conflicting that makes me feel... powerful. It makes me want to break that last thread of his control.

"Then don't." I let my hands slide over his shoulders and down his chest and ribs to his back, sliding over the curve of his ass. I bring my lips to his ear. "Show me how much you've wanted this—fuck me."

He pulls back achingly slow. With the next thrust, I pull him toward me. He manages to hit a spot so deep it steals my breath, cutting my moan short. My entire body trembles.

Our joining changes from an expression of our feelings to something carnal and filled with an insatiable need, afraid we will lose what we don't take here and now.

He does it again and again, faster and harder. I lift my hips to meet his. With every forceful thrust, he claims me—body, heart, and soul.

We move together, hands roaming over each other, needing to memorize every inch of each other. I grip his shoulders, nails digging in. His mouth claims my breast, biting and sucking on my flesh as his hips pound relentlessly against my own.

The sounds of our passion fill the clearing. Tension builds, coiling into a tight spring, urging me closer to the precipice.

My eyes flutter closed, only to snap open when he grips my chin. I meet his gaze, dark and intense.

"Don't look away," he says. "I want to see how beautiful you are when you come for me."

My breath hitches with every forceful, claiming thrust. His cock throbs as he pounds into me again and again, relentlessly pushing me further toward mindless ecstasy.

We lose ourselves in the slide of our slick flesh, the way we move together as if we were made to take pleasure in each other.

Every caress of his hands, every kiss, and every gaze he lavishes on me makes me feel loved in a way I've never known and never thought I could have. I didn't think anything could match the way he used his hands on me. But this… this feeling is *so much more*.

The eye contact feels far more intimate than the physical act itself. Though I'm not sure if it's because this is my first time knowing a man this way or because we are no longer hiding from what we feel.

Joon's hips pound an unrelenting rhythm against mine.

"Joon…" His name transforms into a sharp moan as the building sensation uncoils with a snap.

My body tightens, and between one heartbeat and the next, I shatter around him. Wave after wave of ecstasy crashes over me. He continues moving, making every sensation more intense. I arch my back, gasping and moaning, but I never once look away. Joon holds me together.

His rhythm changes. Speeds up. Maybe it's the intimacy of our eye contact or that I am just sensitive from my orgasm, but I am acutely aware of the way his cock thickens inside me.

With a sound of passion, agony, desperation, and possessiveness all rolled into one, he finds his release, joining me on the tail of my own.

Our frantic movements slow as we come down from the height of pleasure. Even after it fades, we remain as we are, clinging to each other.

He kisses me lightly on the lips, then along my jaw and down my throat. Unlike before, when his kisses were filled with desire and need, now they are sweet and filled with affection.

Joon gathers me against him as he sits up, pulling me into his lap. He rests his forehead against the side of my neck. I reach up and comb my fingers through his hair.

I lean forward to kiss his temple.

He is strong. More powerful than anyone I know, yet he is vulnerable in my arms. Underneath his hard exterior, he is someone who wants the same kindness and compassion we all do.

My heart aches for him. How lonely he must have been all this time, and I'm struck with an overwhelming desire to protect him.

We both lost our parents, but I had people who cared for me. I was never expected to carry on as if nothing happened, nor did I have countless people depending on me.

Somehow, he has felt comfortable enough around me to let his walls down.

As we hold each other, he sighs, letting his mouth trail lazy caresses over my skin. Not with need but a longing to hold onto the moment. To stay where we are, in our private world, free to be who we choose.

I sense the subtle shift in him, and I wonder if it's the same thing nagging sensation rising in the back of my mind. Reminding me that I have always been destined to lose the ones I love.

And no matter how we fight to hold on, this cannot last.

CHAPTER THIRTY-ONE

JOON

I watch Violet's lesson from a distance. Half the time she was given has already passed. The entire thing is a pointless charade, yet she puts her entire heart and mind into it.

She is already sufficiently adept in poise and speech to get by in any situation that may arise. She will not need to know calligraphy, how to speak the old language, or the complicated dance of when to eat or drink at a table full of nobles of varying ranks.

I can easily think of far better ways for her to use this time. Ways that involve her hands, mouth, and body.

Iseul corrects Violet's pronunciation, then demonstrates how to do it properly, explaining the error in great detail, as she does.

Violet reaches down to pat the demon at her side. Iseul's sharp eye catches the movement and lectures her on the importance of focusing.

"These lessons are more painful to watch than when you suffered this torture," Imugi grumbles.

"That, I can agree on."

Iseul is enjoying her role. Perhaps a little too much. I am glad she was never in charge of my lessons. Only she would have been brave enough to be so unapologetically strict with me in a way no one else in all of Arum would dare.

As soon as Iseul's back is to her, Violet flicks a glance my way and gives the demon another pat on the head. She snaps back to attention, feigning innocence just before Iseul turns back around.

This time, Violet's movements are flawless in timing and execution. A small trill of pride fills me.

"If you continue to smile like that, I will have no choice but to have you checked for a head injury," Imugi mutters. "It's unsettling."

Iseul claps once and says something I cannot quite hear. Whatever it is makes Violet's face light up, only to fall in disappointment. They move to the far end and sit at a low-legged table, almost out of sight.

It is just as well. It is nearly time to meet with the council.

I step, nearly stumbling when the world tilts for half a heartbeat before righting itself again.

"What is it?" Imugi demands. They rise off my shoulder and hover before me. The demon's eyes glow with a flash of power, scanning me.

"It was nothing more than a slight misstep," I wave off their concern.

They grumble. "Perhaps you ought to siphon before the meeting."

I shake my head. "There is no need. I have more than enough power for a while yet."

Imugi remains where they are as I walk, only to be stopped when they say, "It's been weeks since you last sensed it—perhaps you need more than before to sense the true location for this final piece? It has been missing longer than the others. It will only continue to weaken the longer it remains separated."

My shoulders stiffen.

Violet is worn from the little amount of travel we've done searching for the final shard after the trial—both as an excuse to give her a respite from the near-daily tedium of lessons and a vain hope that it will call to me.

She pretends that all is well, trying to distract me with her flirtations, but she cannot hide the way her face is becoming gaunt or how the dark circles under her eyes have only deepened.

Even alternating between suppressing her episodes and my ceaseless need to draw on the dwindling power of the frost bloom has done nothing to reduce the toll it takes on her.

When I last siphoned four days ago, I felt the way her heart stuttered. The weakening beat.... I was never saving her, only slowing the inevitable. At most, I helped her retain control over her emotions by keeping her from feeling the effects until the episode subsided.

I am her curse, stealing the last of her life force, little by little, with every deadly kiss—every bit the monster they say I am.

Worse, because I whisper in her ear that I love her and that I am hers and hers alone, all the while dragging her closer into the cold, lifeless arms of the Otherworld.

I continue walking.

Any chance there is of saving her lies with breaking this demon damned curse.

Imugi catches up, gliding through the air beside me. "Each shard has been weaker and their calls shorter than the last—we knew these final ones would be the most difficult. It is thanks to Violet that you found the last two in a shorter span of time than with any of your other wives." They pause before grudgingly adding, "I suppose she deserves a little credit."

I peer at them from the corner of my eye. "If I didn't know better, I would think you almost approve of her."

They snort two white plumes of smoke from their nostrils. "I most certainly do not—she smiles too much. No one that unfortunate should be so disgustingly cheerful all the time." They clear their throat. "But I will admit that she is useful."

Our conversation drops as we pass through the gate to the Central Court. There is a bustle of activity as clusters of servants wait along the path between the Formal Hall and the Temple Tower.

I catch the hiss of whispers they fail to hide as they all part to let me pass.

"It's him."

"He's too handsome to be as cruel as they say."

"Did you see that scar?"

The incessant gossip is cut off when I enter the Temple Tower. I remain in the hall outside the doors of the main room, waiting for my opportunity.

"It is time to begin. If you would, please take your seats," a woman's voice I do not recognize calls out.

Two seconds go by.

Voices hurry to finish what they are saying.

Five seconds.

Conversations draw to a close.

Seven seconds.

The padding sounds of leather-soled shoes fade.

After ten seconds, I slide the door open and stroll in. Imugi remains behind, waiting in the hall.

My footsteps are soundless on the carpet that runs

through the middle of the room to the single empty seat around the table.

The king sits silently at the far end, and on the long edges of the table, the officials are in the process of taking their seats, three to each side.

Everyone, including my uncle, wears the official garb of the heads of state. The robes are made from a heavy material that has the appearance and shimmer of thick morning frost. It fits loosely, wrapping around the front of the chest, and is secured by a wide ribbon belt around the waist, knotted at the left hip, and bearing the symbol of their status and position on one of the dangling ends.

A sword crossed with an arrow for Kwan, the Minister of Hunts, and a balance scale for Ailan, the new Minister of Justice. Her face is unfamiliar to me, having only been recently selected as the replacement for Ilseong.

These two are positioned to the right and left of the interim king.

The next two are Molan, the Minister of Ceremony, and Jinshi, the Minister of History and Knowledge. The former, with the emblem of a dragon twisted in a sideways eight, eating its tail, and a quill resting over an open book, for the latter.

To the left of the empty seat is Seojun, Minister of Commonwealth, bearing the emblem of a skeleton key.

And to the right is Yeona, Minister of Shields, with the emblem of a shield. She is slight and somewhat timid in her demeanor, but rather than physical strength, her position requires powerful magical ability to continually reinforce the shields throughout and around the palace. She is a few years my junior, but that doesn't keep her from taking her job seriously, perhaps more than anyone else on the council.

The seventh position is the head of them all, a role that can only be filled by the standing monarch, marked by the symbol of a crown.

My uncle watches me without drawing attention to my approach.

The six officials turn, noticing me as I approach the table. One by one, they drop into their chairs with matching expressions of shock plastered over their faces. Only the Minister of Ceremony remains standing. She holds herself tall, shoulders back, chin lifted in a haughty air.

"What is the meaning of this interruption?" Minister Molan demands. "This is highly irregular. You cannot barge in here without notice and disrupt official business."

I pull my chair out, but instead of sitting, I lean forward on my fingertips and let my head list to one side. "Can't I?"

She blinks as if she is only starting to realize who she is talking to.

"I am the *Crown Prince*, am I not?" I say to help her along.

"Y-yes, Your Highness." She clutches her hands in front of her and bows at the waist.

"However, I did give notice... before the trial."

"Ah, yes," my uncle speaks up. "His Highness did inform me upon my request. It must have slipped my mind with everything that has happened in the weeks since."

Molan's lip quivers until she pinches her mouth into a tight line. She gives a sharp nod to the table as she finally sits. "Very well. As long as His Majesty is aware, then this meeting may now proceed."

I straighten to my full height and keep my voice clear and even as I project, so no one can later claim that they did not hear or understand. "I came here today to inform you of my intentions." I pin each of them in place with my stare. "My wife has nothing to hide, and I will not abide baseless rumors or actions against her. However, as a show of good faith, I will introduce her to the council and higher nobility in one month's time—months earlier than is customary."

My uncle gives me a barely perceptible nod of approval from across the table. The council members turn toward each other, looking for guidance in each other, and finding little.

Not one heard the hollowness of my words. I doubt either of us will still be around to see it through. With any luck, we will have broken the curse. Otherwise, Violet will likely be too weak to get out of bed. If she is even still alive.

Without her, there is no hope of breaking the curse, and either it or the broken bargain will kill me.

Yeona surprises me by being the first to react. She stands, though it adds little to her height.

"We appreciate the burden she has accepted by sacrificing her time on our behalf. We thank you both for this gesture after the transgressions Lady Hawthorn has suffered." She finishes with a deep bow at the waist.

The added barb at the end hits the intended mark. Molan's mouth twists before she can correct it.

Yeona's stature was a source of grief when she first took up her position after her father died nearly four years ago. She was one of the few who appeared distressed when the former Minister of Justice used Violet as his pawn.

The others stand, offering halfhearted murmurs of agreement and bows.

Outside, a powerful gust rattles against the windows as if objecting to the show made purely out of customary obligation.

I turn my back on them and grip the back of the chair until my knuckles turn white, as a force from deep within strains against my magic.

It only lasts a second. Then, without another word, I rise and take my leave.

This is far from over.

By the time I reach the hall, the wind outside has become a steady howl. Servants rush in from outside, seeking shelter from the sudden, brutal storm.

I shove my way through the clot of panicked bodies as the force within continues to push and strain against its bonds.

A patch of scales rolls over the back of my hand before disappearing. I burst through the doors and into the squall.

"Get Violet," I say through clenched teeth. "Bring her to me, now."

Imugi is off before I finish speaking.

There was always a warning in the pasty—always when my power got too low. It came on gradually. Days or weeks in advance. A little over a day at worst.

The dragon would stir, slowly stretching out as it awakened, gathering its strength once more.

This time, there was no sign of the impending uprising. I have an hour—two, if I am lucky—to quell this storm. There is no other choice. I must siphon before it is too late.

The whole of the Central Court is void of life. No one to question why I am out here or why I run as if a harmony of demons is on my tail.

Agony pierces my scarred eye. Sharp and hot, a needle heated to the point of glowing. Partially blinded by pain, I collide with the entrance to my apartments.,

"Get out!" I shout. "Now!"

They rush past me and into the storm, preferring to brave it over my wrath.

I stumble the rest of the way to my room, using the wall as a guide and support. The prickle of shimmering scales breaks out from my neck and up one side of my face before sinking below my skin.

Ringing fills my ears, muffling the sounds of the world around me until they are distant and undiscernible.

The dragon thrashes and fights to break free, stretching the limits of my power, fraying along the edges. It feels as though the dragon is dragging razor-sharp talons along my insides.

Staggering inside, I collapse onto my hands and knees. I barely feel the pain as my knees crack against the floor.

Sweat dampens my brow. I fumble for the smallest thread of magic to open the passage to the mirror that won't aid the dragon's escape and press my palm to the wooden slats.

With every shard found, the Winter Dragon has grown stronger.

Heavy footsteps rush to my side.

A man kneels, his hands tug on me, urging me to my feet.

Mingi.

He's speaking, but I can't focus on his words.

What is he saying?

The wild beast threatens to overpower me, perhaps for good.

Another voice—this one lighter, more soothing, calling my name.

My left arm seizes. Bones crack. Break. Lengthen then reform. I stare at where my hand used to be. In its place is a claw, covered in shimmering scales made of ice and frost, ending in long, deadly points.

I was wrong. It is already too late to stop this.

That gentle voice calls again.

Violet.

Hide—I must hide from her—Can't let her see. I shove Mingi away and trudge down the first steps. "Stop her," I rasp over my shoulder. Even my voice is no longer mine. "Do not let—"

But it's too late.

Too late.

I am always too late.

Burning agony pierces my eye as the Winter Dragon peers out. It pins her in place.

I only have a heartbeat to see the fear and hurt on her face before I am consumed from the inside out. The deafening roar of the dragon fills my head as it rips free of my hold.

Everything goes black, and I fall.

CHAPTER THIRTY-TWO

VIOLET

"You did well today," Iseul says. Today, she has her hair pulled back into an intricate knot, held in place with a silver comb.

I try to smile, but it feels more like a grimace. She gives me far too much credit. "I butchered every word."

My response elicits a laugh from her as she stacks the books and notebooks, waving me off when I try to help.

"The old language is not easy to master if you were not born hearing it. Even most fae prefer the common tongue outside of ceremony and tradition." She places a hand on my forearm. "You haven't been practicing for long—trust me, you're doing great."

"Is it really necessary for me to know this?"

"Perhaps, not the most necessary thing, but it will only help you. Once you have the basics down, I will teach you how to say a few useful key phrases, as well as ones to listen for." Iseul leans forward. A stray strand of hair comes loose, dangling in front of her face. "This might be an act, but this way, if anyone tries to insult you to your face and lie about it, you can properly put them in their place."

I've never had much talent for languages, but Iseul has a good point. "I appreciate it."

"I don't like to see people bullied just because someone thinks they are better than them. Status, wealth, and popularity don't determine someone's worth," Iseul says quietly, then quickly shakes it off.

There is pain beneath her words, and I wonder what happened in her past that has made this so personal to her. My heart swells. I want to find whoever hurt her and teach them a lesson.

The implied violence of that thought surprises me.

Once more, I try to help her tidy up the materials from our lesson, which earns me an admonishing tap on the hand.

"Go." Iseul points down the path toward the library. "I can take care of this on my own. Besides, I know you want to do your own studies."

Trying to argue with her would be pointless. I pat the slumbering demon at my side as I stand. Bear stirs, blinking their large, round eyes. Sleep vanishes from their expression instantly, and they jump to their feet and hurry to follow.

I wave to Iseul as I step out from the cover of the pavilion beside the water's edge.

"Try not to strain your eyes too much," she calls after me.

It feels good to stretch my muscles. I'm not used to studying with such rigid posture.

The old language is a beautiful mix of soft and crisp sounds that take effort to discern at first. What adds an extra challenge is the different sentence structure from what I'm used to. Perhaps if I focus on mastering that first, the rest will be easier to learn.

Bear hides under the edge of my skirt, trotting along with

me—as if no one will notice the small, moving bulge at my side. Though I suppose it's good enough since no one has asked about it.

The library is quiet as usual. Scholars will come and go throughout the day, getting what they need and returning it later. No one speaks to or approaches anyone else. It seems the proper library etiquette of allowing others their peace and privacy is the same among the fae as it is in the mortal lands.

All who choose to study here do so in one of the designated spaces. Small open rooms without doors with a single table and a cushion between it and the windowed back wall.

I search the shelves for anything that might have more information about Joon's family. Trailing my fingers along the spines, I scan the titles carefully, but I have already gone through them all. Several times over.

That torn-out page in Joon's family records still bothers me. Historical texts are sacred. Written by saint touched scribes who vow to record only verified truths without biases. It's forbidden to change or destroy the records, regardless of how unflattering some might look. Whether royal, noble, or peasant, rank holds no sway over the scribes.

I move on to another section, picking a book at random, and flip through the pages. Then a few more. These appear to be stories written about nobles and royalty, with language typically used in fiction.

The book at the end is leaning against the others, propping them up. Its gilded lettering along the spine is worn and flaking, making it impossible to read the title. I read the first page. It's a story about a woman courted by a prince she did not love.

I grimace. It sounds like a tragedy. There is enough sorrow in this world without reading about it for enjoyment.

I reshelve the book, but my hand lingers on it as the author's words linger. In a strange way, it calls to my heart. They painted such a vivid picture, imbued with nearly tangible emotions in only a single page, that I am reluctant to walk away.

Giving in to the strange impulse, I take the book to an empty study area. Within a few sentences, the story has me enthralled.

But she had already fallen in love with the prince's brother, the king. Not wanting to cause a rift between the two brothers, she rejected them both.

Convinced she was his True Mate, the king secretly sought her out. Their romance bloomed through their clandestine trysts until she became pregnant. By then, they knew neither of them could, nor wanted to, live without the other, so they married.

Heartbroken, the prince left for distant lands.

Months later, the queen gave birth to a young boy. Two years later, they welcomed another son whom they named.

They lived happily for many years, until the day a Shadouk infiltrated the castle.

I remember reading about the Shadouk in a book of lore. A demon cursed creature that devours the soul of a living person in exchange for a dark, twisted power that was never meant to exist. Some say it is purely the stuff of myths, others say it is the abomination created by bonding oneself to a demon.

"My Lady, you must come with me. There is no time."

My head jerks up as I'm startled from my reading by Imugi's sharp hiss. "What—"

"There is no time. You must come now," they repeat. Imugi abruptly turns and glides away, expecting me to follow.

Joon—something's wrong.

I scramble to my feet and race to follow. Bear quickly catches up, taking their usual place. Rather than taking the inner passages that meander past several other buildings, Imugi passes through the doors to the outside for a straight path.

Flecks of ice pelt down as the wind tugs my hair and clothes, trying to steal the breath from my lungs. I shield my face with my forearm as I run.

The storm had swallowed the beautiful day in the short time I was in the library. Wailing gusts push against me as if trying to keep me from reaching Joon.

It's a short distance, but I am gasping from the exertion by the time I reach the main entry.

Imugi pauses, watching me. Probably to see if I will follow or faint.

I nod and motion to keep going, following the sound of Joon's and Mingi's muffled voices.

"Joon," I call to him. I want him to know I'm here. "Joon!"

There's another voice, one I don't recognize. Too deep. Too raw. "Stop her! She can't—"

I pass through the open door and stop in my tracks.

Joon and Mingi are the only ones in the room.

Shimmering scales break out across Joon's skin and disappear—the same as the iridescent sheen that flickers over patches of his skin every time he's siphoned.

Joon stops partway down the steps leading to the underground cavern, holding the mirror. Our eyes meet.

Mingi races over, tugging on my arm, but I refuse to be moved.

Because one of the eyes staring at me does not belong to him—it is not the deep, endless blue that I could drown in—but the summer blue of the Winter Dragon's eyes.

My gaze drifts down to the arm he clutches with his other hand, but that is not his either.

Betrayal tightens my throat.

The Winter Dragon isn't some beast he keeps locked up—

Before I can think of anything to say or do, Joon's body shudders, and then he's gone. Disappearing into the depths below the castle.

Yanking free from Mingi's grasp, I spin on my heel and race for my room. I catch myself in the open doorway and stare at everything that is not mine.

He lied.

He's been lying to me this entire time.

He talked about the dragon as if it were something separate from him, something he controls—rather than a part of him.

He attacked people, freezing them—my parents.

He did this to them.

The betrayal threatens to suffocate me if I stay.

I grab my cloak and run, half-blinded by the bitter tears that sting my eyes.

Imugi sails through the air and hovers before my face, blocking me before I can step outside.

"Get out of my way," I grind out. My teeth are clenched so hard, my jaw aches.

"Where are you going?"

Joon once said the dragon killed his wives, not him.

Another lie, I think bitterly. How gruesome were their deaths? I need to see the truth of their fates for myself.

My heart seizes. Did Joon kill them because they learned his secret too, or had they simply outgrown their usefulness?

"Where is the royal crypt?" I demand, ignoring their question.

"In the chamber below the Temple Tower. Why?" Iseul asks from behind.

I don't know how she found me, but I'm thankful for her timing.

"You cannot go there!" Imugi hisses.

Bear growls, bunching their body in preparation to pounce to my defense.

I duck under the hovering demon and slip outside. The wind has died down some, but flecks of ice still whirl through the air. I barely feel the sting against my face, determined not to let anyone or anything stop me from getting to the crypt.

A shadow passes overhead, drawing my eye to the large shape.

Through the haze of white, the Winter Dragon weaves through the sky. With a roar, it does a somersault and circles back, coming straight for me.

The part of me that wants to live screams for me to run, but another part knows I am too slow—too far from any shelter—to get away. And my feet remain planted where they are.

I squeeze my eyes shut and brace for whatever is to come and hope that my end is quick. Several seconds pass, and nothing happens. I swallow my fear and force my eyes open.

The Winter Dragon hangs, suspended high in the air, gazing back at me in much the same way that Imugi does. The beast's eyes blink slowly.

Two icy antlers that curve back, sprout from the snowy mane that travels down the length of his—*Joon's* body—long body. His scales glitter like freshly fallen snow in the moonlight. His mane and whiskers move gently as if suspended in water.

He is stunning.

We are held captives in this moment that stretches on as we gaze at each other, neither able to look away.

A bell gongs in the distance. Shouts break through the storm in the spaces between the ringing. Voices grow in volume. The spell over us shatters.

Joon turns toward the sound of guards running toward us and roars. He flies for them, sending a blast of blue flame overhead as he soars past and into the northern sky.

No, not flame... *ice*.

It shatters in the air and rains down over the palace soldiers, who shout out in alarm. Mingi and Iseul call my name as I pass the gate to the Central Court.

By the time I reach the Temple Tower, my legs are tired and I'm out of breath, but I keep going.

A lone man, dressed in ceremonial robes, moves slowly through the hall, stopping to light each sconce.

"Where is the royal crypt?" I shout.

He flinches at my volume and gapes as I run at him. I skid to a halt. Recognition lights his eyes, or perhaps he sees I'm about to ask again and wants to keep me from shouting again. Because he finally points down the hall at his back. "Th-that way, My Lady."

I dip my chin in a barely acceptable bow of thanks and continue on my way. Turning the corner at the end of the hall, I hurry down the short passage leading to a set of stairs that lead up as well as down.

The darkness at the bottom is so oppressive, it forces me

to slow lest I collide with something or fall down unseen stairs.

The landing emerges at one end of yet another corridor, with a single doorway halfway down. The only source of light is the sconce across the hall from the double doors.

I brace a palm against the damp stone wall until I'm close enough to see the faint outline of the brick paving.

The faint sounds of a commotion reverberate from the stairwell. Mingi and Iseul are not far behind.

Standing before the doors, gripping the handles, I hesitate. My entire body is shaking from nerves, and my stomach has tied itself into so many knots I think I might be sick.

I don't think I want to do this.

But I have to—I need to know.

With a deep breath, I throw the doors wide before I can change my mind. The sight that greets me is like nothing I could have imagined.

Stone pedestals as high as my waist are laid out in orderly columns and rows. Resting upon nearly half of them are glass mausoleums with the bodies of kings and queens of the past.

A plaque is carved in the stone at the foot of each one, with the name of the monarch, their day of birth, the years they ruled, and the day they died.

I walk down the central aisle. When I near the first, I realize the caskets are not glass but enchanted ice.

Not daring to stop, I make my way toward the archway at the far end of the crypt. What I'm looking for waits for me behind a split curtain that hangs over the threshold, blocking the view on the other side. At first, it appears black, but as I slip through, I notice the shimmer of blue. The silken material cascades down my back and reveals the shrine within.

A shudder rolls through my body that leaves me trembling from a cold that has nothing to do with the cold, damp air.

Seven stone pedestals are lined up along the length of the room with space for more. The first six hold a standing woman encased in ice, making them appear as if they are statues from a distance. The last is empty.

I make my way toward the end. Up close, the details of the women come into sharper focus. Their eyes are closed, with almost peaceful expressions. But their features are gaunt as if their life had been sucked out of them. Every one of them has rounded human ears. Each stone base features a plaque that displays the name, age, and hometown of each woman.

Kiara Price, 22. Cyrindor
Rhiannon Gravelight, 27. Direvale

My legs grow weaker as I read each one.

Leila Threnody, 19. Stone cliff
Florence Ashwood, 28. Elmcrest
Nisha Winslow, 24. Avalan
Cordelia Swann, 21. Holiston

I slow, then stop when I realize the seventh plaque is already engraved. A violent wave of nausea crashes into me, making the world tilt.

My legs give out. I crash to the ground, catching myself with my hands.

Violet Hawthorn, 23. Firnhallow.

He has already begun preparing for my death. Our bargain meant nothing. The evidence before me staring me in the face is a glaring truth I cannot deny, no matter how much I wish I could.

Did he ever intend to keep me alive long enough to break the curse, let alone even attempt to heal me after?

He intentionally deceived me from the beginning. It's impossible to know how much of what he said was a lie or if his tongue is even capable of speaking the truth at all.

If I'd known any of this, I would never have allowed myself to get close to him—I would have guarded my heart.

Which is exactly why he hid the truth.

I don't want to believe it. It's at odds with the man I know—the man I *thought* I knew.

Joon lied about everything. Every word out of his mouth was meant to manipulate me into giving him whatever he wanted.

Pain twists my heart, signaling the start of an episode, but Joon's not around to stop it this time.

I shake my head. It doesn't matter. For years, I relied on my own techniques to stop my episodes. I can do it again.

Concentrating, I focus on breathing slowly, willing my heart to calm. As the onset of an impending episode ebbs, the echo of footsteps nears.

"Violet," Mingi says gently.

I look over my shoulder to find him in the archway, holding the curtain aside, with Imugi hovering over his shoulder. Iseul remains just beyond the door in the room of past kings and queens. Her face is deathly pale even in the dim light as she glances around.

All three adopt an expressionless mask as they watch me, but their presence feels like an admonishment and judgment.

How do they expect me to feel? What do they expect me to think?

I stand through pure strength of will alone and storm over

to Mingi. "Did you know he was lying and manipulating me this whole time?"

Mingi opens his mouth to deliver his predictable denial, but I cut him off. "He is as cruel as everyone says." I thrust a finger toward the frozen women at my back. "Look at them! They are nothing more than trophies—he's even prepared a place for me."

Mingi sighs—*actually sighs*—as if I'm overreacting to something trivial.

"They are not—" he begins.

But I'm not listening. I shove past Mingi, bumping him with my shoulder. Imugi glides effortlessly out of the way to avoid me.

I can't stand to hear more lies. Not from another person I've foolishly come to trust.

Why wouldn't they defend him? They are his loyal subjects. They've told me as much and proved as much with their actions and their words as they went along with Joon's deception.

As I pass Iseul, I let her see the hurt on my face. An expression that says, *I trusted you. I thought we were friends.*

CHAPTER THIRTY-THREE

VIOLET

I STRIDE THROUGH THE HALLS WITH PURPOSE, THOUGH I DON'T yet know where I am going or what I will do, only that I want to get away from all the death and the deceit.

Joon never intended to keep his end of the bargain, which means that it was never binding. Except… I never could speak about it. Or it could mean the only bargain we had was that we couldn't tell others about the verbal agreement we made.

I shake my head. I don't know how to tell what's real or not. There are too many possibilities.

It's possible I misunderstood by assuming things. Yet it's equally as likely that Joon used clever wording to make sure I did.

I try to remember the exact phrasing, but I can't. There is only a vague notion of the whole thing.

Too many emotions are clouding my thoughts, making it hard to think straight.

If I am to die no matter what, then what was the point of any of this? Our bargain, searching, researching….

He used my optimistic nature against me to manipulate

me into falling for him. He said it himself, I needed to be willing.

And it's far easier to kiss someone you love than someone you loathe.

Outside, the bitter air stings my face. The magical storm weakens. Under the dying ghost of wind, I can feel the familiar sensation of Joon's power. The way it traced through my veins when he siphoned and healed me.

Death will come for me whether I return to Firnhallow or remain here, so I might as well be in the home I've known my entire life, surrounded by the few people who genuinely love me. Even if the two most important people are doomed to be forever encased in enchanted ice.

With the Temple Tower behind me, my mind is made up. I will leave this place and never look back. He can suffer as he would have let me suffer. I won't care about his pain—I won't let myself.

Bear scurries out from a bush to their usual place under my skirts. Their presence is a mild comfort. At least there is someone who isn't using me.

Halfway to the gate leading to the Southern Court, I stop and change direction, remembering that I've moved to the Western Court.

Back in my apartments, I head straight for the wardrobe. Nothing of mine from before I arrived at the palace remains. In fact, nothing in this room belongs to me. But I can't very well travel with nothing other than the clothes on my back.

I sift through the various items, selecting the warmest ones and tossing them into a heap on the bed. Annoyingly, it dawns on me that I will have to do more than pack a bag before I can leave. There's transport, money…

Mingi and Iseul are not far behind. His heavy footsteps stop partway inside the room.

"I'm leaving. Don't try to stop me," I say.

"Despite what it looks like, the prince and the dragon are not the same," he lectures, in a tone that says he thinks I'm being childish.

My hands still. I glance at him as I cross over to the bed and begin folding. Whatever he sees in my face is enough to keep him from saying more.

Iseul steps forward and touches Mingi's arm. "Let me talk to her."

He clenches his jaw. He doesn't argue, but he doesn't leave either. Instead, he waits by the door and continues glaring.

"He cannot entomb them as we would those who have passed because it is not a true death," Iseul begins softly. She pauses to let it sink in.

My head snaps up. "He lied to me about the dragon." I snap. "He's the reason I've been alone for years—he took my family from me." I hate that my voice cracks. Tears flood my eyes and spill down my cheeks. I can't fight them, so I don't even try.

"Joon and the dragon are not the same," Iseul repeats her brother's words as she inches closer. "The curse affects them both, so neither of them is in control. It turned the dragon into little more than a wild animal searching for the shards on instinct because it knows they will both die without them."

I curl my fingers into the top I'm folding, and close my eyes, breathing deep.

My emotions are a whirling mess. I am furious and hurt. I want to hate Joon for this—I should hate him, but I don't know how to stop the ache and longing in my heart.

"No human would have ever been frozen if they had not attacked. The more the humans attacked the Winter Dragon, the more people it would freeze. It was a vicious cycle." Iseul is beside me now. She reaches her hands out to take one of mine and eases my grip open. "It was defending itself. The dragon never wanted to harm anyone. It wanted the shards."

Without evidence to the contrary, we believed Joon sent it to attack us, and so we attacked in what we thought was self-defense.

Try as I might, I cannot argue with what she says. But I've seen for myself how the storms are a side effect of the curse, coming on when it weakens Joon's hold on his power. I've looked the dragon in the eye twice, close enough for it to encase me in ice, and twice I have walked away unscathed.

Bear perches on the bed, looking between the three of us. They tilt their head and make an uncertain chirping sound.

Even though my parents are among the many who fell victim to the dragon, they were also among those who attacked. Fear causes people to react before they fully understand. The fault lies only with the curse itself and the one who cast it.

"He said he would fix things," I say quietly. It's an oversimplification of our bargain because, even now, I can't talk about it, which only frustrates me further. "He planned for my death all along—" I break off, choking down a sob.

"Oh, Violet…" Iseul hugs me from the side. "I know it looks bad, but believe me when I say he never wanted any of this to happen."

My body goes rigid in her arms. "Why do you continue to defend him?"

"He saved Iseul's life," Mingi bites out, marching over. "When everyone said she wasn't worth the trouble—that we were worthless, that our lives meant nothing simply because we are orphans—he refused to listen."

Iseul holds up a hand in a calming gesture to her brother. He heaves a sigh but relents.

"Because of that, we pledged ourselves to his service.

However, we wouldn't have if he were truly cruel." She uses my earlier words against me, and though she says them in a gently teasing way, the barb still makes me wince.

I try to hold on to my hurt and remain steadfast, but they chip away at my defenses, weakening my resolve. But their fealty claws at the dregs of doubt in my heart, past the pain and betrayal.

Iseul and Mingi are loyal to him for a reason, a voice in the back of my mind whispers.

"I truly believe it's different with you. *He* is different with you. Whether you believe it or not, he cares for you," Iseul adds. "He trusts you."

And I have trusted him this whole time, haven't I? Not only has Joon protected me, he's comforted me when I needed it, even though that was never part of the bargain.

Which is it, Violet? Is the bargain real, or has everything Joon has done been of his own volition?

Either way, he was the one to offer me protection when I only asked to live.

My head pounds from the back and forth.

I don't need anyone to tell me who Joon is. The more time I spent with him, the more I realized how few people have bothered to know him.

"The people have always seen Joon as a monster. There has never been a time when his people cared for him or respected him, but he has never wanted this for them. Our Joon does not have long, and he is doing everything he can to break the curse."

Monster.

Guilt blooms in my belly, rising and twisting my insides into knots. I said I love him, yet I am no better than anyone else if I am so quick to believe the worst.

The two siblings and Bear wait in silence for what I will say or do next.

Indecision wars within me, freezing my tongue and rooting my feet where I stand. I am torn between my feelings and his betrayal. Between wanting to run and wanting to stay.

"The dragon was last seen to the north, weaving erratically," Imugi's voice cuts through the tension. "The storm is following him toward the Maldan Ice Wall. Something is wrong."

My heart lurches.

Worry squeezes my chest. Despite everything, I don't want to leave without knowing if Joon's all right.

I deserve to hear the truth from his lips as he looks me in the eye.

More than that, I don't *want* to leave him.

Why? I am alone because of him.

But he has been alone from the beginning.

"I'm going," I say firmly. The tightness in my chest eases.

Mingi scowls as if he wishes he could kill me with just a look, then he spins on his heel and stalks out.

I turn toward the wardrobe, this time with specific items in mind, and add them to the pile on the bed. I don't bother going behind the changing curtain or into the other room.

Iseul's eyes go wide when she sees me stripping. She rushes over to the door and closes it before rushing back to my side.

"Violet…" she pleads. She doesn't bother trying to help me. Her silent protest.

I intentionally made it unclear so neither of them understood what I meant. But it still takes me until I am finished changing to build up the courage and find the words.

I pick up the remainder of the clothes I gathered and hand them to her.

Hesitantly, Iseul takes them, uncertain of my intentions.

It turns out, changing your mind once you've made a decision out of anger is every bit as hard as admitting that you're wrong.

Caring about him—wanting to make sure he is all right and wanting to confront him about it all doesn't erase the betrayal or anger I feel. It does, however, add layers of complication.

"I am going to get him. Will you come with me?"

Iseul brightens and grasps the bundle, eyes shining. "Thank you."

We ride, following Mingi's trail, racing the wind that threatens to cover it first. Bear sits at my back, under my cloak, clutching the belt I hooked onto the saddle specifically for them. The terrain is treacherous in places and will only get worse as we approach the storm.

Within a half hour, we spot Mingi in the distance and catch up to him within another few minutes, flanking him.

He glances at us in turn, face passive, then rides faster without a word. We match his pace easily.

It's another hour before the Winter Dragon is visible through the wild flurries. The long, pale body twists and turns in the air, releasing roars of anger and frustration.

All three horses stop on their own, not wanting to get nearer. I dismount and carry Bear over to Iseul.

"Hold them for me?"

"What are you going to do?" she calls over the wind, but I'm already moving toward the storm.

"Stay back!" Mingi shouts at the same time. "You'll—" he

cuts himself off. The unspoken warning hangs in the air, loud and clear. *"You'll end up like the others."*

I hold up a hand. "It's all right."

I have no idea how true that is. I don't even have a plan beyond following my gut about my earlier revelation.

Flecks of ice pelt my body as the swirling tempest doubles in strength within the sphere surrounding the Winter Dragon. My cloak whips, snapping with the violent gusts.

Using my arm to help shield my face, I step into the heart of the storm.

"Joon!" I call at the top of my lungs. The sound is snatched from my throat before it passes my lips. I lower my arm and try again. "Joon! You have to stop!"

The dragon twists back on itself. A single bright blue eye narrows in on me. There is a moment, no more than a fraction of a second, where it pauses.

With a roar that rattles the ground beneath my feet, it spirals higher toward the clouds in tighter and tighter circles before diving. The dragon swoops, leveling out and sending waves of snow cascading to either side as it barrels down on me.

The massive mouth opens as if preparing to send out a blast of freezing flames. But I stand my ground, willing Joon to see me from within.

Deafening silence fills my ears as everything ceases entirely. I peel open my eyes, unsure when I closed them.

Several yards ahead, the dragon hovers about as high as the top of a forest canopy, gazing at me as it had back at the palace. It's even more massive up close than I realized.

My body trembles. I tell myself it's from the cold as I walk forward, one slow step after another, getting as close as I dare.

"It's all right." I am amazed when my voice comes out calm

and gentle. Holding out a hand, I continue speaking, "You can stop now."

The dragon descends as gracefully as a feather and lands. I close the remaining distance, still murmuring assurances until I'm able to rest my palm on the massive muzzle.

The scales are unexpectedly warm. *Just as he is now.*

So different from the night we met…

I stroke the top of the long snout, stunned into silence at the beauty of the dragon—the scales shimmer like frost over deep blue ice. Its white mane is like a pile of down surrounding the two antlers that sprout from the top of the head, jutting backward.

The electric-blue eyes gaze at me, then grow heavy and close, but I keep contact as I move. The dragon releases a deep sigh, and with it, a light that emanates from within so bright I'm forced to turn my face away.

When it fades, the dragon is gone, and in its place, Joon curled within the imprint left behind in the snow.

Mingi races forward and kneels before the prince. He throws a hooded cloak over him and helps him to his feet.

Joon mutters his quiet thanks as he straightens his clothes, keeping his eyes downcast, refusing to meet my eye.

I move back out of the way. Seeing him like this makes it hard to hold onto my anger.

A myriad of emotions shuffle over his features when he finally looks for me.

Mingi is saying something to Joon, too low for me to hear from where I stop. He cuts off abruptly when he realizes the prince is not listening.

Joon rises and walks toward me as if drawn by some unseen force, unable. His uneven gait shows just how weakened he is.

I pull in a breath and hold it. After such an immense use of power, Joon needs to siphon, and even with my battered and bruised heart, I know I will do it if he asks.

He stops just before reaching me, then calls over his shoulder, "I want a moment alone with Violet."

"This is not the time nor the place," Mingi protests.

Joon shoots him a look, making it clear that it wasn't a request.

Neither of us speaks until Mingi rejoins Iseul back at the horses.

"Violet..."

"You lied to me," I say harsher than intended.

Joon averts his gaze. "I never lied to you."

"Not outright, no, but you deliberately misled me." As soon as the words are out, I see what I've missed all along. Joon had every reason to mistrust me when we met.

No one in their right mind would tell a thief their secrets.

"You have every right to be angry, but how could I tell you after seeing your family? It seemed too cruel." Joon takes a step closer and holds his hands out to the side, beseechingly.

With those words, my anger melts away.

He wanted to spare me that pain. *That* is why he promised to free everyone from the dragon's cursed ice after we already agreed to the terms—not as an incentive or blackmail, but to atone in the only way he was able to *because* he couldn't bear telling me everything.

I think part of me realized the truth when he killed Minister Ilseong, and every time I saw the flashing shimmer of scales race over his skin when he siphoned.

Joon sags, taking a half-stumbled step before catching himself with a wince. He is worn out and in pain. It's strange seeing him so vulnerable.

My feet carry me to him without thought. When I reach for him to offer him support, he wraps me in his arms, body curling around mine in a hug, pleading for a type of compassion that has been lacking in his life for too long.

Unable to deny him, I return the embrace. "You should have told me."

"I wanted to." His voice is small.

"You still deceived me," I say halfheartedly.

Every inch of him radiates defeat, unbefitting of the man I know and love. Joon pulls away, releasing me. "I tried to tell you I was a monster."

So much hurt is an awful burden for one heart to carry.

Were our situations reversed, would I have been able to tell him, or would the fear of losing him have been enough to hold my tongue?

"You are not a monster, Joon."

"What does the truth matter when the world chooses to believe the lie?"

"No matter how many believe it, it does not change the truth. I have seen the truth. I know who you are, and I love you. Faults and all, just as you love me for mine."

His gaze snaps to mine, lips parting.

Whatever else needs to be said can wait. I take his hand and pull him with me toward the horses. Iseul holds Bear against her, wrapped in the edge of her cloak, while Mingi waits, holding the reins of the horse Joon and I will share.

We mount and begin the trek back to the palace. The two siblings ride ahead, giving us privacy to talk further.

Joon's arms circle my waist, clutching me as if he's afraid I will disappear if he lets go, and he rests his head on my shoulder.

We are silent for so long that, for a moment, I wonder if he's fallen asleep.

He turns his face, bringing his mouth closer to my ear. His

breath is warm against my neck when he says, "Why do you forgive me so easily?"

"None of this is easy, Joon. I thought the worst of you. I almost left." It isn't everything, but it's enough. "I forgive you because I think I would have done the same. Because I want to forgive you. Because I have made mistakes, too. Because I love you, and I can't just... stop. I don't want to waste what time I have left in this world holding onto anger instead of you."

Joon's arms tighten briefly. "I do not deserve you, or your heart," he whispers, then presses a kiss to the side of my neck.

He is wrong. He deserves to be surrounded by love.

My throat tightens as emotions threaten to choke me. "Everyone deserves to be loved—even cursed princes."

CHAPTER THIRTY-FOUR

VIOLET

It's evening when we return. We are fortunate that it's late enough in the season that the sun is still up.

Joon dismisses Mingi and Iseul as soon as we reenter the Western Court, leaving me to escort him to his room. If I am too weary to speak more than a few words at a time, then it is a miracle Joon can hold himself upright at all.

I wait for him to enter, watching to make sure he can make it the rest of the way on his own. "Get some rest."

He catches my wrist before I can leave. "Will you stay for a while?"

I'm not confident I'll be able to get back up once I am off my feet, and I need to wash up before I no longer have enough energy. When I asked the same of him, he stayed with me without hesitation.

"Let me wash up first." I turn toward the door.

"Use mine," he counters with a yawn. "I want you close."

"All right." I sigh. It makes more sense than going to my own apartments for the same purpose.

Joon refuses to budge until I disappear into the bathing

room. I emerge a short time later, wearing one of his silk robes that puddles around my feet, to find him collapsed on the bed, still fully dressed.

I trudge over and tug on his arm in a pathetic attempt to get him up. "You should change."

"I will. I need to gather my strength first." Joon sighs and rolls onto his side, pulling me with him.

His arms encircle me, holding me against him. I don't even bother fighting it. I'm too tired, and his firm body, the lines and dips of his muscles that even now tell of his strength pressed against me, feel too good to pull away.

"I am sorry, Violet," he says into my hair. "If I am honest, I did not expect you to come."

"I almost didn't," I admit.

He stiffens briefly, then asks, "What changed your mind?"

"I…" *I didn't want to leave you.* The words are there on the tip of my tongue, but they stick.

But you will, an inner voice whispers.

One way or another, I will have to leave him.

"Everything," I say eventually.

As if sensing all my unspoken words, he holds me tighter. "All that matters is that you were there." Joon ducks his head and kisses me. "I swear I will never lie to you again. There are no secrets I have that I will not share with you."

Blinking, I take in the man holding me and the unfamiliar room. Slowly, everything comes back to me. I don't remember falling asleep. I hadn't meant to.

Sun streams through the window. We slept through the evening and all through the night. Though at some point, he must have gotten up to wash and change. The scent of soap lingers on his skin, and his chest is bare.

A groan rumbles from Joon's chest. "Where are you going?" he mumbles, not bothering to open his eyes. "Sleep more, it's still early."

"You need to siphon."

Joon hums in agreement. Rather than sitting up, he drags me on top of him, smiling sleepily. His fingers tangle in my hair as he pulls my mouth down to his. The kiss is slow and sweet.

His other hand roams over me with a touch that is pure comfort. His tongue traces my bottom lip, coaxing me to open for him. The press of his fingers quickly turns needy, skimming over my breasts and over my ass.

It's enough to send liquid heat racing through me to gather at my core. And when his hands grip my thighs, I let him part my legs around him, not caring how the robe falls open to expose me. My desire heightens when I feel his length straining under me.

Still, he doesn't siphon.

"Joon," I say against his mouth.

His response is to hold down my lower back as he rolls his hips, grinding his cock against me as he slips a hand under the robe to grip my ass.

I shift in a half-hearted effort to gain space so he might focus on what I'm saying. His hold on me tightens as he kisses and nips down my neck. Any resistance fades away.

He hums, pleased by my response. The hand on my ass finds its way between my legs. Fingers graze the extremely sensitive skin along my core, teasing, until I'm writhing.

Then he siphons. Like before, he alternates between pulling the power from me and easing his power through my veins before an episode has a chance to start.

Joon has barely taken any, but before I can comment on it, his fingers slip inside me, turning my words into a moan. There is no hiding how ready I am as he begins moving in and out.

He brings me to the edge of pleasure, keeping me there until I let out a plaintive whimper. His hand leaves me to pull the collar of my robe below my breasts as I tug his waistband just low enough to free him from his night pants. Our need is too strong for us to bother with fully undressing.

With him free, I sit up and gaze at him.

"Take your pleasure." His hands grip my thighs as he waits for me.

He lets out a breath as I take him in my hand and guide his tip to my entrance. I sink onto him until every inch of his cock is buried inside me. His fingers dig into my flesh as my body stretches to accommodate him. Then, I begin to move, taking my time to savor the way our bodies fit together and the sweet agony of each movement.

His thumb moves to my clit and moves in small circles, sending a jolt through me. His touch makes it impossible to go slow any longer. The sensations he adds to my movements are so intense. I try to escape them, but he follows every shift I make.

My release rips through me in shuddering waves. Before I can come down from the high, Joon lifts me up and slips from me. The world tilts and I'm on my back.

"You are fucking exquisite when you tremble around my cock." He holds himself above me, positioning himself as he holds me with his intense gaze.

My insides clench with the need to have him fill me again. To move inside me. He doesn't make me wait long. Driving his hips forward, he enters me hard and fast. My breath snags at the abrupt fullness of being stretched to accommodate all of him.

His hand travels up to my breasts, caressing and lightly pinching the peak just to hear the sounds he can pull from me.

He moves with a fierce possessiveness. There is nothing gentle about the way he takes me, though he is careful not to hurt. He leans down and kisses his way down my neck to my shoulder and bites down just hard enough to add pleasure to every primal thrust.

He hooks a hand behind one of my knees and brings it up to rest over my shoulder. It allows him to go even deeper.

We don't bother with words, letting our bodies do the talking. There's nothing but our moans and the sound of our bodies coming together, chasing away all thoughts of anything other than him.

Joon studies my every reaction. Each gasp and whimper I make unravels his self-control. He speeds up to an almost punishing pace, winding me tighter. It's not long before he has me gasping from the unbearable need.

I feel his desperation, a mirror of my own, to hold on to this thing we found in each other and fight against the forces that will rip it away. The cruelty of saints to give us a taste of something so coveted and rare, knowing it was never meant for us.

Every time he buries himself, it's as if he's trying to claim me so thoroughly that not even fate itself can have sway over me without his permission. And I crave it as desperately as he demands it.

I arch my back as I teeter, suspended over the edge in that endless moment right before the fall. My fingers curl, nails digging into his back as I cling to him. He takes the hint and goes even deeper. We surrender ourselves to the moment and to each other.

It's enough to send me plummeting into the exquisite ecstasy of my climax. My lashes flutter as I fall, and I think I see a shimmering strand between us. But I lose it as he drives into me with increasing force. His rhythm faltering as my body clenches around him and I cry out my release.

Even when my orgasm fades, everything is so sensitive that my body shudders in the aftershock of every powerful stroke of his cock. He lets out a sound from his throat, a groan of part pleasure, part utter possessiveness. He thickens inside me, and I can feel every throb as he finds release.

Gradually, he slows, then reluctantly slips from me. Joon gathers me in his arms as he collapses beside me. He holds me, my limbs tangling with his, as he trails kisses over my neck and shoulder.

"I want countless mornings of waking up just like this," Joon murmurs against my skin.

Affection swells in my chest. I never dared to want something so permanent before. It would be easy to let myself dream that it could last longer than the brief moment of our lives.

And all the more painful when it never happens.

No matter how much I want to tell him I want the same, I can't bring myself to encourage something that will only bring both of us more heartbreak in the end.

"You didn't siphon enough," I remind him. My voice is lazy. Almost slurring with the weight of sleep.

Joon nuzzles into the crook of my neck. "Have dinner with me tonight?"

The request is so tender and innocent compared to what we just did that I pull back to look at him. His eyes hold more adoration than I deserve.

How will I ever bear to leave him when the time comes?

I push a stray lock off his forehead, running my fingers

through the long, black strands that fade to the color of frost at the ends. Soft as silk.

I cup his cheek. He touches me in ways no one ever has—creating a desire, an insatiable need within me I never realized was possible. He makes me long for things I cannot have. He makes me believe I could live a life as ordinary as anyone else's, one where it is not pointless to give my heart away.

We knew this arrangement would be temporary from the beginning. Already, I fear it's too late for us. With every look and touch and word, he further deepens his claim on my broken heart, turning our illusion into a star-crossed fate.

The second night of the new moon allows the stars to shine impossibly bright in the cloudless sky. The air is warm again, making tonight perfect for dinner beside the gentle stream. We sit on the uncovered section of the pavilion overlooking the water. The protective barrier over the Western Court outer garden shimmers faintly when the flames of our fire send tiny motes of ash into the air.

Joon has never looked stronger. The reason why brings a flush to my cheeks, which can easily be attributed to the milky-colored frost wine we share if he notices.

After the first siphoning this morning, he proved to be stubbornness-made-flesh when I pressed the issue of his not taking enough power. Joon eventually gave in and siphoned again. His ploy became obvious when our limbs tangled again before he had barely even siphoned.

Half the day passed before he finally siphoned all he

needed. I can't complain, as the process was far from a hardship on my behalf.

My stomach clenches at the memory of him taking me over and over, his hands traveling over every inch of my body as if trying to memorize it, the way we worshiped each other with our mouths.

Even from across the table, I can still feel his touch on my skin—can still feel him moving over and in me.

I swallow thickly and take another sip of the wine. When I look up, I find Joon watching me with a sensual smile and eyes that shine like deep blue flames. I wonder if he knows where my thoughts are or if his are the same.

Determined to focus on this moment, I offer him a placid smile. I pluck one of the many pieces of bite-sized finger foods and pop it into my mouth and chew, pushing those thoughts aside for now.

Joon continues his story, one of the few, clear memories from his childhood he has. How he used to sneak pastries from the kitchen and then take them to Iseul and Mingi before he brought them to the palace.

We take turns sharing pieces of our lives that once felt mundane and unimportant but now feel sweet and significant as we talk over good food and good wine. It's as much learning more about each other as it is listening to the sound of each other's voices.

Tonight is for the present alone. I do not let thoughts of what must come to pass, or what cannot be, infringe on our evening.

"I have been meaning to ask how you found the book that told you of the frost bloom," he says thoughtfully as he brings his drink to his lips.

The change in topic takes me aback. Then I smile inwardly. He's asked before, but things were different between us then. There is no malicious intent behind his curiosity.

"I found it in the back room of the archives when I was working. It must have been mixed in with the antiquated texts by mistake."

Joon sits a little straighter and arches a brow. Suspicion flickers in his expression. "Are there more?"

"No." I frown down at my glass in concentration. "Not that I noticed. I've been through half the main library, and all of the back room shelves, but it is possible I missed others."

"I am glad to hear it." He takes another sip of his drink, never taking his eyes off me as I do the same. A gentle curl forms over his lips. He is smiling more and more these days. I would like to think that I could be the reason for it.

"Tell me about your work. What does one do cloistered in the back room of the archives?" Joon wrinkles his nose. "Please do not tell me they kept my wife busy with mind-numbing tasks such as dusting," he says with faux horror.

If more people could see this side of him, I know he would win his people over in a heartbeat.

"There was *some* dusting, but I mostly rebound and repaired books."

Joon nods, keeping the smile plastered across his lips until it takes on a strained edge. "That is… much better than dusting."

Laughter bursts from me. "I suppose to a prince, it might sound tedious, but I enjoy working with my hands, and taking something worn and making it like new again."

Joon's teasing fades into an expression of warmth as I speak.

"I studied in my spare time, filling countless notebooks with everything that could be useful, from common illnesses to rare conditions." I smile inwardly. "Over the past few years,

I've had a few opportunities to help neighbors and acquaintances. Even if I couldn't find answers for myself, I enjoyed being able to help my city." I sigh wistfully. "I loved being able to help others get well with my own two hands..."

Realizing how long I've been going on, I pause to look up. Joon's chin is propped in his palm as he leans on the table. He watches me closely, with such intensity, I feel self-conscious.

"Why are you looking at me like that?"

His smile is sleepy. He inhales in a deep, contented way. "You are beautiful. More so when you speak of things you are passionate about."

I can't help the slight blush that creeps over my cheeks. "Anyway... even though it's not the same, I also enjoyed working at the archives."

From there, my story morphs into memories of my surrogate family, skipping the ones surrounding the time when my parents were entrapped in the cursed ice, and focusing on the times before and after. Now is not the moment for that. Right now, I want to relive the happiest times.

Joon moves to my side of the table as I finish telling him about the time Sebastian put a frog in Talya's handbag when we were in school.

He leans toward me, trailing kisses from my shoulder to the column of my throat.

I trail off. "You are very distracting," I murmur.

He hums. "I find I am not fond of you looking so happy when speaking of other men."

"He's a friend. If anything, the two of them are like the siblings I never had." My explanation reminds me of what I'd read. "Oh, I nearly forgot. There is something I wanted to tell you."

Joon nips at my earlobe before pulling it between his lips.

Small bumps race over my skin. I hum at the warmth that spreads within. "Joon..."

"Moan my name like that again, and I might not be able to control myself out here where anyone could happen upon us." Joon's voice is a sensual growl as the hand on my thigh inches upward.

"This is important," I insist weakly. It's getting harder to remember why by the second as I melt into him.

He nips playfully at my neck, then slowly draws back. All I can manage is a weak, plaintive sound of protest.

Demons and saints, this man will be my complete undoing.

"What is so urgent?" Joon's eyes and tone show concern.

I sit straighter and turn to face him. "I've been looking into your family history—"

"You have?"

His bewilderment makes me wonder if I overstepped. "Is that all right?"

He shakes his head. "It is fine, just unexpected. Most don't bother unless it is to confirm a date or some other small detail." He considers me for a moment. "I suppose those living in the mortal lands would not be so familiar with recent fae history."

I relax, relieved to hear that. "When I was researching, I noticed something—" I hum, trying to find the right word. "—*peculiar*. A page was removed from one of the books. And there was something written that didn't make sense because it contradicted—"

"Your Highness," Mingi calls out from the far end of the pavilion. His footsteps thud loudly as he runs toward us.

Still looking at me, Joon holds up a hand to him. "We are in the middle of something."

"Demons have breached the palace walls," Mingi says, not

heading the order. "They are swarming the Grand Hall and Southern Court."

He commands our full attention.

"Everyone with lesser magic who cannot defend against demons must go to the Temple Tower," Mingi tosses me a meaningful glance. "Immediately."

Joon and I are on our feet before he finishes.

Talons click against the pavilion floor as Imugi and Bear arrive seconds later. Bear nearly crashes into me as the two demons reach us.

Joon takes my hand and pulls me along with him. "I will meet you back at the gate once I escort Violet."

"There's no time," Mingi protests. "Barriers are down and more fail every minute."

Joon continues dragging me along. He's not listening. I plant my feet and use my full weight to stop him. "I can make it to the tower on my own. I'll be fine—Bear is with me."

Joon ducks his head and kisses me. "I will see you soon, and then you can finish what you were telling me."

He doesn't hesitate to trust my ability to do so.

I smile. We will see each other again soon, right after this is over.

And then, just as he said, I will tell him everything. A gut feeling tells me what I found is important. I'm not sure exactly how, but perhaps he will.

He inhales as if he is fighting the urge to kiss me again, but refrains. There is no time for prolonged goodbyes.

Joone turns to Mingi, once again, transforming into the prince he is. "Fill me in," he says as they race toward the gate that will take them to the Southern Court.

"Minister Yeona was found murdered moments before the first barrier fell."

CHAPTER THIRTY-FIVE

VIOLET

I hurry down the path toward the gate to the Central Court with Bear at my side. I can't quite run. The muscles in my legs are tired—weaker than I'm used to. It would be easy to play it off as a side effect of the drink or from sitting for so long, but I can no longer ignore the way it has gradually crept up over the past several months.

Will Joon and I break the curse before I die? Or will this traitorous heart give out on me first?

No, I admonish inwardly. I cannot allow myself to think like that. *I can't give up now. We have to break it. For my family, for Arum...* for him.

The gate to the Western Court is partially open when I reach it. Bear squeezes through first, then motions for me to follow. As I step in the direction of the Temple Tower, the demon pulls on my skirt. Trusting their judgment, I allow them to tug me along the path behind it that runs parallel.

We enter one of the enclosed walkways. The route is darker and longer, but as long as the shield remains, it's safer.

Outside, the guards' shouts clash against the howls from

the wild demons they battle. I can't fight my unease as the eerie din echoes in the otherwise abandoned passage.

Bear dashes behind a nearby corner to hide as the strong and steady gait of heavy footsteps approaches. I slow, waiting to see who it is.

King Sameun enters the junction at the far end, where another hall runs perpendicular. He spots me and changes direction. He is nearly as relieved as I am to see a familiar face.

"Your Majesty, what are you doing here? You should be in the Temple Tower," I say.

"I came looking for you when everyone from the Northern Court made it to the tower except you."

He is alone.

"Where are your guards?"

He smiles, but it doesn't quite reach his eyes in such a somber moment. "I am more than capable of taking care of myself. My people are more in need of their protection."

Belatedly, I realize Bear isn't hiding under the cover of my skirt as usual. I hope they will be safe wherever they hide. They might be small, but they are still a demon.

A loud crash in the distance shakes the ground.

"Come, we must hurry." The king reaches out and hooks our arms, leading me the way he came. "Joon asked me to find you."

Even though he isn't looking at me while he speaks, I nod in response. When my mind finally catches up, I realize we've taken the long corridor along the northern wall of the Central Court and have passed the Temple Tower.

"Where are we going?"

The king sends a quick glance over his shoulder. "To the Eastern Court. It will be safer for us there."

I open my mouth to protest, but he knows what I'm thinking before I can get the breath to speak it.

"There is not enough room for everyone. It was meant as a safeguard for the royal family and the officials."

We make the rest of our trek in silence, the king holding onto me the entire way. At every crash and breaking of wood or stone, he pauses to listen.

Once or twice, I think I see a movement out of the corner of my eye, or hear a faint whisper close behind, but when I look, there's nothing there. My imagination is running wild, conjuring up images of demons that lurk within every shadow, preparing to pounce.

The Eastern Court is quiet. The shield overhead shimmers with the strength of its hold. Yet everything within is in disrepair from years of neglect.

Once manicured plants are now overgrown, taking over paths and lawns. Vines and branches tangle together as they vie for the same spaces. The wooden structures are cracked and splintered, with some support pieces in the process of collapse. Their painted surfaces have weathered and faded, leaving a ghost of their former beauty behind as they decay.

The sounds of fighting continue to fade as we gain distance. Still, the king doesn't release me until we're inside the old hall, and the door is shut securely behind us.

I release the tension that's taken up residence in my upper back, leaving my muscles aching.

"Follow me," he says, motioning with his hand as he walks quickly down the corridor.

I hurry to keep up, not wanting to fall behind in this unfamiliar place.

There is a distinct lack of voices and light in the room ahead. And when the king slides the door open, my suspicion that we are the only ones here is confirmed.

A shiver passes over me. "Is there no one else?" I ask, barely above a whisper.

"More are coming. It won't be easy for them to get out of the Central Court with all the barriers down." The full volume of the king's voice is a stark contrast for the last fifteen minutes.

He crosses to a dark shape on the wall. With a slight flick of his wrist, metal and stone scrape, causing an unseen chain reaction.

Lights burst to life, trailing from where he stands and spreading out through the massive throne room.

A thick layer of dust coats the two wide thrones perched atop a low dais, and the wide runner cutting the room in half from the door to the bottom of the steps.

Not quite sure what to do with myself while we wait, I wander closer to the dais. Beneath the layer of neglect, it's easy to tell that the throne room in the Central Court is nearly an exact copy. But where the other has harsh edges that mimic the shapes of ice crystals, this one has softer, rounded lines like that of curling wisps of frost or mounds of freshly fallen snow smoothed over by a gentle wind.

"I would like to offer you my sincerest apologies for what happened during your trial."

The strong resonance of his voice, much closer than before, startles me. I whirl around and find the king barely more than an arm's length away. I hadn't heard him approach.

"Minister Ilseong had been a long-trusted advisor. He has never failed me before. I did not think him capable of betrayal." He gazes at me serenely. "I do hope you will forgive me."

I swallow thickly. The role the king played that day is something I have tried not to think about. It chills my blood to remember how he was all too willing to let that Minister kill me in front of the entire court without so much as an opportunity to defend myself. Joon's intervention is the reason I'm standing here now.

He might be asking for my forgiveness, but he is still a king, and I don't see that there is much of a choice here. Though if it means making sure our future interactions are not strained, then I don't see a reason to hold a grudge.

"Of course, Your Majesty. You were only looking out for your people." Before I can stop myself, I add, "I am only glad the misunderstanding was cleared up before it was too late."

He hums, glancing around the room in mild curiosity. "Are you nervous about your upcoming presentation?"

Again, he takes me off guard. Making small talk at a time like this feels a bit odd. The king is not concerned about the demons infiltrating the palace grounds in the slightest.

"A little," I say, not wanting to come off as arrogant. "I don't want to be an embarrassment."

Other than my lessons with Iseul, I have not given it any thought. Mostly because Joon and I are so close to ending this curse, and I want to believe we will succeed before then.

My heart flutters as a light pressure tightens around it. The sensation isn't painful, yet it has persisted since this afternoon.

"I've heard you have not been feeling well lately," he says.

I blink uncertainly, worried he found out the truth of my condition. He nods to my chest. My hand stills over my heart, where I was absentmindedly rubbing the ache.

I lower my hand to my side and clear my throat. "I am well. It's just a habit I have when there's a lot on my mind."

The ground shakes with another loud crash, rattling the chandelier above us, and letting us know the fight continues beyond the walls of this court. The king looks up, and the firelight flashes in his eyes, making them appear to glow red for a brief second.

When he returns his gaze to me, it is the same shade of gray they've always been.

"There is something I would like to give you."

The thought of the king gifting me with anything seems unnecessary, especially when I've done nothing to earn it.

He takes hold of my wrist before I can refuse, reaching into a pocket with his other hand. His thumb rests on my pulse point as he shoves a vial into my palm.

I curl my fingers around it, yet his grip on me remains.

"Have you been in the library again lately?"

"No," I answer, unable to take my eyes off our hands. My breath stutters as a pulse cascades through my body, like a heartbeat that is a little too strong.

"I have never seen a human study so diligently on their own here. I must admit, my curiosity is piqued as to what it is you are hoping to learn."

The longer I look at his grip on me, the stranger it feels. I try to tug my arm lightly, not enough to offend, but to bring it to his attention that he has yet to let go.

"The royal family line," I say, the words flowing too freely from my lips. The unfiltered level of honesty stops me in my tracks. It was a truth I only intended to share with Joon for now. I haven't even said as much to Iseul yet.

The strong hand wrapped around my wrist is distracting, but that alone isn't enough to explain the slip of my tongue. Perhaps the soft haze of alcohol in my system is having a stronger effect on me than I first thought.

Slowly, I drag my gaze up to the king's passive expression. As he watches me, his head lists slightly to the side. There is something unnatural about the movement, though I can't put my finger on it.

I pull harder on my hand, but his grip only tightens.

Another pulse surges through me in panic. My heartbeat quickens, becoming a sharp beat, striking against its cage of bone.

"You look pale, Lady Violet. I meant this draught to fortify you for your presentation, but the excitement of the night has taken a toll on you. Perhaps you ought to take it now. It will make you feel better."

He means well, but his gift cannot stop or lessen an episode. I have tried countless draughts over the years, among other things, and the only thing that could ever stop them once they truly began is Joon's magic.

My lips don't even have time to form a sound before there is yet another pulse. As I open my mouth, I can feel the agreement on the edge of my tongue.

"I think I will… save it for the presentation," I manage to get it out with some effort. "I am all right."

The king's fingers tighten. He tugs on me, and I stumble closer.

I gape at him for this strange change of demeanor. A sickening feeling twists my insides into knots.

He pins me with his narrowing stare. All kindness and pretense evaporate, as cold detachment takes its place, turning his features into hard lines. "There is something… off about you."

This time, the pulse is strong and painful, striking me like a punch to the chest. There is no mistaking it for anything other than what it is. It is not an episode coming on due to the usual reasons, but one forced into being by this man's powers.

He tilts his chin, the angle making the points of his ears appear like small horns. His eyes flash again—the red light coming from within, not the reflection of fire.

A cold smile spreads over his mouth as the king brings his

face closer. Something dark edges his expression. "So *that* is where it is," he murmurs, but not to me.

"Where what is?" My teeth chatter through my question.

He ignores me, continuing to speak to himself as though I'm not even here. "I was wondering how my nephew could keep a human heart from destroying itself."

My throat tightens.

How does he know about my episodes? Joon wouldn't have told him... would he?

"I don't know what you're saying." I pull roughly on my arm, trying to get free and no longer caring if I offend him.

He blinks and finally seems to see me again. "I suspected as much after I sent for you. You were weak. I needed to get you alone to know for certain. If we had not been interrupted, I could have put an end to this far sooner. A human with a heart condition should have ended up bedridden for weeks at a time—or dead. Yet, you always managed to find your feet as if it were nothing," his voice rises in pitch, taking on a sinister glee.

I struggle to follow his line of thought as he continues to ramble vaguely.

Sent for me... interrupted... The episode in the throne room. *That's* how he knows.

"I knew there was something strange about you!" he barks a sharp laugh. "But I never would have guessed *this* is how you did it! No wonder he has kept you so close all this time, doting on you as if he cared."

"Let go—you're hurting me." I loathe how weak my voice sounds when I want to scream the words.

The king sends a violent pulse through me, releasing his grip.

Unbalanced, I stagger back. The vial slips through my fingers and shatters at my feet. Even as I hunch over, gasping for each pathetic breath I take, the urge to apologize is nearly automatic, but I bite it back.

He doesn't seem to care as he nods toward the broken mess. "Would you like to know what it does?"

I don't answer. Whatever was inside it is now ruined.

"It would have marked your life force for the Winter Dragon," he goes on eagerly. "It is a pity you will not get the chance to share the same fate as the other women." The king smirks. "You would have made a nice edition."

"Why?" Even though I already know, I cannot help asking anyway.

"Unfortunately, it is necessary to put a stop to it before you ruin everything." He stalks closer. "If you succumbed to the demons in that garden, then I would not have been forced to push him to present you to the court so soon."

My heart squeezes. It steals the breath from my lungs and freezes my muscles. Spots bloom across my vision. The moment stretches endlessly as the shapes of things he hasn't yet said hover just beyond my grasp as the full extent of his actions falls into place, one by one.

The king, seemingly oblivious to it all, continues to speak. "Minister Ilseong nearly succeeded, but who would have guessed the prince with the frozen heart would come to your rescue?"

Black veins pulse from his pupils, cutting through his irises and over the whites of his eyes as if poison in his blood spreads within.

"At first, I thought you were nothing more than another warm body for my nephew to use and discard… Who would have thought you would be his true weakness?"

His words are cruel. Meant to cut. To drive a wedge between Joon and me. Whether his words are true or not doesn't matter, because beyond a brief moment of jealousy, I don't care about Joon's past. I never truly did.

I shake my head as I back up, trying to put distance between us, even as he follows.

The demon attack. The look of betrayal on Minister Ilseong's face was because the accusation about the pearl had been the king's idea.

"Tonight." The word is barely a sound on my lips, but he catches it.

"Pity the Minister Yeona had to die. She was young, but she was shaping up to be one of the best Arum has ever seen."

In my stunned silence, he closes the distance. His hand whips out, grabbing my hair. "If you had only left things alone, it would have dissolved with his death." The king leans in. "Forgive me, but I cannot allow him to get that final shard from you."

"I-I don't have it."

My mind is reeling, trying to process everything he's said, amidst the agony racking my body.

He knows about the shards and the curse.

No...

The danger, the deaths, the attacks, the—

He didn't try to kill me to keep Joon from breaking the curse—he wanted me dead because *he is the one who created it.*

"Oh, but you do." He chuckles as he circles a finger, pointing at me, inching closer. "Right—" The king jabs my chest. "—in there."

At the touch, a pulse of power zaps through me, as sharp and hot as lightning.

"If you die, the shard and the magic within dies with you, then the prince will at long last fall to the curse."

Demon shit.

I have to stall. Soon Joon or Iseul or Bear or Mingi will

realize I'm not where I should be—they will realize something is off.

"You… it was you."

A smirk unfurls across his face, dripping with poison and condescension.

Black veins continue to spread, out from the corners of his eyes, down his cheeks, and neck.

My gaze is pulled from the grotesque markings to the area just over his shoulder as a dark shape rises up behind him. Two eyes, burn red like angry flames.

The demon hovers, body undulating in the air. Their shape is nearly identical to Imugi's, but this one lacks the beautiful shimmering visage of winter come to life—they are the color of ash and rotting leaves with spiky scales.

I know precious little of the royal family's connection with demons. But after what little time I've spent around Imugi and Bear, it is woefully clear that there is something very, *very* wrong with this demon and their bond with the interim king.

The world sways.

Hurry, Joon, I need you.

"How could you? *He's family.*"

The king's expression twists into a scowl. "He had everything—the crown, a bonded demon, and the future that rightfully belonged to me—but that wasn't good enough. He took *her*, too," he snarls.

Who is she?

Flecks of spittle fly from his mouth as he speaks. The veins continue to pulse just below his skin. "If she would not be mine, then I would take the throne. It was just a matter of ridding myself of those brats."

I am grasping for breath now. My heart beats against its cage of bone like a blacksmith's hammer. Dizziness churns my stomach—or maybe it's the knowledge of everything this man has done.

My knees give out. Fire burns my scalp as I'm held aloft by my hair.

He took her, too.

I loved her first.

I don't know the people he's talking about, but I know the missing pieces he hasn't said.

Could the story I found in the library be true? Everything fits... but *how*? Who would dare write it and then place it in the royal library?

If I can just get near the door, perhaps I can signal for help.

Gathering my rapidly fading strength, I manage to get my feet under me. I take a step back, then another. The king moves with me, hand still fisted in my hair.

The demon hisses, their burning eyes flash.

The king releases his grip with a rough jerk to the side. I stumble and take the opportunity to turn.

A large hand wraps around my neck and pulls me back. The king's fingers tighten, clamping down with crushing force.

Sickening power rips through me as though shredding my flesh with razor talons, cutting into my neck, down to my chest, digging and clawing toward my heart. My vision goes dark.

Then the hand is gone. I fall backward, crashing into the wall, and collapsing to my hands and knees.

The king is still speaking, but I can't understand him.

Pain far worse than anything I've known, doubles over on itself.

I can't breathe.

I can't scream.

Nothing can slow or stop this episode. Not even Joon's

power. I know without a doubt that this time, I will not recover.

As if summoned by that very thought, a vision of Joon emerges from the shadowed doorway. A hallucination. A dying dream to offer some semblance of comfort as my short life finally ends.

I can almost hear him call to me.

Joon doubles before my eyes. Two princes run toward me…

What had the king said?

…a matter of ridding myself of those brats.

I focus on the final word.

Brats.

The first son.

Realization hits me as I crumple to the floor.

CHAPTER THIRTY-SIX

JOON

The demons in the Western Court are whittled down little by little until only a few remain. Bodies of higher demons lay in broken heaps of knobby spines and too-long limbs. Fissures form around the killing wounds of their flesh, like cold ash.

The formless, lesser demons, too stupid to flee, are easily struck down with sword and arrow. Night forged silver cuts through them as if they had no more substance than fog.

A thick, billowing cloud of black gathers to my side, forming slowly, condensing into the shape of another higher demon. It solidifies and lunges, attempting to take me by surprise.

I duck under the swing of the crooked arm and sidestep as deadly talons plunge into the earth where I was standing half a breath before. My grip tightens on the hilt of the dagger as I bring my fist up.

The demon meets my eye and releases an ear-splitting screech as I drive the point of my blade through the center of that blood-red orb. Their cry abruptly cuts off as they slump at my feet. Dead.

I turn to check on Mingi. He fights at my back, cutting down two more demons with a single swing of his sword.

My attention is yanked toward the gate, where a guard points, shouting to his companions. The one next to him lifts her sword.

The demon they eye races toward me, ducking and swerving. I squint.

They are no ordinary demon.

Bear?

Instantly, I know Violet is in danger. They would not have left her—not risk their life to find me otherwise.

The guards converge on Bear, slowly gaining.

I race forward. The four of us meet at once. I drop to one knee as Bear crashes into my chest. Raising my arm, I catch the blade of the sword coming down—ice crackles, coating the metal in a layer, inches thick. I use the added weight to throw the guard off balance and into the other.

"Take care of the real threats!" I shout over the din.

The ice recedes from the first guard's weapon. The pair exchange puzzled glances. Even though they have no way of understanding the situation, they nod and comply.

"You should be with Violet," I admonish, hoping against hope that they only wanted to be brave and help.

But as the demon points eastward, a powerful ache takes shape within my chest—the demand of our bargain—issuing a warning.

Instantly, I am up and running for the gate to the Central Court.

Mingi matches my stride. "The threat is under control here," he says. "Those not needed to hold the shield will join us at the Southern Court."

"Go without me. I will catch up—there is something I must do first."

Mingi doesn't respond. His silence is objection enough, but when we pass the gate, he gives me a look that expresses more than we would have time to speak.

Imugi is at my shoulder, moving with me as easily as if we were still.

"Go with him," I say. "Keep him safe."

After a reluctant hesitation, they oblige.

Bear leaps from my hold and bounds ahead, looking back to make sure I follow. Free of their weight, I speed up.

The demon angles away from the Temple Tower, instead changing course toward the Eastern Court. It's hardly noticeable at first, but the gate is open just wide enough for a man to pass through.

It should be sealed off. It has been since—

I shake off the thought. There is no time to think of that now.

Bear slows as we enter the ruins of my childhood, stalking toward the old throne room.

Their caution tells me all I need to know.

We slip quietly through the main doors. As I close them to keep the sound of fighting from alerting to our presence, a voice I know too well filters down the hall.

Anger and confusion war for dominance among the disbelief, turning my blood into rivers of ice.

Moving silently, I hurry closer to the light spilling through the open door.

"I am sorry, but you will have to die sooner than expected." The words are low but clear, spoken with a cold detachment. It is nothing like the man I have called family since he came to the palace. Yet the voice is undeniably his.

Without seeing inside, I know he means Violet.

Entering the throne room only confirms what I suspected.

The reasons for his betrayal make no difference. If he has harmed Violet at all, I will kill him.

Violet is on her hands and knees, gasping for breath through a violent episode.

"I will not allow you to ruin everything I have worked to accomplish!" Uncle's shout rings throughout the massive room.

It is what he'd said to me not that long ago. But now I can hear the true meaning behind it.

Violet struggles to lift her head.

Blood roars in my ears, nearly drowning out her name as it rips from my throat. My feet carry me to her of their own volition.

My uncle swivels his head and looks at me through two solid pools of pitch. Black veins crawl from his eyes, across his face like fine roots of a plant, extending over every inch of exposed skin.

Demon cursed.

Every fae learns how to identify the signs from the moment we are born so that we will know it upon sight. A warning to those who would risk bonding with a demon without the aid of the Master of Ceremony in an attempt to stand as a challenger to the throne and usurp the reigning monarch.

The higher demons searching for the opportunity to become a greater demon through such a connection are rarely a match to those who seek a life the fates did not ordain. The mismatched power taints life force, poisoning both fae and demon from the inside out. For some, it takes weeks or months. Others can take years or decades.

Uncle's mouth stretches into an unnaturally wide grin,

causing his lips to split at the edges and ooze thick rivulets of dark blood. He rushes forward.

As we speed toward collision, I reach for my night forged silver dagger and grip nothing but air. I don't remember where or when I dropped it.

With a curse, I gather my dwindling power—so much of it already used up—and wait for the right moment.

The king stretches his arms out, hands flexing into claws. Dark talons burst from his nails. Their tips glint with his own blood as they angle for my throat.

A heartbeat before we meet, I send the full force of my magic into him. A demon in the form of a dragon darts up, positioning themselves between him and my power. The magic crystallizes on impact, driving the demon into my uncle's chest. They crash to the floor, locked together by the ice. I don't spare a second for the loss of the only family member I had left.

Violet is all that matters.

I fall to my knees at her side and gather her into my arms. She curls into me.

"Y-you're… real…" she says through raw, agony-riddled gasps.

Sending my power to soothe her comes without thought. I press my palm over her heart and let rivers of it glide through her veins and tendrils to wrap around her heart.

Violet's brow relaxes.

I wait, watching closely to see if it worked.

She takes a breath, deeper, less pained than before. I press my palm to her chest once more.

I will use every scrap of power to heal her if necessary.

I cannot lose her.

Violet's fingers wrap around my wrist, moving my hand away. She shakes her head. Her lips form the word "no," but her voice is silent. The struggle to collect the energy is apparent on her face.

She swallows and licks her lips. "The last shard. It's—"

"We can get it together—as soon as I heal you."

Again, she shakes her head.

The look in her eyes fills my insides with dread, pooling in my gut with the oozing, sickening weight of what she will say.

"My heart."

"Let me heal it—" I cut off at yet another shake of her head.

"My episodes." Violet taps her chest. "You must take it out."

I do not understand—I do not want to, but she forces it upon me. Bile burns my throat. "I can't—you know I can't. It will kill you."

Pushing her hand out of the way, I replace it with my own and prepare to heal her again.

"Won't work… this time."

"You don't know that," I snap.

Violet smiles sadly. She sees through my anger for what it can't hide. "You must take it, or it will die."

My head pounds. "I don't know what to do."

"Break the curse, Joon." She erupts into a coughing fit, and when it passes, there is blood staining the corner of her mouth.

"You must siphon," Imugi hisses. I hadn't noticed when they arrived.

Bear leaps and swats at them, but Imugi dodges out of the way.

"No!" I grind out through clenched teeth.

Violet's fingertips graze my cheek, wiping away the moisture of a tear. That ghostly touch commands my full attention to return to her. She is unnaturally cold. "There's time… heal me… after you break the curse."

It is a lie. We both know it.

As much as I want to yell that she is wrong—that it is not as she claims, there is no ignoring how it is the only thing that makes sense.

For some time, I have suspected that I was not healing her, only easing the pain of the episode. Though reduced, the damage done was still there, below the surface.

It explains why she has become weaker so much faster than she should have, why shadows have taken a permanent place under her eyes—it's why her face has become gaunt over the short time she's been here...

With every siphoning, the shard shifted.

The first time she came to me—the first time I felt her soft lips moving over mine—I took the power of the frost bloom from her and unknowingly called to the remaining shards scattered throughout Arum. I called to the one buried deep within her heart, slowly pulling it toward me.

Loathing over what I did to her this morning crashes into me. I was so careless. So caught up in possessing her, rather than taking only what was necessary. Over and over, I dragged Violet closer to the brink of death while making her believe she was safe beneath me.

I send power into her, willing her body to fully heal so that perhaps it will force out the shard, and she can finally be whole again.

Violet's arms fall to her sides, her back arching from the current of magic coursing through her.

When it is over, she takes the first full breath since I found her.

"Your family records—a page is missing."

"Don't speak, save your strength."

"Just listen. A name was removed. There are mentions of..." Violet's lashes flutter.

She might be able to breathe now, but she is still fading before my eyes.

I can numb her pain, but I cannot fix her as I am. I am too weak.

Even some things are beyond the reach of magic.

I have failed her.

"... Second child. Brother," she finishes.

I have no idea what she's talking about. It could be delirium.

"I will look into it," I swear hastily. "I will have everyone look into it if I must."

"Joon," she says my name softly and smiles. She always smiles—even clasped within the Otherworld's grasp, she smiles—but it has never felt more like a lie. "Don't be like that."

I scowl down at her.

Violet releases a sigh that is a weak imitation of her laugh. "Don't blame yourself—we both agreed to this." Energy continues to fade from her voice. "Don't let it be for nothing... *please, Joon.*"

She uses that word against me—the one that rendered me powerless to her since the night we met—knowing I cannot refuse her.

I squeeze my eyes shut, searching for a hint within our bargain to guide my hand. But when I need it most, there is nothing there.

We have reached a point in our bargain where I cannot fulfill my promise to her, and regardless of what path I choose, the result will be the same.

"And keep me alive until the end *of it."*

"I will do all you have asked. In exchange, you will freely bind and obligate yourself to me until my task is complete."

When I spoke those words, I thought only of finding the

remaining shards. That was my only goal, because once I did, breaking the curse was a given.

Every other vow I made to keep her safe had never been a binding part of our bargain. I said I would allow her to keep her life, but that is not the same as personally keeping her alive. Now that I know the location of the final piece, we have reached the end.

If I had known I would love her, I would have spoken with more care. I would have ensured she could live.

Desperation claws at me, rending me apart from the inside.

"There's no time. She is dying!" Imugi hisses above.

Violet squeezes my hand, halting me before I can lash out.

There is no fighting this. If a solution exists, it is too late. All I can do is what Violet asks of me.

I adjust her, helping her to sit straighter in my arms. I brush the loose strands of dark hair away from her face.

"I am sorry," I whisper.

"Don't—I don't regret a second with you."

Leaning in, I bring my mouth to hers. I kiss her, memorizing the feel of her lips, her taste, her touch. The way she fits me, it's as if the Guardians of past kings and queens created her for me.

I press my palm over her heart and ease the threads of my power into her.

Then, for the last time, I siphon.

Now that I know what to look for, I can feel the shard moving. The pull of it and the slight resistance. The way the call of it radiates out in all directions.

I soothe the pain of the shard, slicing free of the home it made within her heart for the last fourteen years.

Violet gasps. Her body jerks as the shard comes free from her chest.

I pull back and ease her to the ground, retaining the soothing flow of power.

The shard hovers over her, glinting with her blood. It is such a small, insignificant thing, yet it has caused immeasurable damage.

I reach out and grip it in my fist. The jagged edge of broken glass slices into my palm.

Tears escape from the corners of Violet's closed eyes. Her breathing is shallow. Uneven. Gasping uselessly. The wound in her chest closes, healing shut, but she continues to fade.

I scrape the dregs of the well within me for more power.

Watching her slip from this world is unbearable. The magic thrashes, wild and writhing against my hold. It summons a storm of wind and ice to howl and scream my pain and rage.

Streaks of bright blue snap and crackle over my skin like bolts of lightning as I edge dangerously close to draining every last drop of power I possess. Shimmering scales break out, traveling over my hands and racing up my arms, leaving trails of crackling ice in their wake.

She is slipping away. I grit my teeth.

I can't let her go.

I can't lose her.

The ice is to her ribs when I realize what I'm doing. But I don't stop. I let it spread. Let it wrap around her, enveloping her, weaving strands of the curse into the ice inching up her chest. Her shoulders. Her neck. When Violet is fully cocooned within the ice chrysalis, I release the flow of magic.

It's not unlike the others, but this time, it was not the dragon's doing but mine. My power. My control.

Tremors rattle my bones from exertion.

Footsteps clatter through the hall, stopping just inside the throne room. I don't move or look up.

"What happened?" Mingi crouches before me.

"I have the last shard." Each syllable tastes like ash in my mouth.

Mingi starts to speak, probably to ask where it was this whole time, only to press his lips in a tight line when Iseul's hand alights on his shoulder. She shakes her head and motions to Violet's body with a nod.

Not enough.

I couldn't save her. I was not strong enough.

But you could be. The voice is not mine but every bit as familiar. One I have not heard in an age.

I stand abruptly. "Stay with her."

"Where are you going?" Mingi calls after me.

I am already gone, sprinting blindly across the palace grounds, heedless of the world around me.

Before I know it, I find myself in the underground cavern, darting for the mirror in the center of the silver lake.

I cross the narrow walkway. My gaze lands on the smooth surface of the water, summoning the memory of my brief swim with Violet in the water.

Everything. Violet has touched every facet of my life. There is nothing I can see, nowhere I can go, that will not remind me of her.

Stopping before the mirror, I force my fingers to unfurl from around the final shard.

CHAPTER THIRTY-SEVEN

VIOLET

THERE IS STILL SO MUCH I WANT TO TELL HIM. BUT AS THE world dissolves into shadow and ice, I must content myself with what I could express to him through our last kiss.

Warmth is drained from my body, leaving me numb as the nothingness swallows me.

I don't fight the absolute eternity that stretches before me.

I couldn't.

Even if I wanted to.

So, instead, I welcome it with open arms.

CHAPTER THIRTY-EIGHT

JOON

THE JAGGED GLASS RESTS AGAINST MY PALM, COATED WITH MY blood and hers. Rough edges grind as I press it into place.

Blue light shines behind the cracks, growing brighter and brighter. The sheer intensity forces me to shield my eyes. It retreats back into the glass with a sharp hiss of air. Between one heartbeat and the next, a ring of power explodes out. The force of it throws me back. I land several feet from the water's edge. My head cracks against the hard-packed earth. Stars explode behind my eyes.

The weight of invisible shackles falls away. It's as if I've spent a lifetime pinned at the bottom of a lake beneath a boulder that has finally shifted and rolled away, letting my consciousness rise to the surface. Waking. Whole and alert.

I am free from the burden that has held me as its unwitting prisoner for so long.

When I blink, I am no longer in the underground cavern, but in a secret, narrow room within the Eastern Court with Eojin at my side.

My little brother makes the face he always does right

before he laughs. I motion for him to remain quiet. Eojin covers his mouth with both hands, shoulders shaking with silent giggles.

We were not allowed to join Mother and Father at dinner tonight to see our mysterious uncle, who had left Arum before I was born, and now returned at long last.

Sneaking into the spy's room with Eojin to let him have a look at the mysterious man we've yet to meet is little more than an excuse to satiate my own curiosity.

If we are caught, I will be punished with extra lessons, lectures on behavior, and exercise. But for my brother, this is nothing more than a fun trick to play on them.

I brace my hands on the wall and peer through the small opening.

A dozen crystal candelabras were brought in to provide adequate lighting for the late meal. Ornamentation, typically reserved for celebrations and monumental occasions, decorates the room. Rare plants have been cut and fashioned into elaborate garlands, ancestral tapestries hung, and rare vases and paintings are displayed throughout the room.

He must be someone very important, I think.

The three of them sit together at one end of the long table set up in the center of the throne room—Father at the head with Mother to his right, and Uncle on his left with his back to us. They talk and laugh as they share a drink over food no one bothers to touch.

They are too far for me to make out what they are saying.

Eojin tugs on the hem of my jacket to get my attention.

"I want to see, Brother," he mouths.

"In a moment," I reply silently, then turn back to look through the hole again.

A shape moves beside Uncle's feet. I squint, trying to see better. They inch out from the shadows beneath the table until their head pokes its way into the light. The long body slowly glides up, behind the back of the chair, out of everyone else's view.

This must be Uncle's bonded demon.

They share the same young dragon form as Imugi, and Eojin's and Father's demons, Mandu and Kyo… except it's wrong.

All demons within our family line have been a shade of blue, from nearly white to nearly black. This demon is different. They are shades of burnt red with dark, ashy splotches all over their body. And the scales that should be smooth and shining are dull and spiky.

Mother gasps, jumping to her feet. Her chair clatters to the floor with a sharp clatter. Father rises with a shout. Father rushes to Mother's side, taking her hand.

Uncle calmly sets his cup down and dabs his mouth with a napkin before rising. Each movement that the stranger makes is slow and intentional. The odd demon rises up behind him, hovering in clear view, undulating in midair over his shoulder.

Our parents back away, horror written on their faces.

When Uncle shifts, giving me a partial view of his face, I understand why—black veins streak down his face and neck, disappearing below his collar.

Demon cursed.

My heart pounds deafeningly in my ears. I do not think I could hear what Uncle is saying even if I were right beside him.

He jerks forward, bracing against the table and clutching his chest with his other hand. His back curves and strains against his clothes. The hand on the table elongates and transforms, growing larger. Fingers turn to claws with razor-sharp talons. The muscles in his arm ripple and expand, ripping through his sleeves, changing into something else entirely.

He releases a blood-curdling yell that becomes a roar as the dragon within him bursts into being. His spiked scales shimmer like the coal and embers of a smoldering forest fire.

"Jooooon," Eojin whisper-whines my name. "What is—"

I clap a hand over his mouth to silence him, vehemently shaking my head, then quickly peering into the throne room again.

Uncle's demon is looking in our direction, eyes darting for the source of the sound. Their head tilts at different angles, attempting to perceive us.

Demon shit.

I don't fully understand what is happening, but I know we need to get out of here and find help.

Eojin tries to push my hand away. My fingers press into his soft cheeks as I take his other arm and drag him from the secret room. He stops struggling against me almost immediately, as I am never intentionally rough with him.

In the hall, I pause long enough to whisper, "Stay silent, no matter what happens."

Tears fill his eyes, but he nods obediently. Guilt spikes through me at the fear crumpling Eojin's young face. But there is no time to comfort and coddle him. I take his hand and drag him out into the night. We race over the open grounds and slip into the Central Court.

None of the three bonded demons are anywhere to be found.

Where are they?

A scream rents the air.

Mother.

Guards come running, but our parents' personal spies reach us first.

Hyeon grabs me by the shoulders, roughly shaking me. "What happened? What were you two doing in there?"

My mouth moves, but no sound comes out as the rush of guards passes.

"Hyeon, up there!" Yuna shouts, pointing to the sky.

Two dragons leap into the night in a tangle of fire and ice. One a pale blue, the other a mix of blood-red and dull gray.

"Sound the alarm!" a guard shouts. "The queen is dead!"

"What in the Otherworld?" Hyeon breathes. He watches in horror as the two dragons twist and slash against the night sky.

The stories of the shadouk rush back. When an attempt to bond with a demon fails, they will slowly poison each other's life force until they die. But if the demon is far more powerful, they can live on after killing their bonded, able to use the empty husk as a puppet to do their bidding.

Our uncle will kill us—no, he is not our uncle. Not anymore. The realization is the jolt I need to regain my senses.

"Shadouk," I hiss, shoving my brother at Hyeon. "Take Eojin as far away as you can."

"What about you? It's not safe for you," Yuna says, trying to drag me with them.

I pull back, shaking my head. "He only needs one of us—hide Eojin. I will send for you when it is safe."

A chill settles in my bones. I will live long enough to hand over the throne. It's a truth I cannot bear to say aloud.

Eojin sniffles and rubs his eyes. he is only seven, yet I glance at Eojin, sniffling and rubbing the tears from his eyes. He is only seven, yet I must place a heavy burden on his shoulders.

"Prepare him for the crown, just in case."

Yuna nods. "I'll take care of the details of our disappearance."

"We will wait at the Guardian tree on this day, each year," Hyeon says.

Yuna grips my shoulder and nods. "Be safe, young prince."

I watch them slip into the shadows, their movements barely noticeable. Once they disappear into the Northern Court, I run to the Temple Tower.

The ceremonial disciples startle and gape as I burst through the door. "Hide!" I shout.

Some inch away, wanting to heed the order, but most remain rooted in place by confusion.

The Minister of Ceremony comes running. "Your Highness, what is the meaning—" He is interrupted by the tolling of the bell. It sets off a chain reaction of smaller alarms throughout the palace.

"All of you—hide and do not come out until it is safe."

Minister Ilseong bows his head, then quickly turns to usher the disciples toward the stairwell that leads down into the royal crypt.

Smothering silence falls as a dragon's roar cuts off. Seconds feel like an eternity as they tick by. The world holds its breath.

A heavy thud shatters the quiet. I feel it through the soles of my boots more than I hear it, finally breaks the dreadful silence. The tolling bells cease, leaving my ears ringing with ghostly echoes in the sudden hush.

The triumphant screech of a dragon I do not recognize.

My hands tremble as I enter the main chamber and rush to set the lights aflame. Then I walk to the center of the room and wait, preparing myself for what comes next.

Minutes pass. Long and endless. The sound of my shallow breathing is my only company. I flinch as the doors to the

Temple Tower are thrown wide with a bang, shattering the silence.

I take a deep breath. Release it.

Then I sprint forward.

Uncle passes over the threshold and into the main chamber seconds before I get there, forcing me to skid to a stop.

"Who are you?" I demand, feigning ignorance.

Eojin and I were to meet him in the morning. Now, an entirely different future awaits us with the dawn.

He blinks, then smiles. "I am your uncle, Your Highness," he says calmly.

He has changed. The demon curse markings have disappeared, and there is no sign of his bonded demon.

"What are you looking for?" he asks.

"Uncle? I thought you were with Mother and Father. Where are they?" I ask. "What is happening? Have you seen my brother? I was in the library when the alarm sounded. I cannot find him—he knows to come here if the alarms sound," I ramble on as if I had not witnessed a thing.

Uncle's gaze narrows, searching my face.

Does he know I lied?

"He probably ran to his rooms."

My blood runs cold. I must remind myself that he needs me alive.

No one will obey him without a member of the royal family to carry out his will.

"I came here from the Western Court. He—"

"I think I know where he is hiding." The shadouk reaches for me, but I step aside under the guise of looking around him. "Earlier this evening, I overheard him talking about a hidden room there."

There is no such place. Even if Eojin had not been with me, he would have shown me the second he discovered it.

"Eojin never mentioned—" My voice is weak and quiet, lacking any quality a Crown Prince should possess.

"Brothers do not always share everything," he counters. "Come along, Nephew, there is no time to waste."

To object would give away what I know. The only choice is to go along with him. Perhaps I can lead him away…

Outside the Temple Tower, save for the distant shouts of the guard captain giving orders.

I trail behind the shadouk through the long corridors with my head down, like an obedient prince, deferring to a respected elder. My gaze darts, searching for signs of Eojin's escape, even knowing that if they were successful, there would be nothing to give them away.

Every so often, he glances back. I do my best to offer a trusting smile, though too much uncertainty roils within me to know if it is believable.

We enter the building where Eojin and I share our connected apartments. The entire Western Court is abandoned. It's unnaturally quiet—a city of death and destruction.

He leads me into the study in my apartments.

I swallow the lump in my throat.

The shadouk stops and crouches. He glances over his shoulder, motioning impatiently for me to come closer.

His hand is pressed to the ground, fingertips sinking below the surface. There is no secret room before him—only dirt. It fills me with dread. Stories of humans burying their dead inside the earth fill my mind.

For several minutes, nothing happens.

I nearly leap out of my skin when he inhales sharply, and bright, red light shines from his eyes.

Be not afraid, prince. I am with you, my guardian's voice speaks reassuringly within my mind.

A rectangle of crimson light cuts through the dirt, opening at our feet. A faint, sickly light radiates from below, casting a barely there outline on the narrow steps leading into the depths.

"Go on," the shadouk urges. "Find your brother. I will be right behind you."

Determined to save my brother, I swallow my fear and descend.

The soft slide of leather soles trails behind, carrying the heavy presence, growing heavier and more oppressive with every heartbeat. Each breath seeming to say, *Run. Run while you still can.*

An eternity seems to pass, though in reality it is only minutes by the time we reach the hard-packed earth at the bottom. We emerge into a yawning cavern with a dark pool in the center. A long, narrow strip hovers above the water from the shore to a platform in the center, where a tall mirror frame stands.

Large swatches of moss grow in random patches along the rough walls, emitting the sickly, strange light that allows me to see where I'm going.

A young boy sits hunched and leaning forward before the mirror with his legs crossed.

Brother?

"Eojin!" I call, running for him.

I race over the narrow path. The water that I first thought was black, sloshes over in thick crimson waves. I wonder if it's an illusion, or the blood of all those who've died tonight. It's not until I reach the center platform that I realize the boy is not sitting before the mirror, but within.

I whirl around, ready to bolt, only to find the narrow path back to solid ground blocked.

"What is this?" My voice shakes, betraying the terror gripping my spine.

Black veins pulse within the whites of his eyes, swallowing his winter blue irises and spreading like ink into the whites until he stares at me through two shadowy voids.

"It is only the two of us now, Nephew." The shadouk walks forward along the glass. Each heavy footfall sends a wave of red liquid washing over it. "The rest of the family is dead."

Not Eojin.

I shake my head. "That's not true."

"Oh, but it is," he growls the words with malicious glee, letting the ruse slip away.

My hands ball into fists as I stand before the towering monster disguised as the uncle I've only seen through paintings. "Why?"

"Because I loved her first. Yet she chose your father instead, when *I* am the *firstborn*. This—the crown, the throne, and all of Arum is mine by rights—*she was mine!*"

I gather my energy, preparing to call upon my dragon.

"Now I will take what is mine," he calls.

The demon from the dinner lowers from the darkness above. Their eyes shine, molten. Red irises form in the depths of the shadouk's, pushing through the inky voids. More black veins spill from his eyes and across his face, spreading down his neck and under his collar, and over the backs of his hands within seconds.

He lifts a hand, summoning a glowing red orb above his palm.

Imugi's snowy form darts from the stairwell, soaring toward me as fast as they can. But the other demon sees them and swoops, slamming into them. The impact flings Imugi against the wall with a resounding crack.

The sound echoes in my ears, growing louder with the wail of crackling power that strikes me a moment later. My body rises into the air, lifted by giant, unseen hands. The power solidifies and turns into ropes of thorns that pierce my skin.

My guardian's screams fill my head as my own echo in my ears.

I collapse in a heap on the ground, breathless. The air feels too heavy, as if taking the shadouk's side, trying to keep me down. It takes everything I have to get up again.

The monster chuckles, amused by the effort I exert on such a simple thing. He points to the ground and swirls his finger, motioning for me to turn. My body obeys his command as if it is no longer mine to control.

The boy in the mirror lifts his head and gracefully gets to his feet. He turns, the upper part of him shrouded in a shadow that cuts diagonally across his torso.

He takes a step forward. The unnatural umbra melts away, revealing his face.

It is not my brother, as I'd assumed…

My reflection stares at me. His head lists to the side in a jerking motion. Vines of bloody thorns, wrapped around his limbs and body, push outward. The mirror's surface ripples as his hand passes through it.

A cold smile stretches over the lips of the other me a second before his fist plunges into my chest. He rips his arm back to whatever nightmare realm lies on the other side of the glass.

Slowly, he unfurls his fingers, revealing my pearl—the connection to both my guardian and my magic. I lunge, only to slam into the hard surface. I claw and scrape uselessly at the glass.

Dragon! I call to the guardian within me. *Dragon*!

There is no answer beyond a restless writhing that lets me know he is still there.

The boy within the mirror holds his free hand, open above my pearl. His fingers undulate, pulling on invisible strings. Light blue light shines as he works my power from it.

He throws the glowing orb of magic. It smacks against the glass, seeping in and seeps in, becoming one with it. A cold grin stretches over his mouth right before he hurls the pearl. I flinch at the loud crack and watch in horror as it fuses with the mirror.

The soft crunching of cracking glass feathers outward, growing louder and faster as fissures race across the surface.

Then, silence.

Three heartbeats… four… five.

The shards explode in a fierce explosion.

Blinding, searing pain slashes over one eye. My hands fly up, hovering over the area.

"Your memories will be gone within minutes, and soon the pain you feel will be a distant dream, half remembered," my uncle's voice whispers into my ear.

The writhing inside me stretches. Shimmering scales break out across my hands, then disappear with each thrash of dragon's claws.

"Soon, everyone will know that you killed your family because you were too impatient to wait to sit on the throne."

"That's… not true," I grind out as I fight to keep my guardian contained.

"When the world wakes, they will know of your treachery, but I will be by your side, watching as you fail to regain the broken shards of your power until the day you finally succumb. When that day comes, I will take great pleasure in ripping out your throat. And all of Arum will cheer me as I claim my crown, once and for all."

"No!" I scream.

In my anger, the tenuous grasp I had on my guardian slips. The dragon breaks free, sending my consciousness plummeting into darkness.

There is the vague sensation of flying over the palace—a roar summoning a massive storm to envelope the entire kingdom. Images of the fae lands and cities blur past. A blast of ice cuts through the forest, clearing the way.

I wake, cold and afraid, the next morning with Imugi at my side. We are on a platform surrounded by a small pool of water that looks like a sheet of silver. Before me is the polished metal backing of the broken mirror with lines forming a map of the missing pieces.

With a groan, I sit up. The cut running through my eye from brow to cheek stings with the rawness of it. My hand goes to my eye, fingers brushing over the sharp edge still protruding. My heart stumbles.

Blood seeps from the wound like a crimson river. I grip the shard with both hands, ignoring the pain of the jagged edges that dig into the tender skin of my palm.

A scream rips from my throat as I try to remove it in a single pull. But my hold is slippery from the new injuries. Bit by bit, I make progress. Each attempt is agony. Several times, I stop to wretch from the pain.

Finally, it slips free, and I let it drop.

Imugi breathes a puff of fog over my face, instantly dulling the pain. My skin tightens as it stitches itself back together.

Carefully, I press the shard against the mirror backing. It shines and stays in place. I feel a fraction of my power return to me.

How do I know to do that?

An instinct? No.

I squeeze my eyes shut, frowning as I struggle to remember.

A curse...

"You! You did this!" The words are a harsh whisper in the back of my mind.

The one I cast.

Why?

There are holes in my memory—too many to understand. Something went wrong. I ended up tangled up in its threads. *How?*

Every muscle in my body screams in protest as I climb to my feet and leave the cavern.

Outside is chaos. Shouts and screams fill the air as those who are able hurry to tend to the injured.

The death bell on the Temple Tower tolls out.

My family is dead.

I run to the Eastern Court. My uncle is there. He catches me before I can do more than glimpse the remains of my parents, mutilated beyond recognition. Two more adult forms lie beside them, and one the size of a child, only a few years younger than me.

My brother...

No... that's not right.

I am an only child.

CHAPTER THIRTY-NINE

JOON

MEMORIES CYCLE BEFORE MY EYES, RETURNING FASTER AND faster, until they are a blinding blur. Each one is faded and tattered along the edges with the passage of time.

The clues were always there. Lost and obscured in twisted dreams that evaporate with the morning dew—lies muddled with enough scraps of truth to make them more convincing.

Was the body of that child really my brother? Were the other two Hyeon and Yuna, or were the figures by their design?

I blink, and I am before the mirror again. The cracks heal as the curse begins to unravel from the very spot that anchored it all this time. Blue light shines from the edges, radiating with the pulse of a strong heartbeat.

As it fades, a pearl—perfect and whole—pushes out of the glass. I catch it before it hits the ground.

My magic thrums in my veins, strong and unfaltering.

The guardian within stirs.

But not like before. He is calm. At peace again. He is finally free of the pain that imprisoned his mind.

We are united again, at long last, as we were always meant to be.

I missed you, old friend, I say through our connection.

And I, you. The dragon's voice is deep and gentle. A comfort I had forgotten existed.

It is over.

I cannot help staring at this small, insignificant-looking thing—whole for the first time in far too long. There is a faint shimmer of a warmer hue than the pure icy color I remember.

Perhaps it is tainted by the blood that has soaked my hands over the years, or a scar left behind by the curse… or maybe it is the mark of Violet's sacrifice.

I hold it to my chest, closing my eyes as the connection between my pearl and my essence takes root once again. As it was meant to be.

The curse continues to untangle, releasing its hold over the land and the people. The first victim of the Winter Dragon's ice thaws and begins to wake.

Concentrating on the curse, I mentally sort through the tangled strands. When I find the oldest of them, I pull, willing it to come undone faster. Then I move to the next and the next.

The last hundred fray and snap in rapid succession. I feel it working through the human cities, feel each of my previous wives waking.

My feet barely touch the ground as I race back to the old throne room. I need to be there, ready for when Violet is freed.

Mingi and Iseul wait beside Violet's frozen form. They

turn their gaping expressions on me as I sprint toward them. I pass the shadouk, relieved he cannot bring harm to this world any longer.

"I... Your..." Mingi begins and fails to collect his thoughts.

"Both of you, go assist whoever you can as the curse continues to break," I order in a way to help their scattered thoughts find purchase.

They bow quickly. But Iseul hesitates, lingering behind as Mingi jogs off to obey.

"What will you do with her?" she asks. Her eyes sparkle with unshed tears.

Mingi calls to her from the doorway. Iseul bows again, then hurries to catch up without waiting for an answer.

The gentle trickle of water from the stream comes in from a broken window near the back of the room. I use the sound to calm my thoughts and focus.

My power comes to me with an ease I never thought possible. Stronger than I ever knew before the curse, when I was still coming into my full potential.

It bends to the shape of my lightest command. I had forgotten how it was supposed to feel—an extension of myself rather than attempting to control the flow of a wild river slipping through my fingers. Impossible to hold for long.

I ready myself for the moment the curse unravels around Violet.

The gentle rustle of fabric comes from somewhere nearby. A sigh.

Magic ripples over Violet. The broken spell has finally reached her. I must act the second she is free or risk losing her for good.

My attention snags on a movement out of the corner of my eye. I ignore it at first. But then my head snaps up as it draws near.

The shadouk stalks toward us, slowed by the snapping and crackling of bones and joints. He doubles over in pain as his body transforms.

Demon shit.

I assumed him dead—he should have been with the nature of the blast I struck him with… except his demon blocked part of it.

There are seconds to decide my course of action.

Gently setting Violet on the ground, I rise, ready to cut down this monster with a single blow. I divide my power, taking only enough to stop the threat ahead of me while saving everything else for her.

I position myself between Violet and the demon cursed creature ahead of me. Whether I heal her first or deal with him, I will need to move fast.

The unnatural creature laughs with my uncle's voice. A horrible, wet, raspy sound. "I see you finally succeeded at something for once in your life, Nephew. It's inconvenient, but I will make things right once I am rid of you."

"You killed my family," I snarl. If I can distract him with words, then I can save my power for Violet instead of warning him to keep his distance.

"One must sacrifice something of great value in order to gain power." He shrugs. "What could be more poetic than the brother who took everything from me?"

The ash and rust colored demon shakes off the rest of the ice shell and joins the shadouk. Both watch me from identical red eyes.

My uncle's fingers blacken and stretch, turning into talons. "Before the first kings became kings, they sought out demons and bonded to them. Thus, the fae were born into this world." Scales, soot gray and coal red, break out across his face and neck. The charred veins spread, growing and cracking his scales as they pulse beneath his skin. "I realized that if I were to claim my birthright, I must follow in their footsteps."

I flick a glance at Violet. The ice is thin. It's only a matter of minutes before it's gone entirely.

"But upon my return..." His breathing becomes labored, the register of his voice dropping two octaves as he continues, "My dear brother left me no choice—I had to force his hand."

His arm transforms into that of a dragon. The shadouk takes a jerky step closer. Then another. Some of the ashy scales flake off.

I flex my fingers, feeling my magic spark and dance between them.

"If he had abdicated, then your mother could have admitted to loving me as I knew she did. But he refused—it's his fault she died!" One eye turns pitch black, with a red slit pupil cutting through the center. The other eye is bloodshot, though it remains human.

"You are delusional. She loved my father. They were happy together."

What stands before me no longer resembles one of the fae. It is a horrific homunculus made from parts of a dragon and a man, twisted and fused together.

One side of his mouth is stretched wide, nearly to his ear. Razor-sharp teeth push out, sending the others falling to the floor. His left arm is too long and bent in such a way that it appears to be snapped in half, while the opposite is that of the guardian he claimed against the will of the saints.

There is a crack behind me.

Finally.

I drop to one knee as the last of the ice evaporates.

"Enough of this. It is time to send you to the Otherworld and reunite you with your family." The transformation completes, ripping through him as the grotesque dragon overtakes the rest of him. With a screech that splits the air, he ascends.

Mingi, Iseul, and Imugi reappear in the doorway, stopping short when they see the dragon.

Our eyes meet. I dip my chin. A sign that no matter how things play out, I trust them to know and carry out my will. Then, I send my power into Violet with every ounce of strength I possess.

The violent force of the shadouk's tail strikes me in the chest, sending me flying. It circles, preparing to swoop again.

Imugi moves in front of me. They would risk themselves knowing they cannot win.

"Protect them," I say.

My bonded demon, and life-long friend, turns their sorrowful eyes on me. There is no time for argument or hesitation. They bow their head, then cut through the air to do as I ask.

Knowing those I love are safe frees me to fight this battle. I call my dragon to the surface. The transformation is seamless —a sigh of magic tingling over flesh.

I glance at Violet once more. Her lashes flutter open. She sighs. Then her eyes close, and she stills.

No...

It had worked, but only for the briefest second. Now I cannot be with her in these last moments. I can only take some small comfort that the others can offer some comfort as she slips into the Otherworld. If only I had another minute, I could have saved her.

Rage bubbles up, and I turn it on the one who ripped her from me.

Cutting through the air, I aim for the shadouk. My talons pierce his scales and dig in. I drag him with me, soaring higher, through the ceiling and into the night.

He struggles against me as I heave him toward the Maldan Ice Wall until nothing but darkness and barren tundra surrounds us. I fling him, letting the points of my claws rip into muscle and bone as he tumbles into the frozen earth.

Half-clotted blood stains the snow. But the shadouk still lives. He leaps up, taking flight.

We collide. Snarling. Biting. Shredding. Neither of us is willing to concede.

This will only end when one, or both, of us dies.

CHAPTER FORTY

VIOLET

Light shines against my eyelids. Squinting and blinking against the brightness, I push myself into a sitting position. Pressing the heel of my hand to my temple, I attempt to quell the thundering headache.

Everything feels different, yet as I look around my room, nothing appears to be out of place or changed.

Bear dashes from across the room and leaps onto the bed, sliding over the blankets and curling up on my lap. They are a bit too big and too heavy, but I appreciate the sign of affection, so I allow it. I pet the top of the demon's head.

Strange, how they can look like every other wild demon, while managing to be rather cute at the same time.

The door slides open, and Iseul sticks her head in. Her face brightens when she sees me. "You're awake."

She turns to someone out in the hall, speaking too quietly for me to hear before entering and hurrying to my side. Her hands grip my shoulders as she looks me over several times with an expression of disbelief. When she's satisfied, she drops onto the edge of the mattress with a heavy sigh.

"How are you feeling?"

Iseul doesn't wait for an answer before her arms are around me, pulling me into a tight hug. Bear grumbles and wedges their way between us, becoming the center of the embrace.

Iseul pulls back. We share a smile.

Mine quickly fades. "My head is splitting," I groan. "I feel like I nearly…." I trail off.

"What's wrong? Do you feel like you're going to be sick?" Iseul asks, noticing the change in my demeanor.

The pulse in my veins kicks up as everything comes back to me.

A demon. The one who cursed Joon and Arum. "The king, he—"

"Is dead," she finishes for me, holding up a hand. "His body was found a few hours ago. We were there for part of it, but Imugi filled us in on the rest of the details… including your bargain with the prince."

I hold my breath.

"He broke the curse," she answers my unspoken question.

Iseul has mentioned the king and the curse, but I can't help but notice that she has not mentioned Joon. He is not here—if he were all right, then he would be. I know he would.

I am afraid to ask. Afraid to know the truth. But of the two, not knowing is far more unbearable. "Joon?"

There are so many questions tied up in that one word.

Where is he? Is he on his way? Is he hurt? Is he…

No!

He can't be—he broke the curse.

A knock on the door has Iseul jumping to her feet. She hurries to answer as if she can't get away fast enough.

Once again, she exchanges a few words with someone I can't see. A moment later, she returns carrying a tray and sets it down on the bedside table. Pale tea fills a small crystal pot with a matching cup beside it. Next to that is also a shallow, wooden bowl containing something that resembles a dark broth.

Iseul hands me the bowl first and stands there, expectantly.

I hold it and return her stare.

"Drink." She won't tell me another thing until I do. She doesn't need to say as much—it's clear in her tone and body language.

I bring it to my lips and oblige. The mix of herbs combines to create an aromatic, earthy, yet bright flavor with a slightly bitter aftertaste.

There are notes of things I don't recognize, and I am instantly curious. It isn't the worst medicine I've taken, but it is a bit too strong to be considered pleasant. By the time I hand Iseul the empty bowl to inspect, my headache is gone, and I make a mental note to ask about it later.

I wait for Iseul to answer my question. When she doesn't, I ask again, "Where is Joon?" I can't keep the desperation from my voice.

It only increases my apprehension further when Iseul's gaze darts around, as if she is looking for someone.

"Why won't you tell me? Is he all right?"

She looks down at the bowl in her hands. "We should wait for Mingi."

"Tell me what happened," I snap.

Iseul sighs and finally meets my gaze. "How much do you remember?"

I force my shoulders to relax. It's still difficult to believe.

Closing my eyes, I try to find clarity in my thoughts. "The king—" No, not the king. Not anymore. I look to Iseul for guidance, but she only shrugs as if it doesn't matter what I call him. So, I continue, each word coming slowly, "He cursed Joon. Somehow, he figured out the final shard was inside me —he was going to kill me, before Joon…"

My throat tightens. I shake my head.

This… this isn't right.

Removing the shard should have killed me. I try to sort through the haze of memories, but everything is too unclear.

If Joon broke the curse, then… then what?

"How am I alive?" I'm not entirely sure if my question is for her, myself, or Joon, wherever he is. "Joon couldn't break the curse without killing me," I say slowly.

"Do you remember anything else?" Iseul prompts.

Again, I shake my head.

She sighs, pressing her lips together as she decides what and how she fills in the missing pieces for me. "He encased you within ice as he took the shard. He made it part of the curse, but…"

"But?" I prompt when she trails off.

"His ice is different than the dragon's. It…" Iseul trails off and is silent for a moment before continuing, "That alone should have killed you."

My weakened heart. The shard. The ice. The shadouk. So many things working against me, trying to end my life. It is no small miracle that I am alive.

My throat goes painfully dry as alarm presses in on my chest like a heavy weight. But the feeling is stunted by a shocking realization—the strong, negative emotion that would typically set off an episode feels different. No sharp pain or pressure clamps down on my heart, only anxiety.

"Mingi and I talked about it," Iseul adds as if sensing my distress. "We think all those times he used his power to heal you when siphoning, somehow imprinted some of his power onto your soul. Enough that his magic couldn't kill you.

Depending on how much, it's possible you could be immune to some glamours."

I lack significant knowledge in the workings of magic, but the logic is sound enough to stifle some of my unease.

Considering I'm no longer injured, that must mean Joon freed me from the ice and healed me *after* breaking the curse.

Not being able to remember all the details leaves me theorizing in order to make sense of things, with no guarantee that I'm right about any of it.

"Then he is alive." It's not a question. It's true. It *has* to be. Even if he's hurt or trapped, I need to believe he is alive and well, trying to make his way to me.

Iseul swallows and licks her lips.

But… if that's the case, where is he? Why is Iseul doing everything to avoid saying?

Another knock on the door interrupts our conversation. I scowl at whoever is on the other side as Iseul takes the opportunity to avoid telling me what I want to know.

A woman steps in and announces Mingi's arrival.

Iseul rushes to meet her brother. They exchange hushed words. From my vantage, the two of them are either disagreeing or plotting.

I would like to know what they are talking about that they don't feel the need to let me in on it.

Pushing the blankets off, I get to my feet, taking a moment to ensure I am steady. My muscles feel strong and rested. In fact, my entire body feels strong. I don't remember the last time I felt this good.

I quietly make my way over to the siblings. The siblings are so engrossed in their conversation that they don't notice me until I clear my throat. Iseul and Mingi startle and gape at me with identical expressions.

"You should stay in bed and rest. You're not—" Iseul says.

I hold a hand up to stop her. "I have rested enough. Right now, I want to know what you are hiding from me. Where is Joon?"

Imugi's pale form slips through the wall like morning mist. The demon's eyes lock onto Mingi. "Sightings of the second dragon have sparked confusion and unrest. Speculation of a second curse is already spreading through the city. It is only a matter of days before it reaches every city in Arum."

"Have the captains send their men to squash the rumor before it has a chance to leave the walls of the capital," Mingi orders.

"What should they say?"

"Anything—whatever they must to ease the tensions for now. The threat has been handled and is no more."

I push between Iseul and Mingi. "Second dragon?"

Imugi blinks twice. "Yes. In order to become one with a guardian, the Traitor King bonded with a higher demon." They gesture to themselves with their tail. "But they were greedy and did not care that their natures and powers were ill-suited. Even the most powerful will end up demon cursed with the wrong fit."

Flashes of scales flicker in my hazy memory. Ash and rust.

I thought it was only the Traitor King's demon. But had it actually been the dragon within him? If he and Joon were the two who were spotted, then—

My stomach tightens with desperation. "And Joon?"

"Their dragons fought," Imugi says, confirming my theory. Frustratingly, there is nothing in their tone to hint at the outcome.

"There is time for talk when everything has settled," Mingi interrupts. "We must focus on keeping the people at ease now."

Imugi stiffens. They remain where they are, though they heed the unspoken command to stop talking.

I round on the two fae. Iseul stares at the floor, lips pressed into a tight line, while Mingi sighs and swears at the demon under his breath.

His reaction makes me think that I might stand a better chance at pulling the truth from him.

"Tell me what happened to Joon." I clench my fists so hard, my nails dig into my palms. The sting grounds me, preparing me to hear the worst.

If Joon were fine, they would have said so.

He would be here now.

I would sense if he were hurt or worse. Wouldn't I?

"There is nothing to tell," Mingi says.

I take a calming breath, which does absolutely nothing to help.

Demons and saints protect this man because I will send him to the Otherworld with my bare hands if he gives me another non-answer.

"What does that mean?" I ask through clenched teeth.

Mingi's eyes narrow with suspicion, as if he can hear my thoughts. "It means that we cannot tell you what we do not know. We do not know where he is or…" He takes a half step back, then another. "Or what condition he is in."

All the fight leaves me as that last part sinks in. The meaning underlying his words is crystal clear despite his attempts to soften the blow.

They don't know if he is dead or alive.

Deep down, I am terrified of the worst. But I cling to the shred of hope I still have left.

I glance at Imugi. Their expression is strange, but I don't know the demon well enough to read them. Worry? Sorrow perhaps?

Considering their lifelong bond, not knowing one way or another must be hard on them.

Their wintery gaze meets mine for a breath. The demon offers me a minute nod, then turns and floats from the room, passing through the closed door like smoke.

"I will return by evening," Mingi says quietly to Iseul.

"I am going with you," I say.

Iseul elbows her brother in the ribs, giving him a pointed look that communicates a scolding and a reminder about me all at once. He returns her look.

"It's only been one day," he says to me. "You should rest for now, Violet. We will keep you updated."

"While I appreciate your concern for my well-being, I am fine."

As if in a show of support, Bear bounds off the bed and comes to sit beside me.

Mingi and Iseul watch me. Unmoved.

"You cannot expect me to spend the day lounging in comfort and doing nothing when he could be out there, hurt or dying." I decide to change tactics. Frustration isn't getting through. "I need to do this." My voice holds a tremor I couldn't hide if I wanted to.

The two of them consider my plea. Mingi's expression hardens. I think he's about to object, but Iseul speaks first.

"Then I will go as well." She offers me a half smile. "If it becomes too much for Violet at any point, I will bring her back to the palace."

Mingi rolls his eyes in brotherly annoyance but doesn't argue.

Mingi takes the lead, with Iseul and I flanking him. I opted to ride Joon's snow-white mare. I've never ridden her alone, but Star Runner and I are familiar with each other.

Beyond what is necessary, no one in our little search party is in the mood to speak. Our shared goal eclipses all other thoughts.

The air feels heavy, as if the elements themselves are holding their breath, waiting for Joon to reappear. Thick clouds blanket the sky, casting a melancholy gloom over the world. It all comes together, fitting the mood of our little search party.

Bear snuggles against my back under the shelter of my cloak. Their warm body helps fight against the chill.

After nearly two hours, we reach the area Mingi indicated would be the beginning of today's search.

He slows for a moment and stares at a hilly area ahead of us, before guiding his mount to skirt the area. Iseul follows without question.

I stop. There is something on the other side of the hill. But why avoid it when we will end up there regardless?

For too long, everyone has been careful with me. I could understand why when the shard caused havoc with my heart, but that is no longer the case. While sudden and powerful emotions could trigger episodes, that didn't mean I was in danger from all feelings. I am tired of being treated as if I am weak and frail.

I will not shrink and wilt by witnessing the harsh realities of the world. No matter how uncomfortable or painful they may be.

Iseul calls to me as I urge Star Runner forward on our original path. Even without Joon, she is the perfect steed. Part of me wonders if she understands the intent of our mission. A moment later, the pounding of hooves follows.

As I crest the hill, another, smaller one comes into view. At first, it appears to be little more than a mound of dark ash, as if there was a recent fire. A powerful odor hits with my next inhale. The reek of rot lingers on the air.

Not fire. Death.

Mingi pulls up, cutting me off. "It would be better to go around."

When I try to go around him, he moves to block me again.

"Why?" I demand. "You wouldn't bring me anywhere near here if—"

"It's the Traitor King," Iseul says.

Immense relief floods through my body.

"I searched the immediate area for any trace of the prince yesterday. He is not here. If you truly wish to see the carnage, then I won't stop you. However, you will gain nothing by doing so."

I relent. The urge to see the other side has been satisfied with that honesty. Even clinging to hope, I still need reassurance to quell my fears.

We begin our search in the west and ride east, then move north, before riding west again, zigzagging across the kingdom, leaving no swath of land unchecked. Somber silence remains our companion with each arc taking us further and further from the palace.

Mingi and Iseul use their magic to leave markers that will allow us to readily identify the ground we covered.

After several hours, we break to build a fire and eat a small meal. I chew and swallow, barely tasting the food. Worry makes it difficult to get more than a few bites down. The only one whose appetite is unaffected is Bear's. I sneak them pieces of meat and potatoes that they happily gobble up until my plate is cleared.

I stare into the flames, holding my hands to the heat even

though I don't feel the need to warm myself. The cold hasn't gone past a surface level easily banished with a bit of movement. A thought briefly crosses my mind, wondering if tolerance to the cold is another side effect of Joon using his powers on me.

I turn my hand over and stare at the base of my middle finger. Tilting it this way and that, I can't help but hope to see the faint shimmer of the thread that binds me to Joon. That if the light hits just right, it will still be there, a whisper of spider silk, letting me know he is waiting for me, somewhere.

The second part of the day is much the same as the first. We've yet to find the smallest sign or clue that could tell us one way or the other of Joon's fate.

The westernmost edge of the fae lands is a steep slope into an inhospitable tundra beyond. Grounds that are nothing but deep ravines with spikes of rock jutting up several stories high. Ice has formed over everything with sharp edges and points. Storm clouds cover the wild lands as if they are trapped, lashing wind over the landscape in their anger as they kick up a haze of snow.

"We should turn back now if we want to make it back to the palace before nightfall," Mingi announces.

Going back now feels like giving up, even if I know it's not. There isn't enough daylight to do another pass today. Dying will not bring us any closer to finding Joon.

"In addition to the added travel time, each pass we do will take more time than the last—so don't expect to make as much progress as today," he adds. "We can't risk missing anything."

I set my jaw and nod. Already, I feel my heart demanding the impossible of me.

Mingi and Iseul steer their horses toward the palace, but I remain in place a moment longer, staring into the wild.

Perhaps it's only the need to believe that we are still somehow connected. But something inside me is wound tight, as if we are just on the verge of finding him.

I have to believe we will succeed. For as long as we don't find his body, there is still a chance that he is alive.

"Tomorrow," I whisper a promise to Joon, hoping it will find its way to him. "I will find you tomorrow."

Then I turn and follow my companions.

CHAPTER FORTY- ONE

VIOLET

Once more, we make the trip back to the palace. A heavy presence hovers over me from behind. Weighing me down. I lag behind Mingi and Iseul, mostly ignoring their conversations that fill the silence.

After a week of searching from sunup to sundown, we have failed to find so much as a scratch to hint at Joon's whereabouts. It's as if he never existed at all. Even Star Runner seems to drag their feet in disappointment.

I promised to find him, and day after day, I fail to keep my word.

"—need a contingency plan. The officials are upset that a new Minister of Shields has not yet been appointed. A few of them have already requested an audience with him to discuss the matter."

Pieces of their conversation reach me as they adjust their pace to prevent me from falling too far behind. I listen with mild disinterest. Those in positions of authority will always find something to take issue with the hopes that the solution will bring them more power.

"Demons take them, they frustrate me to no end," Iseul snaps, gesturing wildly with her hands. "Even when they are told he is recovering from defending them against the Traitor King."

The two of them continue talking among themselves as they flank me, half a horse length ahead.

"It was only ever meant to be a temporary solution to buy us a few days. We are pushing it." Mingi shakes his head. "Infighting will begin unless they see someone on the throne. Arum needs an active ruler, and soon."

"But who?" Iseul asks. "There is no protocol for a situation like this. Not just anyone can take up that mantle."

"I know," Mingi bites out, though it's clear his frustration is not aimed at her.

Blinking, I sit straighter in my saddle. Their conversation finally succeeds in pulling me from my dejection.

The night Joon and I had dinner, I wanted to share something I'd found during my research. Except we were interrupted, but I never got the chance. It had completely slipped my mind after everything came to a head. And ever since, I have been singularly focused on finding him.

"I know what to do," I blurt, cutting them off.

Both turn to me with matching expressions of bewilderment.

My heart races in a way that makes me feel alive without the pain that used to bring the fear of death with it.

If I'm right—and I know I am—then this will give us all the time in the world to search for Joon without the pressure or demands of politics.

I urge my horse into a run, racing toward the palace.

Within seconds, the thunder of hooves follows.

Once we are inside, I will explain everything at once.

Soon, we are bearing down on the palace gate. The guards

scramble to allow us entry when they realize we're not slowing.

At the stables, the young groom who always seems to know when he's needed ahead of time already has the reins in hand before I dismount. He nods to signal that he will take care of Star Runner, leaving me free to run as fast as my legs will carry me through the grounds and toward the Northern Court.

Wisps of hair cling to my face, damp with sweat. Scholars murmur at the commotion I cause, quickly moving out of my way as I completely disregard library decorum.

While Mingi and Iseul catch up, I gather what I need, grabbing the royal family's most recent record on my way to the book that holds the key to everything. It's in the exact spot I found it, leaning at the same angle as it was the day I found it. The fine layer of dust that settled on the exposed front cover is undisturbed, as if I'd never touched it.

"What is this all about?" Iseul asks between gasps.

At the same time as Mingi asks, "What are we doing here?"

I shove the first book into his hands, opening it and flipping to where the torn edges run down the center crease.

"Look." I run my finger down the fold. "A page is ripped out."

Mingi stares at me with a straight face. "You should have given it to one of the scholars—"

"Why would someone need to remove a page?" I ask pointedly as I flip back one page to Joon's name. "To hide something. And look here, it says, 'first son,' not just 'son.'"

"I'm not sure what you're getting at," Iseul says softly with a hint of guilt.

I lean in. "They had a *second* son," I whisper, then straighten, waiting for them to understand.

"Violet," Iseul says my name slowly. She wrings her hands

and exchanges a look with her brother. "He died the night of the curse with the rest of the royal family."

Turning, I grab the book behind me. "Something else is going on here. I first picked this up thinking it was something else."

I open the cover and quickly flip to the story. But before I can show them, the words rise in a puff of glittering smoke as they begin to fade from the parchment. Then the pages themselves. On and on until my open palms are empty.

By the end of it, my hands are shaking, holding nothing but air.

"What did it say?" Iseul whispers.

I tell them what I remember of the story, comparing it to the nearly identical way the Traitor King spoke of Joon's parents, the monster attack, and how the prince sent his brother away.

Iseul sucks in a sharp breath. "It's too convenient for it to be coincidental, especially since books don't simply evaporate into stardust."

Mingi hums thoughtfully. "I believe you're right. As the oldest prince, Sameun would have normally been the heir, but he lacked sufficient power because he could not form a demon bond upon his birth."

The siblings fill in the gaps of what I don't know, building off each other's thoughts.

"He obviously forced a bond with one before returning." She shudders. "Even if it was the only way to access his guardian, he had to know he would become a shadouk."

Mingi nods. "The past is absolute and cannot be rewritten, as history is the source of the guardians' magic. No mortal magic has the power to take it from them."

Iseul grabs my hand in both of hers. "The Traitor King couldn't just remove the young prince from the record books.

He had to erase Prince Eojin from the memories of everyone who ever knew him. He couldn't change the past, so the curse could only move the memories somewhere else."

Another thought occurs to me—I might be grasping at straws, but if there's even the slightest possibility that any detail from my time here can help, then I will go over every detail, no matter how minor it seems.

"You said I had Joon's power in me and that there is a chance I could see through glamours?"

"I did," Iseul agrees. Her brow furrows at the sudden change in topic.

"How would I recognize it?"

She presses her lips together. "I suppose it could look like they shimmer in certain lights."

"Then I know where to find him." I grin and shift closer. "Joon and I rode through a town to the south, and there was a young man hanging a sign. At the time, I thought it was from the sunset, but I think it was a glamour." I scrunch my nose, trying to remember the name. "I think it was... Lummi."

Mingi flips to a different page in the book he still holds. He turns it around to show Iseul and me. On the late queen's page, he points to the name of the place she grew up in before she married the late king.

It is the same.

"Something tells me you are correct," Mingi murmurs. He snaps the book shut as a scribe passes by and catches him by the arm. "A page has been removed from this one."

The scribe takes it with both hands and bows. "I will see it restored immediately."

"Have them double-check to make sure no other records are missing. Then add the details of the Traitor King's rule and his crimes."

"Yes, of course." The man bows again, then hurries off.

I don't think about the implications of this other prince becoming king. It can be sorted out once we bring Joon home.

I lead Iseul and Mingi through the streets of Lummi. The damp chill of night still lingers on the morning air.

We left the palace as soon as the first rays of sunlight stretched over the horizon and forced the wild demons into hiding for the day.

Food shops are already open for the day, preparing for the rush that will come once the businesses selling other goods open their doors.

I stop across the road from a modest bookstore with a sign hanging over the sidewalk that reads: The Dragon's Tome. The newly painted letters are still bright and vibrant with color. Even the name is an obvious clue.

Two windows, situated on either side of a narrow door, display books on risers.

An arm reaches over the top and replaces one of the books with another before disappearing into the shadows within.

Motioning for the others to follow, I cross and push open the door. The bell above the entry rings our arrival.

"I'm sorry, we're not open yet. If you would—" the young man trails off when he turns toward us.

For a heartbeat, I am too stunned to breathe. The prince's features are nearly identical to Joon's. So much so that I feel as though I am staring at a younger version of him. But where Joon's eyes are two different shades of blue, sharper, deeper, and shadowed with the weight of the curse, his brother's eyes are large and bright, still unwearied by the cruelty of the world.

His gaze skips from me to Iseul and Mingi, then, with a frown, settles back on me.

"Prince Eojin," I say, stepping forward. "I am Violet Hawthorn, and this—"

"I know who they are," he interrupts, though not unkindly. His voice is soft with awe. "I was wondering if or when someone would come."

"We need to speak with you about an urgent matter, Your Highness," I say before the moment can become a happy reunion.

During the ride here, Iseul and Mingi reminisced about their days with the two princes and the antics all four of them would get into.

Prince Eojin nods and gestures to a table against the wall with cushioned bench seats. "Let us sit and speak as equals. I have not been a prince for a long time now."

He locks the door and draws the curtain over the door before joining us, taking the remaining seat beside Mingi, opposite Iseul and me.

The way Eojin looks at the siblings, especially Iseul, seems to hold extra meaning. Perhaps he is reliving memories from their shared childhood.

"How did you find me?" he asks Mingi.

Mingi nods in my direction. "She did."

Eojin turns his attention on me, full of suspicion. "You, I don't know. Tell me, what is a human doing traveling with fae? And how is it that you were the one to track me down?"

"I'm Vi—"

"I know your name. I want to know *who* you are."

After so much time with Joon, the younger prince's prickly demeanor is not quite what I'd expected. Knowing his position, I can't blame him.

"I am Prince Joon's seventh wife," I say matter-of-factly. It pleases me inside when Eojin's brows jump higher in surprise.

"Impossible. We fae do not take multiple spouses."

"It's a long story," Iseul draws out the first word as she offers a smile that is more grimace.

Leaving out the intimate details, I explain everything from the beginning—my condition, my theft, and the bargain with Joon. I explain how I discovered the clues in my research, and the book with the true history disguised as a fairytale. Iseul and Mingi help fill in the details. All the while, Eojin sits back listening with rapt attention.

"Joon killed the Traitor King the night he broke the curse," I finish.

Afterward, the young prince is silent, as if lost in thought.

"Why did you stay here after your memories returned?" I ask after a while.

Prince Eojin shrugs, then leans on the table with folded arms. Most of his princely demeanors have faded, leaving traces behind that can only be found if you know what to look for.

"I have spent more years in this life than the one I was born into. It's simple, but it's a good life." Eojin gazes out the window to a distant point only he can see with his mind's eye. "There is no need for a spare to complicate matters. With the curse broken, my brother can take the throne."

Iseul jabs me in the ribs below the table.

"That brings us to the matter we've come to discuss with you," I say.

Eojin sits straighter, his expression hardens. Perhaps he can sense the gravity in my tone.

I swallow the lump in my throat and steel my spine for the part I must say next. "We found the Traitor King's body, but we haven't been able to find any trace of Joon. We've searched and can't find a trace." Warm pressure builds behind my eyes as tears build, threatening to drown me.

Iseul gently squeezes my hand, then takes over. "For now, everyone believes he is recovering, but there's no telling what chaos will break out if anyone discovers the truth about the crown prince."

"I cannot claim his crown while he lives," he says.

"That is why we must declare him dead—"

"No." I nearly choke on the word as I get to my feet. They had "I won't give up on him even if you do."

Iseul tugs on my arm, having me sit back down. "We're not giving up. This is necessary to prevent unrest while we keep searching."

"If Joon returns to claim his birthright, then I will abdicate," he says. "I will do everything in my power to aid you in your search. However, it will be difficult to do so if the world believes him dead."

"What do you suggest?" Mingi asks.

"I will return, in full support of my brother. Then, after a few days, I will announce that his condition has worsened and he will need to be placed in stasis until we can find a solution," he says, meeting my gaze. "Depending on public opinion, it may prove difficult to place him on the throne when he's found. Though not impossible if the people's memories have returned as well."

I dip my chin, grateful for the prince's thoughtfulness.

Prince Eojin's return is met with a mix of joy and skepticism. But any doubts about his validity are squashed when his bonded demon emerges from hiding. Mandu is the bright blue of a summer sky with a mane so pale it shimmers like moonlight.

With his demon's assistance, Eojin quickly regains any confidence he might have lacked from his years away from the palace and falls back into his natural roles with ease.

Over the following days, a numb detachment comes over me. Each one a blur and an eternity. I watch the coronation beside Iseul and Mingi, though I can barely bring myself to pay attention.

I wait for the search for Joon to resume.

As King Eojin restores order. One of his first official acts is to bestow power, nearly equal to that of the royal bloodline, onto Mingi and Iseul for all they have done for the kingdom. The decree instantly elevates their status to nobles and eradicates the stigma they once carried as orphans. I am truly happy for them. They deserve recognition for their loyalty.

One of his first official acts is to enact a system that will create better conditions for orphans, which will give current and future orphans an equal opportunity to find a good place in society, rather than being relegated to the edges, barely scraping by. Forgotten.

By the time the palace repairs are complete, the king has familiarized himself with the running of the kingdom, using his years among the people to find ways to improve laws and policies.

Eojin shocks the kingdom by declaring the border between the human and fae lands open for the first time in centuries since its creation. The decree is unexpected, receiving mixed reactions of reservation and excitement. Many on both sides of the line begin migrating immediately, eager for the potential prosperity and trade.

On and on, time passes without wavering. Refusing to slow.

I go through the motions I must, moving through the world, but never truly part of it. I am stuck, unable to move forward or back.

Even when everything has settled, the only time I feel like myself is when I ride over plains and tundra, searching for Joon. Mingi and Iseul spend an increasing amount of time with the Eojin, join the last true king's personal spies, Hyeon and Yuna, in near constant discussions about possibilities for the future, as they help him adjust to a life he was never prepared to live.

Clutching the near-empty bag in my hand, I slow Star Runner and stare up at the Maldan Ice Wall. The top reaches so high into the heavens that it's lost among the clouds.

After months of searching, I have finally reached the end of Arum's northern land. I pull out one of the markers Iseul created for me and toss it down, then I turn and head toward the palace.

I am weary but not defeated. I can't shake the feeling that I'm getting closer to finding Joon, even though there's no logical reason to believe so.

Upon my return, I head straight for the throne room. The guards are used to the routine. With a nod, one turns to announce me, then motions for me to enter.

I stride in, stopping at the foot of the dais, and bow to King Eojin. Instead of the usual cue to rise, there is the gentle susurration of his robes sliding over the steps as he descends.

His hand alights on my shoulder. "I am glad you see you return safely."

I straighten.

"Tell me what you have to report," he says. He is giving me a rare courtesy by hearing what I have to say, when a simple glance can tell him everything he needs to know.

"I reached the Maldan ice wall... My results are the same. However, there are still the southern lands to search."

Eojin nods. "I am sorry to hear that. I was hoping it would be different. It has been a long time since I last saw my brother, and I would like to see him again. I miss him."

"I will go rest now," I say. "I want to begin as soon as the sun rises."

"No," he says softly.

I freeze. "W-what do you mean?"

Eojin smiles kindly. "My brother is lucky to have someone who loves him as you do. I will always be thankful for your unwavering loyalty, but it is time for you to return to your family. I am sure they are waiting for you."

I am shaking my head before he finishes speaking. "Please don't ask me to give up on him," I plead.

King Eojin clasps my hands. "If Joon returns half the love you have for him, then you know he would not want you to abandon your own life."

Tears burn my eyes.

I do miss my family. After all, I bargained with Joon to live and have them restored. They must wonder if I am even still alive at this point.

I don't want to admit that he's right. It feels like leaving him for dead.

"Do not fret. We will not stop searching. One way or another, we will find out what happened. I will send for you the moment we learn anything. You have my word."

"Thank you." I bow.

He nods, signaling that our meeting is over.

I bow at the waist again, then turn to go make my preparations to leave the winter fae lands behind.

STARS

Stars glitter against the endless night.

The kings and queens of the past gaze down on the world below, watching the world and the stories of the people unfold.

In a corner of endless night, a spark ignites as a star shimmers, finding its new home.

CHAPTER FORTY-TWO

VIOLET

Iseul squeezes me within an inch of my life. She holds the embrace until stars dance before my eyes. Tears spill down her cheeks when she finally pulls back.

"It's going to be so boring without you," she complains.

"I will miss you, too." My own tears slip free. "But we can write and visit each other."

Iseul sniffles and shrugs. "A poor substi—*oh*!" Her entire mood shifts mid-sentence. "I have something for you. Well, I suppose it's for you and Bear."

She pulls out a leather collar, crouching to fasten it around the demon's neck.

Bear sits back on their haunches and tries to angle their head to see it better. A faint shimmer surrounds their body, adding a ghostly outline of a dog. I can see past it as I could when Joon cast his glamour over us.

"A glamour?"

"I commissioned it a while back, but it took a while to complete. Now, when people look at them, they'll see a dog." Iseul beams.

I throw my arms around her. "Thank you!"

Mingi clears his throat. Our goodbye is cut short with the reminder that he's waiting to escort me to Firnhallow. The reality of the moment casts a shadow over our mood.

Iseul and I pull away.

"I'm sorry I can't go with you. King Eojin asked me to stay." A subtle blush colors her cheeks. "Now that things are in order, we finally have a chance to catch up."

"I'm glad," I say. "After everything that's happened, I'm sure there's a lot to say."

"I'll come visit you, I promise!"

"You are welcome anytime. All of you."

Mingi sighs impatiently. I take that as my cue and pull myself onto Star Runner. She's the only other horse besides Zazu Moon that I trust with my life.

King Eojin offered me an excessive sum of coins for everything I'd done, but I declined. I already have what I sought from my bargain. But when he offered to give me Joon's horse, I couldn't refuse.

Iseul lifts Bear up into my arms. "Be a good little puppy, all right? I'll try to come see you soon," she says, patting them on the head.

She backs up, waving, then turns and runs back through the palace gates.

Already missing my friend, I watch her until she's out of sight, then turn Star Runner toward the east, where the human lands lie beyond the old border.

There is the notable absence of someone I'd hoped to say goodbye to. But I haven't seen Imugi since the morning after Joon broke the curse. Perhaps they are searching for Joon in places the rest of us can't venture.

I don't ask about them, not wishing to jinx them with bad luck, and choosing to believe they are well.

“I’m ready,” I say to Mingi.

He closes his eyes and summons a road for us, cutting through the forest trees ahead. Even with the new roads between the lands with outposts set up to make travel safer for humans and less magical fae, this way will cut a two-day-long trip down to hours.

By the early evening, we finally reach the edge of the human lands. I move off the fae road and turn to Mingi.

“Thank you for escorting me… and everything else.”

“I can take you the rest of the way,” he offers.

I shake my head. “It’s only an hour from here, and I’d like to have some time alone to organize my thoughts.”

My parents have been trapped for what feels like a lifetime, and I have been in the fae lands for what feels like another on top of that.

He nods in understanding.

Mingi and I don’t exchange parting words as we go our separate ways. Other than caring for Joon, we were never close.

Bear and I pass the area where we had our first encounter, and I can’t help the smile that tugs my lips. I was so afraid of them then. My past self could never have imagined that I would bring them home to stay with me one day.

I pause at the top of the hill overlooking the edge of town. It looks like the same home I’ve always known. The same businesses, the same lanterns that ring the city to keep the wild demons from venturing too close, the same bustle of people going about their day. Yet, somehow, everything feels different.

So much has changed that I’m unsure how I fit in my old life anymore, only that my place isn’t where it used to be.

“I suppose it is not this place, but me, that has changed,” I murmur.

It's easy to believe that it's much the same for Iseul, Mingi, and King Eojin. Perhaps, we all feel some variation of being set adrift from everything we've always known.

Bear lifts their head, then leaps down to walk alongside me, taking on the role of a faithful dog.

As we make our way through town and near the gate of my childhood home, I wonder if perhaps I should have sent a letter ahead of me.

Does my family still live here? What if they heard about the Choosing and assuming I died, moved away? Illogical thoughts race through my mind the rest of the way, only to vanish as I turn onto the drive.

The moment I pass through the gate, the front door is thrown wide, with Mother and Father rushing out to meet me.

Just as my feet touch solid ground, Mother wraps me up in a fierce hug, with tears streaming down her face. Father joins us, his eyes glassy and red, and wraps us both in his strong arms. Then we all talk at once, our voices a tangle of questions and words of relief.

When we eventually separate, Mother reaches out and wipes my face. "Are you hurt?"

"I'm all right," I assure them. "The prince didn't hurt me. He..." I hesitate and push down the ache that rises in my chest. "He healed me."

My parents exchange concerned glances. I can't blame them. If it hadn't happened to me, I would have a hard time believing it as well. I am one of the handful who ever got to know the true version of him.

"Is *he* the reason you couldn't return sooner?"

I shake my head. "There was something I had to take care of first."

I tell them a simplified version about the curse and my

time with Joon, leaving out the part about the bargain and the more intimate details, and downplaying the extent of the danger I was in. There's no point in upsetting them when everything turned out well in the end.

"We should go in and let you get settled," Father says, waving to someone behind me.

I turn to find a hired groom jogging toward us. As soon as I see his pointed ears, I recognize him as one of the young stable hands from the palace.

The young man smiles brightly and bows his head.

"It's you!" I say.

There were many times when I caught sight of him leaving the stable after preparing food, water, and always ready to care for Star Runner after a long day of searching.

"Lady Iseul arranged this job when she learned I wanted to move to a human city. She said you'd need my expertise," he says, holding his chin high.

Though we've never spoken before, I can't help feeling a surge of affection.

I laugh. "She's right. I would never have been able to do an adequate job without you." I reach up and stroke the Star Runner's long nose. "You're part of our family now, so let me know if you ever need anything."

"Violet?" Mother calls from the porch, motioning for me to hurry.

I say a few more words in parting to the young fae, then hurry to catch up with my parents.

Bear hesitates when at the threshold, before I remember that demons need to be invited before they can enter a home. "Well, come on," I say. "This is your home, too."

"Who… is this?" Mother quirks a brow.

"This is Bear. A friend gifted them to me, to keep me safe."

I leave out the full truth. My heart is not yet ready to share memories of Joon.

"Them?" Mother mouths the word, catching my slip.

I smile nervously and plead silently for her not to say anything. She gives me a look that says she won't, but fully expects me to go into detail later.

Father seems blissfully unaware of the reality as he frowns down at the little demon. "I don't want an animal in the house," he says.

Bear turns their face up, blinking large, sorrowful eyes at him. They *definitely* have the puppy act down.

Mother puts a hand on his shoulder and says, "It's fine. Bear was a gift." Then to me, she mouths, "You owe me for this."

Bear leaps up and races inside, disappearing into one of the rooms. Their talons even sound like dog paws as they explore.

"All right," Father grumps, only half serious. "But it better not make a mess."

I step out into the bright afternoon and close the door to my patient's home near the border of the neighboring town Winterfell. Tendrils of the sun's warmth cut through the late winter air, whispering the promise of spring.

Even something as simple as delivering draughts to help ease the ache of arthritis for an aging couple fills me with a deep sense of contentment.

It's hard to believe that a year has passed since I finished my apprenticeship and opened my own practice. For over a year, I studied under Physician Wilkes in Avalan. Countless hours with days that began with the sun cresting the horizon, and continued long after it set, I worked to hone the knowledge from my years of research into something useful.

Bear stands guard beside Star Runner. I climb into the saddle, then we start down the road, beginning the several-hour ride home.

Halfway back, a light snow begins to fall. I reach out my palm to catch a few flakes. Sometimes, when it snows, I like to think Joon is sending me a message from the Otherworld.

It's hard to believe that several weeks have passed since I received word of his death. The world has taken on a surreal veneer. Were it not for my work giving me purpose and the support of my family and friends, I think it would have destroyed me completely.

A flash of white against the darkened backdrop of the woods in the distance catches my attention. When I look, there is nothing more than large snowflakes fluttering gently to the ground.

Bear makes a small noise, then darts ahead and disappears into the trees.

"Wait!" I call, racing after them, but they don't seem to hear me. By the time I enter the cover of branches, I've already lost track of Bear.

I continue for about a mile before coming to a halt. They must have seen a forest animal they wanted to play with. Bear knows how to get home. They *are* a demon after all, and are perfectly capable of taking care of themselves.

The woods often remind me of Joon and the many times we rode through them together as we left the palace to search for the shards. At the time, it had been less than ideal—a necessary obligation. One that gradually transformed into deeply significant moments long before I ever realized it.

My life is good, now. It's what I wanted for so long. I am content and happy with the path I've chosen. It's what I've always wanted. And yet, I don't think I will ever stop missing him.

So, while I travel between the trees, I let myself remember to feel close to him again, even for a moment, without holding back. Fat tears slide down my cheeks as easily as smiles curl my lips. I mourn, but I do not despair. Joon wouldn't want his loss to burden me any more than I'd want that for him, had our fates been reversed.

Near the end of the woods, a man comes into view. He walks the road in the opposite direction, leading away from Firnhallow. I hastily swipe at the trails of salt on my face.

As the distance between us shortens, I slow Star Runner. He reminds me of Joon. Then again, everyone and everything reminds me of him.

The white mare steps on a branch as I guide her to the side. The loud crunch breaks the quiet, catching the man's attention. I barely look away fast enough. He might get the wrong idea if he catches me staring.

But my gaze is drawn to him again against my will. I don't realize I've stopped until he comes to a standstill several yards from where I stand.

The stranger lifts his head enough that I can see his face unobscured by the brim of his hat for the first time. For an eternity, my heart ceases to beat.

"Joon?" His name is barely more than a breath.

"Hello, Violet," he answers.

It's his voice… with his face—

Then I'm on the ground and running. Crashing into him.

He's here... he's alive and he's here.

Sobs wrack my chest, and I'm helpless to stop them. Joon holds me until the way of emotion finally runs out, able to breathe and speak again. His arms slip away when I pull back.

"Are you really here?" I ask, voice raw.

Joon smiles sweetly and brushes his fingertips over my face, using his power to cool my feverish cheeks and already swollen eyes. "I am."

Tears burn my eyes anew. "Where have you been?"

"Above the Maldan wall, here the celestial heavens and the earth touch."

"How is this possible? The king's letter… he said—"

"Do not blame him. Eojin only did as I asked."

"You… you've been alive this whole time?"

He nods. "Yes."

"Why didn't you find me sooner?"

"You deserved the chance to create a life you wanted for yourself without worrying over me."

"I worried anyway. I would have done so for the rest of my life until I knew what happened to you."

"That is exactly what I did not want for you." He sighs. "I thought I could be happy if I knew you were doing well. I did not intend to show myself today—that if I did, it would only make things worse."

"What?" I can hardly believe my ears. His admission feels like a betrayal. Every beat of my heart spreads hurt and disquiet through my veins. "You let me believe you were *dead* and would have let me go the rest of my life thinking that?" I shove him.

He stumbles back several steps. Bear comes from out of nowhere and moves behind him, causing Joon to trip and fall, landing on his back in the snow.

"Then why come back at all?" I stomp over to him.

Joon's gaze darkens a second before his hand snakes out and snatches my wrist. He tugs hard, pitching me forward, but he catches me in his arms and rolls, pinning me with his body.

He dips his head, resting his brow against my shoulder, and sighs. It reminds me of another time. A time when we clung to each other in a temporary world of our own, hidden within a forest. When we allowed ourselves to take what we wanted and gave freely.

Just like that, with such a simple gesture, he has me.

He meets my gaze with a soft, wistful smirk. "I thought it obvious."

"Tell me anyway," I say breathlessly.

After a moment, he gets to his feet, pulling me along with him effortlessly.

"I came for you. The second I saw you, I knew I could not live one more day without you." He rests his forehead against mine. "It is terribly selfish of me."

"It is," I agree. My voice is barely audible.

"Would you deny me if I begged to stay by your side for the rest of my life?"

For the briefest moment, my heart soars only to plummet.

"Joon..." I can barely utter his name. I swallow and step back, needing distance to say what I must. "I can't... I can't leave—There are people who count on me." It is a truth that physically pains me to say out loud. "I cannot go back with you."

He steps forward. "I will not ask you to leave your life here again."

"Then, would you be content traveling back and forth, only seeing each other on rare occasions?" I shake my head. "I don't know if I could share you with the world. I don't want to spend more time missing you than being with you." His face becomes a blur as tears obscure my vision. "I could not ask you to give it up—not after everything you've endured. But I couldn't bear a lifetime of goodbyes."

"It was no hardship to let go of something I never wanted. After seeing the way my uncle had controlled others, I could not stomach the thought of wielding that kind of power. Arum deserves a ruler whose heart is with them. How can I give that to them when it is with you?"

"Yet, you must," I whisper.

"You are the dawn that banished my prison of eternal night. My salvation. My heart. I would endure the curse a thousand times over just for a chance to love you."

"Joon…" I bite down on my bottom lip, willing myself to stay strong as he mercilessly breaks down my defenses.

"It was not a decision I took lightly, nor was it one I would have anyone else make on my behalf. In truth, it is a choice I made long ago." He cups my cheeks, angling my face up. My tears escape, sliding over his fingers. "It is already done."

My eyes snap to his, not sure I heard correctly.

"The Winter Dragon is with the guardians of the past among the stars."

"How can that be?" I shake my head. "I thought it happened only if you…" I trail off, unable to say the final word.

"Yes. It was a death of sorts. It was part of the reason I didn't return until now."

"What does that mean for you?"

"It means that I am a fae with lesser magic, I am afraid." He smiles, then winks. "Well, maybe a bit more even without my pearl, but not as powerful as I once was."

Silence settles between us. This feels like a dream, but if it is, then I don't want to wake up—not if it means losing him all over again.

"You once said that you loved me and that you were mine. Is that still true?" Joon's brows crease as his eyes search mine.

I open my mouth to say, *Yes, of course it is,* but a spark ignites, and instead, I say, "That depends."

He frowns. "On?"

A smile forms on my lips. "My family and friends. I don't know how they would react if I let a man freely claim me." I feign mild disappointment.

"Freely?" he says, donning his own wicked smile. "I am already yours. I have simply come to collect my wife in reciprocity."

I flex my hand. The shimmering thread of magic, once tied to our fingers, is gone. "Our marriage was always meant to be temporary. It ended when the curse broke and both our promises were fulfilled," I say quietly.

"My heart says you are my wife still. I do not need a bargain to tell me as much." Joon presses his lips to the spot just below my ear. The delicate kiss sends heat sluicing through my body.

"I'm not so sure anyone else would agree," I say. My eyes close as his mouth explores my skin.

"The world can think what it wants of me. Nothing will stop me from claiming what is rightfully mine." His lips move over the column of my throat, leaving a trail of kisses between nips and flicks of his tongue. "One way or another, I will have you as my wife again. You are the fate I choose, just as I am yours."

My back bumps up against the rough bark of a tree. "I suppose there is not much for me to do but accept my fate," I say.

"Then say it. Say that you are mine, and I am yours."

This moment reminds me of another. When we pretended during a time when I would never live a normal life, and he was destined for one far outside my reach, when being together was nothing more than an impossible dream. But now it is ours to seize.

"I am yours, and you are mine," I say.

"For the rest of our lives and beyond." He leans forward.

"For the rest of our lives and beyond," I echo, just as Joon's lips descend on mine.

EPILOGUE

VIOLET

"Are you sure about this?" Joon grimaces. "Perhaps I should wear something nicer?"

I glance at him from the corner of my eye. This might be the first time I've ever seen him look so uncomfortable. "There's nothing to worry about."

He looks like he wants to protest, but after several false starts, he presses his lips into a tight line and sighs in defeat.

"You've never met anyone's family before, have you?" I ask slowly.

Joon lifts his chin, adopting a false haughtiness. "I have… just not in this context."

"This will be casual. I want them to meet you first. Humans don't usually go around marrying someone they just met."

He frowns. "But we didn't just meet."

Stifling a laugh, I say, "*We* know that, but they don't. The man I married was declared dead after defeating the Traitor King." I press my palm to his chest. "I haven't known *this* Joon for long."

"All right, I concede to your point," he says reluctantly.

I take his hand, then half-drag him inside my parents' house before he can delay again. I'd moved into a small cottage near the northern side of town after I finished studying under Physician Wilkes, but this will always be home to me.

Familiar voices drift from other areas in the house. They have company. I briefly wonder if I should have given them notice rather than dropping in on a whim. I push the doubt away. It's too late now anyway.

I want to talk about Joon with my family.

"Mother? Father? I'm home," I call out. "I brought someone I want you to meet."

A rush of people comes from the kitchen in the back all at once. Mother and Father lead the way with Talya, Sebastian, and his fiancé Lilly, and Mr. and Ms. Byron following.

Everyone begins talking over each other. Joon takes half a step back, positioning himself slightly behind me.

"Why don't we all take a seat in the drawing room while we wait for dinner?" Mother suggests, speaking loud enough to silence the rush of questions.

Chatter immediately resumes as everyone files into the next room, eager for an introduction.

"You will stay for dinner, won't you?" she asks Joon.

"I would not want—"

"It's no imposition at all," she says with a knowing smile as she joins the others.

"I see where you get it from," Joon mutters under his breath.

I feign offence. "Get *what* from?"

"Your unfailing positivity."

After making sure no one can see, I rise on my toes and

press a quick kiss to his lips. While he's still stunned, I pull him into the drawing room.

I gesture to my friends and family, naming each in turn. "Everyone, this is Joon."

There's a round of murmured greetings that feels far more strained than I expected.

"Umm, Violet," Talya says a little too sweetly. "Perhaps you would like to give us all a little more context? You've never brought a man home before." He laughs nervously, then quietly, she adds, "And when you do, he's fae."

Oh... Oooh.

I suppose it would be jarring. Humans and fae have only begun to work together again. There hasn't been much time for more romantic notions to develop between the two groups.

When I look at him, all I see is the man who makes my heart skip a beat when he smiles, who understood me in a way no one else could, long before we fell in love. The man I have been tied to for more than half my life through a curse that became a boon.

Talya turns to Joon. "You see, our little Violet has given herself very little opportunity to meet a human man, let alone a fae. So, we are understandably confused—especially when she's never mentioned anyone to us before."

He gives me a sideways glance.

"Joon only moved to the area recently. We met by chance on my way home yesterday."

Everyone stares, waiting for more.

"He was my protector at the palace," I rush to say. "And gave me Bear for added protection."

My father sends Joon a glare. "That was you? I was wondering if we would ever meet the one responsible for that little *gift*."

I press my lips into a hard line to stifle the laughter bubbling up. Father has finally figured out that Bear is actually a demon, as I knew he would. I could only hide their little *quirks* for so long.

Talya's sharp gaze bounces from Joon to me several times. "Is there something between you two?"

"We are frien—" I start to say, but Joon cuts me off.

"I intended to make her my wife as soon as possible."

I choke on the bluntness of his response while everyone is rendered speechless.

"Joon!" I hiss.

He meets my gaze with an entirely serious expression. "You already agreed when we discussed it earlier."

"You didn't have to tell them that *yet*," I say in a harsh whisper, even though everyone can hear.

"I will not lie to the people who love you."

Heat creeps into my cheeks.

Talya snorts. "Protector, my foot," she mutters under her breath.

Sebastain sits forward on the edge of his seat. "I—uh, that is—our families have been good friends for so long, we are all practically family at this point."

There are nods of agreement around the room.

"So, I'm sure I'm not the only one curious when I ask what it is that you do," Sebastian continues awkwardly. "For work, I mean."

"I would hardly call it work, but—" There is a wicked glint in Joon's eye, and I can tell that whatever is about to come out of his mouth next will have an all too obvious double meaning that no one will miss.

"He hasn't figured that out yet," I blurt before he can finish. "He only arrived in town a few days ago."

Joon gives me a wink before addressing the room. "I was

thinking I might become an apothecary. I enjoy gardening, and with my connections back at the capital, I will have access to rare seeds that would be useful to Violet's work."

"That's wonderful!" Mother beams.

With introductions made and the most pressing questions out of the way for now, Joon and I take a seat. Several lighthearted discussions spring up around the room, each of us moving from one to the other with comfortable ease.

It warms me to see my family welcome him with open arms. I appreciate the way he walked into this unfamiliar situation, willing to adapt for my sake.

When the head cook announces dinner is ready, Mother herds everyone toward the kitchen. She slips her arm through Joon's, dragging him along while peppering him with questions.

Talya holds me back, waiting to speak until we are alone.

"He must truly love you to give up his crown," Talya says.

My heart skips a beat. "He's not..." I trail off.

Talya cocks her head and fists her hands on her hips, daring me to continue the lie. When I don't, she says, "It's a little obvious." She tilts her head toward the window, where Imugi and Bear play fight in the yard. "Why else would a bonded demon be here?"

I send a sharp glare at Imugi. They were supposed to stay out of sight.

"Honestly, Violet, I'm a little hurt you never confided in me."

I flinch, knowing I would feel the same in her place. "I'm sorry. We thought it best to let that part of him go. It might be common knowledge that he defeated the Traitor King, but there are many who still think of him as cruel."

Talya heaves an overly dramatic sigh. "Fine," she drags the

sound out. "I suppose I can understand that. You both have my word that I'll take this secret to my grave."

I throw my arms around her. "Thank you."

"We'll talk about why you haven't told me about that demon posing as a dog later," she whispers.

I pull back, knowing that it's pointless to lie, but at the same time, there are only so many people willing to tolerate a while demon when most would gladly rip a human to shreds.

"Oh, come on. Did you think I wouldn't notice a dog changing from male one day to female the next? Besides, when have you ever seen a dog jump from a second-story window like it was nothing or climb up the side of a house?"

"You noticed that?" I laugh nervously. I'll need to have a chat with Bear about being more careful later.

"Violet," she says my name with the exasperation of a mother dealing with a toddler. "You know I love you like a sister, but there are times I wonder about your sanity."

"Hey!" I pout playfully.

"At least I can rest easy knowing you'll have Joon to keep you from getting into too much trouble on your own. *And* I fully expect to hear the full story from you—that Choosing business is looking more and more suspicious by the second."

I laugh. "Deal."

"Bargain with me," Joon says with a desperation that matches mine when I'd once said that to him.

I rise from crouching over a small bunch of wild herbs and turn to the fae behind me. He's far closer than he was a moment ago.

"Bargain? For what? Why?" I ask with a light laugh.

"Your hand. Your heart."

I smile and tilt my head, trying to figure out if he is teasing me again or not. "My heart is already yours, as my hand will be in two weeks."

Joon's tone turns somber. "By your human customs, yes. I want you as my wife, as human *and fae*."

The moment he gives his wants voice, I know it is just as important for me to know we are bound in all ways that matter. It is the thing that was missing during the past month of preparations, but couldn't name.

"Is there even time to arrange things?" I ask.

He reaches up and tucks a wayward strand of hair behind my ear. "There is nothing to arrange. For the fae, such things are private. Humans have ceremonies and witnesses because they do not possess magic. We need only to speak our new bargain as we did before."

"Then I see no need to wait." My voice has gone breathy and soft with anticipation.

The look of pure happiness on his face only reaffirms what is in my heart.

Bird song fills the woods now that spring is in full bloom. The air is warm and fragrant. It's a time and place I never imagined having with him. It feels like a dream, just as every day since he found me in the forest has. I intend to revel in the passing years I never thought I'd have, and a love I never dared to want before I met Joon.

Joon steps back and takes my hand, holding my wrist in his gentle grasp. The familiar hum of energy dancing over my skin tingles against his cool touch. A shimmering thread appears above our clasped hands, lengthening. The ends elongate, undulating gently as they wait for the bargain.

"For your heart and your hand, I give you mine. I bind

myself to you willingly in this life and beyond," he says. An echo of the promise we made so long ago.

As he speaks his vow, one end of the glittering thread knots around his middle finger. It is the same as it was the first time, only now it's brighter. Brilliant and warm.

"For your heart and your hand, I give you mine." As I repeat after him, the other end ties in a knot around mine. The thread catches the light, shimmering a mix of silver, black, red, and cobalt with its movements. "I bind myself to you willingly in this life and beyond."

The words have barely passed my lips before his mouth is on mine. My hands snake their way up his arms and around his neck. He lifts me by the waist, my legs wrapping around his.

The desire I feel for him is intensified by all we have overcome together. When I try to say as much, his tongue slips past my lips, stroking mine, and all thoughts leave my mind. All that is left is our need to claim each other.

Joon pins me against the rough bark of a tree with his body. One of his hands finds my breast and caresses, squeezing gently before trailing down and over my thigh. He finds the hem of my skirt and slides his palm underneath, then back toward my hip and curving around to my ass. He does the same with his other hand, continuing until he reaches my core. He strokes me. Once. Twice. I moan as two of his long fingers plunge inside me with no more warning than that.

My body has missed his touch—hungered for his, the feel of him on me and in me. It's as if I wandered a desert in search of the one thing I needed to feel whole again. Never finding it until now, and I am ravenous.

"Perhaps I should make you summon the entire town with your cries?" he murmurs darkly.

My fingers dig into his shoulder as he nips and licks at my neck, while he continues to work me.

Then, his hand is gone in a too sudden movement, pulling a whimper from me, leaving me empty with a need to fill that space with him.

With those brief touches, he already has my body aching with desire. I don't have to wait long. He frees himself from his trousers and guides the tip of his cock into position. My breath catches in anticipation as he grips my waist and holds me in place as he pushes his hips forward, stretching me in a single, achingly slow thrust until every inch of him is in me.

"Yes, just like that," Joon murmurs, peppering my jaw with kisses between words. The sensual way he speaks sparks something within me that demands he make his claim.

Joon leans back to gaze at me. "Violet, I—"

"If you wish to claim me, then claim me." I rasp. I need him to move, though I am on the verge of coming undone just like this.

A low rumble emanates from his throat. He pulls back, then thrusts forward, hard and fast. A sound between a cry and a moan escapes me as I gasp at the unexpected strength. He does it again and again and again. Each movement is deliberate and forceful as he obliges.

"Otherworld, take me, I have missed the way you feel."

I try to smother my sounds as he threatens to follow through on his earlier words.

"Moan all you want, Wife. I will take them all for myself."

With that, his mouth is on mine. He swallows my cries of passion with his kiss that claims me just as fiercely as he fucks me against the tree. Raw and primal. Each thrust is a possessive claim that marks our hearts and souls, solidifying the vow we made to each other among the trees.

We move together, proving that we are made to fit

together, to move in tandem, and ensuring every inch of me will crave him for eternity. Every touch, every breath, is an expression of our emotions. The sorrow, the longing and regret, the worry, and the relief. But most importantly, the joy that our hearts are finally whole now that we're together again.

It's as if we were born already knowing each other's souls —as if the saints created me for the sole purpose of having him command my heart, and his for me. Our hands grasp and grip, fingers tangling in hair. We hold tight as we explore the maps of each other's bodies.

Joon growls and bites my neck hard enough to leave teeth marks but not to bruise. His mouth licks and sucks where he bit, soothing the area that is now just tender enough to send bolts of pleasure to my core, making it all the sweeter.

The fire within me coils, winding impossibly tight. And with one more thrust, it breaks. Wave after wave of pleasure washes over me. I cry out, and he consumes the sound with his mouth just as he consumes my body with his. And then he moans as he finds his release, his pleasure, mixing with mine.

We chose this connection, first out of desperation, then gladly once more, because it is what we want—a decision made without the influence of outside forces. We cling to each other as we always have, but this time we will not let go. Our paths were never intended to cross, but by some twist of fate, they did.

I faced more danger helping Joon break the curse than anything else I've done in my life, but I have never been safer than every second I have been at his side.

We were always capable of surviving. Fear blinded us for so long, but together, we were able to become who we needed to be for ourselves. To embrace our strength and determination, and face the curse head-on.

Neither the bargain nor the bond was ever necessary. Only the chance to offer kindness and treat the other as equals, to approach with open hearts and open arms, wrapping each other in compassion that was freely given, not needing to be earned.

Our paths have merged into one we will walk together. Both of us stronger than we could ever be apart. Together, we can overcome anything.

ADDENDUM

Demon Hierarchy

Lesser demons: The weakest classification of demons. No permanent, solid form.

Higher demons: The strongest, natural class of demons. Able to hold their solid form.

Greater demons: The strongest classification of demons. Not naturally occurring in nature. They are created when a higher demon bonds with a human.

Demon power and bonds:

Demons are beings of power, and therefore are non-gendered. They are neither good nor evil, but much like humans, they have the potential to be either and anywhere in between. Their goals and ambitions vary as much as their personalities.

Higher and Greater demons can travel during the day, but their power is weakened. However, Lesser demons are forced to hide in shadows during the day as they are not powerful enough to withstand direct light.

Demon bonded:

A demon bond grants both the preternatural being* and the demon greater power

Demon cursed:

One becomes demon cursed when the demon's magic is incompatible with the life force of the human they intend to bond with. If a bond fails, it is not immediately apparent, but over time, their mismatched energies will poison the other. Both demon and human will gradually go mad, and their blood will rot. This manifests in the preternatural being as black veins becoming visible when they use their power.

Preternatural beings and their origins:

All preternatural beings originated from a demon and a human bonding through a shared goal. Their intention for the power they seek determines the type of preternatural being they become.

The (original) preternatural being and their demon are able to sense whether or not the innate power of the human and a higher demon are a good match and if they are likely to result in a successful bond. They are able to assist in the creation of other higher preternatural beings of their same type. However, the process is risky and may still end in a demon cursed match. Or they may choose to create a lesser preternatural being of the same type, less powerful, and without a demon bond.

The life spans of preternatural beings vary, and while some are able to procreate, not all possess that ability.

*Preternatural beings include, but are not limited to, vampires, all fae, shifters, witches, merfolk, and all classifications of dryads.

Guardians:

Guardians are dragon spirits born to those with the blood of the original fae. Both fae and guardian share a body. The guardian spirit is able to take control in order to defend the kingdom when necessary.

The life of the fae and their guardian are tied. When one dies, so too does the guardian. The mortal soul of the fae goes into the otherworld, while the guardian ascends to the heavens, becoming another star in the night sky.

Shadouk:

A creature born of a toxic bond with a demon. The demon ends up devouring the soul of the living person in exchange for a dark, twisted power.

The Officials of Arum

Minister of Justice

Symbol: Balance scales
Name: Ilseong (deceased)
Name: Ailan

Minister of Ceremony

Symbol: Dragon twisted in a sideways 8, eating its own tail
Name: Molan

Minister of Hunt

Symbol: Sword crossed with an arrow
Name: Kwan

Minister of Knowledge

Symbol: Quill resting over an open book
Name: Jinshi

Minister of Commonwealth

Symbol: A skeleton key

Name: Seojun

Minister of Shields

Symbol: Shield

Name: Yeona (deceased)

Crown of Arum

Symbol: Crown

Name: Sameun (deceased)

Name: Eojin

THANK YOU

Thank you for reading Wicked Prince of Frost. It's always so much fun to explore new worlds and old, and to watch my characters come to life on the page.

If you enjoyed reading Wicked Prince of Frost, then please consider leaving an honest review on Amazon, Bookbub, or Goodreads.

Reviews are so, so important for helping other readers decide whether or not to read a certain book. They don't need to be long or super descriptive. A single sentence or a few words is all that's needed. Positive, neutral, or negative feelings are all valid. All I ask is that you be mindful not to spoil the story or the ending for your fellow readers.

Stay in touch and be among the first to learn about new releases, cover reveals, character art, special offers, exclusive content (first few chapters, bonus scenes, and spontaneous shorts), and more by signing up for my newsletter!

www.aliwinters.com/newsletter

SERIES YOU MIGHT ENJOY

ADULT TITLES

SHADOW WORLD GOTHIC EPIC ROMANTASY:

The Vampire Debt series:

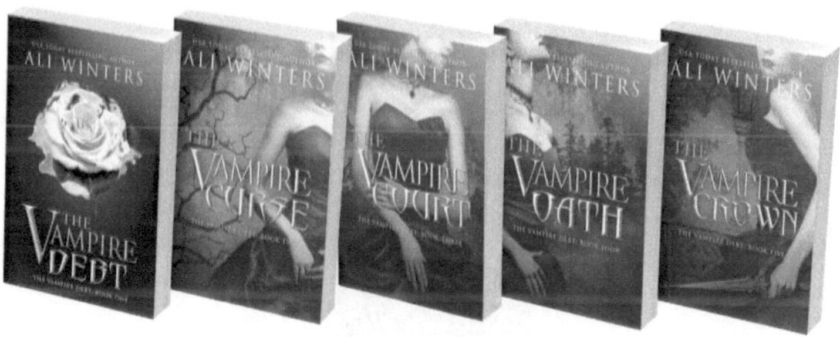

It is a truth universally acknowledged that a single Vampire in possession of a good fortune must be in want of a mortal snack.

Learn more: **www.thevampiredebt.com**

SHADOW WORLD: STAND ALONES:

WICKED PRINCE OF FROST: an epic gothic romantasy

He promised to heal her broken heart, but if she's not careful, he may just end up taking it for himself.

Learn more: **www.aliwinters.com/shadowworld**

THE VAMPIRE TRAP: A Shadow World novella

When a series of murders breaks out across the city of Sangate, all evidence points to the most powerful vampire in the city.

Learn more: **www.aliwinters.com/shadowworld**

STAND ALONES:

HIGH STAKES: A stand alone Urban Romantasy novella

Elle Darling takes a bounty on an item retrieval job that sounds simple enough, but soon becomes deadly when the secret surrounding it is one many would kill to possess. She could end up losing her job or worse… her life.

Learn more: **www.aliwinters.com/standalones**

YOUNG ADULT TITLES

THE HUNTED SERIES:

A Reaper and her mortal enemy must team up to save the balance of life and death before all is lost. Unfortunately, to succeed, one of them must die.

Learn more: **www.aliwinters.com/the-hunted-series**

IN THE END DUOLOGY:

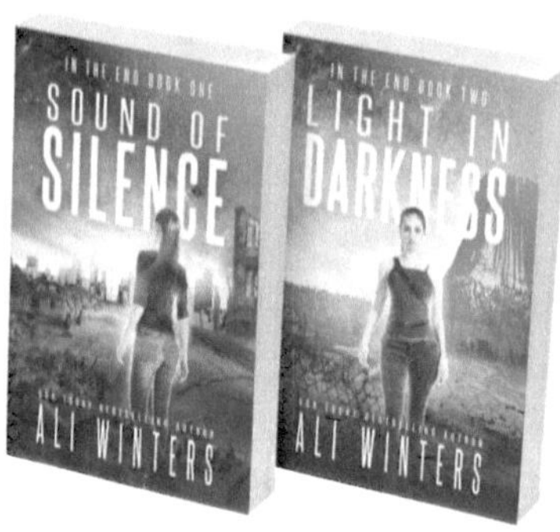

We thought we were alone in the universe. Turns out we were wrong. Dead wrong. —This book is a Romeo and Juliet retelling and contains insta-love, aliens, a virus, and zombies.

Learn more: **www.aliwinters.com/sos**

FAVOR OF THE GODS: a short story

"Like Icarus, you flew too close to the sun. Someone had to bring you back down to reality. You don't belong with princesses, heroes, or demigods."

Learn more: **www.aliwinters.com/standalones**

CAST IN MOONLIGHT

Welcome to Havenwood Falls, a small town where nobody is

what you think, where truths pose as lies, and where myths blend with reality.

Cast in Moonlight is a stand alone novella in the shared world of Havenwood Falls, a multi-author collaboration.

Learn more: **www.aliwinters.com/standalones**

ABOUT THE AUTHOR

Ali Winters is the USA TODAY Bestselling author of several series filled with romance, magic, and adventure. She enjoys breaking down characters to build them up so they find their true strengths.

Her first love will always be fantasy, but she fully admits to being obsessed with coffee and T-Rex, and has a weakness for love interests that walk the line between gray and villainy.

Connect with Ali online

www.aliwinters.com

facebook.com/authoraliwinters

instagram.com/authoraliwinters

bookbub.com/authors/ali-winters

tiktok.com/@authoraliwinters

www.ingramcontent.com/pod-product-compliance
Lightning Source LLC
Chambersburg PA
CBHW020242030826
48979CB00030B/2478/J
* 9 7 8 1 9 4 5 2 3 8 2 9 1 *